The Harlequin's Legacy
BOOK ONE

ANDRÉS ROSAS HOTT

RED MOON PUBLISHING

BOOK ONE

© Copyright 2024 - All rights reserved.

The content contained within this book may not be reproduced, duplicated or transmitted without direct written permission from the author or the Red Moon Publisher.

Under no circumstances will any blame or legal responsibility be held against the publisher, or author, for any damages, reparation, or monetary loss due to the information contained within this book, either directly or indirectly.

Legal Notice:
This book is copyright protected. It is only for personal use. You cannot amend, distribute, sell, use, quote or paraphrase any part, or the content within this book, without the consent of the author or Red Moon Publisher.

Disclaimer Notice:
Please note the information contained within this document is for educational and entertainment purposes only. All effort has been executed to present accurate, up to date, reliable, complete information. No warranties of any kind are declared or implied. Readers acknowledge that the author is not engaged in the rendering of legal, financial, medical or professional advice. The content within this book has been derived from various sources. Please consult a licensed professional before attempting any techniques outlined in this book.

By reading this document, the reader agrees that under no circumstances is the author responsible for any losses, direct or indirect, that are incurred as a result of the use of the information contained within this document, including, but not limited to, errors, omissions, or inaccuracies.

Cover Design: Ary Fajriyanto
Interior Illustrations: Ary Fajriyanto
Book Design and Typesetting: Enchanted Ink Publishing

The text type was set in Garamond Premier Pro

ISBN: 978-91-989715-2-1 (E-book)
ISBN: 978-91-989715-0-7 (Paperback)
ISBN: 978-91-989715-1-4 (Hardcover)

Thank you for your support of the author's rights.

WWW.REDMOONPUBLISHING.COM

I extend my immense gratitude to Ary Fajriyanto for his exceptional talent in creating captivating cover art and illustrations for my novel.

As both author and art director, my main goal was to breathe life into the narrative through compelling visuals, with a strong emphasis on vivid storytelling. The illustrations were intended to create an enchanting experience, truly capturing the essence of the world I had imagined for the readers.

Special thanks to everyone, including my family, who played a crucial role behind the scenes, dedicating so much of their time and effort to bring this fantastical endeavor to life.

"One is you, yet you are no one."

— Marcél Rosas Hott

CHAPTER ONE

Pascal was late. Again.

He stepped quickly over fallen logs and ducked low beneath swooping evergreen branches. Though the wilderness was dense in this part of the forest, he navigated it with remarkable ease. His footsteps as light as a whisper over treacherous mossy rocks. With each exhale, misty clouds formed in the shake of his breath, the biting cold of winter creeping all the way through the thickness of his coat. He pulled his collar tighter to forbid the chill from entering even more.

Yet, as he walked, his mind strayed from his course, far from the natural beauty surrounding him.

He muttered under his breath as he walked over the gnarled roots, every step a cautious dance. He slipped and slid in his frequent efforts to stoop under even more pointy twigs of evergreen that sought to block his path, to grab him as he passed. Pascal had taken this route countless times before, and today, that thought was a frustrating one.

After spending the majority of his life at the orphanage, he wanted nothing more than to leave, to see the world, to taste all that lay unseen and undiscovered. He would soon have that opportunity. Yet, knowing that he'd soon be graduating also left him uneasy.

Can I even handle surviving on my own? He wondered. *I've always had the comfort of Mistress Alma and the orphanage to look after me.*

The bittersweet longing left him conflicted and a little insecure, truth be told. How would he know when he was ready? What threshold would he finally cross?

The forest, usually a great source of comfort and solace, felt somehow different on this day. It seemed to be echoing his inner turmoil, causing him to lose all sense of time.

The sun stretched over the tree line of the Quiet Wilds, reminding him that his walk should have ended about fifteen minutes ago. He picked up his pace.

Great. The last thing I wanted to do was disappoint Mistress Alma. And miss dinner.

The final approach was quick, as he nearly ran the remaining half-mile. Once he spotted the entrance, he slipped in with stealth. The mess hall was already full. He'd have to wait for the perfect moment to sneak inside.

"Have you seen Pascal?"

Whispers spread through the orphanage's mess hall like wildfire as the children ate their typical meal for a Wednesday night: potatoes and vegetable stew. A classic, one that Pascal didn't want to miss.

When he peered around the corner, he spotted his friends Clarion and Danton exchanging a knowing glance. Surely, they were assuming he'd been caught up in his exploration outside the orphanage grounds. Which he had. In fact, that was exactly what he had done.

His eyes wandered down the table to Tania, one of the older girls at the orphanage, just as she was motioning for Mistress Alma. *Damn.* Of course, Tania would notice his absence. She never knew how to keep quiet about these sorts of things.

Removing her pince-nez glasses, Mistress Alma scanned over the mess hall. She rubbed at her eyes, which seemed to be sore at the day's end, a fact that proved fortunate for Pascal. In her scan, she'd somehow managed to miss Tania's raised hand. She circled the room slowly and met children along the wall, all beaming in her presence.

Then, she turned on her heel to stride toward the kitchen, her simple brown dress and jacket flowing behind her.

Poor Tania was stretching her arm ever-higher, looking fit to burst from her efforts, but still, Mistress Alma did not see. That was a relief. Though, the win was short-lived; it was just a matter of time before she realized Pascal wasn't present and that he was late again.

Once she disappeared into the kitchen, Pascal exhaled, his eyes glinting. This was the perfect opportunity. Yet, when he glanced around the mess hall at the tame expressions the children wore, he couldn't suppress the urge to liven up their evening a bit more. After all, he'd been working on a few tricks that he could hardly wait to show them. Why not come in with a bang? He'd probably get in some amount of trouble anyway...

He walked around to the main mess hall entrance and burst through the doors with as much dramatic flair as he could muster. He flipped into a handstand, pressing his palms against the floor, and then strutted through the mess hall on his hands.

The room erupted in laughter. Pascal could never do things quietly.

"Pascal!" Tania snapped, her eyes wide. She emitted a short-tempered gasp. "You're late! Where were you?"

Maintaining his balance perfectly, he chuckled; from his angle, her frown looked like a smile. "What do you think? Am I getting better? I think I could do this all day."

Clarion climbed off the bench and crouched beside Pascal to look him square in the eyes. "It's pretty good...if you want a face as red as a tomato," he teased.

"Well, it's a bit of a strain," Pascal answered. He puffed out a labored breath. "Still pretty cool, right?" He swiveled around on one hand, all while glancing up at Tania.

Her hands on her hips, she scoffed. "What would be 'cool' would be for you to arrive on time."

Pascal returned her sneer with a devious grin. He wouldn't let her deflate his ego, especially not when he had perfected such an interesting trick.

Sighing, Tania rolled her eyes. "Fine, it's pretty good. Now, would you please sit down?"

Without missing a beat, he flipped himself upward and swiveled around mid-air before sticking the perfect landing. The room erupted in applause, though he saved his bow for Tania and Clarion. As he straightened, his eyes met Tania's, and he let out a hearty laugh.

He glanced about the room; some of the kids giggled at his strange antics, while others watched Tania's scolding with envy. Upon turning back to face Tania, he cocked an eyebrow, which earned the expected groan. Her eyes narrowed in suspicion.

Pascal shot Tania a wink before he executed three handsprings, followed by a sprint toward the end of the mess hall for the big finale, something he'd been practicing in his spare time. Without slowing his pace, he ran up the wall and backflipped.

This time, even the nervous children cheered, no one concerned with making too much noise any longer. After all, the trick *was* incredible. That much was undeniable.

Unimpressed as always, Tania asked, "Do you want dinner?"

Pascal let out a laugh as he tried his best to catch his breath. "Sure."

"I'll get you a bowl," she groaned before stomping off toward the kitchen.

He took a seat on the bench with Clarion and couldn't keep himself from smirking. "She's not *that* mad."

Clarion scooted into the space beside him. "Nah, just annoyed. Don't mind her, Pascal, really. You should do it again."

That was more than enough to persuade him. *The crowd wants what the crowd wants.* He cast a confident smile to Clarion and rose from his seat once more. Then, after a final deep breath, Pascal ran toward the wall and backflipped once more.

This time, his jump was higher, which caused him to land too close to the tables. His foot caught the edge of the bench and jarred the front row of children with the harsh force of his landing. When the bench jumped, it caused one boy at the end to lose his grip on his bowl of stew. The bowl flew through the air like a frisbee and smacked into the back of Danton's head.

"Oi!" Danton howled, the back of his jacket now very drenched in stew. He twisted around and grabbed a hunk of nearby bread. Before Pascal could step forward to do anything, Danton hurled the bread at the boy, who watched with wide eyes. The bread hit him square in the forehead.

Pascal's stomach tightened. *Crap.*

Silence blanketed the room. No one dared to move. The boy picked up the piece of bread and analyzed it for a long moment before he chucked it back at Danton.

Within seconds, the entire mess hall erupted in an uproar. Pieces of bread and potatoes flew through the air, whizzing past Pascal's head. He ducked and dodged flying food from every direction. Walls were splattered with stew. If the potatoes weren't mashed before, they were now.

Pascal slipped away and ducked toward the entrance. He was stopped by the opening of the doors.

"Good evening, Grandmother," a familiar voice called. "I was wondering if—"

A half-eaten piece of pie glided through the air and smacked the poor, unsuspecting victim in the face. The children burst into synchronized laughter.

Pascal froze. He recognized the face beneath the pie: Baptiste, Mistress Alma's grandson who was a few years older than Pascal. And now, Baptiste had pie slathered in his strawberry-blond hair.

"What's going on here?" a voice bellowed from across the hall.

In an instant, everyone else in the room froze also. *Now* Pascal was really in trouble.

Mistress Alma stood, her arms crossed, her eyes blazing furiously, her lips pulled into a tight frown—almost as tight as the gray bun she wore pulled high atop her head. Tania stood beside her, a steaming bowl of stew in hand and a scowl harsher than Mistress Alma's on her face. Go figure.

Behind Mistress Alma stood Michel, the cook. He shook his head in warning when his eyes landed on Pascal.

Baptiste cleared his throat from the doorway as he swiped a piece of the pie from his cheek and licked it from his finger. "Not bad," he mumbled, looking about the room. His eyes widened at the sight before him. Food covered nearly every surface and every child.

"Maybe this was a bad time..." he said as he sheepishly ran his hand through his hair, now covered with bits of apple pie.

Mistress Alma stood unamused, though Pascal swore he saw a glint of humor in her eyes at her grandson's state of disarray. Yet, she shook her head then, that humor disappearing. "Children, clean this mess up while I talk with Baptiste."

Cook Michel, a silent and broad-shouldered man, began to fill buckets of water and pass them around. Pascal was grateful for the help, though guilt had settled in by this point. The mess was all his fault after all.

The younger children wiped down the walls and tables as the older kids mopped the floor. Tania, between delegating tasks, handed Pascal his bowl of stew. "It'll be cold by the time you finish cleaning. Maybe if you'd been here on time..."

He shot her a smile and tossed a hunk of dirty bread in the garbage. "I don't mind it cold."

She rolled her eyes and left in search of more cleaning supplies.

After everything was cleared, Baptiste—now free of apple pie—returned with Mistress Alma, who wore her typical worried expression.

"Children," she called. The room quieted at the sound of her voice. "I'm disappointed with your behavior this evening. You took the house rules for granted, caused a commotion in the mess hall, *and* wasted food. If something so unacceptable ever happens again, you will be stripped of your afternoon privileges."

A few gasps escaped the children. She glanced around the room, earning silent nods and mutters of agreement. Still, concern lingered in her eyes, in her creased eyebrows, in her tight frown. "Now, I have some important news. Pay very close attention, everyone."

She was met by a chorus of nods and wide eyes.

With a sigh, she continued. "Governor De Moura has announced that all children will henceforth require an escort. Recently, children have gone missing in and around the city. Therefore, no one is allowed to travel to Pivot or anywhere outside orphanage grounds without a chaperone. Are we clear?"

Again, everyone nodded.

She clapped her hands together with a forced smile and scanned the mess hall. It was by no means sparkling, but the food had been cleaned up. "I think it's about time we call it a night. Let's all get settled and put our night clothes on."

Just as Pascal and the rest of the children began to shuffle about and depart, she spoke once more. "Pascal," she said, turning to face him. "Please have a seat. I'll be back in a moment, and we can discuss what happened."

He nodded solemnly, and she turned to walk with Michel to the kitchen. With his shoulders slumped, Pascal slid onto the bench to eat his cold stew. *I lied. I don't like it cold.*

Baptiste sat beside him and rested his arms against the table. "Tough night, huh?"

Pascal nodded, clearing his bowl after only a few minutes and pushing it away. The food sat heavy in his stomach.

Mistress Alma returned with her food, Cook following her with a bowl of stew and two plates of apple pie. Baptiste graciously accepted the bowl and began to blow on the steam to cool it down. Cook left for the kitchen once more, brought in a few mugs of tea, and disappeared again.

Mistress Alma took a seat across from Pascal and folded her hands as she waited for her stew to cool. Her soft eyes met Pascal's. "Late again, huh?"

He averted her gaze, hand resting on the back of his neck. "You knew?"

Her head tipped down, eyebrows raised. "I'm a mother to an

orphanage of children. I have eyes in the back of my head, on the sides, and everywhere in between."

Baptiste snorted a laugh and pulled the plate of pie closer. "It's true. The woman sees everything."

"What happened?" Mistress Alma asked, ignoring Baptiste's comment. She blew on her spoonful of stew and then took a small bite.

"It was an accident," Pascal explained. "I tried a wall run and backflip which I'd done successfully before that...I may have landed wrong and hit the bench. The stew went flying, hit Danton, and well, you know the rest..."

"I see," Mistress Alma said.

For a moment, there was quiet. Baptiste heartily finished off his pie as Mistress Alma ate a few bites of her dinner. Then, she spoke again.

"If there was anything you would have changed," she asked, "what would it be?"

"Well, perhaps I shouldn't have tried the backflip in the mess hall...during dinner," Pascal replied, trying to hide his unease. "Or done handstands."

"Everyone loves your acrobatics," Baptiste said. "But maybe dinner isn't the best time for them."

"Definitely not," Mistress Alma assented. "You're very skilled at what you do, Pascal, but let's try to keep it appropriate. Understood?"

Pascal nodded. "Yes, ma'am."

She tipped down her glasses. "Showing up on time is also a good idea."

Pascal's cheeks reddened. He nodded silently.

"Got distracted on one of your walks?" Baptiste asked with a chuckle. This immediately earned him a scolding look from his grandmother.

"Something like that," Pascal replied.

"I hope you aren't leaving orphanage grounds again." Mistress Alma's blue eyes were sharp as she raised her eyebrows at him.

"I didn't go far," Pascal admitted with reluctance. He looked away, sighing. "I've seen everything around the orphanage. I want to see more, to see what's beyond the Misty Peaks or on the other side of the Untamed Highlands to the north. I'm not a child anymore, Mistress Alma. Even Pivot is more exciting than here. I'd love to go back to the market with Baptiste."

"And you will," Mistress Alma said. "But I simply cannot have you traipsing about without a chaperone. Once upon a time, when the other homes for orphans were run by scoundrels, you might have gotten away with it, but I built this home to provide a loving and safe place for you and the children. *Loving* and *safe*." Her eyes narrowed to provide emphasis.

Still, he wasn't about to give up. "What about Tania? She's practically a chaperone." It was a stretch, but worth a shot.

Mistress Alma just stared.

"Alright," Pascal relented. "What about Baptiste?"

"No, no," Baptiste said with a wave of his hand. "Keep me out of it. I'm a busy man these days, what, with the trading trips I've had to take."

Pascal nodded, well aware of Baptiste's work as the owner of a small freight airship. In fact, he'd considered asking Baptiste for a job after he left the orphanage.

One day I'll do it. I'll see Pivot on my own and explore all the corners of the city. He'd thought about it often: a visit to the bustling market, walking past the shadowy alleys, the glittering Carnival.

The Carnival.

Thoughts of the bright tents and mysterious caravans always lifted Pascal's spirits. The circus ring, the fortune teller's tent...it all sent goosebumps along his arms. His favorite part of the extravagance was the puppet theater that told stories about Harlequin and his endless battle against Mephisto, the great evil.

"Pascal?"

He'd drifted off. "Yes, ma'am? Sorry, I was thinking."

"You've been thinking a lot these days," she said. "I know you're getting to an age when all you see is the horizon. The world seems so exciting, and the dangers aren't obvious to you yet. You'll forgive me for wanting to keep you safe just a little longer, Pascal. That goes for all my children, even Baptiste."

"Yes, ma'am."

"It is easy for you to get caught up in having fun, but there are others around you who look up to you, who live by your example and guidance," Mistress Alma continued. "I know you didn't ask for that kind of responsibility, but it comes to all of us. To me, to Baptiste, and even to you."

"One day, you'll have your own adventure," Baptiste said with a smile.

"You've always had a passion and a curiosity for life," Mistress Alma said sternly. "But life is also about caring for the people around you, always having their best interests at heart."

"I know," Pascal said, familiar with the lecture. "Protecting the people you care for."

"Indeed." Mistress Alma gave Pascal a warm smile. "Well, seeing how late it is, I suppose I should let you go. It's a school night, don't you forget."

Pascal nodded and gave Baptiste a friendly wave before rising from the bench. With a parting nod, Baptiste shoveled a forkful of pie into his mouth. Mistress Alma cast Pascal a warm smile and then turned to face her grandson.

Pascal meandered away from the dining area and down the hall. As he passed a window, he paused to look out over the kitchen garden and the square dirt yard which accompanied it. Snow still lingered from the snowfall a few days ago. A few of the older kids were in the midst of a snowball fight, squeezing in some last-minute play before bed. Clarion attempted the handstand Pascal had pulled off earlier but gave up very quickly and moved on to doing a cartwheel.

Pascal debated going out there with them, but his mind was muddled. Instead, he made his way to the front veranda. No one else would be out there. They never were.

Just as he'd hoped, it was empty. The wide, wooden veranda stretched over half the length of the orphanage's large facade. In the middle of the veranda, stone blocks formed simple stairs which led down to the long U-shaped lane that connected the building to the road.

Pascal took a seat on the steps, and the cold stone sent a shiver through his body. What a day. After school, he'd zipped through his homework and bolted out to the secret treehouse Baptiste had helped him build years before. Then, he'd slipped under the fence and wandered into the backwoods.

Yeah, the thrill of exploration had been fun, but there was an emptiness that accompanied the enthusiasm.

Maybe I should ask Clarion or Danton to join me next time. Pascal desperately wanted to share the experience with someone. But Clarion doesn't like walking. Danton gets scared too easily. *Perhaps Tania? No, Tania can be a stick-in-the-mud.*

The toe of his shoe dug into the dirt as he listed the different people he could ask followed by the reasons they wouldn't work.

Minette would say yes, but she's always too busy bossing around the younger girls.

The truth was no one would really be enough to fill that void. Even if he found someone to explore with him, he'd already spent years exploring the edges of the orphanage.

I need more. It just doesn't hold the same appeal as it did when I was three.

His earliest memory was of exploring the orphanage grounds. He strained to recall the day he'd arrived, and he could never remember the face of the person who brought him to that place.

Why was he there? What happened to my mother and father?

The question replayed in his mind, tormenting him with questions that would never be answered. As usual, he pushed the thoughts away and focused instead on how much Mistress Alma, Michel, and Baptiste had made him feel at home. Thanks to the other children, he'd never been alone, though loneliness was still his constant companion also.

As he grew older, it became harder to push those questions away. Pascal knew those questions could never be answered by staying at the orphanage.

A door to his left shut. Mateo, the woodsman, emerged from the shed to the right of the drive. The shed was now a silhouette against the blueish hue of twilight, the waning daylight slowly disappearing, allowing the night to take claim. The woodshed was full to bursting, but once every two weeks or so, the tall, gruff man would come around to check the stores and chop some wood for Mistress Alma and the orphans.

Mateo reminded him of Michel. When Pascal was a young boy, he thought they were brothers. The thought was humorous now; he knew better. Mateo had a longer, thick gray beard, and his eyes were edged with gold, unlike Michel's which were darker.

Though Michel was a large man, Mateo looked rugged. His black great coat was currently tossed over the side of his cart, revealing a simple cream shirt and diamond-embroidered neckerchief. His rough leather boots were as dusty as the knee-patches of his pants. Mateo's hand rested on an axe stuck in the center of a nearby log.

"Mateo," Pascal called, hopping up from the stone steps. "Are you cutting us more wood?"

"Pascal." Mateo waved back with a smile. "I see someone has been trying some woodcutting themselves."

"Danton and I do some when Michel's busy," Pascal said with a grimace. "I still haven't quite gotten the hang of it."

"Requires a firm grip, a good eye, and a strong back," Mateo said, holding out a sturdy fist. "And some practice. You'll get there one day. How about you bring me some more while I get to cutting this pile here?"

Pascal nodded and brought out more stacks of wood while Mateo chopped his own pile. After he'd created a small mountain of timber, he sat on the back of Mateo's cart and watched him chop each log.

"How was your day?" Mateo finally asked as he straightened to wipe the sweat off his brow.

"It went...well." Pascal shrugged nonchalantly.

Mateo quirked an eyebrow at the lackluster response. "You seem more thoughtful than usual."

"I just have a lot on my mind," Pascal admitted, blowing out a breath. "I showed off a little in the mess hall, and I ended up launching a food fight."

"I bet Mistress Alma wasn't pleased." Mateo chuckled as he hacked at a piece of wood. "Let me guess, you got a lecture?"

"Yeah." Pascal nodded, looking away. "I was thinking about what she said…how things change when you get older, how the world changes. Or maybe the *world* never changes, but the way you see it does."

Pascal paused. How could he say this in a way that would make sense?

"The backyard seems smaller now than it did before. Been here since I was just a kid, I just…I can't wait to get out and see Vale and Pivot and everything for myself."

"I understand that." Mateo reached for another block of wood and chopped it into manageable pieces. "You want to explore the world. And you will, trust me. In fact-"

"Pascal?" Mistress Alma's voice called from the veranda. "Oh, Mateo! Good to see you."

"Alma," Mateo said with a wide grin. "I was just borrowing Pascal for a few minutes. He's helping me carry some wood."

"Is he?" She cast them an amused look. "Alright, well, do be sure to go around to Michel. He'll have dinner for you."

"Thank you, ma'am." Mateo tipped his head politely.

"Pascal?" Mistress Alma called, her voice half-question and half-command.

With a sigh, Pascal hopped off the cart and shrugged at Mateo. "I'll see you around. Maybe next time you can give me some tips for chopping wood."

"Next time," Mateo promised with a wink and a grin.

Pascal smiled, though all he could think about was his desire to someday hear what Mateo had been about to share. He followed Mistress Alma inside.

"We have a busy day tomorrow," she said as she slowed her steps, waiting for him to catch up.

"We do?" Pascal's eyebrows furrowed, and his head tilted to the side. "Is someone coming?"

She smiled with a small nod. "A new boy. I hope he'll be able to settle in smoothly. And as one of the older boys, it will be your duty to welcome him."

Pascal's eyes lit up. This was exactly what he'd been wishing for. "I'll do my best."

"I know you will." Mistress Alma chuckled and drew him into a quick side hug. When she released him, she patted his shoulder. "Now, up to bed with you!"

Pascal bid her goodnight and made his way up the staircase toward his dorm.

CHAPTER TWO

THE BELL RANG, AND PASCAL JOLTED OUT OF THE pleasant daydream he had wandered into during his least favorite class: history.

Pivot is a place where many species live and work, everything from humans to dragons, elves to dwarves and fairy folk. But the world withdrew from magic, and as a result, creatures associated with or able to wield magic became increasingly rare. Pivot now focused mainly on technology, science, and innovative advancement. On the rare occasion that Miss Lucía told the students a story about the chronicles of Pivot, the exploration of the Quiet Wilds, or the treaty with the dragons, Pascal would actually tune into what was going on in class.

But today? Everyone worked on their latest writing project, which so happened to be a rather boring report on Pivot's recent affairs. In the past decades, Pivot had enjoyed a run of peace and prosperity without any revolutions or battles. That sort of history made for dull reading and even duller writing.

He'd assumed that writing about the current governor, Mariana de Moura, would be easy. Miss Lucía required everyone to talk about what important changes Governor de Moura had brought to Pivot. *How would I know?* Pascal had wondered when given the assignment. *We're hardly allowed to visit the city.*

Besides, there were more important things to think about. Namely, the new boy.

Pascal knew his name was Pierrot and that he wasn't like the other kids. Pierrot seemed like a ghost. Somehow, he'd slipped in and out of the mess hall that morning without being noticed by any of the other children. Throughout the day, every time Pascal had tried to spot Pierrot, he'd failed. It was honestly impressive.

After gathering his things, Pascal headed outside. School was over, the bell had rung, and he could move on with his day. Standing on the school's rickety wooden stairs, Pascal stretched lazily, taking in the outdoors. He enjoyed the feel of the sun's warm rays on his head. A gust of cold wind shook nearby tree branches.

With two hops, he bounded down the stairs and followed the rest of the children down the road. Though he typically walked home with the other orphans, Pascal's mind was miles from the light chatter that surrounded him. Instead, he slowed his pace and turned to look back down the gravel road. Far behind the group, a slight figure trudged alone.

Pascal squinted, though he already knew just who this figure was. The student wore a navy-blue coat and a thick, knitted scarf on top of a worn-out blue sweater. The coat was the same one all the orphans wore to school, the only uniform item Mistress Alma required. It came with a pair of black pants and sensible leather boots.

Now, Pascal came to a stop, watching the distant face grow nearer and nearer. *Yup. It's Pierrot.*

Finally, the elusive newcomer had made an appearance. And honestly, Pierrot looked miserable. His light brown hair fell over his eyes, which remained firmly fixed on his feet. Even the bulkiness of his coat couldn't cover his thin frame. Pascal estimated him to be thirteen or fourteen.

Just then, a farmer's cart rumbled past, carrying a family of four children who waved at a nearby group, hurrying home along the muddy road. Classmates shouted goodbye to each other cheerfully. A few ran alongside the cart for a bit before tiring.

Cocking his head slightly, Pascal looked from group to group. No one had waited for Pierrot. They ignored him. *How strange.* Rarely were orphans so unwelcoming, though they could be a bit cagey at times. If no one else would speak to the new guy, he'd be the first.

"Hey!" he called out. "You're Pierrot, right?"

He didn't answer. His eyes remained glued to the road, and he kept walking. Pascal waved, but Pierrot walked right past him.

Maybe he was lost in his own thoughts. Or he could be scared. Shy, maybe? Most kids were pretty uncomfortable when they first arrived after all. Pascal hurried to Pierrot's side and fell into step with him. Pierrot didn't respond, but Pascal noticed the kid's hands tighten around the straps of his bag.

"Things probably seem a little scary about now," Pascal said, keeping his voice level and calm. The last thing Pierrot needed was someone pestering him. "I came here a long time ago. But everyone remembers their first day, you know? You feel lost and scared. Everything is new, and you're expected to know the routine right away. It's not easy."

Pascal shoved his hands in his pockets and allowed Pierrot to set the pace. Sure, the silence between them was a bit uncomfortable at first, but after a bit, Pascal felt himself drifting off into his thoughts as he usually did. He enjoyed the company.

Walking down the road with Pierrot felt almost like one of his usual hikes, but better.

When they reached the top of the hill, Pierrot stopped and lingered. In a few minutes, they would reach the orphanage gate. Pascal looked with fresh eyes at the place he had always called home, trying as he could to see it as Pierrot might.

The large piece of land was bounded by a long meadow in front, a few trees dotted here and there. At the end of the lane was the orphanage itself. Beyond the orphanage stood even more land which sloped up a hill into thicker trees, a river, and the back fence. Beyond that fence lay a dense forest: the Quiet Wilds.

To Pascal, it was all he knew, so familiar he could probably navigate it with eyes closed. To Pierrot, it was uncharted territory.

"I want to say that things will get better," Pascal said, breaking the silence. "And they will, probably. But in the meantime, if you want to get away and explore the forest or find a quiet place to think, don't be afraid to ask. I know all the best hiding places at the orphanage, and exploring the woods is always a great escape."

Pierrot hunched his thin shoulders and continued down the road without saying another word. Pascal followed a little more slowly. Would Pierrot take him up on his offer?

He's different, but that doesn't have to be a bad thing. Different is okay.

As Pascal made his way down the snowy lane, he spotted Clarion, Danton, and a few of the other younger boys standing by the porch steps, breathing into their hands and shivering in the cold.

They were clearly waiting for him. At the sight of Pascal behind Pierrot, Clarion let out a whoop and darted down the stairs. Pierrot gasped in surprise at Clarion's shout and skittered to the side, hands repeatedly clenching and unclenching the strap of his backpack.

Pascal noticed this discomfort and raised his hands in an effort to calm everyone down. It was no use. His friends gathered tightly around him.

"Where were you?"

"You're late again."

"Mistress Alma said we need to stick together on our way back from school."

Pascal ignored their comments and looked past them in search of Pierrot, who had since darted inside.

Sighing, he turned to the boys. Perhaps he could get Pierrot to open up some other time.

But Pierrot wasn't in the mess hall when the dinner bell rang.

Tania wore a concerned expression as she and Mistress Alma huddled near the far windows. After grabbing his stew from Michel, Pascal approached Tania to search for some answers.

"Pierrot had a rough first day," she said quietly. "He struggled the entire day at school. Miss Lucía already sent a note to Mistress Alma about it. She sent Clarion to fetch him for dinner, but he refused to leave the library."

Pascal remembered the walk home and the way Pierrot had reacted to Clarion's shouting. There was something nagging at the back of his mind, an answer to a question he hadn't yet asked. If he just had some peace and quiet, maybe the answer to the Pierrot question would come to him.

Just some peace and quiet.

Pascal straightened and quickly approached Mistress Alma, who was overseeing the youngest orphans with Minette at her side.

"Mistress Alma," he said. "I have a question about Pierrot."

"Pierrot?" Mistress Alma turned immediately. "Did he come down after all?"

"No." Pascal shook his head, and her face fell slightly before she recovered her usual expression. "But I was wondering if I could have permission to go talk to him?"

"Talk?" Mistress Alma asked skeptically. "I don't know if talking with Pierrot would help, I'm afraid."

"I just need some peace and quiet," he admitted. "If I sit with him in the library, at least he won't feel alone. Maybe I could bring him dinner? Just this once?"

Her shoulders relaxed a little as she smiled. "Very well. That would be helpful. Thank you, Pascal. Ask Michel for Pierrot's dinner. He should have it ready."

Pascal sped around the front hall to the orphanage's library. The cozy room was located on the opposite side of the building, below the boys' dorm. Upon popping his head inside, he caught sight of Pierrot curled up in a window seat with a large book in his lap. Just by Pierrot's posture, Pascal could tell that he felt at home in the library, more than he had at school by far.

Peace and quiet. Maybe Pierrot feels it's easier to think here too.

"Pierrot," Pascal said as he held out the bowl of potatoes and vegetables. "Michel sent some food for you. Mistress Alma didn't want you to go hungry, so she said you could eat here today. I guess everyone talking in the mess hall can be loud, huh?"

After setting the bowl on the window ledge, Pascal took a seat in a nearby chair. He watched as Pierrot's shoulders slowly relaxed, though his tight grip on the book remained. After a short while, Pierrot nodded, as though silently thanking Pascal. He reached for the bowl and began to slowly eat, still focused on his book.

Pascal mused over the puzzle in silence. If Pierrot didn't like the rambunctious mess hall, how long would it take him to get used to the commotion? Would Pierrot be allowed to eat in the library until he was accustomed to large groups? How would Pierrot get used to the noise if he never left the library?

Shoulders slumped, Pascal absently stared at the puzzle, his eyebrows furrowed. His mind ran through his questions, unsure of where to begin looking for their answers. He didn't want Pierrot to think he was frowning at *him*, so he loosened up and forced a smile.

After Pierrot had finished eating, Pascal took Pierrot's bowl to the kitchen. As he made small talk with Michel, Mateo appeared in the doorway, an empty plate in his hand.

"Ah, Mateo. Done already?" asked Michel.

"It was delicious as always," Mateo replied. "Thank you. It was good to get a meal in before I hit the road."

"You're going?" Pascal asked, stepping forward in haste. He suddenly felt a weight settle on his chest.

"I've stayed two days and a night, a long enough time to impose on my hosts. Can't stay forever, my boy." Mateo chuckled heartily as he clapped Pascal on the back. "Come on, don't be so down. Help me harness Old Betty to the cart."

Pascal followed Mateo out, and together, the two finished hitching the old gray mare to the woodsman's cart. Pascal's fingers brushed through Old Betty's thick mane, and he stared wistfully down the empty lane to the road.

"Remember what I told you the other day?" Mateo asked, as if reading his mind. "It won't be long until you're out there. For now, you have your hands full helping Mistress Alma. And that's a good thing. It'll distract you."

"I suppose so," Pascal answered with a sigh. He leaned against the cart and looked at Mateo, his hands flopping to his side. "It feels like these walls are getting smaller. I know I need to be patient, but I want to see more. I need more."

"And you'll get more," Mateo said, leaning against the cart. "But you need to be careful, Pascal. The world is a dangerous place. Children have been going missing lately. Who knows what lurks in those woods, waiting to snatch them up? There have been stories cropping up of wild animal attacks across the country, even in the Quiet Wilds."

"The Quiet Wilds?" Pascal asked, his curiosity piqued. "I was just in the woods earlier. What's wrong with them?"

Mateo's lips pulled tight, and he shook his head, looking toward the forest. "Maybe it's just the winter season, but something about the forest feels off, more so than it did during other years. Like part of the forest is silent or dead." His voice was barely above a whisper. "The air is charged with tension, and the animals have grown quite discordant. Their strange and aggressive behavior feels out of place. I just ask that you remember even the most tranquil places can hide unsettling secrets." He was quiet for a moment. "The Quiet Wilds is a place of the unknown, like the deep oceans. No one really knows what lies in the waters. Perhaps no one should."

"You sound like a captain," Pascal teased.

Mateo's lips curled into a smile, but his eyes still seemed serious. "We all have pasts. Some more unexpected than others."

Pascal pondered this. He'd never known Mateo outside of his role as woodcutter who helped out at the orphanage. Surely though, his life had been something else before he'd been here, hadn't it? What else had he seen beyond the orphanage's grounds.

Mateo pulled him from his thoughts. "Anything happen today? I heard you got in late from school."

"I was walking with the new boy," Pascal said. "He's..." He stopped and reconfigured what he planned to say to avoid any cliché turns of phrase. "He's finding it hard to fit in right now. As far as I know, he's not like the other kids... but I don't know. I just hope he can get used to living here."

"Time will help," Mateo said. "After all, he just arrived, didn't he?"

"Yeah," Pascal agreed, an unsatisfied frown creasing his eyebrows. "I wish I could help him."

"Hm." Mateo clapped his hat on his head and adjusted his diamond-patterned neckerchief. He peered down at Pascal and then rested a broad hand on the kid's shoulder. "I think you should trust your instincts on this one, Pascal. Rely on your good sense."

Pascal nodded slowly at this. "I trusted my instincts earlier today. It helped me figure out that Pierrot doesn't like noise. I brought him his dinner in the library, and he ate. But even though I understand that, I don't know how to help him. The orphanage is never silent, and the mess hall is always the noisiest place of all of them. How is he supposed to get used to it?"

"Maybe you can ask Mistress Alma to go easy on the boy," Mateo said. "I'm sure she would understand if you explained your theory to her. She's a good woman with a heart of gold. I bet you know that more than I do."

"Of course!" Pascal brightened at the thought. "Maybe she doesn't realize. I'll go talk to her. Thanks Mateo."

Mateo hopped up from his position against the cart, a sad

expression on his face. "Well, it's been good talking to you, Pascal, but I need to get going. Maybe next time I come around, you can introduce me to this new friend."

"I'd like that," Pascal said as he stepped back to let Mateo mount the cart. "When do you think you'll be back?"

Mateo shrugged and placed a hand on Pascal's shoulder again, this time allowing it to linger. "I'm not sure. But while I'm gone, please be careful, Pascal. I know you want to have a little adventure of your own—hell, it's in your blood—but you need to watch yourself out there. With the missing kids and the woods…" He paused, taking a deep breath. "Just be careful."

Pascal nodded, and Mateo gave his shoulder a gentle squeeze before releasing his hold. He hopped onto the cart, behind Old Betty. And with a lighter heart, Pascal watched Mateo rumble down the lane and shrink into the distance.

Pascal turned on his heels and darted inside to find Mistress Alma in the main parlor surrounded by a circle of younger children quietly working on puzzles or reading. At the sight of Pascal, she rose and joined him just outside the parlor door.

"Did you find Pierrot?" she asked.

"I did," he said. "Once I sat down and thought about it, I realized Pierrot doesn't like the noise. When he walked home with me, he didn't talk, but he wasn't upset or anything. Then, we got to the porch, and Clarion yelled. It startled Pierrot. He isn't trying to be a bother, but the noise hurts him. I just think he needs more time to get used to it."

"I see," Mistress Alma said quietly. Pascal could nearly see her thinking. "That does support what Miss Lucía had to say. Perhaps we can give him special permission to eat in the library for the next week or so."

"I can sit with him," Pascal suggested. "I'll keep calm and quiet. That might help him get used to people."

"No jumping or leaping or handstands?" Mistress Alma teased, her eyebrows raised.

Pascal shook his head.

"Well then!" Mistress Alma clapped her hands together with a small smile. "I suppose you boys sitting together would work out well. Over time, he'll get more used to you and to the orphanage at large."

"I hope so."

CHAPTER THREE

LIGHTNING FLASHED, AND THUNDER RUMBLED OVER-head as dark clouds blotted out the setting sun and unleashed a torrential rain. What remained were dull orange and gray tones, now saturated by the downpour. The wind whipped the tree branches into a frenzy. Paloma peered through the bushes, her dark eyes wide.

She knew the place well: the maze of bushes and trees, the narrow dirt path, and the looming mountain spur that towered over the edge of the forest. Monstrosities shifted in the shadows. What they were, Paloma never had time to figure out. Instead, her gaze fixed on the circular doorway rimmed with flames that had appeared on the path moments before, spewing fire sparks that sizzled as they bounced off the damp mud.

The bodies of her parents lay motionless. A dark silhouette stood above them, a solitary figure enduring the cascade.

Another bolt of lightning split the sky in two. The harsh, white light illuminated the glade in a flash. Paloma caught a glimpse of a cruel face, a sinister smile, and two eyes of red flame. The sight of such cheekbones alone was burned into her memory.

Paloma's chest tightened as the figure slowly turned toward the bushes she crouched behind, raindrops trickling down her face. Her heart pounded, the rhythm echoing through her ears. She wanted to scream but couldn't find her voice, her breath stolen from her by the chilling encounter. And what good would a scream do? Who could rescue her now?

She made a choice: she jumped to her feet and bolted through the trees, away from the monstrous figure, rain pelting down on her. Branches and brambles tore at her skin as she ran, but she didn't care, despite how much her body stung. The raindrops mingled with the sweat on her face as her lungs burned, but she forced herself to keep breathing, to keep running. Footsteps crunched the underbrush behind her.

With a sharp gasp, Paloma's eyes flew open. She breathed deeply, her body hunched over on the straw bedding that surrounded her. Tears that silently slipped down her cheeks, and she could taste their salt.

She rubbed her face then and let out a quiet breath. She wrapped her arms around her knees, which were pulled to her chest, and rested her head upon them.

It felt as if it was yesterday.

Gradually, her breathing evened, and she felt calmer. She raised her head to look around her tiny bedroom. The makeshift room was just a nook of crates and barrels, but this abandoned warehouse was what the Rejects called home.

A dingy window cracked open to her right and let in a gust of spring breeze along with the mouth-watering scent of fresh bread. The clatter of carts and horses on the cobblestone below and the faint chatter of voices poured through the window.

Winter was finally over, and spring was in bloom. Pivot had woken up.

"Paloma?" Mira called. "Paloma!"

She rubbed her temple and took a deep breath, ignoring the call of her name. Her legs swung out of bed, and she got dressed with haste. There was no time to fret about her dream. She rushed to a bucket of water to wash her face, not waiting to spend as much time in front of the cracked mirror as a sixteen-year-old probably should. As she dragged her chestnut-brown hair back into a ponytail, Paloma tucked a few wayward strands behind her ears and pinched her cheeks to disguise their pallidness.

Mira and the younger Rejects had already gathered around the rickety table and were scarfing down their meager breakfast by the time she met up with them. For many in this group of orphans and runaways, the simple scraps and warehouse were worth it to be free of their horrible families or orphanages. Sometimes, they were joined by truants from the area called the Stews. This was what they called children who still had families but who were bored with school and chores.

In the corner, Claudio, Clément, and Maldavo stood, their arms folded. They didn't look too happy about Paloma's late arrival. Paloma smiled at the younger children anyway, doing her best to ignore the boys' disapproving glares.

"What happened?" she asked.

"The usual." Mira glanced over at Maldavo, who shook his head sharply in response. "Maldavo will tell you. I'll watch over the rest."

Paloma nodded. "Thank you, Mira."

Clearly, Maldavo wanted to speak to her right away. "Let's go to the roof," he said within seconds of her approaching.

Maldavo was a wiry teen with curly black hair and dull brown eyes. As Paloma's right-hand man, he usually ran scouting missions with Claudio and Clément. Whenever his scouts found out about an opportunity to scavenge food or loot supplies, he and Paloma would plan a mission to acquire the items.

"Did you find out about the shipment?" Paloma asked as they walked, leading the way to their favorite spot on the edge of the flat roof. "Was Irina hiding close to the docks?"

"No sign of Irina," Maldavo said with a careless shrug. "We did get a good look at the boxes though. There were quite a few that seemed promising."

Paloma frowned at the news. Irina had recently gone on a scouting mission and hadn't returned in days. The older girl was one of the Rejects' better scouts, and there was really no way Irina would have gone off on her own for so long. The thought of Irina being caught—or worse—left an unease in Paloma's stomach.

"How many guards did you say there were?"

"Six," Clément answered. "More than usual."

"That's...not good." Paloma clicked her tongue as she thought. When she realized how much noise she was making, she began to chew on her bottom lip instead.

"The city guards have been more uptight than usual," Claudio added before spitting once over the edge of the building. "Maldavo told me to check out the market. I was hanging around Doralin Blackcoat's shop 'cause the boxes were bound there. Anyways, that's when I heard rumors of some kind of...I dunno, disturbance? Something's happening to the north, in the Untamed Highlands."

The hair on Paloma's arms stood on end. "The Quiet Wilds?"

Claudio nodded as he looked out over the town. "It can't be the dragons. I mean, not since Pivot made peace with them."

"A sorcerer, maybe," Maldavo suggested with a shrug. "Or a mountain troll. They'll have it sorted."

"Do you think it's related to Governor de Moura's announcement about the missing kids?" Paloma asked, her eyebrows pulled into a tight frown. Now that the thought had come to her, it wouldn't leave. After all, that would make sense, wouldn't it?

Maldavo rolled his eyes. "Who cares? What we really need to worry about is how we're going to get past the six guards."

Paloma nodded, her face strained. "Perhaps we should lay low. Wait for everything to calm—"

"What?" Maldavo growled, his knuckles turning white from his tight grip. "And give up this chance? The packs looked like they might even have cloth."

"We just need some more blankets, Mal," Paloma said mildly. "Hardly worth risking imprisonment for."

"There could be more there!" His arms waved in desperation, irritation building with every denial Paloma offered. With a sigh, his arms fell to his side, and his voice lowered, transformed into a wheedling tone. "We should at least try. I'm sure you could think up a good escape plan."

"Hmm..." Paloma tapped her chin. "Let me think."

Silence fell. The four teenagers sat, looking over the city of Pivot. Far in the distance, the market's banners waved through the sky victoriously. The airship dock's towers and the distant spires of the governor's castle loomed behind. Squinting, Paloma noticed the massive, colorful tent. The Carnival was back in town.

Wide streets led out from the city center. The tenement

buildings where the poorest citizens of Pivot lived were between their warehouse and its place in the city's central district. A cloud of smoke always seemed to hang over the tenements.

Paloma was struck again by how bright the center of the city looked compared to where they lived. The roofs around them were battered, torn, weathered. Their own warehouse, although occupied, looked abandoned, thanks to the broken windows and doors which hung from their hinges. It was a good hiding spot for the Rejects, but still, their safety was dependent on strategic planning and careful defenses.

Their safety was all dependent on her, she knew. As leader, she had to ensure their safety and provide food and supplies.

They'd hoped to acquire some blankets and bedding for the newest additions to the Rejects. Doralin Blackcoat's Emporium of Fine Goods was expecting new stock, as was typical this time each month. Usually, the Rejects would be able to create a small distraction and sneak off with some goods. This time, however, recently increased presence of city guards made Paloma hesitate.

A big diversion could work. But they would have to be careful. She'd need to send Clément, Claudio, and a few others to lookout positions with prearranged signals.

"I have a plan," Paloma finally said. "But everyone will need to follow my instructions to the letter. Mina will remain here with the youngest ones, but we'll bring the usuals: Nate, Allie, and the rest."

"It's being delivered tomorrow morning," Maldavo said. "We could swoop in bright and early when the guards don't expect it."

Paloma thought for a moment and then slowly nodded. "Tomorrow morning," she agreed. "I want to have a strategic meeting with everyone. Let's pull out the map and talk."

"Maldavo found out about a shipment."

Paloma looked around the table where Maldavo and eleven other Rejects had gathered. "It looks promising, so we're going to try to intercept some of the stuff as it's off-loaded in the alley behind the Emporium."

She moved her thimbles into place and then took a handful of jacks and a couple of dice in her hands. She set them out as visuals for their plans.

"When?" Nate, one of the Rejects' most clever lookouts, asked. He blew away the blond hair that fell over his face as he studied the map.

"Tomorrow morning, bright and early," Paloma answered. "Around the sixth bell, an hour after sunrise."

"The largest cart is scheduled to arrive at half-past," Maldavo interjected.

"Right." Paloma gave Maldavo a look before pointing back to the map. "Nate, Clément, and Claudio will stand here, here, and here on the lookout. You'll wait for the signal which will be a low whistle like this." She demonstrated. "Allie, Ivan, and I will distract the guards. Maldavo and the rest will go for the supplies."

"What?" Maldavo frowned. "I should be the one distracting the guards. You can—"

"Maldavo," Paloma said to cut him off. "This is for the best. *Believe me.*"

"Getting stuff is lame," Maldavo said as he folded his arms. "And I have a new dagger to try."

The mention of a dagger sent a shiver along her spine, and Paloma froze. For a second, she was unable to move at all.

But after a few seconds, she forced the thought away and regained her focus. "We aren't trying to kill people, Mal!" Her voice rose a little. "There's no need to bring something like that."

"What's wrong with a dagger?" Maldavo shot back. A sneer crossed his face as he glared at her. "If I was running this mission, I wouldn't be settling for some sissy job."

"This isn't about being cool or being a sissy. It's about getting what we need. No more and no less. Carrying a weapon like that will invite disaster. What would happen if you hurt someone?"

Maldavo fell silent, but he continued to glare.

She let a hint of frustration escape with her exhale. *Great. Now, he'll spend the next hour or two sulking.*

Unlike the other Rejects, Maldavo had also been around since the gang's creation. Though they were the same age, he had always looked at the world with simpler eyes. He relied primarily on his strength and physical power to get him through challenges, while Paloma preferred to use her street smarts and acrobatic ability to evade city guards. The idea of drawing a weapon on a guard horrified her. An artful Reject would never need a weapon of that sort!

Paloma forced a smile as she looked at the ring of solemn faces around her. "If we follow my plan, we'll get what we need easily. Got it?"

"Got it!" the rest of the Rejects chorused. Clément and Claudio glanced at Maldavo, who simply grunted in response. The other boys glanced at Paloma, and she shrugged. He'd come around like he always did.

Once everyone's questions were answered, the group broke up for the day. Maldavo disappeared with Clément and Claudio, no doubt off to pout somewhere.

Meanwhile, Paloma joined Mina in handing out their meager dinner of potatoes and beans they'd scrounged from the market's dustbins. It wasn't the best, but it was better than nothing. They'd grown content with settling for such things.

When the night fell, the Rejects who played in the streets trickled in to their cots, ready for sleep. The warehouse grew quiet in their slumber, leaving Paloma alone with her thoughts and the pressure to make tomorrow work. So many what-ifs plagued her. Eventually, the very scope of these worries overwhelmed her so much that she finally passed out.

THE GROUP WAS READY BEFORE THE SUN PROPERLY rose over the eastern edge of the docks. Beneath a gray-purple sky, Paloma, Maldavo, and the rest of the group gathered outside.

Today, Paloma tied her long, wavy hair back in a tight bun. She made sure to choose clothing she could easily move in: dark pants, a simple cotton shirt, and a thin jacket. Her sensible leather boots were battered now, but they would provide her with solid footing if they ended up on the run.

The Rejects split into three groups and carefully traced their way through the back alleys of Pivot toward the western side of the market where Doralin Blackcoat's Emporium lay. Clément, Claudio, and Nate positioned themselves on the roofs which surrounded the Emporium, just as they'd planned. Maldavo and a few others hid around the corner, a block away from where the carts were being unloaded.

Paloma, Ivan, and Allie were the only ones to openly saunter through the market. Only a few vendors were open this early:

breakfast merchants and grocery stands who peddled homemade biscuits and various flavors of jellies and jams, enticing the passing laborers. Paloma's mouth watered, but she didn't spare them any glances.

With fewer adults around, the teens were quickly noticed by guards who gathered about the Emporium. Allie threw a couple of tomatoes she had nicked from one of the grocery stands. Ivan blatantly began to pry open the door of a nearby stall. Paloma, a familiar face to the guards, simply walked past, which drew attention right away.

Instantly, the three of them scattered, taking care to run quickly but not too quickly. Five of the guards took the bait. As Paloma leaped over stalls, sprang across low walls, and hopped along rooftops, she glanced back to assure she was being adequately followed. All she had to do was divert the guards a bit longer, lose them in the back alleys of Pivot, and then return to the Emporium.

She thought she heard a low whistle from Nate, hopefully a good sign. Glancing to her right and left, she noticed that Ivan and Allie were already disappearing down their respective alleyways, following orders directly.

Heart singing with excitement and relief, Paloma scampered down the alley she had chosen for herself. Behind her, three guards shouted angrily, but she refused to stop. Instead, she sped up, forcing them to run even faster as she hopped over short fences and swung from one handhold to the next along the alley walls. Before they knew it, the guards had followed her into an empty warehouse, only to find the doors locked behind them.

Paloma slipped out through a hidden exit, leaving the guards banging on the doors. With a merry skip to her step, she quickly returned to the market and hurried to their prearranged spot.

When she arrived, her eyes widened in fear. The Emporium's doors were thrown open. The cart was half-empty, but there was no sign of Maldavo or the others. Paloma looked around, frowning, only to spot a ring of city guards quickly closing in on her.

In the open square, there weren't many options for hiding places. She bolted for the alley where the cart stood, only to be cut off by more guards who raised their winched crossbows and flintlock rifles.

"Stand down, girl," a man's deep voice resounded behind her.

Paloma whipped around and glared at the speaker: Captain Roscoe, the burly, black-bearded commander of the city guards. He stood before her, hands on his hips, a victorious smile on his face. She'd been caught.

Paloma stepped back. Two strong pairs of hands roughly grabbed her shoulders and arms, and she jerked forward to shrug them off. They didn't let up, and their grip only tightened.

"No!" she yelled. "Let me go!" Her heart pounded like thunder as her panic surged. She couldn't go to jail. She couldn't let them take her. Too many people depended on her.

Kicking and shouting, Paloma yanked as hard as she could. It was of no use.

"If you don't calm down, we shall have to cuff you, girl," Captain Roscoe said. "You either come quietly or…"

He let the statement linger in the air.

"You have no right!" Paloma protested. "I did nothing wrong!"

"Hmm," Captain Roscoe said, ticking his words off on his fingers, one-by-one. "Let me see. Trespassing on private property. Robbery and theft of various goods. Inciting children to delinquent behavior. Conspiring to steal from the Emporium..."

"Conspiring to steal—?" Paloma gasped.

How did he know that? Her gaze darted around the market, seeking out familiar faces within the shadows. If the Rejects were following her backup plan, they would distract the guards long enough for her to escape. Yet, there was no sign of any of them. *Had the other Rejects also been captured? But how were they gotten rid of so quickly.*

Something shifted within the shadows. Her gaze immediately fixed on a nearby building, where a handful of faces peered out: Maldavo, Clément, and Claudio, along with Nate and Allie. Paloma breathed a sigh of relief. At least they were safe.

Yet, the thought did not bring her as much comfort as she hoped when she caught sight of the expression on Maldavo's face. He looked smug, almost happy, at her predicament.

He didn't... Maldavo wouldn't!

Her mind raced. *But wouldn't he? He's always questioned you. You knew it would be a matter of time before he would challenge you. You thought he wouldn't be able to outsmart you, but he's definitely smart enough to know how to get others to do his dirty work for him.*

The realization was a punch in the gut that knocked the breath right out of her. Paloma slumped, biting down on her lip as the guards surged forward to cuff her. She couldn't even bring herself to fight back. Angrily blinking back tears, Paloma struggled to keep her disappointment hidden from Captain Roscoe. And when Doralin Blackcoat, a dwarf, came out and gazed at Paloma with an inscrutable expression, Paloma didn't say anything then either.

"No parents, no living kin," Doralin said, scratching her chin. "Where's the girl to go?"

"Prison, if I had my say." Captain Roscoe spat at the ground to emphasize his point. "But knowing the guv, she'll end up at Mistress Alma's with the rest. If they can keep her, that is. We'll see. I'm not holding out hope."

"And the others?" asked one of the city guards.

"We'll catch them," Captain Roscoe said, flapping his hand nonchalantly. "Let them go for today. Without her to lead them, rounding them up will be an easy matter."

His words cut through her heart like a dagger. *The man was right.* Without Paloma, the Rejects were done for. And now, it sounded like Paloma was headed for the last place she wanted to be: The Skystead Home for Orphaned Children. If the orphanage was like the others that the Rejects hailed from, it would be worse than prison.

But it's not over, she told herself. *Once I get there, maybe I can find a way to escape. Maybe there'll be other kids there who want to join the Rejects. I'll fight my way out of there, and then I'll...I'll...*

She'd find a way to return. But after Maldavo's betrayal, would things ever be the same?

CHAPTER FOUR

"Good morning, sleepyheads!" Minette's cheery voice jolted Paloma out of whatever formless dream she'd been lost in.

She woke with a gasp and groaned softly as the foggy maze of dreams melted away to reveal the wooden beams of the girls' dorm at the orphanage. For a moment more, she lay against the thick, goose-down pillow and traced a trail with her hand across the edge of the soft blue and red blanket covering the bed.

It reminded her of the blankets she had been dreaming of getting for the newest Rejects. Her heart sank at the thought of them. If Maldavo and the city guards had their way, the Rejects wouldn't be Paloma's problem anymore. She hadn't intended to leave them to survive on their own; she'd always wanted to do nothing but protect them from all harm.

She blew out a breath, refocusing her energy on the most pressing problem: what to do now. Paloma had thought that she would escape the orphanage easily on the day of her capture, but since her arrival, she'd realized life here wasn't as bad as the other orphanages some of the Rejects had escaped from. Honestly, her life here was much easier than it had been before.

She couldn't remember the last time she'd slept in such a nice bed. For as long as she'd been living on the streets, taking care of the Rejects, life had been hard. They only ever had rickety cots and straw beds to sleep in. The mattresses at the orphanage were far more comfortable than the thin pallets of the warehouse.

Although her bed at the orphanage had given her more restful sleep, it still didn't erase her unease. The cruel face that had loomed over her parents' bodies hadn't reappeared in her dreams recently, but her nights remained filled with dark forests. Such things, though faceless, were still terrifying.

"Paloma?" A little girl approached Paloma shyly. "Breakfast soon."

Before Paloma could say anything in response, the girl retreated. Paloma found it hard not to smile. It had become routine for the girl to announce breakfast to each of the new boarders especially, and the girl's shyness momentarily had Paloma regretting how abrasive she'd been initially. The regret passed. She couldn't get attached to this place.

Slowly, she got up and slipped into the new clothing Mistress Alma had given her. The thin, navy summer jacket wasn't her favorite, but she liked the deep red blouse and black skirt with small, red polka dots. No doubt it was a hand-me-down from some well-to-do young lady from the city, but it possessed a touch of flair that she nonetheless appreciated. Just in case Paloma wanted to explore the woods later, she added a pair of gray shorts underneath.

As she surveyed herself in the mirror, Paloma tied her hair into a quick bun before turning away. She realized that one of the older girls about her age, Minette, was watching her. All of the younger girls had already lined up to follow Tania down the main staircase to the mess hall. With a half-smile towards the spy, Paloma trailed behind the group, listening to the girls chatter in line in front of her.

As Paloma ate the hearty breakfast served by the ever-silent Cook Michel, she looked about the hall with appreciation in spite of herself. When she had arrived at the orphanage, she'd struggled to fit in. Even the always-sweet Minette and the ever-exuberant Pascal had gotten a tongue-lashing when they dared to say hello.

Though her arrival had been relatively recent, it was still clear that much had changed since then. As one day trickled into the next, Paloma felt the cloak of anger and sadness beginning to melt away around her. Perhaps she would always experience pangs of betrayal and disappointment when she thought about Maldavo and the Rejects, but she was no longer afraid of the orphanage. That much she knew for certain.

When she had first arrived in the company of two city guards, the grand facade of the building had intimidated Paloma. The place sported a wide veranda and double oak doors with heavy knockers. Of course, it had been intimidating. Yet, once inside, Mistress Alma had greeted them and invited the three visitors into her private study opposite the main entrance doors. The woman was kind, clearly, though she did seem as though she'd be strict when such a thing was necessary.

After her admission into the orphanage, Paloma had been shown the large mess hall in the west wing, where everyone ate. Mistress Alma told her that the east wing consisted of two parlor rooms, where prospective parents could come to meet the children, the library, and other smaller playrooms where the children relaxed during cold winter nights. A garden and large yard lay between the east and west wings and served as the preferred play area for most orphans. On the second floor, the west wing was dedicated to the girls' dorm and bathrooms, while the east wing housed the boys. Mistress Alma, Cook Michel, and other part-time staff stayed in the middle rooms above the front hall. The layout was relatively easy to make sense of, and she did so within a few days.

Now, Paloma stared out the mess hall window at the vegetable garden. *It isn't so bad. In some ways, I almost enjoy it. I wonder what the Rejects would say about that.*

However, knowing her ragamuffin family was out there made it impossible for Paloma to fully embrace her life at the orphanage. She worried for them. Of course she did! She had been their leader, and leaving behind people you cared for like that was never simple. Plus, in the back of her mind, she was sort of waiting for something awful to happen here. The Rejects had trained her to believe such things were inevitable in places like this.

But so far...nothing.

Although it would have been an easy matter to scramble over the orphanage fence and head back to Pivot, she knew the city guards would severely punish her if she were caught. She would play along for now.

At least school is over, she reminded herself. *It would be much worse if I had been going to class.*

Paloma repressed a shudder at the thought. Because she'd never spent a day of her life in school, Mistress Alma believed she needed to do some catch-up work. As a result, Paloma was given quite a bit of summer homework and spent mornings with the other kids who had summer homework from their teachers, all of them quietly grumbling to themselves at not being allowed to enjoy the summer sun. Still, it was better to learn at the orphanage than elsewhere. The people here were kind.

The other teens studied various trade skills to prepare them for work after the orphanage. But since Paloma had so much catching up to do, she didn't get to practice the work she'd do as an adult. Instead, she was carefully monitored by the ever-studious Tania as she attempted to learn many years' worth of education in one summer. Or, at least, as she tried to

Paloma struggled to focus constantly, but again and again, she was restricted to the library to go over her homework with Tania. Today, every now and then, she stared out the library window and wished she was somewhere else.

"I want to go outside," she said today, looking up from her notes.

Tania laughed. "That sounds like something Pascal would say."

"Really?" Paloma asked, perking up at the thought of another like her.

"Yes," Tania said. "He loves exploring in the forest... and beyond, if you believe his tales. I mean, I'm sure he'd invite you on his next trip if you asked."

"It sounds fun." She tried not to look too excited at the possibility.

"Just ask him," Tania said. She held up a thick textbook in lieu of changing the subject. "For now, let's get caught up on history. What do you know about Pivot's past?"

With that, Paloma was forced into the textbook until half-past eleven. When their study time ended, Paloma's energy returned, as though it had just been waiting for this moment. Quickly, she helped Tania stack up the books and return them to the shelves. And it was then that she noticed a quiet, brown-haired boy poring over a thick volume, his finger slowly moving across the page.

What was his name? Paloma wondered. *Pierre? Piet? Pierrot? Something like that.* Tania had mentioned he didn't talk or respond to anyone but Pascal and Mistress Alma. Still, from the looks of him, he was just like any other kid.

Paloma ignored her curiosity as best as she could and finished putting the books away before following Tania to the mess hall. Along the way, they talked about Tania's dreams of going to a teacher's college.

"So, that's for me and Minette," Tania said. "Then, there's Clarion and Danton. They'll probably go into the trades: airship dock workers, blacksmiths, something like that..."

The girl trailed off as the two of them entered the room. A spectacle was unfolding before them.

Pascal was upside down on top of a table, as usual, performing a special handstand on his elbows. Paloma watched as he pushed himself up dexterously onto his hands and then swiveled about, his face burning bright red from the reorientation.

"Oh, Tania! And Paloma!" he shouted in greeting.

Tania huffed and set her hands on her hips, though she did roll her eyes in amusement at Pascal's antics.

"And then there's Pascal," she said humorously. "He'll no doubt end up at the Carnival."

"The Carnival," Paloma echoed.

"Carnival?" Pascal hopped off the table at its mention. "Are you two planning to go?"

"Mistress Alma hasn't mentioned any trips to Pivot," Tania said. "I was just telling Paloma that you're probably headed to the Carnival as soon as you turn eighteen."

"Well, that would be nice, but I could also own my own airship. Embark on an adventure. See where the sky takes me. I might end up a local legend in Vale."

Paloma saw Tania's lips thin at Pascal's clearly fantastical dreams. Still, the fact that Pascal was so optimistic warmed her heart in a way she hadn't expected. Tania and the others scoffed at Pascal's hopes, and she found them a tad bit hard to believe, of course. But there was something disarming about the way Pascal grinned. Tania's disapproving stare melted away, and a smile tugged at Paloma's cheeks.

"That sounds nice, Pascal," Tania finally said, her tone deceiving her words. Paloma couldn't help but wonder if the fake-kindness had something to do with her. "Just don't get yourself killed in the process, alright?"

With that, Tania moved down the tables to talk with Mistress Alma.

Pascal shrugged and smiled sheepishly at Paloma. He leaned in, a clever smirk on his face, one eyebrow cocked. "Do I sound that crazy?"

"A little," Paloma said, pinching her fingers together to match the smallness of her tone.

"Pierrot!" Pascal's gaze shifted just beyond her shoulder. "Glad you could make it. Did you get some studying done this morning?"

The quiet boy from the library slipped past her elbow. In his hands were the two colored balls he always carried. Although he wasn't as skilled at juggling as Pascal, Pierrot was quite competent, from what Paloma had heard. Instead of answering Pascal's question, the boy nimbly rolled his blue ball from one side of his hand to the other. Paloma couldn't help but smile.

"Good to hear," Pascal answered, as though somehow reading Pierrot's mind. "My morning felt so slow. I mean, I thought it'd last forever."

"What were you up to?" Paloma asked.

"Master Geraldo gave a talk on caring for horses," Pascal said. "He's the farmer from the next field over. Some of the younger boys said they might be interested in farming, so he came in to talk."

"Horses can be fun," Paloma said with a shrug.

"Not when Master Geraldo talks about them." Pascal's posture shifted into a slouch as he stuck an invisible piece of straw between his teeth and took on a farmer's drawl. "There're only so many things, m'girl, that you can talk 'bout a hoss 'afore it gets dull, y'know?"

A burst of laughter erupted out of Paloma before she could catch herself. Even Pierrot, who was always solemn, grinned widely.

The other children who had been listening in started to mimic Pascal's impression of Master Geraldo, sticking their bellies out and slouching about the room. Luckily, Mistress Alma swooped in before chaos could fully take over and hustled everyone to their seats for lunch. Paloma could've sworn she saw Pascal shoot her a wink.

After lunch, Pascal and Pierrot slipped out the back kitchen door by themselves. Paloma hesitated. Could she follow them? Pierrot never talked to anyone, and from the stories she'd heard, he was very shy. Would they even want someone else along? The last thing she wanted was to feel unwelcome. Sure, Tania said Pascal liked to explore with friends, but would Pierrot be alright with the change?

Just then, Pascal turned from the door and waved to Paloma with a grin. Her cheeks flushed, and she waved back lamely before darting back into the mess hall.

Yes, she told herself, catching her flustered breath. *Another day.*

DAYS TURNED TO WEEKS.

Paloma hovered on the fringes of the orphans' various social circles. Although she was friendly toward Tania, Minette, and Pascal, there was a barrier between herself and the others at the orphanage. Was it her long years of living on the street? All the suspicions and fears she'd built up that couldn't be laid to rest? She wanted to feel that sense of belonging…but could she? Was it even possible when the Rejects were still out there?

On a day halfway through summer break, Paloma left the mess hall after breakfast, lost to her idle thoughts. Would she make it through the reading she was expected to get done? Maybe she should go to the library to get started.

Paloma came to a screeching halt before she could even make it to the stairs.

In the entrance hall of the orphanage stood three familiar faces: a group of younger Rejects! All of them looked petrified, but when they caught sight of Paloma, their relief was palpable.

It's just like the first day I arrived, she thought. *But they'll have me to rely on. I can help them.*

She moved forward and welcomed the Rejects with open arms. Since they were younger, under the age of ten, they had no idea what had led to their capture. They didn't know about the larger dynamics of the organization and the greater world around them. Des, Leo, and Maria could only tell her that there had been a raid on the warehouse. Most of the children had escaped, but the few who were slower had been easily caught by the guards. Once they'd been captured, they'd lost track of the others entirely.

Yet, the raid wasn't the end of it, Paloma realized quickly. This time, the guards seemed determined to ferret out as many kids as possible. Over the next few weeks, handfuls of Rejects were brought in on a regular basis. Paloma checked the front hall every morning, whether she was going to the library or not.

One day, she saw Allie, Nate, and Mira with Little Bea in her arms. Their faces were pale, eyes dark with exhaustion. Allie's face was blank, but Paloma could tell she was nervous by the way she clutched the edge of her threadbare sweater. Nate's blue eyes were round saucers on his thin face. The four trembled, clutching each other, as though they'd be forcibly separated if they let go for even a moment.

Paloma's heart sank with worry. All of them looked more scared and hungrier than before. When Paloma had led the Rejects, no one this young had been this hungry. Nate had obviously lost weight since the last time she'd seen him, and even Bea's bright red cheeks looked thin. Without thinking, Paloma rushed forward.

"Mira!" she said. "Nate and Allie! What are you doing here?"

They stared in shock.

"P-Paloma?" stuttered Mira, her eyes wide as if she had seen a ghost.

Nate and Allie stared down with guilty expressions and hunched shoulders. Nate looked particularly miserable. Paloma sighed and rapped the young boy on the forehead.

"I'm fine, thanks for asking," she said dryly. "I've been here since the day I was captured, so whatever you did, Nate, don't feel too bad. It's not like I've been languishing in prison. Things really aren't so bad here."

There was a tangible relief, though Paloma could still see the tension each of them held in their limbs.

"Maldavo said the mission went wrong," Mira said. "I've been so worried for you. I thought—"

"Oh, the mission certainly went wrong," Paloma said grimly, an edge in her tone. "I'm sure Nate and Allie could tell you all about that."

"But we—I mean, Maldavo, he..."

"He's an ass," Paloma answered, "and an idiot. I don't care what he did to me anymore. I'm sure you're here because of some poor planning on his part. Am I wrong?"

"No," Nate said gruffly, shuffling his feet, eyes still trained downwards. "Maldavo's mission last night didn't go well, and we weren't able to shake the guards. Most of us scattered, but I stayed behind with Allie to help Mira pack...and then..."

"We were caught," Mira said, still holding tightly onto Bea, who had begun to cry, from hunger no doubt. Mira bounced the baby up and down in an effort to calm her. "Then, we were brought here. I mean, what's going to happen to us, Paloma?"

"Well," Mistress Alma's voice answered before Paloma could speak. "How about we start with some breakfast? I think Little Bea here would like some food."

Upon the advent of Mistress Alma's calm gaze and welcoming smile, Paloma relaxed a little. The guards doffed their helmets and bowed politely. Behind Mistress Alma, Minette stood, her bright eyes fastened on Little Bea. Mira watched the young girl for a moment with wary eyes and then nodded stiffly.

Once everyone was eating, Paloma cornered Mira and asked for more information. Mira, watching Minette dote on Bea, had relaxed her posture a bit. No doubt, she realized that the orphanage was far from the evil place the Rejects had always thought it to be. Paloma knew that this moment of realization meant Mira would probably be a bit more willing to answer questions.

"What happened? *Really?*"

Mira stared at Paloma for a long moment, as though trying to discern Paloma's game. And then, moments later, she spoke, seemingly accepting of the answer.

"After you were captured, things went from bad to worse," Mira confessed. "Honestly, I should have known this was all Maldavo's fault. He was strutting around like he owned the place, even though everything was falling apart. Like he was happy that you were gone. I didn't understand. Maybe I didn't want to understand."

"He set me up and compromised our mission just so he could become the leader," Paloma said. "He showed his true colors, those of a cruel, cowardly boy. And he's no real leader, not even a bit. He never deserved the Rejects, but I never worried. I never thought he'd do anything of that kind."

"Well, when you didn't return, we feared the worst," Mira said, shaking her head. "Maldavo tried to make plans, but you know how he is. Every single one of his missions ended failed, and we lost one or two Rejects each time. I mean, we couldn't even find a place to stay by the end. Anyone who went back to the warehouse was in danger of being caught. I mean, you probably know that already. Most of them are probably here."

"They are," Paloma said, "but they couldn't tell me the whole story. Well, Claudio probably could if he wanted to, but he refuses to talk to me."

"Maldavo's minion," Mira said with a scoff, her voice filled with annoyance. "He's probably still scared of Maldavo. You know how he and Clément were always at Mal's beck and call. Even though it was and is abundantly obvious that Maldavo doesn't have half of your street smarts or sense of strategy."

"As things got tougher, I suppose Mal made poor judgments," Paloma guessed, voice soft.

Mira nodded. "You know he'll end up here. It's only a matter of time. Then, you'll have to watch your back. For now, Claudio is no danger to you."

"I know," Paloma said, looking away.

She imagined Maldavo entering the backyard, sneering and scoffing at the rest of the children. Maldavo, the one always stupid enough to carry a knife around. Just the thought gave Paloma a headache.

"Forget me," Paloma said with a wave of her hand. "I can take care of myself. I'm more worried about everyone else. He'll try to bully people here into doing what he wants. I mean, Mistress Alma won't accept that."

"And you'll be here too, right? You can stop him."

"I'll do my best."

Deep down, though, she wondered whether her best would be enough. *I didn't see his betrayal coming. I should have given Maldavo more thought, but I underestimated him.* He's always been an idiot, certainly, but a dangerous one? She wondered if she would be able to stop him, given a second chance.

She couldn't keep her mind from going to his knife. He could very well still have the weapon when he arrived at the orphanage.

Paloma took a deep breath to calm herself. Knives always had that effect on her, much more than any other weapon. Ever since, she'd used one to defend herself when she was assaulted by a man on Pivot's streets in her childhood. Not knowing what else to do, she had wrestled her attacker, grabbed hold of his knife, and drove it straight through his heart, killing him.

It was an act of self-defense.

She knew that, she did. Yet, it wasn't enough to eliminate the trauma that still lingered on the edges of her consciousness.

Just the thought of the cold metal pressed against her skin sent a shiver through her body as she relived the horror all over again.

But worse were the evil thoughts that clung to that fear, an even greater darkness waiting to claim her. *Why couldn't it have been the man who killed my parents?* It was a question she'd asked many times, a wish she'd made repeatedly for many years. What she would give to have driven that knife through *that* man's heart.

CHAPTER FIVE

"WHO'S IN CHARGE AROUND HERE?"

That voice. It was familiar.

Paloma turned to see the backyard door swing open, and it was confirmed. Her worst fears had manifested: Maldavo strode into the large, square yard, Clément following him closely. He strutted about with a scowl on his face, asserting his dominance like an animal.

Paloma stepped in front of Mira and Minette as they supervised the younger children playing in the dirt. Maldavo's eyes darted to her immediately upon her movement. His lips curled into a dark grin, and he spat on the ground, his furious gaze meeting her level stare. The children in the yard instantly hushed.

Maldavo folded his arms slowly. "So," he repeated with belligerence, "who's in charge around here?" His stance and nasty expression threatened danger. She knew he'd play some sort of game like this.

Not even five minutes, and he's already starting trouble. He stood at his full height, towering over the younger children. To them, he probably looked intimidating, and he knew it.

Paloma, however, wasn't impressed. She crossed her arms and cocked her hip to the side with a smirk. He looked down. *Maldavo, the bully, avoiding my gaze.* The coward. Of course, he wouldn't openly cross her. Of course, he knew her power. Instead, he was going to pick on the weaker children. She'd expect nothing less from him.

If he'd just shut up and follow the rules, they could find a way to put what happened in the past. Of course, she'd never trust him again, but at least they wouldn't be at war. But she knew there was no way Maldavo would go for something as simple as that.

Claudio moved over to stand at Maldavo's side right away. Paloma rolled her eyes. Of course, Claudio and Clément would tag along without question. The three had always worked and fought together. Clément, though, was usually the quietest and smartest one of the three. Maybe he would think twice after everything Maldavo had done. If Paloma could turn any of them, it would probably be Clément.

I'm delusional. He's obviously chosen his side.

Paloma glanced at Mira, who stared at Maldavo with disgust and held Little Bea close. Minette's mouth gaped, and her eyebrows raised. She clearly couldn't believe someone like this had entered their space. Had the orphanage ever had troublemakers like Maldavo?

"Nobody?" barked Maldavo.

More children moved back, leaving a wide clearing around him which only made him seem even more powerful. A few more of the Rejects hesitated, looking to Paloma and Mira for leadership. In the strained silence, Claudio whispered something into Maldavo's ear.

Maldavo's gaze finally settled on Paloma. Maldavo smirked and gave her a toothy grin, his chest puffed out in confidence. It was all an act, a facade he could use to look tough and boost his ego.

Paloma stepped forward silently, her posture relaxed but defensive. Her hands tightened around her elbows as she kept her arms crossed. In response, Maldavo eased back a hair. He seemed reluctant to lose ground, though he was also clearly unwilling to stand up to Paloma in this moment. She knew far more about this turf than he did.

Her lips curled in satisfaction, but before she could say anything of her victory, she heard a distant shout and a rustle. The hedge that lined the backyard parted, and Pascal's head popped out comically from among the leaves, followed by Pierrot's.

At the sight of Pascal, Clarion stood up and said. "Pascal! Come meet the new kid!"

"We have more?" Pascal asked, his tone laced with excitement. He had never been ambivalent about meeting a new orphan, that was for sure.

He clambered out of the hedge and cartwheeled toward Paloma. With a friendly smile, he waved at Maldavo, who didn't respond.

"More of the kids I knew," Paloma explained in a dry tone. "This is Maldavo and this is Clément. Close friends with Claudio, as you can see."

"Ahh," Pascal said, as he ran his hands through the leaves that had snagged in his unruly hair. "Glad to have you here, Maldavo, Clément."

"Sure," Maldavo said carelessly. "I'll make myself right at home."

His eyes scanned Pascal and Pierrot, sizing them up. Pierrot, with his reserved, almost-blank expression, didn't get a second look, but Pascal clearly caught Maldavo's eye. Pascal was tall, athletic, and not at all bad-looking, though Paloma would never admit that. His carefree expression and easy-going charm had already melted away some of the tension on the playground, though Maldavo did the best he could to maintain authority and control.

If Maldavo had any sense, he would recognize that he was outnumbered. Unfortunately, knowing him, Paloma's presence and Pascal's natural charisma would only inflame Maldavo's need to prove himself, especially in front of this new crowd.

"Want to play some ball?" Pascal asked suddenly. He grabbed a nearby kickball and bounced it expertly against his knee. "We play a mean game here at the orphanage."

"Give it a try!" Nate spoke up in encouragement, finally regaining the courage needed to speak. Pascal passed the ball to Maldavo, who watched it bounce on the ground and roll away. The game died as quickly as it had begun.

"Maybe another time," Maldavo said with a sneer. "I have to talk with my men."

"Men?" Pascal quirked an eyebrow.

"You wouldn't understand," Maldavo replied with a sniff of disdain.

With that, he strode inside, followed by Claudio and Clément. Pascal nearly let out a laugh, but Paloma glared at him before the sound could leave his lips.

"His men?" Pascal echoed again. "What is going on?"

"He's still on the streets, Pascal," Paloma answered. "At least, in his head, he is."

"But he's here now. He doesn't have to think about stuff that way." Pascal grabbed the ball and tossed it to her, his voice ringing high and nonchalant with innocence.

Paloma caught the ball at the last second before it fell to the ground. "You have to understand, the streets of Pivot are all we ever knew. You don't get anything without power and respect. Whether you gain those things through fear or admiration is up to you, but it's how we think. How we've survived. Can't turn that off so quickly."

"I suppose. You weren't like that," Pascal said, holding her gaze. The silence between them lasted a long few seconds, before Pascal dropped his eyes abruptly. "It's a shame, though. It would've been nice to have another guy to hang out with."

Paloma hesitated. This was a golden opportunity to ask Pascal about his and Pierrot's little excursions. "Well," she said, "if you want—"

"Paloma!" A young girl wailed her name as she barreled into the yard. "Jason took my dolly!"

Paloma turned to the girl. Her discussion about joining Pascal would have to wait. *I already have enough to deal with anyway*, she reminded herself. Maldavo was here.

If Maldavo had arrived during the school year, perhaps things might have been easier. Even though Mistress Alma had planned a summertime schedule of housework, chores, homework, events, and other activities for the orphans, everyone still had a lot of spare time on their hands.

Too much time.

Because of this relative summer freedom, it was hard to keep tabs on Maldavo, who seemed to be hard at work recruiting Nate, Danton, and two other boys into his small gang. Pascal wasn't taking Maldavo's efforts very seriously. After attempting a few more times to find something in common with the new arrivals, Pascal had stepped back.

No doubt he thought Maldavo needed some space. Paloma couldn't disagree more.

It was hard not to get upset all over again about what had happened in the market every time she spotted Maldavo. The memory filled her with determination. That boy was evil, and he was going to ruin the orphanage if left unchecked.

If someone had told the old Paloma that she would get so worked up about Maldavo's impact on the orphanage, she would have thought they were crazy.

However, her brief time at the orphanage had taught her the precious treasure of a secure home. Her nightmares still bothered her a little, of course, but she didn't have to wake up every day worried about keeping the youngest Rejects fed. If Maldavo gave the orphanage a chance, he might discover something of this kind also.

But he wouldn't. He'd never understand. He'd never listen.

Just like what happened to your parents, the voice hissed. *He'll destroy everything.* She couldn't risk having everything taken from her like that again. The anger bubbled deep within her, steadily growing closer to the surface. Her resentment of Maldavo had blurred with the resentment of her parents' killer, merging into an enduring desire for revenge.

M ALDAVO SHOWED HIS TRUE COLORS TWO WEEKS after his arrival.

The orphanage was mostly empty. Many of the children had decided to go paddling in the small stream that ran through the nearby forest. Only a few had remained behind to finish their homework and handicrafts, no one Paloma was particularly close with.

Although she had planned to run out to the forest and join the others, Paloma wanted to make sure Nate and a few of the other boys had been invited.

There were no sign of Nate. That worried her.

She walked over to the door that opened into the boys' dorms in the east wing. Hesitating, she turned and discovered Pascal walking down the hallway behind her. He looked pensive and a but worried.

"Pascal," she said in quiet greeting.

"Paloma." He stopped and looked around, as though he were lost. "Sorry. I was just…"

"Looking for something?" she asked.

"Pierrot," he replied. "We were supposed to meet by the big oak tree after lunch, but he never showed. That's not normal. Pierrot's a stickler about time."

"Is he?" Paloma asked. "I had no idea. Did he get distracted by a book?"

"I checked the library already. He's not there." Pascal shook his head. "I thought maybe he might be in the dorms. But why would he? I mean, he's really very—"

"No harm in checking," Paloma said with a shrug. "I was going to knock on the door myself. Tania and the rest are out by the stream, and they wanted to make sure everyone was invited. She said Clarion and Danton were absent, and they usually show up first for these kinds of things."

Pascal frowned, confirming Paloma's suspicions about the oddity of the situation. "That is strange. Let's see."

Opening the door to the boys' dorm, Pascal revealed the neat hallway lined with doors, most of which opened into spacious rooms filled with neatly-made beds. The layout, the wood floors, and the whitewashed walls looked just like the girls' dorm but barer. Over time, the girls had decorated the walls of their dorm with drawings and cross-stitch projects. The boys...not so much. It was pretty dreary.

Just as she was about to ask where Pierrot's room was, a door further down the hall burst open. Clarion bolted out, yelling incoherently about Mistress Alma.

"Get back here, you little shit!" a rough voice growled.

Claudio. He appeared in the doorway, and, catching sight of Paloma and Pascal, he halted.

At the same time, Clarion cowered behind Pascal, keeping his eyes fastened on Claudio. Paloma's apprehension turned to anger when she noticed the bruise on the younger boy's cheek.

I knew it. I knew he'd be up to no good. Of course, Claudio and Clément were just going to do whatever he said and cause trouble as well. They were their own little mob, and she was going to put a stop to that.

"Pierrot's inside!" Clarion gasped, his heart clearly racing. Between breaths, he added, "Where's Mistress Alma? Those jerks need to be stopped!"

"Maybe in her study," Paloma suggested. "Check there. If she isn't, try the kitchen."

As Clarion ran down the hall, Paloma strode forward. Anger surged through her, tinting her vision with red. Darkness crept at the edges of her thoughts. She would take revenge on Maladavo. She tried to push the sinister thoughts away, but too much rage had filled her. She was ready to knock him down a few pegs.

Before she could move, Pascal forced his way past Claudio. When he made it through the doorway, he jolted to a stop, frozen.

Huddled on the floor was Pierrot. Maldavo stood above him, his thick-soled boot on top of the boy's head. Because Pierrot's arms were wrapped around his head, Paloma couldn't even tell if he was conscious. Bruises riddled his arms, and Paloma winced even just looking at him.

"Pierrot!" Pascal cried.

His usually friendly expression was clouded, and his eyes narrowed into slits, possessing enough venom to strike down even the deadliest snake. Maldavo was that snake. Paloma almost had to do a double-take to make sure she wasn't imagining this angry version of Pascal.

He moved forward, but Maldavo refused to budge. Instead, his foot pushed down harder on Pierrot's head, causing the boy to moan, low and pained. Paloma had never heard Pierrot talk, but she had occasionally heard him make similar sounds when he felt stressed, scared, or overwhelmed. She looked at Pascal desperately.

Without warning, Pascal stepped forward, not giving Maldavo any time to react. He pushed the bully back, dislodging his foot instantly. Maldavo flew to the ground and landed against it with a hard thud. His eyes burned with animosity.

Paloma, in the meantime, glared at Claudio and Clément, raising her fist as if to strike. The two boys cowered, unwilling to move to help Maldavo, as she moved to Pierrot's side.

Gently, she laid a hand on his elbow. "Come on, Pierrot," she said in the softest voice she could summon. "It's time we got out of here."

"I'll take him," Danton mumbled.

Paloma glanced over at Pascal, who stared at Danton in confusion. Apparently, he hadn't noticed the boy either.

With a disapproving frown, Pascal eyed Danton. "What are you doing here? Hanging out with bullies now, Danton?"

"I wasn't with them." Danton shuffled his feet and hung his head, his breath clearly catching at the accusation. "He tried to get me to join all week. He cornered me and threatened to hurt me...but I didn't like it when they started hitting people."

"So, you went along with it?" Paloma spat. "That's a familiar story. I don't even see why you're all picking on Pierrot anyway. He isn't gang material. Anyone can see that."

"He's a weirdo. That's reason enough. He's already on the outs," Claudio said, forcing a laugh as he glanced at Maldavo for approval. He didn't receive much, but he continued on anyway. "Why would you care anyway, Paloma?"

"You need to pick on kids smaller than you for validation? Grow up! Pierrot is different, and so what? That doesn't mean we should be mean to him." Paloma shook her head and turned to the pale-faced Nate, who also bore a guilty face. "After everything you've seen, everything you've done, are you sure you want to hang around with a witless bully like Maldavo?"

"Who you calling witless?" Maldavo chimed in from the corner, where he was busy picking up his pride.

"Maldavo isn't—" Clément chimed in, but Paloma cut him off.

"I'm not talking to you." She glared at Clément in warning. The authority she'd once had over him had not disappeared, and he cowered at her words. "I'm talking to Nate."

Nate looked away for a moment. "I'll go with Danton too."

"The kids are gathered at the stream. If you want to have some real fun, go outside and join them. Standing around watching Maldavo spout his idiocy is a waste of everyone's time. Especially on a day like today."

With a nod, Nate followed Danton out. Pierrot stood between the two boys, having carefully gotten to his feet. Pierrot still wouldn't look up, his face covered in dirt and dried tears.

Paloma looked to Pascal, whose eyes hardened the moment Pierrot stumbled out of the room. Maybe it was guilt or disappointment that the other boys had joined in on the mess, but his expression held such contempt and anguish.

"Maybe I should go find Mistress Alma," he said. "After all, Pierrot might need to—"

Maldavo's thick fist flew through the air and struck Pascal square on the jaw. Pascal staggered. Without his usual grace, he lunged at Maldavo and shoved him to the ground. They tumbled and twisted, but Pascal landed on top. Once there, he swung, cracking Maldavo's nose with his fist.

Within seconds, they were in an all-out brawl.

Pascal and Maldavo grappled furiously with each other, clawing and beating like a pair of wild animals. Both teens were so focused on beating each other up that they didn't notice or hear Claudio and Clément cheering Maldavo on. They stood in front of Paloma, blocking her way, though this action did prevent them from helping Maldavo and ganging up on Pascal in the fight.

Her previous anger seemed to dissipate. She couldn't believe Pascal—friendly, jovial Pascal—was throwing punches. *Who knew he had it in him?*

There was no way this ended well, despite her surprise. Yeah, Pascal could leap, somersault, and dodge many of Maldavo's hits, but his brute strength was lacking compared to Maldavo's beefy fists. Pascal had probably never faced an opponent from the streets. Street fights were dirty, something Paloma had never liked, though she had to admit it was effective.

With each blow, Maldavo wore Pascal down. He grabbed a chair, knocked Pascal to the ground, and then kicked him in the stomach. Pascal groaned and pushed Maldavo's foot away.

When Maldavo tried to straddle and swing again, Pascal reached out his hand.

A flashbang sparked. A brief light flared between them. Maldavo froze, staring.

Pascal blinked rapidly and rolled back to bring himself to his feet. He stared at Maldavo as he clutched his wounded stomach and swiped blood from his lips. Even though he refused to show it, he was in pain. Paloma could tell by his subtle grimaces each time he moved. She had to find a way to end this.

She shook her head. "You never learn, Maldavo." Scoffing, she took a step forward. "Stand back, Pascal."

He glanced at her, fear flashing across his face for only a moment. She nodded with a grin.

It all rushed back to her in an instant: the shady, underhanded fighting she'd learned from the street's finest brawlers. In Pivot's darker alleys and corners, Paloma had learned the bare-knuckle, below-the-belt form by observing the gritty street fights. She learned how to anticipate and evade, how to use her surroundings—whatever it took to win. After that man had attacked her, she vowed to never again be a victim.

She took a deep breath, getting a good look at her surroundings as she raised her fists to her chest. Her level gaze met Maldavo's intense glare. Fighting him would be easy. After years of training with each other, Paloma knew exactly how to handle him. She could predict his moves before he made them.

When he rushed at her, swinging the chair, she easily shifted out of the way. Then, before he could respond, she took the highest leg of the chair and pushed it down towards the ground. Maldavo turned with the chair and lost his footing.

Paloma smiled. Even after sparring with her for years, Maldavo had never learned his lesson. He always resorted to strength over strategy.

He charged forward and swung the chair once more. Paloma grabbed two of the legs and yanked it toward herself, pulling Maldavo off balance. His torso was undefended. Claudio and Clément shouted in warning, but it was too late. Paloma kicked him hard in the ribs, driving the air out of his chest. He dropped the chair and stumbled back.

Paloma threw her full weight behind her fist then and struck him in the chin. Though he blocked her next swing, he missed the kick to his stomach. He choked with pain, doubled over, and delivered the final blow, knocking the bully to the ground.

Maldavo lay there motionless, completely stunned. He wasn't quite unconscious, but he wouldn't be getting up anytime soon. She raised her bruised knuckles in challenge, turning to Claudio and Clément.

"Anyone else want to go for a round?" she asked, her voice harsh and tight with adrenaline.

Claudio and Clément stepped back and wordlessly shook their heads. They clearly wouldn't be giving her any trouble from now on.

"I didn't think so," Paloma spat. "You're cowards!"

Her eyes stared daggers at Maldavo, wishing she could cut him with her gaze alone. Part of her wanted to beat him to a pulp, but she knew pummeling Maldavo further wouldn't help matters in any significant.

Paloma's hands lowered, and her fists uncurled. Behind her, Pascal stirred, opened his mouth, and then shut it, perhaps realizing that silence was better.

"Look at yourself, Mal," she said quietly. "I failed, perhaps, but you..." She shook her head. "Just hopeless."

With that, Paloma strode out of the room, head held high. Pascal, eyes filled with respect, quietly followed her.

CHAPTER SIX

Pascal wanted to say something to Paloma as they walked down the hall in search of Mistress Alma. The way she had stood up to Maldavo had deeply impressed him. He glanced at her, admiration clear in his eyes.

Maybe Paloma would like to join me and Pierrot.

He debated whether to ask her but paused. He'd felt a connection to her a few weeks ago when they'd been leaving for the woods and had winked to prompt her to follow them. She hadn't. *What if she doesn't want to be part of our group? She's been living on the streets, leading the Rejects. Clearly, something went down between her and Maldavo. I mean, she has a lot going on.*

As Pascal hesitated, he looked up to see Mistress Alma and Michel approaching them. Alma's sharp blue eyes took in Pascal's ruffled hair, flushed skin, cut lip, and darkening bruises, as well as Paloma's reddened knuckles. With a sigh, she shook her head.

"Wait in my office while I deal with the others."

Moments later, she returned. She sent Pascal to the kitchen to join Clément and Claudio, so she could speak with Paloma alone. What they talked about, Pascal could only guess, but he hoped that Paloma wouldn't get in too much trouble.

Why would anyone hurt Pierrot? He's obviously not a threat. Pascal blew out a defeated breath. *What happened between Maldavo and Paloma anyway?*

Pascal walked through the kitchen door just as Michel's voice rang out, gruff and irritated. At first, Pascal assumed he was annoyed about the fight and prepared himself for a lecture. He almost chuckled when he heard Michel snap something far more predictable instead.

"Why would she switch it to gas?"

Michel started the stove, and the boys watched in awe.

"It's like magic," Claudio said.

Michel huffed and shook his head. "Science. Magic is nonsense."

He placed a pot of water on the stove and grumbled something about progress and wanting to switch back to wood. The guys helped Michel cook dinner, as per Mistress Alma's orders. They didn't talk much.

Paloma returned as they ate, thank goodness, and she didn't even seem shaken. After dinner, Pascal and Pierrot slipped out through the back door, this time following Paloma as she glided into the backyard. Clearly, she wasn't going to hide her leadership instincts any longer.

It didn't take long for her to notice their presence, and with a sigh, Paloma turned around to stare at them, her hands on her hips. "What?" she asked.

"Oh," Pascal said, his voice suddenly leaving him. Every thought, every question…gone. Paloma was intimidating. She wasn't like the other girls in the orphanage, and he didn't know how to react. "I was…um, well, Pierrot and I were worried about you."

Paloma's hard gaze shifted to Pierrot, who nervously juggled his blue leather ball.

"Really," she said in a deadpan. "I don't recall hearing Pierrot say anything."

"Pierrot can communicate." Pascal leaned forward. "We have a secret language." Raising an eyebrow, he cast a smirk in her direction.

Paloma shook her head with a dry chuckle. "A secret language?"

"It's more like a code. I mean, sure, Pierrot can shake his head and nod, but I taught him how to juggle. When he juggles his blue ball, he's saying yes. If he's juggling his red ball, he's saying no or disagreeing. Or something like that."

"Huh," Paloma said, tapping her finger on her chin. "That's... actually quite clever."

"Right?" Pascal looked at Pierrot with admiration. "He picked it up really well, so when we go out wandering, we can communicate. And of course, now that you know the secret, you'll simply have to join us."

"Oh, will I?" Paloma tossed her low ponytail playfully, her eyes showing how much she enjoyed this game. "Join you in what?"

"Uh, well..." Pascal ran his hand through his hair, resting it on the back of his neck. He was usually self-assured, but right now, he felt flustered. "We could go on a hike?"

"Are you alright with that?" Paloma asked, half-turning to Pierrot.

Pierrot continued to juggle his blue ball and offered a small smile.

"I suppose that means yes," Paloma said, returning the smile.

"Looks that way." Pascal nodded. "So, I hope you'll say yes too."

"I..." Paloma trailed off, looking away as she did. "I suppose the idea of going on a trek sounds fun. Better than wasting my time on Maldavo or lolling about the library with Tania. I have been waiting to get out."

"Great!" Pascal turned to Pierrot and gave him a high-five, his movements quick and eager. Pierrot's grin widened as he twirled the blue ball in his other hand. He turned back to Paloma. "Come with us. I want to show you something."

Paloma nodded, still suppressing her smile. She wouldn't give him that satisfaction just yet.

After popping back into the kitchen to steal a few snacks, Pascal led Paloma across the back lawn. They pushed through the narrow gap in the hedge where a tiny wooden gate stood. Golden sunlight shone faintly through the underbrush, and low branches hung from the elms and oaks that grew on both sides of the stream. Paloma felt all the muscles in her body release and relax at the mere contact with nature in this way.

"Careful," Pascal called out as he confidently hopped from stone to stone across the water. Pierrot followed, obviously skilled with the route. This clearly wasn't their first trek. Paloma moved quickly but carefully to avoid slipping as she tried to catch up. On the other side, the three scrambled up a small incline toward a thicker patch of forest. Pascal soon turned off the narrow path through the trees and pushed through the underbrush.

In this late afternoon light, the forest took on an almost-magical glow. The sound of the stream faded, leaving only the faint chirping of sparrows and the gentle rustle of a cool breeze in the branches. The summer felt kinder here, as though it had no reason to be harsh. As Pascal looked around, he saw the forest with new eyes—Paloma's eyes—and a rightness settled in him.

Pascal wanted to be here. He was happy to be here.

A great oak tree with huge branches that spread in welcome as Pascal slowed to a stop. The ancient tree had three boards nailed to its trunk, the only sign that something was hiding within its great boughs. After quickly scaling the crude ladder, Pascal reached his treehouse.

Paloma followed. She poked her head through the branches until she could clamber onto the five boards Pascal had carefully fastened across two of the largest tree limbs to create a flat ledge. Overhead, another level was accessible by a thin rope ladder. The extra floor also served as a crude roof to shelter against any rain that might fall.

There wasn't much in the way of furniture: three short stools, a wooden box, and a rope ladder. Paloma's gaze was immediately drawn to the scene that was now visible through an opening in the tree's branches. The tree house overlooked a round meadow, a corner of the river which wound through the forest, and the treetops of shorter elms. Pascal took a seat next to Paloma, drew up his knees, and watched the forest with her. He didn't normally pay it much mind. After all, he and Pierrot were here just about every day.

"This is really nice," Paloma said. "When did you make this place?"

"Baptiste helped," Pascal admitted. "I told him about my plan, and he came out to help me hammer the boards down. Mistress Alma let me have these old stools, and Mateo—the woodcutter—gave me the box. I used to pretend it was a treasure chest when I was a kid. Now, Pierrot and I use it to store supplies."

Pascal pulled the chest toward him. Paloma reached forward and ran her hand over the lid. A diamond, inset with four smaller diamonds, was carved into the wooden lid.

"I can see why you would think that," she said. "It gives this whole tree house... I don't know." She shrugged, suddenly looking a bit sheepish. "It feels almost magical." She buried her face in her hands, chuckling to herself.

Pascal watched her with curiosity. *This girl, the one who beat Maldavo's ass earlier, is suddenly shy?* He leaned closer to her and muttered, "It does."

She looked back at him, and he gave her a reassuring nod.

He opened his canvas rucksack and began to rummage about. "Michel threw in some biscuits and a few apples," he said, handing the food around.

The three sat back in contented silence as they enjoyed the after-dinner snack and gazed at the peaceful vista around them. Pierrot rubbed his belly and glanced at the bag hopefully. Pascal rolled his eyes with amusement.

"I don't think Michel put anything else in there," he said. "Let's see."

He rummaged about in the dark depths of his backpack. His fingers happened upon an apple, and then another, and another. Puzzled, Pascal pulled out three more apples with a frown.

"That's strange. I could have sworn that there weren't any apples left."

"Maybe you didn't look hard enough?" Paloma suggested. "Or they got stuck in the corners?"

"No," Pascal said slowly, staring at the mysterious fruit. "It was like they appeared out of thin air."

Pierrot sniffed his apple, bit into it, and grinned. He gave a thumbs up to Pascal. Paloma tasted hers tentatively, then relaxed and gave a thumbs up to indicate it was just like the one she had finished.

"So strange," Pascal mused, staring into his bag.

"Has this happened before?" Paloma asked.

"Sometimes..." Pascal frowned at the tips of his fingers and quickly changed the subject. "Well, never mind about me. I'm worried about Maldavo. And you seem to know more about him than the rest of us."

Paloma glanced over at the bruise on Pierrot's cheek, her face growing solemn. She clutched her knees to her chest and exhaled deeply. "I just hope Maldavo never finds this place," she said softly. "He'd ruin it."

"Yeah," Pascal agreed. "I get the feeling that he just wants to cause harm. To be in control."

"You could say that," Paloma muttered.

"Why..." Pascal stopped and then started again. "Why is he like that? I mean, I understand that sometimes habits are hard to break, and when you grow up on the streets, that's all you know... but he's here now. This is a chance. I don't get it."

"All of the Rejects are probably struggling to feel comfortable right now. But most of them are like me. They just need time. Eventually, everyone will learn to relax and accept the new life that Mistress Alma is offering. Maldavo, though, he's different."

"Is there any reason why?"

Pierrot leaned forward, curious to hear what Paloma had to say. Paloma let out a long breath, rubbed her face, and then thought of a way that she could explain the situation to the two boys.

"So, the thing is, Maldavo and I used to have our own families. We both lost our parents ... I saw mine killed by ravagers," Paloma explained slowly. "Maldavo never talked about how his parents were killed, but I do remember him once saying that he never wanted to think about it. It must have been bad, right?"

"Yes," Pascal said, shock and sadness coursing through him. "I'm—I'm sorry to hear that."

"It is what it is," Paloma said with resignation. "But I think Maldavo doesn't want to end up like his parents. He wants to be strong and never get taken advantage of. He's a fighter and has always wanted to prove himself. I have to admit, I do understand him. After living as we did, it's hard to trust people, especially adults. But I would never bully someone. I wouldn't pick on someone younger or smaller than me. Never."

Pascal nodded. She continued.

"We disagreed on everything," Paloma continued, meditative in tone. "Maldavo always wanted to go in on an operation with guns blazing. He sometimes carried daggers. It worried me. I didn't want to cause that kind of trouble. Sure, we stole stuff, but only what we needed to survive. And I certainly didn't want to fight a guard like that."

"You'd end up in prison," Pascal said.

"Yes," Paloma said. "But Maldavo never listened. He always wanted to lead our operations, but his decisions were usually foolhardy and led to children getting caught. Anyway, we had taken on a couple of new children, and we needed some blankets and things. Doralin Blackcoat was expecting a shipment. Maldavo set it all up." She paused, huffing out an annoyed breath. "And I was an idiot for believing that it would turn out alright."

"What happened?" Pascal asked, itching with curiosity. His head tilted slightly as he grew engrossed in the story, Pierrot's eyes glued to her as well.

"He betrayed me," she answered simply. "We had set up lookouts. I was the distraction, tasked with occupying the guards while he carried out the main part of the mission, but he..." She shook her head. "I learned later that he had gone to the city guard and told them. They played Maldavo because he's a prideful idiot. I was captured, and Maldavo took his chance to lead the Rejects. Well, you can see how that went! Captain Roscoe, I'm sure, was very pleased."

"Unbelievable," Pascal mumbled, shaking his head. "But at least the Rejects are safe now, right? I mean, they have beds and food, so you don't have to worry about that anymore."

"Yeah, but most of them come from orphanages that were... well, they weren't as nice as this one. They were horrible. That's why so many of us are so nervous about being here. After the places that some of them experienced, they think this place is the same."

Pierrot's eyes were fastened on Paloma. Such focus was rare for the shy boy. He leaned forward and poked her elbow.

"What is it, Pierrot?"

He poked her again, and she sat back, releasing her knees. Pierrot took her hand and pressed a white daisy into it. Paloma stared down at the flower for a second. She blinked and tucked the flower behind her ear. "Thank you," she said, and Pierrot smiled.

Pascal couldn't take his gaze away from her face. *She looks so pretty.* His cheeks flushed, and he looked away toward the trees. *Don't make this awkward.*

Pascal cleared his throat. Support was key. He was here to support her, to gather information. "I think I understand. A little bit. Maldavo had a hard life, and that really twisted him. When dreadful things happen to a person, they try to keep them from happening again. I guess for Maldavo and his lot; they think brute strength is the best protection."

Pierrot balled his hands into hard fists and puffed out his

chest, assuming a strongman pose, making a comically angry face.

"Yes. Too powerful," Pascal agreed with a light chuckle. "They become mean."

"They become the things they hate," Paloma said quietly. "If we aren't careful, we might all turn into monsters."

"Is that what you fear?" asked Pascal.

"Maybe a long time ago, when I was young and desperate," Paloma admitted. "But then I formed the Rejects, and I set my dreams for justice aside. I realized I had to focus on helping the others, but sometimes, I wonder. I wonder if a day will come when I somehow find those who killed my parents and make them pay."

"Vengeance," breathed Pascal with a hint of hesitation. "So, if you had a choice, where would you end up working after graduation?"

"I guess I could go into mercenary work," Paloma said. "I have a lot of experience fighting, so I could fight for a living, go into trade, or study piloting. Maybe something that makes good money. Honestly, I'm not sure. How about you?"

"Hmm," Pascal hummed in thought, offering a timid grin. "It might sound silly, but I've always dreamed of being a hero like Harlequin. Mistress Alma thinks I should work on an airship, like Baptiste. I suppose working on an airship would give me the opportunity to get out into the world and travel, have experiences. I just don't want to work a dull or meaningless job, you know? I want to *do* something. Help people."

"Help people?" she asked. "Help them how?"

"I don't know," Pascal admitted, his shoulders slumped. "Like, the missing children. How unsafe is the world that kids can't even go out alone without fear of disappearing? The world needs people to help those who are vulnerable and can't do it for themselves."

"Well, I suppose there are a lot of things to fix out there," she answered slowly, seeming to consider Pascal's bold declaration a bit more seriously. "I mean, maybe the world would be a better place if there were more heroes about. But Harlequin is a fairy tale. Those stories aren't real. Everyone knows that."

"What if they were?" Pascal sighed with happiness at the thought before proclaiming dramatically, "Harlequin, The Master of Illusion, who wielded the slapstick. One day, he finds a love that transforms his heart, and he is freed from his bondage to Mephisto. From that day onward, he fights for justice and thwarts Mephisto's schemes."

"I think you're missing bits," Paloma said. "Isn't there a wise woman also?"

"Oh, you know the story too?" Pascal asked, eyes shining with joy. Finally, someone else who could talk about his obsession. What were the odds?

"Enough of it." Paloma shrugged. "By the market, there's a Carnival. One of the main shows is a puppet theater where they always have stories about Harlequin and Mephisto. Whenever we could, we'd creep in and try to watch for free... until the city guard would see us and chase us out. The Carnival folk didn't care, but anyway... yes. I've seen a few stories."

"Maybe that should be our next adventure," Pascal teased, though excitement bubbled in his chest at the thought. Mistress Alma hadn't taken the children to see the puppet show in years. "What do you think, Pierrot?"

Pierrot nodded enthusiastically.

"Pascal, your dreams for the future are rather optimistic. I suppose I shouldn't be surprised, though. Pierrot, what about you?" she asked, turning to address him. "Do you have any dreams or plans for the future?"

Pierrot shook his head and shrugged. After a few seconds, he mimed a thinking pose.

"He doesn't know yet," Pascal explained. "Pierrot is smart. He can read fast and remember a lot, so I think he could do just about anything, but he doesn't know what he wants to do yet."

"I see," Paloma said. "Well, I'm sure you'll figure it out one day, Pierrot. You might even have a better dream than mine."

"Better than justice on those who wronged you? I don't think there is a more magnificent idea. Right, Pierrot?"

Pierrot nodded.

"I don't think it's a stupid idea," Paloma explained, "but I do think that... I mean, I look at Maldavo, and I can't help but worry. Maybe I'm only a few choices away from going crazy and hurting people too."

A thoughtful silence fell over the group. Finally, Pierrot mimed a sad tear, and Paloma offered the two a comforting smile. They couldn't sit in this feeling forever. It wasn't productive for anyone.

"Look," she said, "it's not all that bad. Sure, life wasn't easy leading the Rejects, but I met so many good people. I learned how to take care of myself and others. I became more confident and skillful—learned how to fight for our survival. Certainly better than Maldavo. But coming here has changed my life a lot, too. For the better."

"Oh?" Pascal leaned in, eager to hear the answer.

Pierrot cocked his head inquisitively.

"Yes," Paloma replied. "You see, now a whole new world is opening up for me, thanks to Mistress Alma, Miss Lucía, and Tania. I'm learning new things, things that will help me find a new life. I won't be stuck with the limited choices I had before. Now, I can choose a new path."

"A new path," echoed Pascal curiously. "To where?"

"I don't know exactly, but maybe it will take me away from going down the path that Maldavo took." Paloma faced him and added, "And then I hear about your dreams, Pascal."

"Oh," Pascal said, looking away as his cheeks grew warm. "I suppose my dreams sound silly."

"Maybe when you say them out loud, they do." A giggle escaped her, and it warmed his insides. She continued in a more serious tone. "But now I want to see where your dreams will take you. It makes me want to join your quest for something more. Maybe we'll find another world altogether."

"I hope so!" Pascal sat up, beaming. His heart fluttered at the thought, and he had to force himself not to leap out of the tree house to do ten dozen handsprings and cartwheels across the forest. What was it about her that made him feel so light and free?

She smiled, soft and filled with a glimmer of warmth he hadn't seen in her before.

With a single nod, he added, "We'll find it together."

CHAPTER SEVEN

Pascal felt cheerful, which was odd. He'd never really reached that sort of high before.

Ever since they shared their hopes and fears in the tree house, including their worries about the recent disappearances, Pascal, Pierrot, and Paloma had become inseparable. And as their trust in each other grew, Pascal had shown Paloma all the hidden places he'd found in his years of wandering around the orphanage's forest. Though she loved the tiny spring tucked in among a circle of weeping willows and the monolithic rock that stood up in a little clearing of white daisies, her favorite was the largest and oldest tree in the northern part of the woods that towered over them. She told Pascal it made her feel so small but in a way that held meaning. He'd pondered the thought, never quite looking at the tree in that sense. That tree had been around for years and survived so much through the span of its life. It gave her hope, and soon, it gave him hope, too.

When Paloma suggested that they sneak away from the orphanage so she could show them places from her old life in Pivot, Pascal was delighted. Ordinarily, he wouldn't give leaving the orphanage without adult supervision too much thought, but with children disappearing from the countryside around Pivot, he knew they'd have to be extra careful not to get caught. The stakes were high; they wanted to maintain the trust and freedom they'd built up with Mistress Alma.

Thankfully, Maldavo was no longer bothering them. Chastened by Mistress Alma's following punishment, Maldavo was kept busy with extra chores in the kitchen, helping with dishwashing and dinner preparation. Mistress Alma did not tolerate such behavior, and Maldavo's behavior greatly saddened her. As a result, Mistress Alma was busy overseeing the more unruly children, allowing Pascal, Pierrot, and Paloma more freedom.

They planned their trip in detail, deciding to visit the market and Carnival. On a sunny Saturday with particularly fine weather, Pascal, Pierrot, and Paloma slipped away from the orphanage grounds and set out to see the sights in Pivot.

As they passed snug homes and cottages tucked amidst the trees, Pascal felt a strange urge to hold Paloma's hand. Maybe it was the peaceful walk through the forest or the way the sunlight peeked through the trees, illuminating her in a warm glow, but he wanted to be closer to her. He glanced at Pierrot, who had a relaxed smile on his face and merrily bounced his blue ball in one hand as they followed the main road into Pivot.

Closer to the city, the trees slowly disappeared, and the houses jammed against each other along a web of narrow roads. As they drew nearer to the center, Paloma took the lead. She deftly wove between the carts and horses, twisting through the slow-moving crowds that made their way in and out of the city.

Impressive, Pascal thought. He and Pierrot stared wide-eyed, mouths gaped, as a horseless carriage would rumble past on occasion. Overhead, airships puttered along as they carried heavy loads to the docks.

Pascal and Pierrot slowed to a crawl. The sight of the tall houses, sometimes four stories high, boggled his mind. He recalled Paloma's stories about her time with the Rejects as he peered down the dim alleys. Piles of twisted metal and wood lay half-obscured in the shadows. Hints of another, more dangerous world where criminals hid from the law.

The boys followed Paloma, keeping to the main streets and avoiding the city guards' patrol routes when necessary. She knew which alleyways were safe and which weren't. Thanks to her, they quickly reached the market, where the crowds were thickest. They could easily blend in here.

As a hub for trade, the market was packed with people from all around Vale: stalwart giants who shook the wooden stalls as they clomped by, thrifty dwarves who loved to haggle, and humans plying their trades.

The air was thick with the aroma of sizzling meats from nearby food stalls, mingling with the sweet scent of freshly baked pastries that wafted through the bustling crowd. Pascal's nostrils twitched as he caught a whiff of exotic spices being sold nearby.

Amidst the chatter of buyers and sellers negotiating deals, a lively street musician played a jaunty tune on his flute, adding to the vibrant atmosphere. Pascal couldn't help but tap his foot to the rhythm, his spirits lifted by the infectious melody.

Colorful banners fluttered in the breeze overhead, casting shifting patterns of light and shadow on the cobblestone ground below. Pierrot's eyes widened in wonder as he took in the kaleidoscope of hues, his gaze darting from one vibrant display to another.

Paloma noticed his wide-eyed fascination and leaned closer. "Fairyfolk and wood elves come in on occasion, bringing in wares from the west," she said, pointing to one stall discreetly. "They usually have some cool stuff. Want to check it out?"

"Sure," Pascal answered with a shrug. "Not that we can buy anything."

Paloma turned to Pierrot, who clutched his juggling balls and nodded shyly.

"It's overwhelming, isn't it?" Paloma asked, tilting her head to one side.

Pierrot nodded again, looking down. Pascal felt a flash of care for her, seeing how her connection with Pierrot had deepened.

"Why don't you check out the book stalls over there," Paloma suggested, pointing directly across the street. "It should be quieter in there; give you a break from all the chaos."

Pierrot's eyes lit up, and he eagerly headed to the small book stall, leaving Pascal and Paloma to wander the market alone. He'd never seen Paloma so excited as she pointed out stall after stall, housing wares and trinkets of all kinds. Pascal stopped and admired a wood-carved figurine of Harlequin, wishing so badly he had the money to buy it. Pulling himself away, he walked over to Paloma, who stared at a pair of bright red earrings.

He imagined what she'd look like wearing the earrings, stirring his stomach, and sending it leaping at the thought. *She'd look beautiful in them.* He stepped closer and leaned in slightly as he said from behind, "You'd look pretty in those."

She jumped and shook her head, waving away his words. "Yeah, right," she teased, punching his shoulder. "Do I look like a girl that wears earrings?" Her cheeks flushed, and she looked away, wrapping her arms around her torso.

Had he made her uncomfortable?

"Say what you want, but I think you'd look pretty," he said, his voice teasing her back.

She watched him for a moment and took a step back, away from the jewelry. "It's the earrings," she said in a quiet voice. "They're just pretty." She walked away from the stand, peering back at Pascal, and gesturing him forward. "Are you coming? I want to show you my own hidden spot."

His lips curled into a smile, and he jogged to her side as she led him around the back of a building, climbing up a rusted ladder to a rooftop. She settled in, patting the spot beside her. He took a seat and looked out at the crowds of people swirling about.

"This is where I like to come and sit. It's a wonderful place to have a bit of peace among the chaos of the city."

Pascal looked out over the city; the sun was bright on the horizon. He'd never seen anything so amazing. "It is," he agreed, glancing at Paloma, who sat with her knees curled up to her chest, resting her head on them as she stared on. "Where are we?"

"We're on the roof of Doralin Blackcoat's Emporium. You can see all the traders and buyers come and go." She pointed to a group coming in, wearing long coats that screamed of wealth. "See them? They're definitely visiting. And them?" She pointed to another group, much grungier than the first, covered in what looked like dirt. "They live just outside of town but come here often to trade their harvest."

So many people of all different kinds. *Just like the stuff sold in the stalls.* He'd be lying if he said it wasn't overwhelming at first—all the sights and smells, the noises, and the people. Yet, it was his chance to see the world in ways he'd never done. This was a place where he could talk to new people, discover exciting stories and places, and learn about strange lands he'd never dreamed of going to.

"Pierrot would like it up here," he said.

Paloma nodded. "We should head back soon to him."

Pascal agreed, though neither of them moved. They were too absorbed in the moment, too swept up in this life that was nothing like the orphanage. Despite all the struggle Paloma had faced, Pascal was a bit envious that she'd had the experience of living in Pivot firsthand.

For a month, they returned to Pivot as often as they could, sneaking out beyond the orphanage grounds to the enticing city. With some guidance from Paloma, Pascal learned who—and who not—to talk to.

Not everyone was friendly. Most merchants and traders didn't spare the time to stand about and chat with nosy teenagers. So, the three of them spent their weekend hours loitering in the massive cobblestone square, passing stalls, and keeping an ear out for news.

Pascal's first friend in the market was Arrio, the beggar. Stooped, yet wiry and strong, Arrio moved about from stall-to-stall begging for scraps. With his ragged gray-brown clothing, he wasn't usually noticed in the crowd. But when Pascal approached him, the old man listened and responded surprisingly cheerfully. In Pascal's eyes, Arrio seemed like a mysterious mage thanks to his wooden staff carved with symbols and geometric designs—specifically, a diamond in the center that reminded him of Mateo.

"Really, Pascal," Paloma said as they walked among the stalls. "Everything seems so magical to you."

"What do you see?" Pascal asked curiously. "If we're seeing different worlds..."

"An old man who couldn't do an honest day's work if he tried," she said. "But at least he's friendly; I will give you that. He's a sight more friendly than Giulia, the witch, and Vizzo."

Giulia, the cloth merchant, and Vizzo, the spice seller, viewed all children with suspicion, especially children who seemed to be up to no good. Although Pascal, Paloma, and Pierrot had agreed from their first visit never to steal or cause trouble in the market, Giulia and Vizzo still scowled at them whenever they passed.

Giulia, a gray-haired woman who put on airs, often wrapped a purple silk scarf about her face as though the children carried an obnoxious stink. Vizzo, a gaunt, grizzled old man, was prone to shouting at them. His thin fingers were quick to reach for a bell that he would shake in alarm if he thought anyone was about to cause trouble.

On the other hand, Barolo, the Carnival ringmaster, had a heart of gold and a soft spot for children. Instead of yelling at the trio, he usually stopped and chatted. After Pascal had charmed his way into the Carnival with multiple promises to behave, Barolo let them explore the Carnival with the promise that they wouldn't interfere with the Carnival folk who were working.

On one of their visits to Pivot's market, they bumped into Baptiste. He'd just docked *The Unbroken*, his airship, and was overseeing its unloading when he noticed Paloma, Pascal, and Pierrot wandering throughout the market.

With a cheerful wave, Baptiste asked after his grandmother, the orphanage, and the other children. When he found out that the three of them were truant, he shook his head and chuckled in amusement, jokingly threatening to turn them in. But each time they returned to the orphanage; they discovered that Baptiste hadn't gotten around to telling Mistress Alma what they were up to. Now, their greeting had become habitual, and his threats a funny ritual. Thanks to a friendly word from Baptiste, the children were now largely left alone to roam as they pleased.

Pascal, Paloma, and Pierrot sat outside the grandest Carnival tent. Pascal's gaze drifted over the bright yellow, orange, and red canvas with its blue accents and imitation gold trim. It was where the best shows were held—acrobatics, dwarven wrestling, the puppet theater—and one of his favorite places to visit.

Now that he was regularly visiting the Carnival, Pascal no longer had to dream about what it would be like to work there. Since Barolo allowed them to explore the Carnival as much as they pleased, Pascal could experience the magic of what went on behind the scenes. Even now, as they perched on wooden chests beside the ring toss stall, Pascal's smile widened.

Paloma had managed to get them to the puppet show in fun time that day, so they watched the new story being performed. Although Pascal had read everything he could find about the tales of Harlequin, Mephisto, and Mephisto's legion of minions, he was transported by the story as it unfolded. It was a short episode, dramatizing the moment when Harlequin met his beloved Columbine for the first time.

Columbine was a beautiful woman with ebony hair and flashing dark eyes who traveled Vale and beyond. If she had been born to a noble family, poems might have been written about her beauty, but Columbine was a poor wanderer who sang and danced for a living. Wherever she went, Columbine's courage and kindness changed the world for the better.

Then, the story took a surprising turn, for Columbine met a mysterious, handsome man who smiled at her and offered her a posy. She recognized the illusion for what it was, however, and simply smiled. As she walked away, the handsome stranger revealed his face, struck deeply with love. It was Harlequin.

With that, the episode ended. Already, the cliffhanger killed Pascal. He was never very good at being patient about such things.

"Do you think he'll follow her? Or will Mephisto send someone else after them?" Pascal mused eagerly, a bounce to his step as he imagined all the possible outcomes.

He spent the next half hour talking his friends' ears off and predicting what would happen in the next episode. Finally, Paloma sighed and gave Pierrot a look. The younger boy proceeded to pelt Pascal with his juggling balls. Pascal subsided with sheepish laughter. His friends were not as obsessed with fairy tales as he was.

I rarely left the orphanage as a young child, Pascal thought. The occasional trips to Pivot had always been the height of adventure, and when Mistress Alma had taken them to puppet shows, he would memorize the stories: the sagas of Harlequin and Mephisto and his many henchmen: Callisto the horrifying wendigo, the banshees, and the fiery Killflare. It felt so real to him. Magic was something tangible, something he could really understand.

"Sorry, you know how I get." Pascal stared ahead absently. "Harlequin has always been my hero. As the herald for Mephisto, he had been so powerful, but then he freed himself to use his powers for good."

"You could say that Pierrot and I know the story," Paloma said, deadpan. "You're doing it again. Hit him, Pierrot."

Pierrot threw his red ball at Pascal's head again, but he deftly caught the ball in midair and tossed it back with a grin.

"Alright, alright," Pascal said, raising his hands in defeat. "I'll stop. It's just so fascinating."

"It is," Paloma agreed. "And I know you want to be like Harlequin, but you don't need to talk about it all the time."

"I'm sorry," Pascal said, looking down.

Pascal's mind drifted to that fight with Maldavo, the moment that mysterious spark of light had burst out. Though he hadn't mentioned it to anyone, a part of him wondered if it had been related to him. How could he not wonder? Things of that nature didn't just happen.

"At any rate," Paloma said, her voice lighter to shift the sudden quiet mood that fell over Pascal, "we'll be able to see what happens between Columbine and Harlequin next weekend, right?"

"Until then, I suppose time will pass by slowly."

"Not if we keep busy," Paloma said. "I still think we should try that trick again."

"Which one?" asked Pascal, hopping off his wood chest. "The handstand?"

"Yes, that one." Paloma nodded. "It was difficult, but I think I could master it with a bit more practice."

"Maybe Cherise will let us use her mat," Pascal said. "Let's ask her."

Pierrot and Paloma followed Pascal through the maze of tents that formed the Carnival. Passing by the Sideshow of Wonders, the fortune teller's tent, and the ring of food stalls, they made their way to one of the areas not open to paying visitors. They approached the acrobats' tent, where Cherise and her dance team often practiced. As they hoped, Cherise stood by the door.

The slight young woman wore a gaudy, sparkling suit and had let her long hair down from its usual bun. Her green eyes were dark with fatigue. When she rubbed her face, her thick makeup smudged, giving her a ghoulish look. Still, at the sight of them, she smiled in greeting.

"Did you want to use the tent for some practice?" she asked.

"If you don't mind," Pascal said politely. "Paloma and I wanted to work on the handstand trick you showed us the other day." Yeah, he already knew how to do a handstand, but he liked having someone from the Carnival show him. It made him feel like he was a part of it.

"Be my guest," Cherise said. "I just got off, so I won't be around. You'll have to be careful, you two. Pierrot, you'll keep them out of trouble?"

Pierrot nodded and gave her a small smile.

"Good," Cherise said. "Have at it."

They strolled into the tent, staying away from the professional equipment as Paloma and Pascal set up the mats and the small wooden blocks that Cherise had given them permission to use. Pierrot was content to sit and watch from the sidelines as his friends hopped, leaped, cartwheeled, and jumped around on the mats.

At some point, Crisanto, one of the trapeze artists and acrobats, joined in. Cherise returned with Enzo, the mime, in tow. With his attention drawn away from his friends, Pierrot watched in fascination as Enzo slowly mimed his way down a wall, through a door, and over to Pierrot's side, where he offered a comically limp handshake.

Pascal smiled with relief. Pierrot was always the silent one in the conversations between him and Paloma, and he worried

Pierrot might feel left out. No matter how hard he tried to involve him, Pierrot remained withdrawn. Though, he seemed to enjoy himself around Enzo, which left Pascal hopeful that Pierrot had made another friend and fit into this Carnival world as Pascal did.

Hours passed before Cherise noticed the time. She and Crisanto snuffed out the lanterns and shooed them out so they could close the tent for the night. Reluctantly, the teens exited the tent. The sun's light rapidly faded as they made their way to the front of the Carnival as an older crowd spilled in for the next round of entertainment.

What I would give to live at the Carnival. Of course, he didn't tell the others that. They'd probably think he was crazy. If anything, he could expect the eye roll he always got when mentioning Harlequin's stories. But the Carnival had become a place where he felt almost at home—like he belonged here.

"Ahhh ... the curious trio returns home," said a creaky voice.

Pascal stopped, causing Paloma to bump into him. Pierrot hung back nervously as an old woman approached: Cosme, the Fortune Teller.

Tonight, the old crone was swathed in black and purple. Her graying hair was tucked away into a massive black turban decorated in silver threads. From the silver chains hung charms—crescent moons, five-pointed stars, triangles inside circles, and faintly luminous gems—matching the charms on her draped, old-fashioned, deep purple dress. Cosme reminded Pascal of a witch from the ancient tales, making him feel simultaneously nervous and excited.

"Madame Cosme," he said with a smile. "Good evening!"

"Good evening, Pascal, Paloma... and young Pierrot. I see that you have been having a fine night," she said.

"You have?" asked Pascal in surprise. "How did you know?"

Paloma sighed but didn't say anything. Pierrot hopped back a few steps and half-hid behind Paloma. Cosme laughed, echoed by Pascal in turn.

"You are young, and it is a day off from school and work, is it not?"

"Let me guess," Paloma said, crossing her arms. "Hugo told you that we were here, and you probably saw Crisanto and Enzo just now."

"That I did." Cosme chuckled, tapping her nose and winking at Paloma. "Quite an astute mind you got there, girl."

"So, it wasn't the Sight after all?" Pascal asked, slightly disappointed.

"Never fear, Pascal," Cosme said, drawing close to him. "I know that your heart seeks adventure. But any skeptic like the lovely Paloma would say that all youthful heart's desire adventure. But in you, the drive to see the world is stronger than most. That, my old eyes can see all too well. I am glad you have found friends to travel with you, for the road ahead is dark and perilous."

"Pascal does have an obsession with adventures," Paloma admitted.

"Dark and perilous?"

"The Sight doesn't show those gifted all the answers. It is but a flash, a moment of truth." Cosme flung her arm in a grand gesture, startling Pierrot. "And that is what I saw—a boy with a mysterious past who faces a dark road ahead, but he bears a light within that he has not yet fathomed. A light that is shared with his friends. Hm, yes, that is what I saw."

"Interesting," Paloma said. "Well, it's getting late, and we need to head home before the night watch starts patrols."

"Right, yes," Pascal agreed reluctantly, staring at Cosme, hoping she'd say more.

Cosme was finished, though. Mumbling quietly to herself, she retreated into her tent to await her first visitors of the night.

After a moment of hesitation, Pascal slowly followed Paloma and Pierrot past the Carnival entrance and out into the main streets of Pivot. His aching legs dragged on the walk home, his limbs sore from all the acrobatic activity. Pierrot looked as though he were going to fall asleep on his feet. Paloma, on the other hand, was too concerned with getting caught by the sharp eyes of the night guards.

A silence descended upon them as they sped along. When they were finally past the city gates, along the country road, the three heard a distant bell toll seven times. Pascal paused and looked back at Pivot wistfully.

Paloma also slowed and let out a heavy sigh. "I thought Cosme was going to hold us up forever."

"She does get a bit chatty sometimes," Pascal agreed.

"Chatty? That's one way of putting it." She paused for a moment, looking up. Then, she spoke once more, her voice low and calm. "Sometimes I wonder about her."

Pascal's head cocked to the side. "About what?"

"I don't know." Paloma shrugged. "About her abilities, I suppose. Is it all guesswork? A con? Or something else? Something magical and real, like you hope?"

"Maybe a bit of both," Pascal said, trying to be as unbiased as possible despite his hopes to the contrary.

"That's more than likely true," Paloma said. "Either way, Pierrot was scared. What do you think, Pierrot? Do you think she was telling the truth?"

With great reluctance, Pierrot pulled out his blue ball and rolled it back and forth in his trembling hand. He tightly squeezed the leather a few times.

"Yes," his face seemed to say to Pascal. "It's true. All of it."

CHAPTER EIGHT

"Pascal!" a familiar voice hissed, interrupting his conversation with Brenson, the Tall Dwarf, and Bati, the Dragon Kin—two performers who worked in the Carnival's Hall of Wonders. Usually, Brenson, Bati, and the other Hall of Wonders' performers would be dressed in their costumes, slathered with paint, and posing in their glass-fronted showcases. Today, however, everyone wandered among the wagons parked behind the Hall of Wonders, laughing with their fellow performers and old friends.

When the trio stopped by the Carnival, the performers eagerly welcomed them in to enjoy their day off together. *It's funny,* Pascal thought. *When I first met them, I'd believed the rumors of the Carnival folk battling as mercenaries. I'd imagined them to be so daunting and dark. Yet, they're actually gentle and kind. Shy, even.*

"Pascal!" Paloma called out again, grabbing his elbow. "The guards are on the hunt. We have to get out of here!"

"What?" Pascal's head jerked around in every direction. "Why—"

Before he could finish, he saw Enzo mime-sprinting in front of Pierrot, telling him to run. Nomu—a water creature who could effortlessly bend water to her will—had also leaped up and turned her gaze toward the approaching city guards. Her piercing dark green eyes remained steely; her lips drawn into a thin line of determination. With a graceful flick of her hand Nomu conjured a delicate tendril of water that danced in the air, beckoning at them.

Pascal, Paloma, and Pierrot hurried toward the side entrance when a shrill whistle rang out behind them. Pierrot froze and clapped his hands over his ears. Paloma readied herself for an attack, but when someone shouted, she dashed away. Pascal grabbed Pierrot's hand and sprinted after her, following as she wove through low-hanging banners and open-ended tents until they reached the Carnival's western entrance.

The door was reserved for Carnival workers, but Torto was near the door and recognized them. The short giant took in the scene and shoved the door open, urgently waving them through.

As they wound past barrels and hopped over wooden crates, the main Carnival gate slammed open. He risked a quick peek back at the sight of three city guards. One of them, a stocky, red-faced young man, seemed very familiar.

"It's Tomás." Pascal panted, catching up to Paloma. "You know what that means." They dove behind a stack of crates, Pascal's arm shielding Pierrot protectively. Tomás was a new recruit for the guards. Quite the zealous officer.

"Ugh! Of course, it has to be him." Paloma grunted, resting her back against a small building. "He won't stop searching, and we'll be running through the city forever."

"We'll just have to go back home," Pascal said with a shrug.

Pierrot nodded, squeezing his blue ball in agreement.

"The West Gate," Paloma said, nodding in that direction. "Come on."

The three plunged into the depths of the market, dashing past rows of stalls. Paloma grabbed whatever she could reach to toss behind her in hopes of slowing them down. One guard slipped into a cart and accidentally dragged Tomás down with him as he fell. Pascal could hear some of the stall owners yelling unhappily at the mess that the guards were making.

Pascal glanced over at Paloma with a wide grin. "Someone's *not* happy," he said with a chuckle.

"Get serious, Pascal," Paloma said, but even she was suppressing laughter.

Paloma darted to the right, pushing past workers as they dashed to the next intersection packed with traffic. A cart full of compost was slowly crossing while two city guards were converging on either side of them.

How in the world are we supposed to get past them?

Paloma didn't skip a beat and sprung upward, leaping across the cart in a graceful arabesque. Then, she fell forward into a roll that brought her smoothly back onto her feet. Pascal followed close behind with his own mighty leap, and Pierrot slid beneath the cart, just barely avoiding the wheels. The city guards fell behind as they picked up speed.

Up ahead in an alley, Paloma grabbed hold of a nearby awning and swung upward. She leaped up the buildings' jutted windows and balconies, climbing to the roofs that connected. Pascal followed, looking down at Pierrot, who struggled to get a foothold on a window ledge. Pascal pulled him up, and they scrambled toward the rooftops after Paloma.

Ahead of them, the city climbed upward. The spires of Pivot's center soared, nothing higher except the airships. They followed along the rooftops until they reached the metal railings that hung from the lowest airship dock. They swung from rail to rail until they reached the rope ladder at the end.

Breathless with excited laughter, Paloma grabbed the metal ladder and scurried to the top, hopping from creaky platform to platform, with Pascal and Pierrot not far behind her. As the platforms widened for the larger ship berths, they ran down one of the upper deck piers and made their way to the far edge. Pascal stopped on the second level to peer over the edge at the guards struggling to climb onto the lower dock. More whistles rang out in alarm.

"They aren't giving up," Pascal called to Paloma. "They must be bored today."

"Really bored," Paloma agreed with an eye roll. "We have to keep going." She climbed to a higher vantage point and looked down. "Too many guards."

Tomás caught sight of them overhead and hollered something incomprehensible.

She didn't wait for him to finish before taking off through the depot's doors, dodging carts and trolleys, with Pascal and Pierrot not far behind.

On the other end of the vaulted warehouse, Pascal caught sight of another airship, and his eyes widened as he recognized the blue and yellow markings on the side.

That's Baptiste's ship!

There was no time to stop and chat. With an unconcerned wave, Pascal flew past Baptiste, whose eyebrows rose high at the sight of the trio barreling past. He shook his head as Pascal waved, running at full speed to the opposite end of the ship, where another airship edged past, readying to make a berth on a dock ahead.

Baptiste looked from one end to the other, making the connection, and shouted out in warning, "Don't do it!"

But Paloma had already thrown herself over the edge of the dock and grabbed at the rope ladder that the workers unrolled. Using her momentum, she swung back and forth until the ladder reached him and Pierrot once more.

They flung themselves over the side of the dock, grabbing on. The workers yanked at the ladder in a panic, attempting to pull it back, but their weight was too much for the workers to heave. Pascal clung to the rope, waiting as the ship crept closer to a nearby rooftop from all the momentum. As they slowly moved overhead, they dropped to their feet in a synchronized roll.

"Down this way!" Paloma panted, hunched over with her hands on her knees, barely able to catch her breath. "We'll have to climb over the wall, but then we'll almost be at the gate."

Pascal nodded. It was a good idea, if they could scale it quickly enough. They leaped from roof to roof, hopping to the ground as they approached the red brick wall. Pascal's lungs burned with every breath of oxygen he took. His energy was depleted, but he couldn't give up. Not yet. Still, it hurt to breathe.

Looking up at the wall, he squinted, tilting his head. *It's high. Too high for Pierrot?*

"You first," Pascal wheezed. "I'll give Pierrot a hand, and you pull him up, alright?"

Paloma nodded and scampered up the wall.

The sound of thick-soled boots crunching the cobblestone announced the guards' arrival, and Pascal heaved Pierrot up to the bricks. Sparing a glance over his shoulder, the guards rushed forward, leaving Pascal no time to escape. Glancing back to the wall, Paloma had just reached the top and frantically flapped her hands at Pierrot in encouragement. Pascal glanced back to the guards, who were closing in on him.

I need to get up there. Now.

He lunged for another part of the wall, grabbing onto the footholds in the brick. Just as he lifted his foot, a rough hand grabbed his ankle and jerked his leg down. On instinct, Pascal kicked, and Tomás let out a loud yelp, followed by, "Dammit!" Still, the guard's grip tightened. That was no good.

Pascal struggled to hold onto the wall without a decent place to grab hold. Leaning down cautiously, he tried to pry Tomás's hand off his ankle but didn't have the support.

"Get off!"

A light flared, an enormous burst, leaving them stunned. Seizing the chance that this distraction caused, Pascal jerked his foot from Tomás's grip and lunged upward, out of reach. Blinking away the white dots that obscured his vision from the flash, he climbed over the wall, and Paloma and Pierrot came into view.

On the other side, they all doubled over, panting and gasping for breath. Pierrot flopped to the ground finally and rested his back against the wall.

"What was that?" Paloma huffed between breaths. "Did you see it? It was definitely you, Pascal."

"I-I don't know," he said, equally stunned. He wiped the sweat that poured over his forehead, the salt stinging his eyes. "It doesn't make sense."

"Well, we'll have to figure it out later," Paloma said, retying her ponytail and gesturing to where Pierrot glanced at the wall, nervously squeezing his red ball. "Pierrot is right. We have to keep moving. I don't know how long it'll be until—"

"Ah, Paloma and her friends," a gruff voice said from the shadows.

Pascal jumped, jerking his head around. Then, his shoulders relaxed. Paloma relaxed in kind.

"Arrio," Pascal said. "I didn't see you there."

His hand rose in a cheerful greeting as he scanned over them. "In a bit of trouble, are we?"

Pascal nodded and said in panted breaths, "The city guards." He winced from the pinch in his side, amplified with every burning breath. "They're chasing us."

"We aren't supposed to be in Pivot," Paloma admitted.

As if following along the line, Arrio glanced at Pierrot, who nodded silently as he twirled his red ball.

"Ahh, sneaking out?" Arrio said. "You're not allowed to leave the orphanage, are you? Not since the children have been going missing?"

Pascal kept the whirl of thoughts he had on the topic to himself. Arrio didn't really want to know, not in that way.

"Hmmm..." Arrio mused, stroking his short, gray beard. He leaned on his staff and thought for a moment. "Follow me," he said, "I have an idea."

He opened the door to a nearby building and ushered them inside a quiet warehouse filled with sacks of grain. The daylight filtered through half-shuttered windows, offering just enough light to illuminate the dust in the air. Arrio gestured to a circle of stools around a small table.

"This warehouse usually has guards stationed here at night, but during the day, it is empty," the beggar explained. "You can safely remain here for a while and rest, as long as you do so silently. I will sit outside and redirect the guards. They should be along now any moment. After that, I am sure you three will be anxious to reach the West Gate. In, in!" With a conspiratorial nod and wink, Arrio disappeared outside.

Pascal, Paloma, and Pierrot sat, rubbing their sore muscles as they finally caught their breath. Minutes passed before they heard a nearby whistle, followed by the familiar clomping of boots. Deep voices rumbled outside the window.

"Have you seen three teenagers running about?" a guard asked.

"Three teenagers?" Arrio asked, tapping what Pascal assumed was his cane against the ground. "Teens, teens..." he mused, pretending to think for a moment. "Ah, yes. I believe I did see a few run past not too long ago."

Pascal's body stiffened, terrified Arrio would give them away.

"I believe they went northeast, toward the Carnival," Arrio answered.

"It's the criminal element, y'see," said another one of the guards. "The girl—Paloma, they call her—she was the old leader of the Rejects, y'know. A lot of distrust among the merchants, especially Vizzo, when they see her around. What if she were to form a new gang? What if she returned to her old ways, stealing and the like? What's happening at the Skystead Home for Orphaned Children? These are the kinds of things Vizzo's always blabbing about."

Tomás sighed and said something indistinct about Vizzo. Then, he glanced up once more.

"That's why we have to look as though we are dealing with it," Tomás explained. "After all, Paloma might not have returned to her old ways, but I am fairly certain Mistress Alma wouldn't allow her children to visit Pivot unsupervised—especially with Governor De Moura's orders. At any rate, I think we lost them, so let us know if you see anything. We may have to make a trip to the orphanage soon..."

"I'm sure Vizzo would be happy to hear that," Arrio said. "And his temper may cool if the children do not show up at the market anytime soon."

"Yes," Tomás agreed. "That would help."

The guards chatted with Arrio for a moment longer and left. When the coast was clear, Arrio whistled softly. Pascal, Paloma, and Pierrot emerged, and he gave them a long look.

"It seems as though you young'uns have become frequent truants." His eyes twinkled with amusement. "These days, folk are on edge. Vale can be an unfriendly place, and old grievances are not easily forgotten. It would perhaps be best if you returned home."

What did he mean by that? Vale is an unfriendly place? And what old grievances? Rather than asking about it, Pascal simply nodded and agreed.

"I was trying to make it to the West Gate anyway," Paloma said. "If they go south, we'll be able to slip out and return home easily. You alright with that, Pierrot?"

Pierrot tossed his blue ball limply. It was clear that he was exhausted. Pascal nodded his assent.

"Let's get home," he said.

WHEN THE THREE ARRIVED AT THE ORPHANAGE, THE sight of the familiar stone building lifted their spirits. What had seemed boring this morning now looked like a sanctuary. They were safe here. No one would chase them, no one wanted them captured or killed. Upon their arrival, Pascal pushed past the hedge that bordered the yard and led the group toward the mess hall.

On the back lawn, a bunch of the orphans had gathered for a game of tag. Tania, noticing their arrival, raised an eyebrow. Danton and Clarion, who were trying to evade a mob of younger children, stared at Pascal with twin wounded looks of betrayal. Pascal sighed. His friends would be unhappy to learn that they'd missed a trip to Pivot.

As Pascal, Paloma, and Pierrot walked into the front hall, however, they froze.

Mistress Alma stood side by side with Tomás. She crossed her arms and gave the three of them a look of silent rebuke. Her thin lips were pursed, and she shook her head. Beside her, Tomás stiffened. He glared at the three children, still red-faced and clearly annoyed by the fact that he hadn't caught them.

"We need to talk," Mistress Alma said. "My office. Now."

Pascal hung his head and trailed behind Mistress Alma and Tomás. Paloma and Pierrot slowly followed. Lining up in front of the desk, the three waited while Tomás seated himself in Mistress Alma's guest chair. The older woman took a seat behind her desk and gave each of the children a look. They all knew what she'd demand before she opened her mouth.

"Explain yourselves," she said.

No way would Pascal let his friends go down for this, so he explained how he led them outside the orphanage. Paloma, however, seemed equally determined to shoulder the blame and explained her role in guiding them through the city. Pierrot remained silent, but he also pointed to himself every now and again, trying to take responsibility, too. Mistress Alma tried to hide a smile.

"While I admire your loyalty," Mistress Alma said, "I would rather have a straight answer. That being said, I suppose I could guess the three of you cooked up this idea together. How long has this been going on?"

"For a month or so?" Pascal confessed. "It was supposed to be a one-time trip, but then… well, I mean, the market and the

Carnival are just so interesting, and a single trip wouldn't let me see everything. So, it ended up being...weekly."

"Did none of you stop to think about Governor De Moura's ban on unescorted children in Pivot?" asked Mistress Alma.

"Well," Paloma answered, "Pascal and I are pretty strong and spry. We can run from anything. And I know the city well."

"That, I can attest," Tomás admitted heavily. "And they never really caused trouble. The only complaints we received were unjustified, but perhaps if the children were to get an official allowance, the complaints might be more easily dealt with. Find an adult chaperone to accompany them, and they should be fine."

The trio stared at the city guard. *Is he serious, or am I dreaming? He actually took our side.* Tomás shrugged self-consciously.

"And there are others who have given testimony, among them Master Barolo," Tomás added. The guard pulled out a small notepad and squinted at the chicken scrawl written there. "Some others from the Carnival, too. Cherise, Crisanto, and Enzo. They seemed to be particularly vocal and even offered to serve as mentors for the children to learn the Carnival trade if needed. Would that meet your requirements, Mistress Alma?"

"Well..." Mistress Alma tapped her fingers against her desk. "It seems as though your time spent in the city has paid off, you three. If the Carnival folk are truly not put out by the proposal, I will accept."

"Glad to hear it, ma'am," Tomás said. "I suggest we make this arrangement with the agreement that these three are allowed to visit Pivot on the weekends. However, there is the matter of their actions today. They ran from guards, knocked over a fruit stand, and evaded and led us on quite the chase. That should not go without reprimanding."

Pascal bit back his excitement, but repressing the smile was impossible.

"Very well," Mistress Alma assented. "No more secret or unauthorized visits. After you three pay off any damages and work off your punishments, we shall make arrangements with your new mentors."

"And I will keep a weather eye on them," Tomás promised. "As best as I can, anyway."

Pascal would gladly accept any punishment, knowing it meant he could finally be a part of the Carnival. Finally, an opportunity for his future had presented itself.

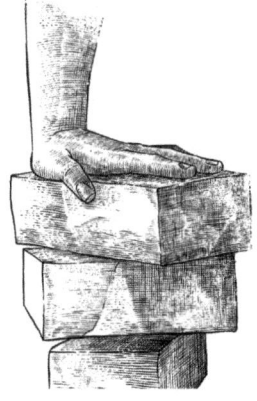

CHAPTER NINE

LIGHTNING FLASHED, AND DARK TREE BRANCHES tossed in the wind, rain pouring down in sheets. Paloma, drenched and shivering with cold, huddled behind the bush. She didn't want to look up. She didn't want to see what always loomed ahead: the unmoving shapes of her parents' bodies, the horrifically twisted faces that hovered over them. Still, the young girl's eyes moved to the scene, unable to help themselves.

Those cheekbones, the dark flaming eyes, the sharp twist of the wide, maniacal smile. Rain pelted down, creating a muddy tableau around her. She would never forget that face. Forcing her gaze downward, Paloma realized with a start that the bodies lying in the mud weren't her parents.

No! Paloma's breath came hard and fast.

Pascal and Pierrot.

Pascal's chestnut hair spilled over his blank face, raindrops clinging to the strands, and Pierrot's blue and red balls lay just beyond his lifeless fingers. Paloma screamed. Bursting out of the bush, she ran forward.

And then she was sitting upright, drawing in deep gulps of air. Paloma scraped at the rivers of tears flowing down her face with shaking hands. Thank God. Thank God that was over.

Resting her head against her knees, Paloma squeezed her eyes as the dream faded. This time, she had been ready to fight. She wasn't just fighting for her friends, though. It was about justice and taking action. She knew that her parents would never come back, no matter what she did. Even if the ravagers were brought to justice, her parents would never return. But if she acted, then at least nobody else would be hurt. Pascal and Pierrot would be safe.

And it's the first time that I saw anyone else there.

The realization hit like a swift punch to the gut.

Shaking the thoughts away, she made her way down to the mess hall and worked through the hearty breakfast served by Cook Michel, despite not having much of an appetite after the dream. For the rest of the day, as she studied and hung out with Tania, Paloma remained locked in pensive thought.

Her quiet demeanor did not go unnoticed. It was Friday, which meant she would meet Pascal and Pierrot in the backyard after dinner. Over the past several days, the three had practiced acrobatic routines together for hours in the yard. Today, however, when Pascal asked her what she wanted to do that night, Paloma shrugged inattentively. Pierrot and Pascal discussed, in their lopsided fashion, their plans for the evening. They finally decided to head for the tree house. Paloma absently nodded.

Pascal's head cocked to the side as he watched Paloma curiously, but she pretended not to notice. Together, the three headed into the forest.

Once they reached the tree house, they took up their favorite positions on the platform. Pierrot unpacked the small basket

Michel had given them, and she helped herself to the canteen as she snacked on a biscuit.

Eventually, Pascal's voice broke into her thoughts. Paloma shook off her reverie.

"Sorry," she apologized. "What did you say, Pascal?"

"You're awfully quiet," Pascal mused, watching her with a knowing expression. Paloma melted under his gaze of concern, both appreciative of his consideration and guilty for making him worry. "Are you alright? Pierrot and I are worried."

"I'm fine," she said with a shrug. "I just... it's been a tough day, is all."

"A tough day?" Pascal asked. "What happened? Was it Maldavo? Did Clément or Claudio say something?"

"No, no," Paloma said, raising her hands in protest. "They've all left everyone alone since I decked Mal. No. It's just something I've always had."

"You're sick?" Pascal's eyebrows pulled in tight, and he leaned closer, grabbing her hand.

Pierrot squeezed his red ball, his expression pinched as he gazed at her. Maybe it was the dark circles that ringed her eyes or her unkempt hair that she normally tied up neatly that gave her away. Paloma rubbed the bridge of her nose.

"No, I'm not sick." She looked away, trying to muster the courage to form the words. "Look, it's weird, but I've always had this same dream. It's an old memory from when my parents were killed. When I was running with the Rejects, I'd have it often. It usually comes when I'm anxious or stressed, but..."

"You had the dream last night," Pascal guessed before she could continue to speak, giving her hand a light squeeze that sent flutters through her body and along her limbs.

"Yes. It happened again," she answered, sliding her hand from his and placing it on her knee. With her other hand, she rubbed her forehead and helped herself to another biscuit. "Just thinking about it... it makes me feel terrible. It's always the same, and there's nothing I can do to change it. And this time, I saw you and Pierrot. Your bodies were...there."

"Oh," Pascal said softly, scooting back to give her space. "I'm sorry."

"I know." She forced a smile, an attempt to look alright, to *feel* alright.

Pierrot nudged her and held out his juggling balls. Paloma chuckled a little and accepted them, juggling the balls in her hands. After a little while, she started to relax and focus on the task.

Watching the rhythmic arc of the balls—upward, downward, and around—some of the tension from her shoulders and neck eased. Just these simple things helped. She could narrow her focus onto the cool breeze, the quiet forest, and the flash of the balls.

Setting them down, she smiled at Pierrot.

"Thank you," she said. "I see why you like those juggling balls so much. They help you shift your focus, don't they?"

Pierrot offered a small smile, and Pascal met it with a larger one.

"Pierrot is smart," Pascal said. "I think we should all have juggling balls."

"I wish juggling could fix everything," Paloma said. "But it helped me remember that what I can do is to remind myself we're safe. If we study and prepare, I know we'll be ready for anything."

"Yeah," Pascal said, leaning sideways to give Paloma an awkward hug. "We're friends, no matter what happens." The comfort of his arms around her shoulders, holding her close, made her feel better.

"Why does it sound silly when you say it?" Paloma teased, giving him a playful smack.

"Because I'm a sap," Pascal retorted, tightening his embrace. "That's what you say, anyway."

"Hm..." Paloma smirked, leaning into his embrace for only a moment before pulling away. "Now, that is true. Brenson and Torto agree with me, too."

"Like they should talk," Pascal said with a grin, glancing at her from the corner of his eyes.

She chuckled and shook her head. Already, she felt ten times better. Just the thought of their visit to Pivot had lightened the mood. Maybe Pascal had something to do with it, though she refused to think about that further, settling on the idea that it was the Carnival that had raised her spirits.

THE NEXT MORNING, THE THREE OF THEM MADE THEIR way into Pivot, escorted by Tomás. After browsing the market, they wandered into the Carnival, where they were released into custody to the Carnival folk. Cherise, Crisanto, and Enzo waited by the entrance, as usual, waving cheerfully.

Paloma's stomach was full of butterflies, and Pascal was more jittery than usual. Not only was the pressure of being caught released from their shoulders but today was their first attempt at a street performance. They'd perform right next to the road, so anyone eating candied apples from vendors or waiting to play ring toss at nearby stalls would be able to enjoy the small show. The trio was escorted inside, and together, they rushed off to the costume tent.

Paloma chose a red-and-black costume studded with faux pearls that hugged her spare frame at the waist and flared out in a short black tutu. A white, frilly collar went about her neck, matching her hair tie, lacy bracelets, and anklets. After applying white makeup to her face, Paloma added pink blush and eye shadow, just as Cherise had taught her. The thick makeup made Paloma look like a doll.

When she emerged from her tent, she found Pascal and Pierrot waiting outside. Pascal, wearing black tights and a diamond-patterned tunic of red and black, appeared very tall and imposing in Paloma's eyes. His only accessories—a white posy and a white-trimmed black cap—were intended to match Paloma's own color scheme. Like her, he wore thick white paint on his face but with clownish patterns traced above and below his eyes.

Next to him, Pierrot looked slight and short in his white clothing accented with black trim. His face had been painted with a very simple white paint, with a single blue tear painted at the outer corner of his left eye. Unlike Pascal, whose hair had been curled, Pierrot's hair had simply been brushed beneath his conical hat, which was tied with a black bow beneath his chin.

Paloma, knowing she had caught their attention, twirled around. "What do you think?"

"Whoa... Paloma," Pascal's eyes lit up as he inspected her from top to bottom. "You look so..." He paused as if unable to form the words. A part of her hoped his cheeks were flushed beneath that white paint, as she could feel hers growing warmer. With his mouth gaping open, he stared at her. "Wow."

Beneath his gaze, she suddenly felt self-conscious but played it off in confidence. "Well, of course," she said with a playful pout. "A lot of work went into this."

Pierrot grinned a little and tossed a red ball at Pascal's head in silent admonition. Paloma giggled as Pascal faked a head wound and collapsed on the ground.

Behind them, Enzo rolled up his brightly painted orange-and-blue organ grinder. He unfolded part of it, showing off a cheerfully decorated drum. When he cranked the grinder and pressed the kickstand pedal, he played the loveliest songs. Passersby couldn't help but listen.

"Let's go!" Paloma called out. "The Carnival has officially opened, right? We should start as soon as possible!"

Pascal and Pierrot didn't need encouragement. Quickly, the three raced over to the spot that had been set aside for them. Laying out the orange and blue mat that Crisanto loaned them, Pascal and Paloma rapidly set up while Pierrot began a simple juggling routine.

At the sight of their warm-up, the passersby paused. Older men with long beards, mothers pushing their little ones, and curious children gathered in a wide half-circle. Enzo played a cheerful tune, which he emphasized with well-timed drumbeats. He knew just what he was doing.

Pascal and Paloma, following along to the music, somersaulted, leaped, and cartwheeled across the mat in perfect synchronization. From jumping jacks to split leaps, Pascal and Paloma tried to outdo each other with each successive maneuver.

The crowd loved it. More onlookers gathered, clapping and cheering, drawn in by Paloma and Pascal's energy.

Then Pierrot eased forward to give Paloma and Pascal a little breather. He completed his first set of juggling—first his colored balls, then three small bats. Sometimes he would hop from one foot to another, juggling underhand beneath his knee. The onlookers shouted encouragement. Stepping in, Pascal began to catch some of Pierrot's balls. For a short while, the two juggled together. Then, one by one, Pierrot handed off the rest of his juggling props, freeing his hands.

Now that he was no longer juggling, Pierrot was able to complete his favorite mime: a man feeling his way along a wall, climbing upward, finding a door, unlocking the door, then slipping through with a jaunty farewell wave. As he slipped through the "door," Pierrot stepped back. By this time, Paloma and Pascal had grabbed the props for the next trick—Pascal's brick handstands.

Pascal assumed a handstand on the mats. One by one, Paloma threw Pascal a brick, which he slowly stacked below his hands. Eventually, to the impressed oohs and aahs of their audience, Pascal was balanced on five bricks beneath each hand. Then, pushing upward, he temporarily released his grip on the blocks, knocking them off one at a time until his hands were again on the ground. As Pascal popped up, sweating, applause broke out.

Enzo's music crescendoed to a finish, signaling the end of the show. Pascal, Paloma, and Pierrot joined hands and bowed in tandem before silently gesturing at Enzo in thanks. The crowd applauded all the performers and slowly disbanded.

Paloma caught her breath and heaved a sigh of relief. *A success! It had been a success. Really.*

She glanced over at Pascal. He wore a wide grin, his eyes twinkling in adoration. Her heart skipped a beat as she watched him laughing and smiling with Pierrot. With his attention elsewhere, she took the moment to sneak a peek, to really admire Pascal and his performance.

Beyond the makeup, the sweat trickled down the side of his face, pooling at the back of his suit. His muscles flexed against the material. He wore the costume well.

Look how happy he is. This performance was like an answer to his dreams. And honestly, it was special for all of them. They've worked so hard to achieve this—something real, something enjoyable, and something no one could take away.

I want this moment to last forever.

The thought remained with her for the rest of the night. After performing on and off for two hours, they parted ways with Enzo.

Paloma, Pierrot, and Pascal changed into their street clothes while Enzo went on to prepare for his next show. Paloma rolled her eyes at Pascal's excitement to see a new episode at the puppet theater before they headed back.

This evening, the story was about the moment that Harlequin decided to pursue Columbine's heart. Once he'd made the decision, a mysterious seer named Ojos Verdes broke the bond that held Harlequin to Mephisto. He could then remain with Columbine, sitting with her at a crackling golden campfire while Ojos Verdes looked on with troubled eyes. She feared Mephisto's Citadel was hidden within a wasteland of decay in the Untamed Highlands. Mephisto followed the orders of an even greater evil.

In the shadowed halls of Dominion, Mephisto felt his hold over Harlequin suddenly snap. With a roar, he sent forth his many henchmen—minions of fire, lightning, and shadow—to hunt down his wayward herald. They sped past the iron gates into the wasteland and the world beyond.

From that time onward, Harlequin and his beloved could no longer linger by the campfires of the other Wanderers. The two lovers were forced to flee, running from place to place to avoid Mephisto's minions.

The audience gasped as each horrific creature emerged, nearly catching Harlequin and Columbine. Each time, the two lovers managed to escape.

One night, however, Harlequin and Columbine rested beneath a broad-branched tree filled with the soft glow of fireflies. Harlequin and Columbine kissed in a serene, magical moment.

Columbine whispered tenderly, "I have news, beloved. The best news ever!"

The curtain fell.

The crowd surged to their feet with applause and cries for more.

"No!" Pascal leaned back with a groan. "What is her news? Do you think there's a way they can defeat Mephisto once and for all?"

"Here we go," Paloma said, glancing at Pierrot with a shrug.

She knew that for the next half hour, Pascal would think of nothing else but the puppet show. After listening to him yammer on about the show and his predictions for a while, Paloma dragged him outside, where Hugo stood and waited with a wide grin.

The tall, aristocratic puppetmaster glanced at them with his deep golden eyes, pushing back a piece of his dark hair. Tonight, he was dressed in his most formal costume—a long-tailed three-piece suit. The deep red and black handkerchief that emerged from his waistcoat pocket matched the red and black, diamond-patterned ribbon that banded his velvet top hat. Smoothing back his hair, Hugo smiled down at them.

"What did you think, Pascal?" he asked. "Was the show exciting tonight?"

"It was!" Pascal's eyes lit up as he bounced in place like a child. "I know you said you won't ever tell me what happens next, but I can't wait for next weekend. Come on, Hugo, please."

"He's telling the truth," Paloma said. "Pascal is always excited about what's going to happen next, but tonight he is practically beside himself."

"I'm glad to hear it," Hugo said with a chuckle. "I didn't think I'd be able to trump the excitement of the first performance you saw, but I suppose I underestimated your obsession."

Pascal shrugged, his face growing red.

Changing the topic, Hugo asked, "How was *your* first performance? I may have stopped by... and you three did spectacularly."

"Really?" Pascal asked, stepping forward. "We were that good?"

A smile curled at Paloma's lips, pleased with the praise. Or was she more pleased with Pascal's reaction and the way he was overflowing with happiness?

"One day, you will perform in the big tent," Hugo said. "With time, your abilities will grow, Pascal. For now, you should celebrate what you and your friends have accomplished."

"You think so?" Pascal glanced at Paloma with uncertainty. She nodded once in agreement, causing Pascal's cheeks to flush once more. He turned away, facing Hugo. "So, are you going to tell me about what happened with Harlequin?"

"Here we go again," Paloma grumbled, letting out a huff. "You and your hero, I swear."

"Sometimes we think of heroes as people who swoop in triumphantly to conquer the enemy, and they save the day in the blink of an eye," Hugo said, squeezing Pascal's shoulder with encouragement. "But that's not really how it works."

Pascal's head tilted slightly as he watched Hugo with scrutiny. Pierrot crowded a little closer, curious about Hugo's words, as Paloma fixed her gaze on the Puppetmaster as well.

Hugo smiled at the three serious faces ringed around him. "Absolutely. The best heroes learn to remain true to their hearts. They stand on their convictions even when times get tough, and they never give up on themselves or their friends. Through thick and thin, they remain loyal. They believe in themselves...and when they least expect it, their hard work and determination will bring the most surprising results."

"Just like Harlequin," Pascal said.

"Yes," Hugo confirmed with a broad grin. "Just like Harlequin. He never gave up. Once he discovered the truth, once he realized who he really cared about, Harlequin knew what he had to do. He never gave up fighting for what he believed in. If you can learn anything from our stories, I hope it's that, Pascal."

The three of them nodded solemnly.

"Now," Hugo said, "you should probably head back soon."

He glanced over at a nearby stall. On the wall, another missing person's poster had been tacked up. It was a black-and-white drawing of a young boy with dark, curly hair. Paloma frowned, remembering when Irina had gone missing. It seemed that the Rejects weren't the only ones who'd had someone disappear.

"Yes," a creaky voice broke into her thoughts. "Another one lost. Poor soul."

Paloma turned about as Cosme, the Fortune Teller, drifted up to their small group. Tonight, Cosme was dressed in black robes trimmed with gold and a gaudy gold turban. Hugo shook his head at the sight of her.

"Cosme," he said in a mild reprimand, "don't scare the children."

Paloma rolled her eyes at the word. *Children. I'm nearly an adult!* Still, an uneasiness settled in her stomach, knowing that until she *was* an adult, she would be deemed a child. At least in the eyes of those around her.

"I speak only the truth," the old woman replied serenely. "A truth and a warning, yes. For all of you, dear children. Watch your paths. I fear a darkness looms."

CHAPTER TEN

"WHAT'S THIS PLACE CALLED AGAIN?" Pascal asked as Paloma led them down the winding cobbled lanes surrounded by nice homes with crisp lawns and wide parks. Though, the truly remarkable feature was the abundance of willow trees that lined the road.

Paloma shook her head, hiding a grin. "I told you, Willowside." She turned to Pierrot, giving him a teasing nudge while gesturing to Pascal. "In case you couldn't tell."

He cracked a smile, in awe of the difference in setting between this part of Pivot compared to the marketplace.

"We still have a bit of time before we need to be back at the West Gate," Paloma said as they meandered along. Ringmaster Barolo had created a small area for them to perform later in the afternoon. Until then, they were wandering about, leisurely killing time. "I want to show you the Stillmere River."

She gestured just beyond Willowside to a river that curved and wound, just as the road did. Past the twists and turns, the river led northeast to the lower section of the airship docks.

"Supposedly, it winds its way from the Stillmere Sea near the Untamed Highlands all the way to the Great Sea, The Southern Abyss."

Freight ships, tugboats, and steamers riddled the congested river, cluttered and chaotic. Pascal tilted his head slightly, looking from the river to Paloma. *Why did she want to show us this so bad?* Paloma swiftly turned on her heels and led them down the road.

"But that's not the part of the river I wanted to show you."

A serene and private part of the river weaved through the heart of Willowside. Pascal's head turned in every direction, gazing at the willows that surrounded him and tapered over the water, just barely dipping their leaves under the surface. A stone bridge connected one side to the other, the seclusion a complete opposite of the river they'd seen minutes before.

Leaning against the bridge, Pascal swiped up two rocks and handed one to Pierrot. "Want to see who can throw it further?"

Pierrot nodded and pulled his arm back to fling the rock as far as he could, the water lilies on the surface gently swaying in response to the disturbance. Paloma clambered up the high stone wall of the bridge to sit at the top. Pascal tossed the rock, skipping it a few times—though he wasn't paying attention. His focus had drifted to her legs dangling over the stone's edge as she wistfully stared at the peaceful setting.

Pascal climbed up to sit beside her, Pierrot following his motion, and together, they watched the dark green water swirl past.

After a few minutes, Paloma turned to the boys. "Do you know what this bridge is called?"

Pascal shook his head, glancing at Pierrot with a shrug. "I didn't know bridges have names."

Pierrot juggled his red ball in response, indicating he was equally clueless.

"It's called the Bridge of Sorrows," Paloma answered, her tone soft. "I know—you wouldn't think it. The water is so lovely, and it all looks so beautiful."

"Did someone die here?" asked Pascal.

"No." Paloma shook her head. "It's just become the spot where people throw away their engagement or wedding rings. Sometimes things don't work out, and when the people of Pivot are sad about lost love, they have a tradition of throwing the rings into the Stillmere River."

Pascal leaned forward precariously, trying to fathom the green-blue depths of the river. Try as he might, he couldn't catch a glimpse of anything. The morning sunlight dancing on the water was brilliant enough to sparkle like precious gems, making it impossible to see the river's bottom.

"I don't see any rings," Pascal said, not entirely believing it to be true. Or maybe he just didn't want to.

"Well, no, you wouldn't. You see, the Stillmere River is very mysterious," Paloma explained. "In this section, it becomes quite deep. Nobody has been able to fathom the bottom. It's that deep and dark. And, there are rumors that something lives deep in the waters, so nobody has really felt confident to try to dive for the rings."

"I don't know if that's more creepy or sad," Pascal said with a shiver, his eyes fixed on the sparkling water below.

"Yeah," Paloma agreed, "me either."

"Imagine losing someone you love..." Pascal said slowly. "Coming out here and mourning your heartbreak. Would throwing away the ring really help?"

"I don't know." Paloma shrugged.

"At any rate, I don't think we have to imagine too hard how it would feel to lose someone. We've lost our families, right? My parents were killed, and yours ..." she drifted off, staring at Pascal. "Wait, Pascal, how did you end up at the orphanage?"

He shook his head. "I don't know the details. All I can remember is a man leaving me there. But even now, his face is just a blur. I was too young to remember much—only three when it happened. Whenever I used to ask Mistress Alma about my parents, she would only say that a man dropped me off, believing he was my father, though she'd never been certain. It's always been a mystery."

"So strange." Paloma watched him with a sliver of pity in her eyes. Maybe she felt bad for him because at least she knew who her parents were. Pascal could only guess. Unable to face the sympathetic pull in her eyes, he turned away. Paloma cleared her throat and faced Pierrot. "What about you, Pierrot?"

Pascal's gaze shifted, but Pierrot refused to meet his eyes. He focused instead on the waters of the Stillmere River and tossed another rock. The gray stone hit the waters with a dull plop and sank out of sight.

Pascal glanced at Paloma, who shrugged in response. If Pierrot didn't want to talk about it, then he didn't have to. He didn't want to pressure Pierrot and hoped one day his friend would feel comfortable enough to share his story. Until then, Pascal wouldn't push.

Pascal hopped off the wall. "Let's go back."

"Yes," Paloma quickly agreed, probably just as eager to change the conversation to something less melancholy.

They headed north to the Carnival, jumping right into their costumes and other preparations for the show. Pascal helped Pierrot straighten his bow and comb his hair before putting on his conical hat. Pierrot smoothed the lapels of his costume and turned about in front of the mirror to make sure that everything was in place before proceeding to the makeup table outside the boys' changing room.

Paloma was already seated before the long mirror, carefully applying white foundation to her face. Pascal took a seat beside her, applying his own white makeup like Cherise had taught him. He glanced at Pierrot, whose face was only inches from the mirror, as he smoothed the makeup across his skin.

Usually, they'd be reviewing their tricks for the evening. Pierrot would squeeze his colored balls or poke Pascal when he wanted to insert an idea into the conversation.

But not today.

He rolled the red ball into his palm in a small circle as he stared into the mirror silently. Sure, Pierrot didn't talk, but he was particularly quiet tonight.

Turning to face him, Pascal asked, "You alright, Pierrot? Ever since the bridge..." He didn't want to bring it up, but he was worried for his friend. "Are you okay?"

Pierrot slowly squeezed his red ball. His right hand rose to pull down the corner of his lips as he mimed an exaggerated frown.

"Your parents?" guessed Pascal.

Pierrot pulled out his blue ball in response. Instead of juggling it, however, he simply held it between lax fingers as he stared glumly at his juggling props.

"Do you want to talk about it? Sometimes, talking helps. But I understand if you don't want to."

Pierrot held up his blue ball as if to say "yes."

"So..." Pascal wracked his brain for a way to figure out the story without making Pierrot uncomfortable. "I guess your story is just as sad as Paloma's and mine."

Pierrot's hand trembled as he began to release his tension by squeezing the blue ball over and over again.

"Did your parents die, too?" Paloma asked in a gentle tone.

Pierrot shook his head slowly.

"They aren't dead? Were they trying to keep you safe from ravagers or something?" Pascal asked.

When Pierrot again shook his head, Pascal and Paloma looked at each other dumbfounded. A pit grew in Pascal's stomach as the information clicked into place.

"It's because you're different." Though he struggled to find the right words, he knew it to be true. "Isn't it?"

Pierrot nodded miserably, and Paloma leaned in to give him a tight squeeze and sighed. "Well, they don't know what they're missing. They must not see how kind and smart you are. They don't see your talent." Under her breath, she spat out a muttered, "Stupid!"

Pascal nodded his head in agreement, placing a hand on Pierrot's shoulder that was still in Paloma's half-embrace. "She's right. There's nothing wrong with being unique. If they can't see that, then I feel bad for them. They're walking through the world with their eyes closed, missing out on getting to know such a great person like you."

Pierrot leaned forward, pulled out a piece of charcoal, and traced a tear at the corner of his eye. Paloma and Pascal met his steady gaze in the mirror.

"You're sad," Pascal affirmed. "I understand why. And it's fine. Just know that I would never leave you."

"Me either," Paloma said, giving him another squeeze. "You're stuck with me now."

Pierrot shook his head. This time, he picked up a cloth and wiped the charcoal tear away. Pointing at Paloma and Pascal, he mimed a stiff little smile. After swooping in for another hug,

Paloma returned to her seat with a big smile. Pascal knew he couldn't take away that pain. It was something that would forever be trapped within Pierrot—a feeling he knew well. Buried deep within, the question of *why* would always remain. It would always plague and torment him, not knowing how someone could willingly leave their child.

He shook away his own dark thoughts and forced a smile. Even though he couldn't strip away that pain, he and Paloma made Pierrot feel better. Even the smallest sliver of happiness was enough to melt away the insecurities and frustration.

"We're always here for you, Pierrot," he promised. "Always."

Pierrot began to juggle his blue ball again, the official sign their talk had helped take a great weight off his mind. Pascal smiled and looked in the mirror to finish his makeup.

PASCAL SWIPED AWAY THE MAKEUP, PLEASED WITH their performance. The cheers and hearty applause rang in his ears as he replayed the evening. The shouts and whistles left him more energized than usual. When he'd looked over at Pierrot during the applause, he'd noticed a tiny red heart marked at the corner of his eye, replacing the typical teardrop. Pascal's heart warmed at the sight, feeling light and blissful.

But it was when he looked at Paloma that his heart skipped a beat. Even now, wiping away the makeup and sweat, the familiar flutters returned. He closed his eyes, envisioning her face: the soft features that contrasted the edginess of her personality.

He opened his eyes, watching her through the reflection. Her hair was pulled back with a few tresses that fell in wispy strands about her face.

Gorgeous. She's simply stunning.

Her gaze met his through the reflection, and her hazel eyes lit up as her lips pulled into a warm smile. Frantically, his heart raced his focus only on Paloma in that moment. And that was when he knew, when he recognized for the first time, that he wanted to be closer to her.

His mind screamed to reach out and touch her, to gently take her hand or pull her into an embrace. *Something.*

And maybe he would have... if Pierrot hadn't poked him in the shoulder, snapping him back to reality.

He tore his eyes from Paloma as Pierrot pointed at Enzo, who had packed up his organ grinder for the evening. Pascal quickly rolled up his mat, and the three of them carried their props to their small tent, neatly packing everything away before rushing off to the puppet theater. Pascal had been waiting the whole week to find out what news Columbine had for Harlequin.

Tonight, she revealed that she was going to have a baby, which meant that their daring escapes from Mephisto's minions would become more dangerous than before. They were aware of Mephisto's rage and resentment over Harlequin's defection and feared the arrival of the blood moon—when Mephisto's minions would gain immense power. If Columbine and Harlequin weren't careful, their lives and their baby would be at risk. Sure, Harlequin had his slapstick, but even with all his power, it might not be enough to protect the ones he loves.

What would typically leave Pascal reeling in excitement had struggled to hold his focus. The final scene revealed that Columbine had a baby boy, yet all Pascal could think about was Paloma. All his senses were attuned to her. The soft cadence of her voice left him mesmerized and entranced when she leaned in close to whisper into his ear about the story. When she handed him a candied apple, he couldn't help but notice the soft brush of her skin against his hand. Even Pierrot's poking and nudges wouldn't pull him away.

I want to spend more time with her. Alone.

Pascal declared to himself that he would find a chance to be alone with Paloma, a chance to talk with her, just the two of them. Yet, his plan was repeatedly thwarted.

After breakfast, Paloma was whisked off for a talk with Minette, Tania, and Mira. She returned only to remind Pascal and Pierrot that they had another day in Pivot planned.

This is my chance to spend some time alone with her. Or so he thought. When they got to Pivot, it was as if everything was working against him. At the puppet theater, Pascal planned to slide in beside Paloma. Instead, Pierrot plunked himself between them. In turn, Pascal spent the entire show thinking about Paloma rather than paying attention to the show.

He'd had crushes over the years, but nothing like this. Paloma made him feel… everything—invincible, accepted, happy. He wanted to do something for her. He pondered on what would make the other girls happy—pretty bows and ribbons, jewelry, clothing—but Paloma wasn't like the other girls. She didn't care about fashion or jewelry. *Not like it matters. I only have a shilling or two. Maybe if we go window shopping, I could get an idea of what she'd like.*

Pascal suggested they stop by Doralin Blackcoat's Emporium. They always had exotic trinkets in little cabinets and mysterious glass showcases, candies displayed behind the confectioner's counter. Hopefully, she would point out something she liked.

Of course, with the way Pascal's day had gone, his plan failed again. He observed her walking past the different showcases, uninterested in anything Doralin had to offer. After finally getting up the nerve, he opened his mouth to ask her, but Doralin Blackcoat appeared, watching Paloma with skepticism as she talked about the increase in fabric and bead prices.

Defeated, Pascal was ready to give up until Pierrot stopped to check out Van's bookstall. The perfect opportunity to be alone with Paloma. Unfortunately, when she moved away from the bookstall, she stepped too close to Giulia's fabric stall. Giulia flew forward and shooed them away with a few choice words.

Paloma led Pascal to an out-of-the-way spot behind Van's book stall where they could sit in peace while they waited for Pierrot to finish browsing.

Pascal glanced at Paloma, and she met his gaze with a smile and a warm sparkle in her hazel eyes. Pushing back a wayward strand of her wavy, dark hair, Paloma's face lit up with happiness. She leaned against the wood backing of Van's stall and gazed up at the blue sky overhead. The sun was setting in the west, casting long shadows across the market. Already, a few of the stall owners were lighting the lanterns that would give the market a merry nighttime glow.

"I'm glad," she said simply.

"Glad?" Pascal asked. "About what?"

"Just glad," she answered. "At first, being taken to the orphanage felt like a nightmare. But now I can enjoy Pivot without having to worry about basic survival. Mistress Alma takes care of that, and I just have to think about me and my dreams and what I want to do with my life." She stared out at the setting sun. Rolling her head to Pascal, she added, "And, I met you. Another thing to be glad about."

Pascal's heart nearly leaped out of his chest. Finally, a small window of opportunity. But before he could reply, Pierrot's ball smacked against the back of his head in greeting as Pierrot pointed upward in warning at the darkening sky.

"I suppose we ought to get back home," Pascal said, a hint of an edge to his tone.

"We'll be back before you know it," Paloma reminded him.

Slowly, the three returned to the orphanage, enjoying the golden sunset as the sun sank behind the western hills and forest. When they came within sight of the orphanage, their pace picked up. Perhaps Michel might have a tasty snack waiting for them.

But when they arrived, Pascal frowned. The kitchen was clean but also empty, unlike the typical evening in which Michel would sit by the hearth, smoking a pipe and enjoying a tankard of light beer. But there was no sign of Michel.

In the front hall, Tania and Minette stood with the older children and teenagers. At the sight of Pascal and his friends, they visibly relaxed with sighs of relief.

"Pascal!" Tania called out. "Thank goodness you're back."

"What happened? Why does everyone look so worried?" He glanced over at Paloma, whose eyes were on Maldavo at the other end of the hall. Though Maldavo hadn't caused trouble in a while, the smug expression on his face left Pascal with a sinking feeling in his stomach that Maldavo was back to his antics.

"Did one of the orphans do something?" Pascal asked.

Mira, who had linked her arms with Minette, shook her head quickly. "No, no. It's Mistress Alma and Michel. They said they were popping down to Skystead for some emergency, but it's been hours since they've left. That's odd, right?"

"It feels odd," grumbled Danton. "Clarion and I went into Skystead to look, but there was no sign of them."

"No sign at all?" Pascal's stomach sank. The muscles in his back tightened as he straightened and looked about the room, the severity of the situation settling in. It wasn't like Mistress Alma *or* Michel to be gone after nightfall.

Pierrot anxiously squeezed his red ball, looking back and forth between Paloma and Pascal. Pascal calmed his features. Reacting too nervously would frighten the younger kids. He needed to slow down and think rationally—if they didn't return by morning, he'd send for the constable.

Taking a deep breath, Pascal steadied his tone. "Though I'm concerned, I don't think we should panic. We are the eldest and need to set an example, run things as normally as possible, and work through this with a level head."

"Agreed," Paloma said. "What are you thinking?"

"We'll send Danton and Clarion to the village tomorrow morning to make a report to the constable. That is if Mistress Alma isn't back by then," Pascal said. "For now, let's put the other children to bed and try to get some sleep. Clarion and Paloma can help me lock up."

"Good idea." Minette nodded. "Tania, Mira, and I can put the children to bed with Danton's help. Maybe Mistress Alma was just held up. I'm sure she'll be back tomorrow morning, and there'll be no harm done."

With that, they scattered to their self-appointed duties. Pascal, Paloma, and Clarion found Michel's extra keys on the usual hook by the kitchen door. Together, they locked all the doors and closed the windows and shutters. Pascal had just slid the key back into place when Maldavo and his gaggle of jerks burst through the kitchen door, scooping up a sack of snacks.

He'd have probably just ignored them if Maldavo hadn't swiped Michel's beer and shoved it into his bag.

"What are you doing?" Pascal asked, his tone filled with more authority than he'd intended. Though, he was pleased with how daunting he sounded. "That's Michel's. Put it back."

Maldavo looked at his friends and laughed. With a scoff, he turned to Pascal and stepped forward, a nasty sneer curled on his lips. "And if I don't?" he asked with his chest puffed out.

Pascal didn't waver. He took a step forward, asserting his own dominance. There was no way he'd let Maldavo steal from Michel. "I said put it back."

"Try and stop me." Maldavo closed the distance between them and shoved Pascal back with enough force to make even Pascal's light feet stumble.

"What's going on in here?" Tania asked, standing in the kitchen's doorway.

"Maldavo didn't like it when I told him to put back Michel's beer," Pascal answered, setting his feet firmly again.

Maldavo's eyes were slits, glaring at Pascal. He lunged forward, ready to swing, but Pierrot swiftly stepped in front of Pascal, blocking his path. Pascal's eyes grew wide, and pride beamed from him to see Pierrot standing up to his bully. Maldavo, on the other hand, only grew resentful.

"Oh, now you want to be a big boy, huh? You think you can square up to me?" Maldavo faked a swing, moving forward just enough to make Pierrot wince, believing he was about to be struck. With a chuckle, Maldavo pushed past them to leave.

"Knock it off," Tania said, hands firmly placed on her hips. "You know you're not old enough to drink, so put it back. Just because Mistress Alma isn't here doesn't mean you can start trouble."

"You want to talk about trouble," Maldavo snapped. "Maybe you should take a look around you." His eyes landed on Pierrot. "He isn't so innocent, you know. I heard Miss Alma say that he killed his brother. Now, *that's* trouble—having a killer here at the orphanage."

Pierrot shook his head, tightly gripping his red ball as he slowly backed up.

"Don't try to deny it, freak. You pretend to be all quiet and innocent, but you're a killer."

Pierrot turned on his heels and sprinted from the kitchen, disappearing from sight.

Turning to Tania, Pascal stared in disbelief. She shook her head and gestured to the doorway. "Go after him. I'll handle this."

Pascal nodded and slipped out of the kitchen to find Pierrot. As he left, he could hear Tania say, "It wasn't what you think, Maldavo. Mistress Alma told me what happened, so you should watch your mouth and apologize for being so rude."

Paloma called out to Pascal, but he ignored her call, heading instead in the direction Pierrot ran. She jogged up to him, asking what happened.

"Maldavo made some horrible accusations about Pierrot, and he ran off," Pascal explained.

Paloma's jaw tightened, ticking slightly in irritation. "What'd he say?"

"He called Pierrot a killer. Said he murdered his own brother."

Paloma stared at the kitchen with a glower. Looking back to Pascal, she said, "Let's check the library."

Together, they found Pierrot pacing around the library, flipping the red ball about his hand repeatedly.

"Pierrot," Pascal called out, rushing forward to his friend. But Pierrot shook his head, looking away. "Come on, Pierrot. Don't listen to that fool."

"Yeah," Paloma agreed. "Mal is a manipulator. Don't listen to him."

Pierrot continuously shook his head and turned around, his arms waving through the air. Unsure what to do and unable to understand Pierrot, Pascal spoke in a soothing tone.

"Pierrot, it's okay. Try to relax. Calm down."

Snatching a scrap paper from a random notebook someone had left in the library, Pierrot scribbled on the page and handed it to Pascal. Paloma read the note over his shoulder. "Accident."

Piecing it together, Pascal asked, "Your brother's death was an accident?"

Pierrot nodded and grabbed the paper, scribbling some more and handing it back. "Sick bear. Attacked," Pascal read. "My fault." He looked at Paloma, whose eyebrows were creased as she read the note silently. "A rabid bear attacked your brother, and you think it was your fault?"

Pierrot nodded again, looking away. He slumped into a chair, burying his head in his hands. Pascal rested a hand on Pierrot's shoulder as Paloma sat across from him.

"Pierrot," she said, her voice gentle. "Don't blame yourself for what happened to your brother. That's not something you can control."

"Yeah, we all know you'd never intentionally hurt someone. You're too kind of a person, too caring, to harm someone on purpose. And you know what? We don't have to talk about it right now. Another time."

They stayed for a while longer, not talking about their pasts but playing and practicing minor tricks. After a while, Pierrot returned to himself and even smiled. Pascal put on a smile, too, but it faded as he walked back to the boys' dormitory to settle down for the night. He couldn't help but feel a deep uneasiness pooling in the pit of his stomach. He *knew*, deep down, that something wasn't right.

In the morning, Pascal, Pierrot, and Clarion rushed downstairs and joined Paloma and Mira in the front hall. When they peered into Mistress Alma's study, there was nothing to indicate that she had returned. Some of the other children searched the back garden, while others wandered the house. There was no sign of Mistress Alma or Michel.

"Well, I suppose we should send Danton and you to Skystead," Pascal suggested warily to Clarion. "I can stay with the others and help get breakfast going."

"What do you think—"

Before Clarion could finish his question, a sharp knock echoed through the front hall. Pascal quickly slid the locks back and threw the door open wide, hoping to see Michel or Mistress Alma on the doorstep. At the sight of a strange man, his heart sank.

It wasn't Michel, Mistress Alma, or even Constable Leon.

A man with an iron-headed walking stick pushed past Pascal and stalked into the front hall as though he owned the place. His dark, glittering eyes passed over the children as though they were invisible.

Then, after a moment, the stranger put his hands on his hips and said, "Well, well, everything looks to be in order."

"Excuse me," Pascal said politely, "everything looks to be in order for what?"

"For new management, my boy," the man said briskly. He threw his walking stick at Clarion, who nearly dropped it in shock at his next words. "I am Master Darco, and from today onward, I will be your new headmaster."

CHAPTER ELEVEN

PALOMA'S EYES NARROWED AS SHE SCANNED DARCO from head to toe. Although Paloma had never put much stock in how a person looked and dressed, there was something off about the man. She folded her arms and trained her gaze on the stranger.

Master Darco was a solid, short man. Like Paloma, he had chestnut-brown hair, but it was cut short on the sides and seemed a little unruly on top, as though he had forgotten to comb it. A scruffy beard ringed his square jaw and slightly sneering lips.

Paloma frowned. If she had passed Master Darco in the street during her days as leader of the Rejects, she might have guessed him to be a racing bookie or a ticket master for underground street fights due to his light tan and his crooked nose, which looked like it had once been broken and badly reset.

Although he was dressed in a double-breasted black suit complete with a row of shiny silver buttons, Paloma figured that Master Darco had seen the rougher side of life. She'd seen many of his types before, but it jarred her to find one in the front hall of the orphanage.

However, Pascal seemed relaxed and chatted calmly with Master Darco about who he was and why he was there.

"It is a sad state of affairs, a sad state, I am afraid." Master Darco shook his head with a grim expression. "Mistress Alma had a great-great cousin once removed. Fell ill, you see, and since it was an emergency, she volunteered to help her family. You know how she is about family. She went off with Michel, but before that, of course, she reached out to the board, and I've been sent in to help run the place until her return."

"How long will she be gone?" Tania asked, popping up from around the corner.

"A few months, I believe," Master Darco said blithely. "Until then, I will need all the help I can get." Darco clapped Pascal on the shoulder heartily. "Can I rely on your help?"

"Um…" Pascal glanced at Paloma, who kept her expression neutral. "Yes, yes, of course."

"So, perhaps someone can lead me to Mistress Alma's office?" Master Darco said. He turned on Clarion suddenly. "What's your name, boy?"

"I—Clarion," the young teen replied.

"Lead the way, Clarion. Bring my cane along."

After Clarion led Master Darco away, Paloma's eyes scanned the orphans that assembled in the front hall, mouths hung open in surprise. Beneath Tania's calm exterior, she looked unsettled. Minette and Mira clung to each other and wiped away tears from the corners of their eyes. Danton frowned at the office door as it shut behind Master Darco and Clarion.

Her gaze landed on Pascal, who had a thoughtful but calm expression. *Did he really not find this all to be alarming?* Behind Pascal, however, Pierrot silently huddled, clutching his red ball. The fact that Pierrot was responding so poorly to Master Darco's presence was a bad sign.

Paloma caught Pascal's gaze. With a small jerk of her head, she suggested that they go somewhere private to talk. Leading Pascal and Pierrot into the library, Paloma shut the door behind them before whirling on Pascal with frightening intensity.

"I don't like this, Pascal. Not one bit," she said in a low hiss.

"Don't like what?"

"Master Darco's arrival," she said as if the answer was obvious. "It feels ... wrong."

"I don't like it either," Pascal agreed. "For Mistress Alma to just disappear without so much as a goodbye..." He trailed off, shaking his head. "It doesn't make sense. Why didn't Michel return to tell us?" He turned to Pierrot. "Pierrot? What do you think?"

Squeezing his red ball rapidly several times, his timid gaze rose to meet Pascal's, filled with anxiety.

"We just need to be careful," Paloma whispered. "We'll stick close to the orphanage and keep an eye on Darco as we figure out what's really happening."

Pierrot perked up, watching Pascal with a newfound hopeful expression.

Pascal exhaled and ran his hands through his hair, ruffling his thick locks even further. "Yeah, alright. I trust your judgment, Paloma. And you too, Pierrot. It's not right how Mistress Alma disappeared so suddenly without talking to Tania or me. It's up to us now. If Master Darco tries something, we'll be here to stop it or help the others if needed."

Pascal's instant support filled Paloma with relief. She was no longer alone, nor did she have to fight with her friends like she had once done with Maldavo when they made plans for the Rejects. Feeling more empowered, she followed the two back to the mess hall, where the rest of the orphans gathered for breakfast.

Once everyone was fed, Tania broke the children into groups. Paloma and Pascal volunteered to help run sporting events outside and keep Mistress Alma's scheduled activities going. That was how things continued over the following days.

WITHIN A WEEK OF MASTER DARCO'S ARRIVAL, HE had hired a new cook, groundskeeper, and two guards.

Miss Myrrah, a thin, dark-haired woman with dull gray eyes, took over the kitchen. Unlike Michel, Miss Myrrah was haughty and suspicious. No child was allowed to enter the kitchen without permission. If anyone caught roaming about her kitchen, regardless of whether they were trying to get a snack, they would be severely reprimanded.

Master Gorgo, the new groundskeeper, was a broad-shouldered, dark-skinned man with dull brown eyes and curly blond hair. Like Michel, he didn't talk a lot, but he didn't seem to like children. When anyone went near him, the man would growl.

The guards patrolled the orphanage grounds nonstop. Weylin, one of the guards, wore a black skullcap with black clothing to match. His skin was pale, and his eyes pitch black, surrounded by shrunken cheeks. However, he was chattier than the other new hires and took a special liking to Maldavo, who talked with Weylin quite a bit.

Anala was a tough-looking mercenary who wore black-studded, leather chest armor with matching gauntlets and shin guards strapped over a sturdy pair of boots. Like Miss Myrrah, Anala was also a young woman, but she was fierce and forbidding. She had sweeping, fiery-red hair that was buzzed short on one side. Though she wasn't talkative when she did speak, her voice sounded kind enough, but she never seemed interested in the children. Paloma guessed this was because half of her face was covered in thick burn scars that marred her otherwise pretty face.

With guards like these, the children might have felt as though the orphanage was safer than ever, but as the days went by, Paloma and the boys realized that the guards were more interested in keeping the orphans in rather than in keeping danger out.

Nate, who still loved to scout and stand lookout, had kept a keen eye on the orphanage's front gate. Armed with a pair of binoculars he had filched from Mistress Alma's storage cupboard, the young boy had noticed something odd—the orphanage's part-time cleaners, Ella and Grandma Bea, as well as Mateo the woodsman and Reggie, the original groundskeeper, had been turned away at the gate.

In hushed whispers, Nate told Paloma what he had seen at lunchtime. His story fueled her suspicions. Master Darco was taking over. But why? Paloma wondered.

When Pascal suggested they sneak out to see if they could find any news in the village, Paloma agreed. *Maybe someone in Skystead will be able to tell us more details about Mistress Alma's family. Or where Master Darco really came from.*

Sneaking out proved to be more difficult than usual. Paloma, Pascal, and Pierrot had to avoid the guards, as well as Miss Myrrah, who now seemed to serve as an informal guard at the kitchen door, watching over the back garden. Finally, they were able to slink into the forest and work their way to the hidden space beneath the orphanage fence. Just like they'd done on their first trip to Pivot, they squeezed under the gap and out to freedom. Within minutes, they worked their way back up to the road.

To the south, heading toward the village, they could see the distant cloud of a cart. Coming from the north, however, was a familiar face—Baptiste. At the sight of the young man, the friends looked hopefully at each other. Obvious relief washed over Pascal's face.

"Baptiste!" He ran forward to greet the young man. "You're here!"

"I've been coming by for the past two days," Baptiste said with a wide smile that didn't quite hide the worry in his bright blue eyes. "For some reason, I'm not allowed to go in. Did something happen to Grandmother?"

"Mistress Alma is gone," Paloma said. "A family emergency, they said. Someone got sick."

"Family?" asked Baptiste, looking confused.

"Some kind of distant cousin, I think," Pascal said. "Do ... you have a distant cousin, Baptiste?"

"I don't know, to be honest." Baptiste frowned. "Grandmother never mentioned anyone else in the family. There was always just me and her."

"Hmm..." Pascal mused aloud. "Master Darco is probably lying."

"Of course, he is." Paloma rolled her eyes. "The real question is, where is Mistress Alma now?"

"So, you haven't seen her either?" Baptiste asked, his worry increasing.

Pierrot solemnly shook his head.

"Not for a week," Paloma said. "Master Darco showed up claiming Mistress Alma had a family emergency and that Michel went with her. Since then, we've had new staff, and there are guards now that watch our every move."

Pascal nodded with wide eyes. "They're creepy, Baptiste. You wouldn't believe it! We thought maybe we could ask around in

Skystead to see if we could find out what's going on. But maybe you could do that for us? And ask the city guard in Pivot and the constable in Little Mead?"

"I can do that," Baptiste agreed, his voice tinged with worry. "I'll ask around and see what I can find out. You three should go back. Don't get into serious trouble over this. But she's missing, and my concern for her safety, intertwined with this situation, is deeply unsettling."

After making tentative plans to meet Baptiste in the same place at the same time in three days, the trio returned to the orphanage as quickly and carefully as they could. Knowing that Baptiste was safe was a great relief, as was his determination to get to the bottom of the matter.

Later that day, they gathered in the mess hall with the rest of the children for supper. Miss Myrrah swept around the room, gazing over them with a cold eye, while Tania, Minette, Mira, and Danton scuttled around with the food. Paloma and Pascal also helped them serve since Miss Myrrah didn't seem interested in helping the youngest orphans with their meals. *She drives me crazy, but there's no point in resisting*, Paloma fumed.

When dinner was over, before the children were dismissed, Master Darco stepped into the hall. At the sight of him, Paloma folded her arms. Her lips thinned to a straight line. She didn't trust the wide grin that spread across his face.

"Children, children!" He raised both arms, drawing everyone's attention to the head of the room. "What a lovely surprise we have today!"

Everyone began to whisper and wonder. *What did Master Darco have up his sleeve?*

"A visitor!" he answered. "He's been away for some time, but the orphanage owes him a great debt for his kindness and generosity. Please welcome our most gracious benefactor—Lord

Dolion Serpentine! Your lordship, if you will." Master Darco bowed low in an ingratiating kind of way.

Paloma rolled her eyes, the annoyance setting in. The mysterious benefactor stepped into the room.

Lord Dolion Serpentine was a tall, spare man with jet-black hair curled and oiled in the latest fashion. His black, finely made suit jacket was offset by a red velvet waistcoat complete with gold buttons, a neat pocket handkerchief, and a monocle stowed away in his waistcoat pocket. He wore old-fashioned black breeches with shining, knee-high black leather boots. His cane, finished with a silver dragon's head topper, was much nicer than Master Darco's.

At first glance, the small smile on Lord Serpentine's face seemed welcoming, but Paloma glanced at Pierrot. The young boy cowered behind Pascal.

Lord Serpentine approached the first table and began to talk with each of the children, asking after their health and ensuring that Master Darco was adequately managing the orphanage. Before the aristocrat could make it to Pascal and Paloma's table, Pierrot had already slipped out to the library. His sanctuary awaited him.

When Paloma and Pascal spoke with Lord Serpentine, she found the man to be quiet, learned, and thoughtful. He asked about the orphanage's daily schedule, where most of the children had come from, and whether any changes needed to be made. Overall, he seemed to be very kind, but Paloma couldn't help the apprehension that claimed her.

After dinner, Pascal and Paloma searched for Pierrot. As she suspected, they found him hiding in his usual place in the library. The young boy was reading through a book on the use of magic. Beside him, thick leather-bound tomes were stacked high. Paloma studied the book bindings: *The Entyre Collection* of *Artimus Rex's Works*. *Wild Wanderings: Exploring Vale and Beyonde*. *A Treatise on the Shadowe, the Void, and the Netherworlde*. *On Faeries and Dragons*. She sighed.

Whenever Pierrot was worried, he hid in the library and read. Paloma wondered how the books helped him cope. Reading wouldn't bring Mistress Alma back, help them figure out what Master Darco was doing, or if she could trust Lord Serpentine. It seemed to be such a passive activity, such a waste of important time.

"I suppose reading is one way to cheer up," she said, sitting down by Pierrot and carefully pushing his stack of books to one side. "You didn't like Lord Serpentine, either? The man seemed willing to at least talk about practicalities."

"Everyone's excited because he's rich and might adopt one of us," Pascal said, his tone practical, unamused.

Paloma nodded. Of course, they are. Who doesn't dream about having a family? Pascal has made the orphanage his home and built his own dreams beyond this place. Others look to the security and opportunity being adopted provides. Pulling herself out of her thoughts, Paloma realized that Pascal was talking.

"In all my years here, I've never heard of a Lord Serpentine," Pascal was saying. "Why is that, and why did we need to have new staff at the orphanage? Why are the guards turning visitors away? Where did Mistress Alma go? And what is going on in her study?"

"I overheard Clément saying that Master Darco holds secret meetings in the study," Paloma said. "But Clément can hardly know the truth. Who knows what's going on in there? Either way, I don't like the secrecy. Mistress Alma was never secretive. Not that way, at least."

"I agree." Pascal sighed, gripping his hair. "But what are we going to do?"

"In two days, we can meet with Baptiste," Paloma pointed out. "Until then, we keep an eye out, I suppose."

"And Pierrot can read," Pascal said, gesturing with his thumb to the stack of books.

Pierrot nodded and turned back to the page he was reading. Paloma stared at him. *Who knows, maybe Pierrot will find something to help us out.* But she wasn't holding much hope.

THE NEXT MORNING, AFTER BREAKFAST, MASTER Darco once again showed up in the mess hall with Lord Serpentine in tow. When breakfast was over, he told everyone to line up in the backyard for another special announcement. Since Lord Serpentine was present, everyone got very excited. It took a while for the children to get in order, but eventually, everyone was outside and lined up from youngest to eldest. Master Darco looked over the group of forty children and smiled in his oily way.

"Now that we are all properly organized," he said, "I can talk to you about how we are going to run the orphanage while Mistress Alma is away on her distressing family business. After Lord Serpentine talked with everyone last night, he told me that many of you expressed worries about no longer following Mistress Alma's schedule. We understand that the recent changes must be very …" Master Darco searched for the word *scary*. "But don't worry! Lord Serpentine had a grand idea."

Everyone waited with bated breath.

"Overseers!" Master Darco said. "For the rest of summer vacation, I will appoint overseers to make sure that our new schedule will go smoothly. You saw how hard it was just to get everyone lined up, so I think we should appoint some overseers right away."

The children looked at each other, stunned. Overseers had never been needed before. Master Darco went on enthusiastically about his idea, detailing what being an overseer would involve—organizing activities, implementing the schedule he would set out, and punishing miscreants.

Paloma's breathing hitched at the mention of punishment. She could trust Tania and the others, but if Maldavo got the position, there would be trouble. Glancing at Maldavo, the boy's expression was a watchful sneer. She could tell that his interest was certainly piqued.

"These overseers will be called team captains," Master Darco continued. "Lord Serpentine will choose one or more if he finds those suitable to lead. Your Lordship." Master Darco ended his speech with a low bow to the aristocrat, who stepped forward.

Within a minute, the oldest children were lined up. Paloma, Pascal, Tania, Minette, and Danton were the obvious choices for team captains, but a foreboding filled Paloma.

As Lord Serpentine and Master Darco paced up and down the line, looking at each orphan skeptically as though he were searching for a sign. Paloma held his gaze defiantly, unrelenting in her suspicion. She noticed Pascal standing calmly, looking curious. *How can Pascal just stand there? How can he not react?*

Master Darco stopped in front of Maldavo and looked down at the stocky boy, who smiled back at him with a confident sneer. When he kept walking, Maldavo gritted his teeth and snarled. Master Darco marched past Paloma to the end of the line and turned. He had apparently already found someone to become an overseer. As Master Darco walked back toward Maldavo, Paloma's heart sank.

No. Not him. Anyone but him.
"Stop," Lord Serpentine said.

Master Darco halted in front of Paloma. For the first time, Lord Serpentine stirred and stepped forward. He moved to Master Darco's side and gazed down at Paloma, who glared fiercely at the dirt beneath her feet. Lord Serpentine's finger rose to Paloma's chin and gently but insistently pressed upward.

Paloma was forced to gaze at Lord Serpentine's pitch-black eyes. She shivered but held her ground. Her lips pressed together in determination as she stared back. Perhaps it was her courage or her silent strength, but Lord Serpentine didn't seem at all fazed by the girl's silent resistance. He smiled. Which was somehow worse.

"My lord?" Master Darco asked. "You believe Paloma should be a team captain? She was, after all, the previous leader of the Rejects."

"Was she?" asked Lord Serpentine. "Hm. Perhaps with time, when we know her better...Who did you have in mind, Darco?"

"Well, another former leader of the Rejects," Master Darco said. "He holds, I believe, a certain..." he paused, as if for dramatic effect, "*strength* that we might need in a team captain. This boy right here, my lord. Maldavo."

"Maldavo," Lord Serpentine repeated, nodding at the bully. "Do you feel that you have what it takes to lead the others and ensure peace is kept until Mistress Alma's return?"

"Of course, my lord!" Maldavo said with a salute.

As Maldavo's confident proclamation hung in the air, an eerie hush settled over the courtyard. A shadow of foreboding enveloped Paloma and Pascal. Paloma glanced over at Pierrot, who was already clearly distressed. Without a word, the silent boy flitted inside.

CHAPTER TWELVE

On the morning they were supposed to meet with Baptiste, Pascal woke to banging noises out in the backyard. Yawning and stretching, Pascal rolled out of bed and shuffled over to the window. Danton had already pushed the window open and was hanging over the windowsill to see further. Easing back, he looked at Pascal with wide eyes.

"What is that?" he asked.

"Let me see." Pascal leaned over the windowsill as the warm summer breeze ruffled his nightshirt.

His gaze was immediately drawn to a square box being erected in the middle of the yard. The walls were metal with small slits that could barely be called windows along the top. It wasn't that big either, only a few feet wide and a few feet long.

At the sound of voices in the distance, Pascal's eyes shifted to the side of the yard. Master Darco was directing Master Gorgo, who was carrying what looked like a heavy iron grate. The muscular groundskeeper set the grate against the box, creating one open wall. He fiddled with something at the corner of the grille and the solid metal box.

"Is it a door?" asked Danton. "I don't get it. What would that be for? Storage? We already have a good amount of storage space in the attics over the dorms."

"I don't think that's for storage."

Danton stared at Pascal in confusion. "What could it be for then? Mistress Alma said we weren't allowed to have pets or anything."

"Pretty sure it's not for a pet." Pascal shifted back. He didn't want to look at it anymore. The whole thing didn't feel right. "I have a feeling... this isn't going to be anything good."

There was something about it—the hard edges, or the idea of tight spaces, and the rusty metal—that made a shudder roll through Pascal. Whatever it was, it didn't look good, and it was standing right in the middle of the children's playing area.

More boys crowded up to the window and clamored to see what was going on. Pascal stepped back, allowing the others to press forward and look out. Across the yard, the windows of the girls' dorms were also thrown open, and more faces leaned out for a closer look at the construction in the yard.

Pascal found everyone talking excitedly when he went down to breakfast. The air was filled with predictions and guesses as to the purpose of the mysterious box. Nobody seemed to be worried, which made Pascal feel even more out of place. *Didn't anyone else get a bad feeling from the sight of that box?*

When Pascal sat with Pierrot and Paloma in the dining room, he relaxed a little. Judging by the hollow smile that was pasted on Paloma's lips but did not reach her eyes and the nervous way Pierrot was squeezing his juggling balls, they were both tense. Pierrot seemed downright scared. Paloma looked as though she had a lot to say.

If Miss Myrrah were nicer, Pierrot would probably try to eat in the library. But he would only get in trouble. *It's a shame, too. Pierrot was getting more courageous and finally felt comfortable eating in the mess hall. And now this....*

Anger burned like fire through Pascal's veins. His eyes narrowed as Maldavo stalked into the mess hall, followed closely by Clément and Claudio. It was just as Paloma had guessed. Things were going from bad to worse.

In the single day since Maldavo had been promoted to team captain, he'd already begun to assert his position over the others—including Tania, who hadn't been promoted despite being the one person at the orphanage who deserved the position the most.

Splitting the children into four groups, he chose two "lieutenants" to help him keep an eye out for everyone. Of course, he'd chosen Clément and Claudio. *How is it possible for them to be even more smarmy and insufferable?*

They marched down the center aisle and took a stand at the far end of the room. Pascal's eyes landed on Maldavo's new stiff, leather jacket, paired with a new belt, an ominous club hanging from it. *What would Maldavo do with that club if given the chance?*

Master Darco sauntered into the dining room for what Pascal assumed was another announcement. Pascal shot a glance at Paloma, who shook her head with trepidation in response.

"Well, children," Master Darco said, "this is a great start to our morning! Everyone showed up on time, thanks to our new team captain, Maldavo, and his men. Hopefully, the rest of our day will go swimmingly!"

The children gave a muted cheer that quickly withered away under Maldavo's glare. Pascal's own applause was half-hearted at best. Paloma folded her arms and glowered at Maldavo, who glared right back at her with a twisted sneer on his face. Pierrot, of course, remained silent, too cowed to respond to anything. Master Darco raised his hands, and the children fell silent.

"Of course, I know that all of you will try your best to be part of our team. Everyone here, I am sure, will be on their best behavior, but ..." Master Darco's gaze seemed to fall on Pascal and Paloma, "perhaps there may be some who struggle to accept these changes. I'm sure that, once in a while, some of you will be naughty. Am I right?"

At that question, all the orphans except Pascal and Paloma shook their heads. Pierrot just hunched his shoulders and gazed miserably down at the half-full breakfast plate before him.

"For our safety and the happiness of everyone at the orphanage," Master Darco continued, pacing down the aisle toward Maldavo. "It's best that we have ways to remind ourselves what happens when we don't behave. You are expected to listen and follow orders. Anyone who doesn't will, unfortunately, face punishment in our newly erected hotbox."

What the hell is a hotbox?

The room erupted in gasps and whispers, especially among the ex-Rejects. Paloma's flat expression, not holding an ounce of curiosity like Pascal, led him to believe she already knew.

I wish I could talk to her, ask her about the hotbox, but Master Darco and Maldavo are paying close attention to the room. Not wishing to draw attention to himself or Pierrot, Pascal silently waited for the interminable speech to end.

Master Darco went on to list an abundance of new rules: no entering Mistress Alma's old study, no leaving the dorms unless specifically called upon or involved in a group activity, no leaving the orphanage grounds, and no tardiness for meals. Failure to abide by those rules meant punishment in the hotbox.

How uncomfortable can it be? Pascal wondered. *Is it worthwhile to flout the rules and leave the dorms to meet Baptiste? Or should we stay in and just hope for the best?* He needed to talk with Paloma as soon as possible.

Before the boys and girls parted for their dorms, the children lingered, talking with each other about the "activities" that their new schedule allowed, which they could participate in under the keen eyes of Clément and Claudio. Many of the children were curious about their new schedule. After the activities, there was a short half-hour break before lunch where they could gather in the dining room, the front porch, or the library. During the afternoon, they were expected to quietly play in the dorms, but they could choose which dorm they wanted to stay in for the afternoon. Later in the evening, everyone would gather for supper and could spend another half hour together in the common areas.

Pascal frowned as he considered the new plan. He wondered if Paloma realized the truth. From now on, their schedules would be tightly controlled and enforced. Unable to stop thinking about the news, Pascal approached Paloma. The two of them sat on the dining room table, feet on the bench below them, shoulder to shoulder, as though they were overlooking the scene. Pascal leaned forward, elbows on his knees.

"How bad is it?" he asked.

"How bad is what?" Paloma spoke in an undertone. She kept her poise casual, as if she was talking about blueberry picking or finishing homework. "Maldavo being in charge and patrolling the halls like we're in jail? Mistress Alma missing? Master Darco and the staff being so cold?"

"The hotbox," Pascal said. "I've never heard of one before."

"Lucky," she replied. After a beat, she added, "It's something I saw in the lower quarters of Pivot, where the poor people lived.

There was a prison, and they had a courtyard. I once looked over the wall, and I saw one. After that, I asked around."

"What did you find out?"

"It's real punishment," Paloma said. "It gets baking hot in there. And you have to sit alone for hours in the heat. You get thirsty, but they don't give you anything to drink. Most people get terribly miserable in there... and if they stay in for too long, if the weather is particularly hot, then... well..." Here, her voice dropped even lower. "They say you can go crazy—hear voices and see things—and then you pass out."

"So, it's best that we don't try to get to Baptiste this morning," Pascal said. "Before, we could sneak out, but with all these new rules and the hotbox, I'm worried. For Pierrot, mainly. He can't come with us, even if we do decide to go."

"Where is he?" asked Paloma.

Pascal sat up and looked around. His eyes ran over the crowd of children. There was no sign of his silent friend, and his heart sank at that realization. *No doubt about it*, he thought with rising panic. *Pierrot has gone to the library. Without permission... and right after dinner, too. He's going to be in big trouble if Maldavo notices.*

"I can distract Maldavo," Pascal said quickly in a low tone. "You get Pierrot from the library."

"Shouldn't I be—"

Before Paloma could finish her sentence, Maldavo whacked the table with his club. The room fell into an instant silence. His stout form slowly pushed through the small clumps of children as he made his way over to Pascal and Paloma. Pascal could feel his heartbeat rising, but he kept what he hoped was a neutral expression on his face.

"Paloma," growled Maldavo, "Pascal. Where's the freak?"

"Freak?" asked Paloma with a bite in her voice. "Who could you be talking about, Maldavo, if not yourself?"

"Shut up, Paloma," Maldavo snapped. "I asked you a question. You keep it up, and I'll have you in the hotbox before you can say 'knife.'"

"Knife," Paloma shot back.

"Who are you talking about?" Pascal interjected. This wasn't the time to get into an argument.

"Pierrot. You know who I mean. The freak." Maldavo turned around again. His gaze ran across the crowd as he looked for Pierrot. "Gone to his precious library, has he?"

"The bathroom, maybe?" Paloma suggested.

"Unlikely, but we'll ferret him out," Maldavo sneered. "Clément, you check the boys' washrooms. Claudio, you come with me to the library. We'll see if the little truant has been busy already, breaking the rules."

"He doesn't mean to," Pascal said, clenching his fist.

"Stay put, Pascal," Maldavo barked out the order, taking his role of authority too far. "If you know what's good for you, you'll stay put."

"As if we would," Paloma said. "He might be lost for all we know."

"Lost?" asked Maldavo with heavy skepticism. "On the way to the washroom?"

With that, Maldavo disappeared into the front hall area, followed by Claudio. Paloma and Pascal, after giving each other a measured look, followed close on their heels. Neither was willing to leave Pierrot to the mercy of Maldavo. When they got to the library, the door was ajar. With a triumphant shout, Maldavo burst into the room. Pierrot curled up in his favorite window seat, looked up, and froze.

Maldavo didn't waste any time. He grabbed Pierrot by the collar and began to shake him as he struck Pierrot on the head and screamed at him.

Pascal didn't hesitate to jerk Maldavo off Pierrot. When Maldavo shouted for Claudio's help, Paloma slyly tripped him to slow him down.

Pascal and Maldavo crashed into the two library tables, knocking over the cart. Unlike last time, Pascal held his own much better, crashing his fist into Maldavo's jaw as he kicked him in the shin.

Maldavo must've realized he was losing because he tried to tear away, but Pascal held him with a tight grip, punching him again until he heard a sharp crack, followed by Maldavo's howling shriek of pain. He clutched his face as blood gushed from his nose.

"Maldavo!" Clément shouted from behind Paloma.

"Pascal hit him," Claudio gasped in disbelief. He staggered to his feet. "He broke his nose."

"Serves him right," Paloma said with a smirk.

Maldavo, blinking away his tears, glared at her with pure loathing. As Clément and Claudio rushed forward to help Maldavo stop the bleeding, Pascal rushed forward to Pierrot, who crouched by the bookshelf, shaking.

"You get out of here, Pierrot," he whispered, helping him up. "Go to the dorms and wait for us, alright? The library isn't safe anymore. We'll find you somewhere new to hide."

Pierrot looked up at Pascal, tears pooling in his eyes. The pain he seemed to feel was unbelievably vast, something Pascal honestly knew he couldn't even conceive of. With only the barest of nods, he slipped past Paloma and made for the closest set of stairs to the boys' dorm.

Paloma, turning to watch Pierrot leave, noticed Master Darco now standing in the doorway. Master Darco's gaze was fixed on the boys, particularly the blood gushing from Maldavo's nose. Judging by the half-smile on his face, Master Darco enjoyed the fight. Shrugging slightly, Master Darco stepped forward and put on an expression of displeasure. "What is going on here?"

"It's Pascal, sir," Claudio said. "He hit Maldavo. I—I think he broke his nose, sir!"

"Pascal?" Master Darco rounded on him.

"He was hitting Pierrot, Master Darco," Pascal explained. "I will admit that I lost my temper ... but it's because Maldavo has never liked Pierrot. He was just using this as a chance to hurt him. Everyone knows that Pierrot needs peace and quiet. The library is his real home. You can't take that away from Pierrot!"

"We will discuss the matter of Pierrot another time," Master Darco said. "Clément. Claudio. Take Maldavo to Miss Myrrah. She can care for him. As for you, Pascal. I'm afraid that this is exactly what I was talking about earlier—such violent disruptions are not what this orphanage needs. It's the hotbox for you."

"What?" Paloma said, shoving forward past the guys. "Maldavo started it when he hit Pierrot! If anyone deserves the hotbox, it's him."

"I was..." Maldavo winced as he tried to speak. Cursing under his breath, he cupped his jaw.

"Stop trying," Claudio said. "It'll make it worse."

Master Darco slashed his arm through the air, silencing the boys. Pascal's heart pounded as he glared about the room, ready for anything, even the hotbox. *If I had to do it all over again, I would.*

"He's going to the hotbox. That's final," Master Darco said. "When he's ready to rethink what he did—"

"I'm not sorry," Pascal interrupted flatly. "I'll never be sorry. What Maldavo did to Pierrot was wrong. If I could punch him in the face again, I would."

"Pascal was only doing the right thing," Paloma said, gritting her teeth. "But if he must be punished, then I say I ought to go instead. Pascal has to take care of the others. The children will miss him, and there will be more problems with him gone. I'll take his place."

"You?" asked Master Darco, his eyebrow rising.

"Yes. Me."

"Pu' 'er in," Maldavo said in a strangled voice as the two boys led him out of the room.

Master Darco hesitated. He cocked his head and studied Paloma, but at the same time, it seemed to Pascal that Master Darco's gaze was unfocused. It was as though he was looking at Paloma and through Paloma at the same time, as though the oily headmaster was hearing something they couldn't.

Looking closer at the man, Pascal noticed that his suit looked soiled that day. The buttons had a mild tarnish to them. Master Darco's eyes seemed to glint like the eyes of a cat in the firelight, glimmering orange.

"You," Master Darco said, now in a completely different tone. It was quieter and more agreeable but more ominous somehow. "Yes, of course, Paloma. If that is what you wish. Pascal, you ought to thank your friend for her courage."

"Paloma, I'll be fine. I can do this! I need you to believe in me. We're friends. We're on the same side."

"No." She shook her head firmly. "Better me than you. Pierrot needs you right now. I'll see you tomorrow..." She paused, looking away. "Or whenever I see you."

Paloma followed Master Darco out of the library with her chin up and her back straight, looking at the world like condemned royalty.

CHAPTER THIRTEEN

Paloma followed Master Darco into the yard without a single glance at the other orphans, who watched from the windows. Grabbing her by the arm, Master Darco shoved Paloma toward the hotbox's entrance, but she refused to go down without a fight. She jerked her arm from his tight grip, a loathing glare on her face, fury burning through her eyes. Paloma pasted an overly sweet smile on her face, as she confidently stepped into the hotbox.

Behind her, Master Gorgo shut the rusty door with a heavy clang. The locks on the side of the box slid shut with a thud. Paloma stood by the grated door and transferred her furious, accusing glare to the groundskeeper.

Master Gorgo grunted. "It's locked up nice and tight, headmaster."

"Good," Master Darco said. "If the girl wishes to take on the punishment meant for her friends, then so be it. She won't be going anywhere for twenty-four hours. You understand, girl?"

"It's Pa-lo-ma," she ground out. Anger bubbled in her chest, though she pushed it down to keep her cool. She refused to let him rattle her. "And I understand just fine, thank you."

"You won't be so fine when the sun rises," Master Gorgo said with a careless shrug. "I'd rest up and save your strength."

With that, the giant man lumbered off, leaving Master Darco and Paloma alone.

"Honestly, you have no idea how lucky you children are. Things could be worse, you know. All you had to do was listen."

"And all you had to do is pay attention to what we need," Paloma shot back. "Pierrot is different. He needs peace and quiet. He wasn't doing anything wrong, and you know it! Maldavo is a bully. Pascal was just trying to protect his friend. If you paid attention and had any heart, you'd understand."

"Dear girl," Master Darco said, "I do hope you gain a new perspective during your stay in the hotbox."

Paloma folded her arms and stared back at him. With a chuckle, the headmaster turned away and walked over to the kitchen door. At least, that was where Paloma imagined he was going. Her view was rather limited. Even though the entire door to the box was made of rough, rusty iron grating, the door was narrow, and the box was small enough to fit only two people. Paloma's view through the grate only allowed her to see the rest of what had once been their playground. No one was allowed out these days, so Paloma was forced to sit in the hotbox alone.

Behind the hotbox, the kitchen gardens were neatly lined up in rows. Usually, a small group of kids would be tasked with tending to the garden and carefully picking the ripened produce. However, no children were allowed out, and try as she might, Paloma could hear no sound of Miss Myrrah moving around.

Paloma remained silent, isolated in her thoughts. At first, she considered trying to escape and looked carefully at the hinges and felt around the edges of the door, testing the strength of the walls. It would be practically impossible to escape, especially without tools.

Recognizing that she was going nowhere, Paloma sat down. A metal bench had been set up along one wall. However, the bench was so narrow, and the space inside the hotbox so tight, that a teen—much less an adult—wouldn't be able to lie down. Some of the youngest and smallest children could probably rest on the bench, but the thought of a small child stuck in the hotbox for hours on end sent a shiver through her spine.

She propped herself in one corner of the hotbox, stretching her legs out along the metal bench, and absently stared at the corner where the walls met the ceiling.

Alone, she sat with only her thoughts to pass the hours that ticked by. Sleeping in such a cramped space felt impossible. *Daydreamers and solitary thinkers might not feel stifled by such limited movement, but I need to move.*

I need freedom!

The memory of how the wind felt on her face was a small consolation as the night disappeared, taking the chill with it. The sun rose over the courtyard, and any cool shadows that remained slowly vanished. Beneath the hot sun, the hotbox began to feel like an oven.

Time went by at an agonizing pace as the heat built up. Sweat poured down her face, the saltiness stinging the corners of her eyes. Dehydrated and hungry, her stomach churned and ached. Dazed and overheated, she couldn't stop thinking about flavored ice, winter, snow, and buckets of water. Anything that was cold.

Paloma dozed off, feeling more and more hot and uncomfortable as the day dragged on. Her light sleep was disrupted by fevered dreams that grew more fantastic over time. It became difficult to distinguish her dreams from her thoughts. Visions of her parents, Pascal and Pierrot, lying dead, swam through her mind and mixed with pulses of anger and hopes to exact revenge. The anger and revenge eventually took center stage to ward off the painful visions of death.

Lunch came and went, although she wasn't given any food or drink.

Of course not, she thought, feeling more miserable and disoriented than ever. *They really want to punish us ... and there is nothing scarier than being trapped in a small box for hours on end in the heat without nourishment. If it was anyone else, they'd be beside themselves within an hour. But I can do this. I can... I can...*

The confidence she possessed when she entered the hotbox, however, slipped away with the hours. As Paloma drifted in and out of sleep, the shadows lengthened. Usually, the cooler evening temperatures would provide some relief, but this was the height of summer, and even the dusk brought only the barest hint of a breeze. As the sun set, it shone its last rays straight into the small hotbox, forcing the temperature even higher.

Unable to escape the sun's rays, Paloma huddled in the corner. The wall behind her was burning hot, and she could no longer rest her back against it. She tried to lean forward as much as she could while balancing on the narrow bench. Resting her head on her arms, she closed her eyes and dreamed.

In her dream, Paloma was running through the forest. This time, the fog evaporated as the trees caught fire. Her parents lay behind her, surrounded by the crackle of orange flame. A *Fa-*

ther? She could not help but hope as she peered out into the shadows.

"Lord Serpentine!" Paloma said with a mixture of relief and confusion at the sight of the man outside the door.

The aristocrat peered through the bars and stared at her with a look of concern. For a moment, his gloved hand rested on the bars, but then he hastily removed it.

"Loma," he said. "I've been worried for you."

"Worried?" she asked.

"Well," he said with a sigh, "when I came to the orphanage, I expected to see many kinds of children, but few stood out as you did, Loma. There is something inside you that I sense. Something terrible, but something great."

"Inside me?" she repeated, confused. Standing up, she moved to the door. It only took a single step before her hand rested on the bars. "Ow," she hissed, jerking her hand away. The iron bars were still white-hot from the sun's rays.

"This is a terrible place," Lord Serpentine said, his eyebrows pulled down tightly in a sad expression.

"Well, you could tell Master Darco that he doesn't need to punish us with something like a hotbox," Paloma said in a dry tone. "Most of the children are already trying to follow the rules."

"And you did not?" Lord Serpentine asked.

"Well," Paloma said, wondering if there was any use in trying to explain it to the orphanage's benefactor.

He seemed nice when Pascal and I talked with him. But another voice within her pointed out *Pierrot doesn't like him either, which means that I need to be careful.*

On the other hand, she countered, *Pierrot hasn't talked to him much, so maybe it was just Pierrot's usual shyness.*

"I didn't mean to," Paloma finally said. "Pierrot isn't like the others, you know. He likes peace and quiet. Reading in the library helps him feel safe. He just wants to read. He's not going to bother you or Master Darco or any of the staff. Maldavo knows it, too, but he hates weak people, and he likes to feel powerful, so he torments children like Pierrot."

"I see," Lord Serpentine said as he shook his head. "A hot-headed boy."

"Yes," Paloma agreed. "I understand that sometimes you have no choice but to fight, but Maldavo is an idiot and a bully. He was cruel to Pierrot, so of course, Pascal stepped in. Pascal is like that. I just... helped."

"Did it make you feel satisfied?" Lord Serpentine asked curiously.

"No... not really." Paloma stopped, hesitated, and admitted, "I like beating up Maldavo, I'll admit. It feels good because he deserves it. Maldavo is evil."

"Ah, you are trying to be a good girl, then. A young lady of honor."

"Honor doesn't get things done," Paloma said impassively, "but sure."

"Hm. There, you are right," Lord Serpentine said. "What is the point in pursuing the higher path? Where is the fun in honor and goodness? In the end, we all just grind our fingers to the bone, eat, sleep, and repeat until we die." He paused for a beat. "Just like your parents, am I right?"

"What do you know about my parents?" Her tone was sharp.

"Loma," Lord Serpentine said mildly. "I have not achieved my position for nothing. My good deeds and generosity are known far and wide. And I hear things in return. The story of your family is well-known thanks to your previous exploits as the leader of the Rejects."

"I suppose you heard something from the city guards and think you know everything now," Paloma said bitterly as tears glittered in her eyes.

"They did say something about the night your parents were lost to you," Lord Serpentine nodded. "A tragic affair. Did they ever catch the murderers, whoever they were?"

"Ravagers," Paloma bit out. "And no. But don't worry about that. When I'm old enough to leave here, I will find them and make them pay. They will see justice. That's the promise I made to Father and Mother... and to myself."

"Justice? It sounds like vengeance to me, Loma." Lord Serpentine smiled then. It was not a kind one, but their gazes met in silent acknowledgment. "That is what I sense then, deep within you. Grief cannot last forever. It fades before the power of vengeance. Yes. I sense your thirst."

"Is that wrong?" Paloma retorted in defiance.

"No, no," Lord Serpentine said soothingly. His smile grew even wider. "Indulge yourself, my dear; purge yourself from the shackles of love, for it weakens your thirst for vengeance that burns with righteous intensity within you. Allow me to guide you down this path where you can unleash the justice you rightfully deserve. Join me, Loma; only then will you be able to choose your own destiny."

Paloma stared at the man in surprise. For a quiet and kind man, Lord Serpentine seemed to have a surprisingly vicious streak. *Still, maybe he just wants to support my cause. He sees how I suffer, how everyone here suffers from loss. I'm sure he just wants to help. Yes. He just wants to help...*

He stood close to the door, his face nearly pressed against

the small window. His voice was barely above a whisper. "Let yourself be beautiful, Loma. I am well aware of the dormant darkness that resides within you. Let the flames of vengeance fuel your thirst and graciously bestow upon me yet another soul, as you have done before, my dear. Together, we can make them all suffer; we shall feast on their delicious souls and dance in a glorious symphony of malevolence."

She jerked back slightly, terrified and in awe. *How could he know?*

"Your parents were in the wrong place at the wrong time, were they not?" Lord Serpentine asked gently. "They were simply traveling, going about their business, and they paid an unfair price for it. I am certain you are more than up to the task of setting the scales of justice straight."

"I know I am," Paloma said. "That's why Pascal and I have planned to work together. We want to help others by fighting for the justice they deserve."

"It sounds like an interesting... scheme. But it will take years to achieve, will it not? What if there was another way?"

"Another way?" she asked curiously.

"Indeed." Lord Serpentine nodded.

He shifted, slowly tapping his chin in thought. Paloma noticed that tonight, the aristocrat was wearing dark clothing, a long coat, and a wide-brimmed hat. It looked as though he had been traveling somewhere cold. Still, despite the fact that he must be hot, Lord Serpentine seemed more than happy to remain standing by the hotbox and talking with her.

After a long day with only her thoughts and nightmares for company, Paloma welcomed his presence. *Besides, maybe he will help me get out of here sooner. Or, even better, offer me his mentorship and help me achieve my dreams.*

But what about Pascal? Another smaller voice spoke up. *Didn't you want to see the world with Pascal? He makes you laugh and smile. When you're with him, you feel as though anything is possible.*

True, but Pascal isn't even an adult yet. He's only ever known the orphanage, which makes him sheltered. There's no doubt that he's got big dreams, but he's still got a lot to learn. I don't have the time. Being with Lord Serpentine would mean that I can get away from all of this.

The more Paloma considered the matter, the better the idea of leaving the orphanage seemed. When she had first arrived, Paloma had been suspicious and afraid, but deep down, she had also felt angry, believing she didn't need anyone to take care of her. She liked being on her own and in control of her life. The idea of following someone else's schedule had been frustrating.

Over time, though, she became used to it. Paloma realized that there was freedom in being taken care of. Mistress Alma's hugs, Pascal's jokes and antics, and Pierrot's gentle company soothed Paloma's spirit—and for a while, she felt happy with her new life and friends. Finally, she'd found a home.

But since Mistress Alma left, things had become difficult again. Master Darco's rules were overbearing, and she hated being trapped in the dorms all day long. Even worse, the injustice of Maldavo's promotion made her sick. Restless and anxious, her nightmares about her parents' deaths had returned with a vengeance, and this time, she couldn't perform with Pascal to forget.

She relived the events again and again without end. Her parents were traveling late at night, trying to get to Pivot before nightfall.

The rain and the bad weather had slowed their cart down. The wheel got stuck in the poorly kept mountain road. When their horse tried to pull the cart out, the wheel had twisted and required fixing. They were delayed and had to press on through the stormy night.

Then... Paloma's memory became foggy. *Mother and Father had stopped for some reason. They were staring at something. Looking at something?*

Try as she might, she couldn't remember. Her mind refused any entrance to the memory. All she could remember were short flashes—lengthening shadows, the heavy rain made visible due to the flashing bolts of lightning, and men emerging from the forest.

Ravagers. It had to be. Her mother shoved her into the bushes, hiding Paloma from the attackers, and her vision clouded even more. She had barely been able to see through the leaves, but what she did catch a glimpse of had frightened her. All she remembered was the face of the man who had killed her parents.

Why am I thinking about this now?

"Loma," Lord Serpentine said. His voice jolted her back to the present. There was something comforting in the way he said her name, a promise that perhaps he might understand what she truly wanted. More than Pascal ever had. "It is clear to me that you are meant for more than doing tricks and basking in applause. The power inside you will fuel you beyond anyone's wild imagination. Your friends cannot ever fully understand."

"Yes, yes," Paloma nodded. "I-I just want to be out of here. I want to be free to pursue what I need to do. I want to make them all pay."

"Make them all pay." Lord Serpentine's smile widened. "My sentiments exactly, dear Loma. Are you willing to come with me and walk the path? I can promise you what your heart desires—and more!"

"Please!" Paloma nodded fervently.

To be free of the hotbox, to be free of the orphanage and its restrictions... to become powerful enough to find the Ravagers. Hope sprang up in Paloma's heart.

"What do I have to do?" asked Paloma.

"Just follow me."

With a wave of his hand, the lock sprang open. Paloma's eyes widened with shock.

"Where—where are we going?" she asked, stepping out of the hotbox and sagging with relief as she escaped the stifling hot air.

"To a place of freedom," Lord Serpentine said, an unusual smirk playing across his mouth.

CHAPTER FOURTEEN

"I know it sounds crazy," Pascal whispered to Pierrot, "but I just don't feel right leaving her there."

Pierrot clutched his red juggling ball. His gaze was fixed on the shadows that disguised the two of them as they sat together in the darkness.

They were hiding in the stairwell that ran between the boys' dormitory and the east wing, where the library was located. Normally, they would have just used the kitchen door to sneak out, but with the guards now patrolling the halls, the two boys had to use their backup route out of the orphanage—the library windows.

Pascal whispered his plan to Pierrot. They could loop around the back of the east wing through the shrubbery to get to the backyard. It sounded easy, but both boys knew the real trouble lay with the backyard itself. There were no trees or bushes to hide behind. The box stood out in the open, in the middle of the flat dirt and grass of the backyard. Behind it was the kitchen garden, but the rows of vegetables wouldn't offer much in the way of coverage.

The younger boy poked Pascal nervously, keeping his eyes trained on the stairs sloping down before them.

"What're you worried about?" Pascal asked. "You think we'll get caught?"

Pierrot squeezed his blue ball once.

"We probably will..." Pascal said in realization. "Maybe you should stay behind, Pierrot. That way, if I'm caught, you won't get into trouble too."

Pierrot tossed his red ball at Pascal. His eyes now accustomed to the shadowy darkness, Pascal easily caught it and exhaled softly, trying to keep calm.

"Well, if you are so set on joining me, and you think my idea won't work, what's your idea?" he asked, keeping his voice low.

Pierrot held up a small metal canteen. Pascal lifted it. It was full of cool water from the bathroom sink.

"Oh," he said with a smile. "That's a good idea, Pierrot. If we can't break her out, at least we can give her some water. You ready to go?"

At Pierrot's short nod, Pascal silently rose to his feet and glided down the stairs. Pierrot followed close behind, hugging the canteen to his chest. After cautiously peering up and down the east wing's hallway, they darted across to the library door.

Inside, they found the library empty, just as they had hoped. Within moments, Pascal slid open the quietest window and slipped out.

The drop to the ground wasn't that far. Even Pierrot was able to land easily with his cargo in hand. Leaving the window open, the two ducked down and slunk between the bushes and the building. They took care to avoid raising their heads in case any of the new staff were patrolling further down the wing. When they reached the far end of the building, they sat and looked around.

From their vantage point, they could peer around the corner of the building into the yard where the kitchen garden and the hotbox stood. Keeping as quiet as they could, they tried to see if Weylin and Anala were skulking about. After a few minutes, they heard a rustling in the hedge.

Pierrot froze, wide-eyed. Pascal eased back and ducked down. Together, they peered through the gaps in the shrubbery and watched as Weylin pushed his way through the thick hedge from the direction of the forest.

After looking left and right, the tall, pale guard paused. Overhead, a great owl swooped down, its long wings soundlessly gliding through the night. Weylin's eyes narrowed. He bent down, hefted a stone, and threw it at the bird. The stone arced through the air unerringly and hit the owl in the wing. The owl tumbled down and struggled to keep flying. It circled about, crying out in pain, before disappearing into the forest. Surely, it would not survive long there. The forest was a cruel place to those who were injured or hurt.

Pascal lurched forward before Pierrot stopped him. There was no reason for Weylin to hurt the bird. Even more eerily, Weylin had managed to hit the owl squarely with the rock. That was a feat in and of itself, and it made Pascal feel even more uneasy about the new staff members.

Weylin moved forward as though nothing had happened. The tall, rangy guard gave a low whistle. There was another rustle, and three familiar faces pushed their way through the hedge nearby.

Maldavo, Clément, and Claudio. Pierrot clutched Pascal's arm soundlessly. Pascal found it incredibly difficult to breathe.

"I'll take the left side," Weylin said conversationally. "You three boys take the right. Give a shout if you see anything suspicious."

"You think Pascal will try something?" asked Maldavo.

"It's a hunch," Weylin replied. "Get going."

The three saluted and made their way across the lawn toward the west wing. That left Weylin to cover the east side of the grounds. Weylin silently watched them spread out. Then he, too, turned and slipped into the shadows. As he turned, a stray shaft of moonlight illuminated Weylin's face, and Pascal caught a glimpse of the guard's oddly glimmering eyes. His breath caught in his throat as a chill ran down his spine.

There's something almost inhuman about his eyes. Just like Master Darco. This is not normal. What the hell is going on here?

Glancing at Pierrot, Pascal noticed that his friend had curled up into a ball, clutching the canteen as though it were a lifeline. When Weylin disappeared out of sight, Pascal laid a reassuring hand on Pierrot.

"Let me take the water," he said. "You stay here and keep an eye out, alright?"

Pierrot reluctantly handed the canteen to Pascal, who slunk around the edge of the building and crossed toward the hotbox. He made sure to move as quietly as he could. Although the windows of the orphanage were all silent and dark, anyone could be looking down at the yard from the shadows.

As he neared the hotbox, Pascal slowed down a little. There was something eerie about the way the hotbox loomed up out of the shadows. The thought of Paloma being trapped alone in that horrifying cage all day made Pascal feel sick. Still, he drew closer.

"Paloma?" he whispered.

There was no answer. Pascal crept even closer, trying to peer into the shadowy box. He could sense remnants of warmth radiating from the box, no doubt from the sun that had beat down on the metal all day long. But Pascal couldn't see his friend.

"Paloma?" he whispered again.

Paloma did not reply.

Pascal set the canteen down, slipping it through the largest opening in the grate so that it stood just inside the door. There was still no response from Paloma.

Did she pass out? His heart began to race at the thought. *Is she sick? Or did they take her somewhere else?*

The hair on his neck stood on end to the sharp rustling behind him. Whipping around, he caught sight of Weylin slinking out of the shadows by the edge of the building. It was as if he had appeared out of thin air. Now Weylin stood close to the wall where he and Pierrot had hidden. The guard reached down and dragged Pierrot up by his hair.

"Let him go!" Pascal hissed, racing forward to kick Weylin in the knee. He staggered and spat out a curse, dropping Pierrot, who rolled out of the way and grabbed the closest pebbles he could find. Pascal repeatedly kicked him in his other leg.

A pebble hit Weylin in the forehead, and he winced, dropping his hold on Pascal's leg. Pascal rolled away, but Weylin lunged for him, slapping him sharply. Pascal aimed to kick him between the legs, but Weylin blocked it, slamming him against the orphanage's stone wall.

Pascal gasped hard; the breath knocked out of him. The now familiar, energized tingle ran through his limbs to his fingertips. Half expecting a flash of light, there was nothing more than a small spark that sizzled to nothing. Weylin slammed him repeatedly against the wall, gripping his throat.

Pierrot flung a handful of pebbles at Weylin's head, who growled and punched Pascal in the stomach before tossing him to the ground. Pascal groaned and pushed himself to his feet, wincing with the movement. Weylin raised his fist and aimed at Pierrot's head. Anticipating the move, Pierrot had already dived out of the way before Weylin's fist could crash against his skull.

However, Weylin was two steps ahead and twisted around, kicking at Pascal again as he grabbed for Pierrot's sweater, choking him with the fabric.

"Let him go!" Pascal cried out, regaining his stance and elbowing Weylin hard in his lower back.

Weylin didn't respond. He jerked Pierrot up by the collar and shook him harshly, giving his head a brutal smack. When he dropped Pierrot, the boy curled into a ball, covering his head, too dazed to fight him off.

"Oh my, my, my," a velvety voice broke the quiet.

Pascal stepped back and froze. Weylin shifted into a defensive stance, clearly attempting to cut off any means of escape. The elegant voice was familiar but left Pascal confused.

What is Lord Serpentine doing out here at night?

The benefactor stepped out of the shadows and motioned toward Pascal and Pierrot. "What have we here?" Lord Serpentine asked as though he was inquiring about the time of day or the weather.

"Two boys up to no good, my lord," Weylin said, his voice husky. "Pascal and Pierrot, just as we thought. No doubt hoping to stir up some trouble."

"We were just trying to help Paloma," Pascal countered. He turned to Lord Serpentine, who seemed to have appeared from nowhere, with his back to the hedge as he stood on the lawn.

Had he just come from the forest? Odd... I would've noticed him coming through the hedge. It's too noisy. Maybe it's because Weylin and I were fighting that I didn't hear.

A deep uneasiness settled in his gut, a shiver running through his limbs and down his spine. Beyond him, the thick hedge and forest rose ominously in the pale moonlight as if shadows had shifted within the shadows. Deep shadows that absorbed the light surrounding them.

"Help Paloma?" Lord Serpentine wondered aloud as if surprised. "Whatever for, my dear boys?"

"She's been stuck in that box all day long," Pascal said. "Without food and water, I bet. Pierrot and I just wanted to…"

"To…?" the nobleman prompted gently.

"Help her," he answered with a shrug. *What else?*

"Help her," Lord Serpentine echoed. "A lovely sentiment, but I wonder what that means, exactly. To give her some food and water? Or to help her escape?"

"Whatever we had to do," Pascal said, stepping sideways to keep Lord Serpentine focused on him and not Pierrot. "We'd do it."

Lord Serpentine eyed him knowingly, remaining silent for a moment before he finally said, "Paloma isn't here. You see, your friend is rather special. Her abilities and her spirit, they aren't like anything else I've seen."

"She is special," Pascal agreed, "but I don't see what that has to do with anything. Unless …" he hesitated, "are you going to adopt Paloma?"

"Something like that. She and I talked. And we agreed that her destiny lies elsewhere. It would be a shame for a girl of her talents and passion to be wasted away here at the orphanage. Paloma's dreams, after all, speak to a bright future for her—a future that coincides with many great things to come."

"Great things to come?" Pascal sharply repeated. "What do you mean by that?"

"My dear boy." Lord Serpentine sighed. "You cannot expect to understand these kinds of things. They are, after all, the stuff of legends, but I assure you that when the moon rises and my master comes, you will understand everything."

"The moon?" The hair on Pascal rose to attention, remembering the familiar story he'd heard at the Carnival's puppet theater. "Isn't the blood moon related to darkness or something?"

He probably sounded like a madman. A child believing in fairy tales. Maybe he was grasping at straws, but something didn't sit right with what Lord Serpentine was telling him.

"Goodness, the child is quite well-read, Weylin." Lord Serpentine's eyes shifted then, and with a heavily lidded gaze, he looked Pascal over from head to foot. "How ... *surprising*. But to answer your question, my boy, there are many reasons why a man such as myself might celebrate the coming of the rising moon."

"Such as what?" Pascal's voice rose sharply. "Is something happening?"

At that, the branches of the trees rustled gently in the breeze. The shadows shifted, and gray figures floated upward over the hedge, like ghosts appearing in a living nightmare. Their rags swung limply in the night breeze—no feet attached to their legs that dissipated into mist. But what truly shocked Pascal to his core were their heads—they weren't human. Some of the ghostly creatures had great antlers that rose from their skull-like faces. Others were hidden by heavy cowls that shadowed their features. The only sign of life that emanated from them were red and white eyes that gleamed in the darkness.

The puppet show! Pascal's heart pounded rapidly in his chest, the realization hitting him hard. *They're creatures of the dark. The messengers and guards who serve the evil Mephisto.* His stomach twisted, consumed with terror and animosity at the sight of the monstrosities that lurked before him, hovering over the hedge and the forest's edge. Despite the pale moonlight streaming down, it seemed that their very presence leached all light from the night sky. Like dark clouds, they hovered over Pascal and Pierrot in oppressive silence—the banshees.

What are they doing here? Not that it mattered. What Pascal needed to focus on was making it through this alive. He and Pierrot were truly alone, a realization that caused him to break into a sweat.

Lord Serpentine's eyes flared a deep red as a sly smile widened across his pale visage. He could no doubt smell the fear rolling off them. Still, Pascal fixed his stance and gritted his teeth in the face of darkness. His mind was clear, his intentions sound.

Wherever Paloma has gone, I am not going to give up rescuing her.

"Whatever you plan to do," Pascal said in defiance, "we are *going* to get Paloma back. There's no way she'd allow this!"

"You will discover the truth about Paloma soon," Lord Serpentine said. "The truth about your friend, the truth about Vale, and much more. Until then ..." the nobleman trailed off.

At that moment, Master Darco emerged from the orphanage. Behind him, Miss Myrrah stood like a white ghost, peering beyond the door with eyes glittering a deep purple. Pascal's hopes for help plummeted at the sight of them. They were both in on whatever Lord Serpentine had planned. It was just as Paloma said—these people were up to no good.

And now Paloma is gone. What are Pierrot and I going to do?

"I see you've caught them, my lord," Master Darco said, rubbing his hands. "I suggest some time in the hotbox?"

"Perhaps. It is, after all, why we instituted the punishment," said Lord Serpentine slowly. "But after everything they've seen, I think there might be a more suitable course of action. They could warn the others, and then we would have a time of it getting the children through. On the other hand, such pure souls must be treasured. It would be a shame to waste them."

"Perhaps it is time for them to join the others," Weylin said with ominous smoothness.

He stepped forward and rested a hand on Pascal's shoulder. Pascal tried to shove off the hand but failed.

"Join the others?" Pascal said, the tension of both of Weylin's hands gripping his shoulders, immobilizing him.

Behind him, Pierrot struggled to rise from the ground. Master Darco marched over and grabbed him by the ear, jerking Pierrot painfully to his feet. Lord Serpentine looked at them thoughtfully and slowly nodded.

"Yes," he said. "Let us take them through to the Citadel. It is their time."

Weylin's hand descended and covered his mouth, smothering his cries. Pascal tried to wriggle out of the guard's grip, but Weylin seemed to have grown even stronger than before. He easily twisted Pascal's arms behind his back and half-dragged him across the yard. Master Darco pulled Pierrot along behind.

A profound sense of helplessness enveloped both of them. The moonlit courtyard offered no solace, its desolation merely magnifying their fear. The feeling persisted as they were being led into a darkness from which there might be no return.

CHAPTER FIFTEEN

"THIS IS A CURIOUS SIGHT." A MAN'S VOICE CUT through the night like a hot knife slicing through butter. There was something about the voice—powerful and ominous.

Pascal twisted about, peering upward in the general direction of the voice. Pierrot kept trying to squirm out of Master Darco's grip, dragging his feet in the dirt as he tried to get away. The headmaster swore in several languages at their resistance.

"Mephisto and his minions, wrangling children in the dead of night. How peculiar," the voice continued conversationally. "I see you've decided to hide behind the appearance of a nobleman, but I'm afraid the stench of evil can't be disguised."

Mephisto? Pascal couldn't have heard that correctly.

All Pascal could see were the pale beams of moonlight streaking down through the ragged clouds. Shadows shifted along the edge of the orphanage's roof. Then, as if pushing a curtain aside, a hand swept the night shadows away, and a man seemed to step forward through the air.

Pascal sheepishly stared at the man who appeared within the darkness like a glimmer of light. He could only make out the outline of the man—tall and broad-shouldered with well-defined muscles and the typical bicorne hat atop his head. The silhouette felt incredibly familiar.

His heart leaped into his throat in relief and excitement. *No. It can't be... Is he really here?* If *Lord Serpentine is Mephisto and these are his minions...*

At first glance, the mysterious man looked as though he might have come from Lord Serpentine's own ranks. *No. Not Lord Serpentine. Mephisto.* But Pascal could sense that he wasn't; his assumptions were proven correct when he caught the shimmer of a subtle diamond tracing along his dark velvet suit.

As he tipped his head in a shallow bow of greeting, his face was revealed, recognizable, yet unknown. Dark, wavy hair fell across his forehead. A light beard fringed his chin, framing a wide smile, and behind a mask of black and silver, his deep, sparkling eyes glimmered a faint gold. Unlike the cold, flat stares of Lord Serpentine's men, these eyes gazed at Pascal with warmth, offering him hope.

Without warning, the mysterious man leaped from the roof, swinging what looked like two flat pieces of wood connected to each other. At first, it seemed quite short, only about two feet long. When the attacker swung it, however, the short bat suddenly doubled in length, rapping loudly as he battered Weylin.

As he hit Weylin, Pascal kicked him in the shins until Weylin finally released him. Master Darco cried out as Pierrot bit into his hand hard enough to draw blood. Pierrot yanked away, fleeing from Master Darco as their rescuer put distance between them and their attackers.

"Thanks," Pascal said.

"You're welcome, Pascal." The mysterious man laid a hand on Pascal's shoulder. "You tried your best, but as you are now, I'm afraid you are no real match for Mephisto."

So, it's true—Lord Serpentine is Mephisto. These are his minions. Which means...

"Harlequin is *real*," Pascal muttered, his eyes shining.

"As old and as real as those standing before you," the older man said enigmatically. "Forgive my late arrival."

Pascal glanced over to Pierrot, who leaned closer to the man. He was comfortable—reacting nothing like how he had with the others. Pascal opened his mouth to speak, but Mephisto's soft cackle cut him off.

"Well, well, well," Mephisto said in a menacing tone. "Look who we have here, ladies and gents. The Lord of Illusion and Trickery himself—Harlequin. Our dear friend, whom we have missed for so long. How have you been, Harley?"

"As well as one might be, Mephisto," Harlequin replied with a bite to his words. His hand slid off Pascal's shoulder, and he stepped forward as Pascal and Pierrot stepped back. Their gaze shifted from Harlequin's shimmering suit to Mephisto, who seemed to have plunged his side of the courtyard deeper into shadow. On either side of him, Master Darco, Weylin, and the banshees arranged themselves, their eerie eyes glowing in the dark.

"I'm glad to hear it," Mephisto said unenthusiastically, not sounding glad at all. "Honestly, dear man, we've been looking all over for you. Surely some of our messages reached you? I did try to leave my calling card on a variety of occasions."

"Unfortunately, I've been busy," Harlequin replied evenly.

"Yes, you have been, haven't you? After the whole matter with the Wanderers and the wise woman, I'd nearly given you up for lost, but I still had to try to win the black sheep back into my fold."

"There is no home for me at your side, Mephisto." Though his voice was steady, his fists clenched tightly at his side. "I learned the truth by the grace of light. I found salvation. I don't need you or your games."

"You found a lie!" Mephisto spat. His eyes filled with a raging inferno that glowed and flickered in the darkness. All vestiges of the cultured, kind Lord Serpentine disappeared, leaving behind something malevolent beyond all comprehension.

Pierrot flinched and shrank behind Harlequin a little more.

"Those women...Ojos Verdes and the other wench, they lied to you," Mephisto went on. "They were like all others, coveting the ancient power and bending your heart to their will. Certainly, at first, they may have seemed to be whatever it was that you were looking for, but surely you have since discovered the truth."

"The only truth I know is that I never found such happiness at your side, Mephisto. Columbine showed me another way, another world. I may have lost her, but I will still walk the path that she opened for me. And that road, I am afraid, will cross yours. For even though we walk apart, Mephisto, we are inextricably bound. Where you go, I will haunt you."

"Oh?" Mephisto eased back a step, and the fire within his eyes dimmed a little. "You are going to stop me? Is that it? Well, old Harley, may I remind you that time is running short. Before you know it, the blood moon will rise, and it will be a night to remember! That, I can assure you."

Harlequin's back straightened, but the resolve gleaming in his eyes was broken and exhausted. *Does he not want to fight Mephisto? Maybe he hoped that Mephisto would change. But if the* stories are true, Mephisto can never change. He and his men are drawn from the Netherworld and comprised of evil. Harlequin is different. He draws on something even more ancient.

"And you, Harlequin ..." Mephisto frowned. "After all these years of running, why reveal yourself today? Are you here to witness the hour of our triumph and celebration? Or is there some other secret you hold? Why appear here in this hole of a place? What are you hiding?"

Harlequin tilted his head as though deep in thought. "The same could be asked of you, Mephisto. What are you doing here in this *hole of a place*? Surely your Citadel would better suit your tastes. Unless you are the one responsible for all of the missing children around Vale and Pivot?"

"Ahhh ..." A devilish grin curled at the corner of his lips. "You caught that, then. I am not surprised, old friend. But of course, you must know the answer, or are you simply too cowardly to speak of it aloud?"

"Pure souls," Harlequin said with gritted teeth. His eyes narrowed, and his gaze hardened.

"Yes, yes." Mephisto stepped forward and raised his hands in a careless shrug. "Pure souls are what we seek. After all, you know that they hold the most potent power. They are the easiest sources of what we need if we are to bring our master to this realm."

"*Your* master. I had hoped that you would abandon such madness after your last failure."

"I will not fail again," Mephisto hissed.

With that, he raised a hand. The three banshees behind him flew forward, only to tumble back as Harlequin's bat swept forward and unleashed a swathe of shadow.

"Run, boys!" Harlequin shouted.

"No!" Pascal yelled back. "We're helping!" He rushed toward Master Darco, Pierrot close behind, reaching into his pockets to draw out the last of his pebbles. Pascal bounded through a series of flips that ended with a high kick to Master Darco's head. It threw the headmaster off balance, cursing obscenities. Though he tried to grab Pascal, he couldn't. Weylin simply slithered into the shadows in retreat.

As Pascal fought Master Darco, Harlequin fought the banshees. Mephisto, on the other hand, stood by the hedge with a smug expression, his arms folded in triumph. That second Pascal glanced toward Mephisto cost him; Master Darco's fist crashed into his face, which already ached from the previous blows from Weylin.

Pascal hit the ground and rolled, forcing himself to his feet. Swiping away the blood that trickled from the corner of his mouth, he gritted his teeth.

Master Darco didn't wait for Pascal and lunged toward Pierrot, wincing when pebbles riddled the side of his face, though it hardly slowed him down. He grabbed Pierrot and shoved him to the ground, knocking the wind out of his lungs.

"Pierrot!" Pascal cried out.

The windows along the east and west wings began to fly open, faces appearing and peeking out curiously. At the sight of the banshees and dark creatures, Danton, Clarion, and many of the children screamed in horror.

As if summoned, a sneering Maldavo appeared around the corner of the west wing, followed closely by Clément, Claudio, and Anala. He rushed Pascal with eagerness, apparently either thrilled at the fight or at an opportunity to get his revenge on Pascal, or both. Clément and Claudio, wide-eyed at the black, shadowy, ghost-like monsters, hung back.

Pascal, however, barely glanced at Maldavo. His focus was entirely on Master Darco, who had slapped Pierrot nearly unconscious. Racing toward Pierrot and Master Darco, he attempted to strike with a kick. Master Darco blocked Pascal and grabbed his ankle, attempting to punch him. But his fist sailed past Pascal.

Two of the banshees dripped black blood as they fled into the forest, while the orphans began to cheer as Harlequin and Pascal pressed on in their fight.

Mephisto howled at the sight before him. "You cannot defeat us," he cried. "Maldavo, come!"

"Yes, Lord Serpentine?" Maldavo bounded forward, coming to a stop in front of Mephisto.

"Now is your moment, my boy," Mephisto said with a wide, devious grin. "Now, you will understand the truth of my power!" Red-forked lightning twisted from within him, though the flicker was faint.

Maldavo didn't seem to care. When Mephisto bent down to embrace him, he glared at Pascal with a malicious smile. Though Pascal called out his name, stunned that Maldavo had really given into darkness so easily, Maldavo didn't respond. Instead, his grin spread, no doubt expecting to receive something great from Mephisto. Mephisto eased back from his embrace, raising his arms as dark shadows surrounded them.

"Don't let the shadows touch you," Harlequin called in warning.

Pascal wrenched himself away. Grabbing Pierrot, he climbed onto the metal grating of the hotbox door so that they both could stand above the ground. Master Darco seemed to vanish into thin air, appearing behind Miss Myrrah by the kitchen door.

Harlequin defied gravity by levitating up to the hotbox roof. With an outstretched hand, he drew Pascal and Pierrot to his side. Pascal's eyes were glued to Maldavo's feet, where a bottomless, black darkness had appeared. The shadows that swirled around Maldavo grabbed at his legs, crawling in tendrils upward.

"It's—it's alive?" Pascal whispered in disbelief. "It's alive!"

"Stay back," Harlequin warned.

Harlequin tucked his slapstick beneath his arm and wove a symbol in the air. His hands rose and fell as he worked his magic, drawing apart the curtain of reality.

He's opening a door to another place! Pascal realized. *Are we running away? What about the other children?*

At the thought, he glanced back to the windows, where the children began to scream in horror, pointing to the playground. Pascal's gaze followed their points to the center, where the shadow had wrapped itself around Maldavo, consuming him.

Maldavo tried to step back, but it was too late. He glanced down at his feet and the shadows that wrapped around him. Stunned, he looked up at Mephisto.

Mephisto's face was deathly pale below his ravenous red eyes, and his clothing had become the bloodiest of red. Even more telling was the cruel smile that twisted his face.

Shock and horror spread over Maldavo's face, and he began to scream, attempting to twist himself free. The inky, black shadows were as thick as tar, arching back to the outstretched palms of Mephisto.

"The soul of the boy will become *my* power!" Mephisto roared. "There is no purity in the child; as such, he has no use for my master. But for me... his dark soul is perfect."

As Mephisto pulled the shadows into him, Maldavo's skin began to disintegrate. Lines of dark power ran from him to

Mephisto, trapped and slowly torn apart, feeding Mephisto his darkened soul.

Maldavo's eyes darted from his friends to Pascal in a silent panic. His desire for power had ended up as nothing more than being used as a tool for someone else's strength. Though he howled and struggled, he was at the mercy of Mephisto and fell silent as his clothing collapsed in a heap.

The pile of garments on the ground was all that remained of Maldavo.

The shadows seeped back toward Mephisto, whose eyes now gleamed with his newfound strength. The red-forked lightning that twisted from him crackled and popped with life.

Pascal fought against waves of nausea. Pierrot sat down beside him with a thud and cradled his head in his arms. Pascal looked around to the windows where the children had disappeared. Clément and Claudio shook with fear, a puddle of their lost supper on the ground before them.

What are we going to do? If that happens to dark souls, then what happens to pure souls?

"Time to go," Harlequin said. "We need to regroup."

Pascal turned to him, dumbfounded by the words. *We can't just leave,* he wanted to say, but Harlequin must have known because he shook his head, a mournful expression on his face.

"We need time to figure out a strategy. We need to go. *Now.*"

His hands parted, drawing through curtains of air that formed a vortex of smoke-filled clouds, discharging blue energy. In the middle, a passage expanded, and on the other side, Pascal glimpsed a familiar alley—one that ran behind the Carnival, close by the north gate.

Pascal hauled Pierrot to his feet and pulled the two of them through the portal that Harlequin had created, not daring to look back. Once Harlequin stepped through, the passage snapped shut behind them, cutting off his view of the orphanage and Mephisto's cackle, accompanied by the booming crackle of thunder.

Pascal was disoriented. Broken. He'd left the others behind. *Paloma. Tania, Clarion, Danton. I left them all!* The orphanage was filled with helpless and pure souls ... targets for Mephisto and the blood moon.

He drew in several deep breaths to regain his composure. In the distance, he could hear the sharp whistle of a city guard, the distant clang of metal against metal, and a cat's angry squeal. A beggar clattered around the corner, pulling a metal cart full of newspapers.

It was almost eerier than the orphanage, as if they had traveled to a different time. How could life simply go on in the city, like Mephisto hadn't just consumed Maldavo?

"Come along, you two," Harlequin said. "Let's sit down and try to figure things out."

He led Pascal and Pierrot around the corner and through the north gate into the Carnival. He drew his hands across his face as they walked. The black-and-silver mask disappeared, revealing laugh lines at the edges of kind eyes.

This part of the Carnival grounds was closed to the public, but the boys were familiar with it after their time as street performers. Normally, at this time of night, everyone would be relaxing around their campfires after a night of work. Tonight, though, people were clustered around various tents and caravan wagons, whispering in hushed voices.

He knows the Carnival's layout well. Cocking his head slightly, Pascal curiously followed Harlequin as he made a beeline for the puppet theater, ducking behind Hugo's Puppetmaster tent.

Pierrot followed him right in, but Pascal hesitated. "You know Master Hugo?"

"Well, in a way." Harlequin smiled. He hung his bicorne hat on Master Hugo's hat stand and whirled about to face the two boys. "You see, I *am* Master Hugo."

"Woah, woah—wait. What? You—you've been here all this time?" Pascal stammered, eyes wide and mouth gaped open.

"One and the same." Harlequin nodded.

"I don't know how I didn't see it before."

"You weren't meant to, my boy." Harlequin clapped Pascal on the shoulder. "It's all part of the trick. One day, however, your sharp eyes will miss nothing, and you'll be able to—" Harlequin stopped and thought for a second. "Well, perhaps we can talk about that later. Right now, I'm curious as to what is going on. I'll go and get us some tea and try to find out what's happening in Pivot. I have a sinking feeling."

"You and me both," Pascal mumbled, trying not to think about Maldavo's grisly fate.

Harlequin slipped out, leaving the two boys to sit inside "Master Hugo's" tent and try to grapple with everything they had learned tonight. It felt as though he had just lived through ten years in less than an hour. He had no idea where to start; there were too many questions piling up in his mind.

Why is Harlequin here in Pivot? Why was he hanging around the orphanage? Is he trying to stop Mephisto again? Is Mephisto really going to summon his master? Is his master Diabolico, like the puppet show mentioned? How many pure souls are required? When is the blood moon happening?

But there was one question that hurt the most, that plagued his mind.

Where's Paloma?

It echoed in Pascal's mind, shredding his heart to pieces at the possibilities. *Was she hurt? Did they take her somewhere? Did they ...* The image of Maldavo flashed through his mind again, but he shook it away. *No. Paloma wasn't evil like Maldavo. She was good. Pure.* But even that thought left a bitter taste in his mouth.

Pierrot poked Pascal and jarred him from his thoughts. When Pascal glanced at Pierrot in silent question, Pierrot held his hand to his ear and stretched up as though straining to hear. Following his silent commands, Pascal focused on the sounds outside the tent.

Brenson, the Tall Dwarf, spoke with one of the dancers about a recent guard patrol. Though their voices were hushed and muffled, Brenson seemed displeased.

"Can you believe it?" His voice rose to a clearer level. "They have the nerve to accuse *Carnival folk* of stealing children! As if we would do something so despicable!"

"And what is the governor doing about all this, I ask?" the dancer insisted testily.

"I heard that she's been sending out the best cannon shooters, the ones who investigate and look for clues. But they came up with nothing beyond what we already knew about the disturbance in the north. They're accusing us because we're different, and they have no other leads. But if there's a link between the missing children and the disturbance," Brenson paused as if shaken by his own words. "If there is a link between the two, we're in serious trouble."

"Do you think the governor will lock down the city?" The dancer's voice began to shrink as they moved away.

"Only a matter of time, I'm afraid," Brenson said. "Only a matter of time, and perhaps she'll institute a curfew to boot. Won't that wreak havoc with …"

That was all Pascal could hear before they were too far to make out their words. Pascal crept to the door and peered out into the shadows of the tents. Uneasiness crept through him. As if they didn't have enough to think about, now the Carnival was being accused of stealing children?

He turned away and pulled a camp stool close to the bright fire, brooding as he sat before it. When he closed his eyes, all he saw was darkness—swirling shadows, screams, and the faces of his friends as he abandoned them.

CHAPTER SIXTEEN

TEN MINUTES LATER, HARLEQUIN RETURNED BEARing a large tray with a pot of tea and three cups. Setting it down, Harlequin poured out the hot sweet tea, added milk, and served the two boys.

Pierrot had pushed his chair further back into the shadows, where he seemed to be content with watching Pascal and Harlequin talk. The silent boy's eyes were fixed on Harlequin in an unnerving way, as though he were fascinated by what he saw. For a boy who rarely made eye contact, even with his friends—much less looked at strangers—Pierrot seemed more forward than usual, leaving Pascal in a conflicting mix of worry and relief.

"You probably have a lot of questions," Harlequin said, leaning forward and cradling his tea between his broad hands. "After tonight, you've seen so much. You'll probably never look at the world the same way again."

"Yes," Pascal answered uncertainly, his voice trailing off. "I don't even know where to start. My head is jam-packed full of questions."

"Start with your first one," Harlequin suggested. "I don't know if I can answer everything, but I'll do my best."

"Why are you here?" Pascal blurted out. "Working here at the Carnival ... and staying here in the city. Even Mephisto was surprised to see you."

"He would be," Harlequin admitted, the glimmer of a brief smile flashing across his face. "Mephisto has been searching for me for a long time. Many times, he nearly caught up with my trail, but he never could hold me down for long. I would always manage to slip away. Responsibilities and other duties held me here in Pivot. As I feared, Mephisto took root in the deep heart of the mountains. There, his power has spread out from the heart of a ruined Citadel You see, Pascal, he summoned Citadel Dominion from the void of the Netherworld."

"How?"

"During the last blood moon, Mephisto managed to gather more power. Now, Dominion has fully manifested itself into our world. From there, the rot has spread. It has created a wasteland, destroying the mountain forests and all signs of life therein. Despite his accomplishments, Mephisto has been biding his time and waiting for the right moment—for the rare blood moon."

"Mateo had mentioned something strange about the woods dying..." Pascal mused aloud. Harlequin's head tilted slightly at the comment, and Pascal added, "He's the woodcutter at the—never mind." Pascal took a deep breath to center himself. "I know that during the blood moon, the influence of evil grows. Under a blood moon, he will be able to... to use pure souls to summon Diabolico?"

"Yes. His plan is to use the power of pure souls to create the Gateway, a passage through which Mephisto's master will emerge," Harlequin explained. "Over the past year, children have begun to go missing. At first, I thought it was a problem for the city guards to handle. A matter related to the black market, perhaps. But during the past few months, I have felt the coming of evil."

"Then you started to keep an eye on the orphanage," Pascal said.

"Yes, well," Harlequin hesitated, then nodded. "Yes."

Pascal stopped and stared at Harlequin. For the first time, it hit him. *He's Harlequin.* The same hero he'd looked up to his entire life. Just sitting across from him on a camp stool. *Is this a dream?* So much had happened at the orphanage it hadn't sunk in that the man who rescued them was the one person he'd always dreamed of being real.

Harlequin leaned forward and unlatched the door of the potbellied stove. Then he stoked the fire, slipped in a piece of wood, and carefully shut the door again. The warm glow of the fire shone through the glass pane in the stove's door, creating a cozy scene.

We're sitting in a tent sipping tea by the fire. Me and Harlequin. How unbelievable!

Harlequin turned his head. Beneath his dark curly hair and straight eyebrows, his deep-set eyes glittered gold, and Pascal suddenly found it difficult to breathe.

"Did you have any other questions?" Harlequin asked. "Best get them in before we start planning how we are going to rescue the others."

"How much time do we have left before the blood moon?" Pascal asked, trying to ignore his rising panic. "Is it tonight? Tomorrow?"

"It has already begun, but the height of the moon's phase will be the night after tomorrow. We still have some time to retrieve your friends and stop Diabolico's summoning."

"We need to find Paloma." Pascal's gut wrenched when he considered Paloma being absorbed by the dark shadows. "She's essential to our team. Plus, she's a hell of a fighter. She used to run the Rejects, you know. I mean—" Pascal stopped, then started again. "Of course, you know. Never mind. We need Paloma."

Pascal recalled Mephisto's words. He'd said her destiny lies elsewhere. *You will discover the truth about Paloma soon. The truth about your friend, the truth about Vale, and much, much more.*

"You care for her," Harlequin guessed.

Pascal's cheeks flushed, and he shrugged. Why was it so hard for him to talk about Paloma this way? His feelings were all jumbled, made worse by worry. The one thing he *was* certain of: Mephisto was right—Paloma was special.

Mephisto had taken her somewhere. Deep down, Pascal knew.

Pascal looked back at Harlequin, at his look of concern, and changed the subject. "And we'll be able to survive Mephisto's defenses?" Pascal's doubt was evident. 'I suppose you'll be fine, but Pierrot and I lack experience in combat. I know a few basic things, but I don't have powers. Well, none that are useful, anyway. If any at all." He still hadn't figured out the flash of light.

Harlequin leaned in, closely examining every detail on Pascal's face and hands. "You have begun to manifest abilities?" he asked, setting his cup aside, his gaze scanning deep into Pascal, searching for the faintest flicker of newfound powers.

After a momentary pause, Pascal mumbled, "Something like that," glancing over at Pierrot, who nodded solemnly.

Pierrot pretended to pull something out of a bag over and over again. Then he bunched up his fingers and spread them out, miming an explosion.

"Fireworks?" asked Harlequin.

"I can sometimes make things appear. Once, it was apples. A couple of times, it's been a flash of light." Pascal shrugged. "Honestly, I wasn't even sure they were from me. I mean, I can't control them at all. I've just been learning how to perform better, how to fight. Paloma taught me a lot, but it would be nice to have her fight alongside us. We fight well together, Paloma and me. We even came up with a special jump-kick move."

Harlequin smiled at him. "Your acrobatics and fighting abilities have greatly improved. However, I don't want you to underestimate yourself either. Give yourself time, and you might be surprised. Your magic and your powers will come, and one day, you will understand just how strong, how special, you are."

"How do you know?" Pascal asked, half in hope and half in disbelief at the idea of one day becoming a magician. Wielding magic had been something of talk, not reality.

"I know this because..." Harlequin glanced down at his feet, suddenly unable to meet Pascal's anxious gaze. "Because, Pascal," his voice was quiet, "you are my son."

Harlequin looked up. Something nameless and deep glittered within his eyes. Pascal froze, his teacup halfway to his lips.

Pierrot's eyes widened and fixed on Pascal. Then, Pierrot slowly rose and edged out of the tent door, giving them privacy. Harlequin gave Pierrot a sharp glance but did not stop him. He turned instead to Pascal.

Staring down at the teacup in his hands, Pascal felt like he had turned into a statue. Harlequin shifted slightly in his seat and waited. After a moment, Pascal turned to the man who had just said the most unbelievable words he could have ever fathomed.

You are my son.

Pascal shook his head and blinked, trying to assimilate the news. Never would he have imagined meeting his father.

After years, he'd come to believe that his parents were a distant memory. And never in his wildest dreams had he imagined that the man he had admired all his life would suddenly appear and claim him as a son.

Harlequin was a legend, a hero—not a father. *Wait.* Pascal reminded himself. *There was the story of Columbine, the beautiful Wanderer who sang and danced with Harlequin. They fell in love—then she revealed her surprise. They were going to have a baby. That baby... it was me? The whole story was true?*

"It's a long story," Harlequin said. "You already know most of it if you were paying attention to the puppet shows. Which, according to your friend Paloma, seems likely."

"Once upon a time," Pascal said faintly, "there was an emissary who was the lead herald in Mephisto's band of minions."

"Yes, in those days, I was clothed in shadows from head to foot and wore a red and black mask every day. I was bound to Mephisto by a spell, sealed with his blood on my mask, and I roamed the countryside with his minions," Pascal's father explained in a subdued voice. "Those were dark days that I can never forget. Even now, I can hear them in my mind—the screams of those I chased into the Netherworld."

At his words, the floor beneath them began to swirl in shadow. Pascal instinctively drew his feet up onto the rungs of his camp stool. The shadow, however, did not reach up. Instead, it seemed to surround them until the fire, the tent, the half-made bed, and the partially open costume wardrobe disappeared.

Now, the two of them sat in what looked to be an empty meadow. The clouds parted overhead, revealing a dull gray moon. A cart had overturned on the road passing through the meadow. The passengers—two men and a woman—fled before the dark, ragged banshees that swooped down out of the sky.

As each of the travelers ran, they found themselves face-to-face with illusions drawn from their nightmares. Then, driven by fear, they fell through a blazing vortex of smoke and fire, a portal summoned by Harlequin.

"Those people," Pascal said softly as he watched the vision play out, "where did they go?"

"Where they belonged, oddly enough," Harlequin said, but he sounded regretful.

"Criminals?" asked Pascal.

"Not all those who steal and lie and cheat have given themselves over entirely to evil, and there are some who live in the noble houses of Pivot who have the most wicked of hearts," Harlequin said. "Rich or poor, we gathered those wicked people to the Netherworld."

"For what?" asked Pascal.

"For Diabolico, for greater power, just as you saw earlier today," Harlequin said. "But one day, that all changed."

The scene shimmered. There was Harlequin dressed in a fine black suit with a cherry and aquamarine diamond-checked waistcoat and a black and red mask. He was striding down a road between farmers' meadows. In the distance, smoke rose from a Wanderers' encampment. Several men were working on carpentry or shoe repairs. An ancient woman was drawing a young lass into her tent for a palm reading. By the fire, a dark-haired beauty bent over a stewpot.

"I was sent to a small tribe of Wanderers to gather a damned soul for Mephisto," Harlequin said. "The way he ordered me—I could somehow tell that this was different. A test, perhaps. Whatever the case, I went there straight away. Instead of waiting for nightfall, I arrived at dusk to understand what Mephisto wanted."

"It was Columbine," Pascal said, breathless. "She's... my mother."

"Yes, your mother." For a moment, his voice seemed to catch, but Harlequin let out a deep sigh and continued, his voice steady if pained. "She was beautiful, and her soul, to anyone with the Sight, clearly shone as pure as a diamond. After years spent in shadow, what could any man do but fall in love?"

Pascal watched as Harlequin of the past approached the fire, bowed deeply in front of Columbine, and took her hand to gently kiss it. Their eyes met.

His mother smiled, an expression he instantly recognized from what he'd seen in the mirror: a puckish, lopsided grin filled with happiness and charm.

The tent flapped open, and the old crone stood there for a moment, watching the two. The woman's deep green eyes glinted with secret knowledge. She let the tent door fall closed and withdrew.

"Carmen knew the truth from the start," his father said.

"Carmen?" Pascal asked.

"You'll have heard of her as Ojos Verdes, the wise woman. She was the leader of the clan and a seer with knowledge of magic and the supernatural. Columbine, having lost her kind, found solace with Ojos Verdes and the clan. Recognizing her true nature, they'd taken her in and allowed her to become one of their own. Under her protection, Columbine would never come to any harm."

In the vision, Harlequin took a seat on a log and accepted the bowl of stew that Columbine offered. Pascal and his father sat and watched the memory unfold, tinged with rose and gold in the falling dusk.

"But there was still Mephisto," Pascal said. "You had to break the bond he had on your soul."

"Ojos Verdes helped with that," his father explained. "Once the curse was broken and my soul freed, my will returned. I could make a choice. The sign of my bondage—my black and red mask—was finally removed."

"The black and red mask," Pascal mused. "I've never seen you wearing one that color."

"As soon as I tore it off, I stomped on it until it broke. From that time onward, the legend of Harlequin was born, and I wore my own mask." Harlequin smiled sadly. "Of course, Mephisto was furious. He became my archenemy and ordered Columbine's ruthless demise—not just to brutally end her life but to inflict profound devastation. The very thought leaves my soul shattered even now. That was Darco's mission. Darco had always been jealous of me and my position as Mephisto's first and most favored soul collector. He was more than happy to inflict pain on me by hunting down Columbine."

"So, the idea was to kill Mother, and then... you'd come back to him?" *What kind of insane plan is that?*"

"Mephisto is pure evil and only understands that," his father answered. "Either way, your mother and I went on the run. When we learned that she was pregnant; however, we knew that we couldn't travel about forever. Your mother—"

The scene shifted to another place and time. Another fire, this time by a wagon drawn deep into the forest. As the wagon's door opened, Pascal watched Harlequin emerge with a small baby in his arms. After a moment, Ojos Verdes looked out and gave the man what appeared to be an order.

There was a heavy pause. The real Harlequin gazed angrily at the illusion. Unshed tears glittered in his golden eyes. Pascal didn't quite know what to do, but he, too, began to feel the weight of sorrow spread over him. He reached forward to squeeze his father's arm.

"Your mother didn't want you to live in fear, Pascal," his father said, voice gentle and clam. "She was determined to love you with all the love her heart could bear. Your mother and I had so many hopes and dreams."

The scene faded, leaving only grass below and stars overhead. In front of them, far in the distance, a small cottage caught fire.

"What happened?" Pascal asked with hesitance. "We never got to that part in the puppet show."

"Darco found her. I was away, scouting for signs of Mephisto's minions. You and your mother were staying at a small cottage when Darco arrived. They…" He swallowed hard and cleared his throat. "They boarded up the doors and windows and set fire to the building. Your mother refused to give you up. I rushed back and tried to force the door open with my magic. Darco and his minions, however, had set about wards, making my power useless. I ended up tearing boards off a window to get to you. She was waiting for me with you in her arms."

"She didn't try to save herself, did she?" Pascal asked, his tears finally releasing.

"She threw you into my arms and gave Darco what he wanted—a fiery death for my beloved. Your mother was the kindest and bravest woman I've ever known. She knew that her death would sate Darco and Mephisto, at least for a time. I think she believed that you and I would be saved by her sacrifice."

Harlequin shook his head, blinking rapidly. His voice wavered as he said, "And she was right, as always. From the flames, or perhaps from some long-forgotten power carried within her people, a wave of white magic spread out. It terrified Darco and the minions, driving them off. They never realized that I had arrived and saved our child. They never found out our best-kept secret—you, Pascal."

The illusion of the cottage in flames died out, leaving the two of them to sit in the dark again.

"Why didn't you stay?" Pascal asked. "You must have left me at the orphanage for a reason."

"Your mother's plan was foolproof, but she could not have foreseen Diabolico," Harlequin said as he shook his head. "I beat it out of Shadowsoul, the coward. Mephisto's master, Diabolico, appeared to him in the flames of a mage fire. It was a summoning of sorts if you will. A way for the two to communicate and plot their dark magic. At any rate, Diabolico wasn't pleased."

"About what happened with you?" Pascal frowned.

"Well, it wasn't just about me. He was apparently unhappy about the state of the world. Your mother and I had worked to reverse Mephisto's evils. We made it hard for Mephisto and his minions to spread their malice or influence others to commit evil deeds. As a result, the Netherworld was not receiving enough souls for Diabolico's liking. Diabolico decided that a door needed to be opened so he could enter the world. No easy matter, thank goodness. Mephisto and his spawn may be able to come and go, but for Diabolico to leave the Netherworld, special preparations must be made."

"The Gateway that needs pure souls," Pascal guessed. "All these years, Mephisto has been planning and waiting for the blood moon. Now, in preparation, he has been gathering pure souls. Maybe he needed more than he thought, so he took over the orphanage."

"Indeed." Harlequin sighed. "If I was still bonded to Mephisto, it would have been my unhappy job to retrieve every child's soul. When I failed to return to Mephisto after your mother died, he came after me yet again to try to renew that bond. I just... after losing your mother, I felt as though I had failed. I had failed to protect the woman I loved, and I would fail to protect you as well. That's what I believed."

"I get it," Pascal said quietly. "It was too hard to fight when you had a small baby."

"Yes. Each time he sent a minion after me, I had to be so careful to make sure I eliminated the minion. I needed to make sure word of your existence wouldn't reach him. If he had found out about you, Pascal, before it was time—" Pascal's father shuddered. "No. I could not risk it. So, before you could remember me, I decided to leave you in Alma's care. She is a good soul and powerful in her own way. Her wisdom and good heart have protected the orphanage for many years. While she cared for you, I could come and go. Baiting Mephisto away from Pivot, allowing him to chase my trail, and sometimes even battling one of his henchmen. It wasn't always easy, but it had to be done."

Harlequin huffed out a deep breath. "Ten years ago, the blood moon waxed full. Mephisto wasn't prepared, and I was able to thwart him due to sheer luck. Maybe it was the memory of you and your mother. I don't know. I just couldn't give up."

"All alone..." Pascal's head drooped at the thought of his father roaming from place to place by himself.

"Not entirely," his father said, setting his hand on Pascal's shoulder in comfort. He winked at Pascal. "I had you, didn't I? I would come around once in a while to see how things were going. Sometimes, you and I would talk, and every time I left, I felt prouder, happier, and even more courageous than when I arrived."

The words rang in Pascal's ears. Frowning, Pascal wondered how his father came to visit. *Had he made himself invisible and watched from afar? No. He said we talked.*

Then, with a rush, it clicked—wise Mateo, whose eyes were edged with gold and who wore a diamond-patterned neckerchief and had a diamond etched into his cart; ever-cheerful Arrio, with his mysterious staff with a diamond in the center; and Hugo the Puppetmaster, with his costume's red-and-black-diamond patterns on his hatband and handkerchief.

All of them had been there for him, listening and helping him out whenever he had asked for it. Pascal's heart lightened at the realization, and he smiled at his father, who grinned back in turn.

"My whole life, you were there," Pascal said. "Even when I thought I didn't have parents, you were there for me." A warmth wrapped around him like a tight embrace, knowing that his father was present the whole time, even when he wasn't aware.

"And now, we face something that will seriously challenge us, even working together. Mephisto fed on that poor child, and his powers would reach their peak beneath the blood moon. Who knows what will happen then? I want you to take this." Harlequin drew something that looked like a watch out of his jacket pocket. It had a dull silver band, but where the timepiece might have been, a small flat circle sat instead. "It's not much," he said, "but it belonged to your mother. I think she would want you to have it."

"My mother's?" Pascal took the band and ran his finger delicately over the flat silver top. There were tiny engravings cut into it—curlicues of flowers, twining branches, and a fantastical bird.

"It's a locket," his father said, pressing against the side. The engraved top popped open to reveal a lock of chestnut-brown hair on one side. On the other side, Pascal saw a detailed painting of a beautiful woman with flashing dark eyes and deep chestnut-brown hair.

"Mother," Pascal said, struggling to find words. "She's..."

"Beautiful?" his father gently asked. "Yes, as beautiful as her soul. Keep it. When you look at her, you can think of us both."

"Where are you going?" Pascal's voice rose in alarm at his father's words.

"Nowhere. Yet." Harlequin smiled. "But we can't take these things for granted. Not when we face Mephisto during the blood moon."

"So, we'll go back and take on the fight!" Pascal said with relief. "We'll save Paloma and the other children and find out where Mistress Alma went."

"Exactly." Harlequin grinned and winked at Pierrot, who had appeared suddenly at his elbow. "I'm sure we'll figure out a way, but we're going to need all the help that we can get."

CHAPTER SEVENTEEN

"Who is going to help us?" Pascal asked.

His father smiled and glanced at the doorway of his tent, where a familiar silhouette stood. Ringmaster Barolo. The red jacket and black pants tucked into his gleaming lizard-hide boots no longer looked as well-brushed and spotless as they would before a show. Barolo took off his hat and threw it onto the hat stand. His curling, sandy hair was dark with sweat.

"Who needs help?" Barolo asked, looking around the tent. "I stepped out of the ring, only to hear the news about the guards. There are missing children about, from what I hear, and now I find two in your tent, Hugo! Is there trouble afoot I ought to know about?"

Pascal glanced up at his father, who stared thoughtfully at the ringmaster. Barolo threw his head back and laughed.

"You and your secrets, Hugo." His chuckle died down, and he winked at the boys. "Or can I now safely call you—Harlequin? He always comes and goes as he pleases, but we never complain. Everyone loves him, and they respect his art. But it is clear to see that whatever you've gotten yourself into this time, you might need some help. Surely you will allow us to help you?"

With that, the ringmaster pushed the tent door open. Even more of the Carnival folk gathered outside the door. Pascal and Pierrot's eyes widened at the sight of the muscular Torto, the grim-faced Brenson, the fierce-looking Bati, and the ever-mysterious Nomu. Beyond them, Crisanto and Cherise were standing with other dancers and acrobats.

Brenson and Torto had already changed out of their costumes and had armed themselves with a great axe and stone hammer, respectively. Bati was always dressed in her leathers, but she seemed to have picked up a pair of whips as well, which now dangled in a coil at her hips. Nomu's pale blue skin was still covered in white makeup, but she sported a high ponytail. Two sheathed daggers hung on her belt, and a canteen clipped to her hip filled with water.

"We're ready," Brenson said. "After the guards burst in here, it was only too clear to us that it would be in our best interests to help in the manhunt for the children. Especially if the rumors are true."

"Rumors?" Pascal asked.

"There have been sightings of little ones being carried away," Bati replied softly.

"Carried away, yes, and to the north," Torto rumbled. "Why to the north, we do not know, but that is what the eyewitnesses have told us."

"The north," mused Harlequin. "Then, my hunch is correct."

"Hunch?" Barolo folded his arms and frowned. "What are you thinking, old friend?"

"The orphanage. It has to be that. I was drawn there tonight—not just to check up on Pascal but also because I could sense a locus of power. What if—but surely not ..." He trailed off, deep in thought, and gazed at the others solemnly. "Great evil has woken tonight and grows stronger by the minute. Pure souls are being harvested for Mephisto to open a door to the Netherworld ... For Diabolico himself."

Everyone gasped in shock. Pascal guessed that everyone remembered the rumors surrounding the disturbance that had spread in the Untamed Highlands in the north. A wasteland that had destroyed forests, it was said. Pascal could see that the Carnival folk were putting the pieces together after Harlequin explained Mephisto's plan.

"Yes. Mephisto," Harlequin repeated. "And, he is collecting pure souls. The children. I believe he is gathering the last of them tonight at the orphanage. If we go there now, I am certain we will find that he has opened a portal between the orphanage and his Dominion."

"And you wish to fight him?" Barolo asked in disbelief. "With only these two boys?"

"If only Paloma were here, too," Pascal griped. "Mephisto has her."

"Then it's a good thing that *we* are here," Brenson said, stepping forward. His lips thinned with determination behind his black beard, and his dark eyes glittered dangerously as he hefted his great axe. "Mephisto. Diabolico. I don't care," he added. "We'll show them a thing or two and teach them a lesson about messing with the townsfolk of Pivot!"

Everyone cheered as Bati, Nomu, and Torto also stepped forward. Ringmaster Barolo held a grim smile. He raised a hand in command and began to organize the rest of the Carnival folk into groups to serve as watches or to volunteer with the city guard. Pascal looked at the four Carnival performers who remained with them. Torto and Brenson were talking about battle tactics and debating the best ones to use against the shadows who had flown off with the children. Bati and Nomu stood quietly and watched, their sharp eyes trained on Harlequin, who began to work an enchantment.

"It'll take a little longer since there are more people passing through," Harlequin explained.

"Maybe I should get a sword or something," Pascal suggested. "Pierrot, how about you?"

Pierrot mutely shook his head. Pascal moved to Pierrot's side and laid his hand on his shoulder.

"Do you want to stay?" he asked. "We'd understand if you did."

Pierrot squeezed his red ball, but his eyes glittered with fear and worry.

"Are you sure?" Pascal asked. "I'm always glad to have you at my side, Pierrot, but I don't want you to get hurt."

Pierrot kept squeezing his red ball. His gaze dropped to the ground, thin shoulders hunched a little, but he determinedly remained at Pascal's side.

Pascal smiled. "Are you worried?"

Pierrot held up his blue ball.

"About me?"

Pierrot squeezed his red ball.

"You?"

Another squeeze of the red ball.

"Paloma?" guessed Pascal.

Pierrot slowly raised the blue ball.

"I'm worried, too," Pascal admitted. "I don't understand where she could have gone, and I don't like what Lord Serp—I mean, Mephisto—said. It has me concerned. The sooner we get there, the sooner we can find Paloma and bring her back."

"And we will be there sooner than you might wish," Harlequin broke in.

Once again, Harlequin looked as though he was drawing back curtains on a stage, but this time, his hands parted, and an opening was created back to the lane in front of the orphanage. As soon as the passage was large enough, Torto ducked down and squeezed through.

Harlequin winced as Torto struggled to fit through the edges of the opening. Brenson, Bati, and Pascal immediately rushed forward and shoved Torto through. With a sharp pop, the giant wriggled out of the portal. He landed on the gravel lane and ran up to the orphanage. Brenson, Bati, and Nomu followed closely behind.

Drawing in a deep breath, Pascal stepped through the portal. Pierrot crowded close behind. Then Harlequin stepped through and closed the opening after him. As soon as the portal shut, the world around them plunged into gloom. Without the cheery glow of the fire in "Hugo's" tent, everything dimmed to shadowy hues of deep purple and black.

Pierrot drew closer to Pascal, huddling behind his friend, as the group quietly looked around.

"Pierrot and Pascal will go straight to the dorms and get the children out," Harlequin said in a low voice. "The rest of us will bait Mephisto's henchmen outside and keep them occupied in battle. The children need to run."

"We'll take them to the village," Pascal suggested. "It isn't too far. From there, everyone can find a way to Pivot. We'll wake the constable and ask for his help."

"I imagine the constable is already stirring," Brenson said gruffly. "The governor has sent the city guards to rouse the neighboring villages. I'm sure your constable will be up soon enough."

Pierrot suddenly clutched Pascal and poked him hard in the back. It was a warning, and Pascal peered into the darkness.

Harlequin followed Pascal's gaze. Both of their eyes hardened at the sight of the coalescing shadows before them.

Three minions glowered at their small group. The creature in the middle looked like a gnarly tree, complete with branch-like antlers jutting out from its head. It released a guttural cry that raised the hair on Pascal's arms. The dark shape to the right hovered just above the ground. He raised his hand, and a cloud of bats began to swirl about his head while the dark creature on the left unfurled six long arms.

Pierrot grabbed Pascal's arm and squeezed hard. Even Pascal found it hard not to shiver at the creepy sight before him.

"Callisto, Darkwing, and Mechawire!" Harlequin cried. He turned to Pascal and Pierrot and pointed at the orphanage. "Get inside!"

At his words, the cloud of bats rushed toward them. Pascal grabbed Pierrot's shoulders and pushed him down while ducking himself before they scurried toward the orphanage porch, arms wrapped around their heads.

"We'll be fine," Torto yelled, pushing Harlequin forward, as well. "You go ahead with the boys. I'm sure that there are others inside that will need to be dealt with. We can hold these three here."

"Very well," Harlequin called as he leaped forward.

He raced past the boys and swung his slapstick, clearing a path through the cloud of bats. As they reached the steps to the porch, Pascal paused and looked back. Torto battled Mechawire, swinging his great stone hammer. Small craters appeared along the gravel lane with every massive thud. Bati breathed a wave of fire, setting quite a few of the bats ablaze. Their piercing shrieks split the night. Meanwhile, Brenson grappled with the gnarled branch-like arms of Callisto the Wendigo, attempting to chop off the desiccated limbs with his great axe.

"Time to rescue the others," Harlequin said briskly.

"Rescue whom, exactly?" A cold yet familiar voice interrupted them.

"Paloma!" Pascal rushed to her side as she stepped out of the porch's shadows. When he realized that she wasn't smiling at him, he faltered. "P-Paloma?" Cautiously, he stepped closer.

She looked tired and dirty, as though she'd been in a fight. His eyes traveled to her rumpled, sweat-stained clothing from yesterday when she had marched off to the hotbox. There was something about the tense way she held herself, the sharp look she trained on Harlequin, that unnerved him.

Slowly, Pascal moved up the porch steps to get her attention. But she couldn't seem to tear her eyes away from Harlequin's face. As Pascal reached the top of the steps, he realized that the orphanage's front doors were open. So was the entrance to Mistress Alma's study.

Pierrot, who had followed him up the stairs, poked Pascal hard in the back, no doubt in response to what they saw. Anala and Weylin dragged Clarion and another small boy, both kicking and screaming, into a cloud of smoke and a fire-wreathed portal in front of Mistress Alma's desk. The blazing portal led to a dark and shadowy dungeon-like courtyard.

"What's going on?" Pascal asked. "Paloma? This is crazy! Are you really not fighting this?"

"Pascal." The way she said his name—so calm and reassuring, yet cold and lifeless—left a heaviness in the pit of his stomach. "Lord Serpentine has his reasons. You just have to listen."

"Really," Pascal said in a dry tone. "How is taking us all away from the orphanage a good thing?"

"We are all going to leave at some point," Paloma pointed out. "One way or another, we will leave. Even you, Pascal, have dreams that will take you away from here. Lord Serpentine is offering us another path, another life, another chance."

"I don't know about that," Pascal retorted. "For starters, he's not Lord Serpentine at all. He's called Mephisto, and he's evil."

"And the man who is with you?" asked Paloma in an emotionless voice. "What about him?"

"What *about* him?" Pascal shot back defensively. "He's my—"

"He is a killer," a velvety voice interrupted Pascal. Mephisto stepped forward from the porch shadows. Harlequin swung the slapstick in warning, but Mephisto came to a stop beside Paloma. She looked up at Mephisto as he rested a comforting hand on her shoulder.

"You can see it, Loma, can't you? Just as I promised, you will have the justice you seek, and after that—why, what else could you achieve, I wonder?"

"The justice I seek?" Paloma turned back and stared at Harlequin. Her eyes widened and filled with an emotion Pascal couldn't place. Everything about her seemed to still, like a snake preparing to strike. "It can't be!"

"What?" Pascal asked with a sinking feeling in his stomach. "Paloma, talk to me. What justice? Are you talking about your parents?"

"It's *him*. Those dark flaming eyes, that cruel smile, and the shape of his face. The man who killed my parents. It's him!" Paloma said with rising anger. Her eyes blazed, and deep within her hazel eyes, Pascal thought he caught a flicker of a red flame.

He watched in horror as Paloma launched herself at his father.

"Paloma, no!"

He dashed back down the stairs toward his father, reaching to grab Paloma's shirt, but stumbled as his hand grasped only air.

Paloma had always been fast, but now she seemed to move faster than the eye could track. In her hands, she held two thin daggers that she aimed at Harlequin's heart.

Before Pascal could call out his father's name, Harlequin leaned back, knocking Paloma off her path and forcing her to the side.

As if reading his mind, she twisted around and kicked him in the shoulders, aiming her daggers at his belly.

Pascal regained his footing and tried to grab Paloma, but she anticipated his move and jumped high, planting her foot on Pascal's forehead. She kicked off and aimed another spiraling attack on Harlequin.

The two battled, though Harlequin deflected each of her attacks, merely repelling her until he could find a way to subdue her.

Just as Pascal was torn to see his father and friend combat one another, he assumed his father was just as torn—not wanting to hurt the person his son was so fond of.

Paloma seemed to guess it as well, for she gave a cry of frustration and renewed her onslaught. This time, her sideswipe caught one of Harlequin's lapels, nearly drawing the tip of her blades across his throat. But he grabbed her right hand and twisted, hoping to drop her weapon. Paloma's grip tightened in response, and she slashed wildly downward.

Her blade drew a red line across Harlequin's cheek and down his chest. Purplish-red fire flared as the blade met his skin, cutting easily through the cloth and creating a jagged wound. Before Paloma could attempt to stab him again, Harlequin whirled about and threw her across the hall.

Paloma gracefully arced through the air, fell to the ground in a ball, and rolled to her feet. Mephisto appeared behind her, clapping his hands with relish.

Pascal's eyes darted to his father, who took in a deep breath as he gazed at Mephisto and fell to his knees.

No! He looked at Paloma, who stood by her new master with a pleased expression. *How could this happen? It's like she's not even there.* Her eyes were no longer the warm hazel that drew him in, entrancing him with her gaze. No. They were dead and dark.

Harlequin was gravely injured, and Pascal had no idea what to do.

I should've known better, Pascal realized in horror. There was no way Harlequin could fight Mephisto with Paloma attacking him. Not when he's too worried about hurting her. *I should've stopped her. But how could I have known? And what about the others?*

He turned back to see those who had been fighting out front running full-speed toward the orphanage, only pausing to beat away Darkwing's bats as the minions chased them. Brenson had a limp. Bati had a trail of blood dripping from above her eye. As they got closer, Pascal could make out cuts and bruises along Torto's body. Though Nomu didn't have any visible injuries, she held a deep fear in her eyes as she shot a jet stream of water at the minions, knocking them over like dominos. But even that attack only held them off for a moment.

We should've brought more people. We're overpowered. There's no way that we can beat them! And Father... Pascal looked down at his father, clutching his face and chest. He was bleeding heavily. More than Pascal expected from a dagger. Maybe the blade was charmed. Either way, Pascal had to get everyone back to safety.

Mephisto stepped forward and looked at Harlequin with a sly grin.

"Now, old friend," he said with a heavy sigh. "I had hoped that things might go better, that you might see reason, but even now, I can read that spark in your eye. You will not come easily, and if you will not see reason," Mephisto's face turned into a snarl, "Then, it is better that you not live at all!"

Mephisto's hands rose, and shadows whispered around him.

"Stay back," Pascal yelled with fright as he realized what was to come. "Don't let his shadows touch you!" Even as he said it, his heart sank. There was no way that his father would be able to move, much less run, in his condition.

"Pascal." Harlequin's voice was hoarse. He grabbed Pascal's hand, a look of insistence in his weary eyes. "You have to go. Leave me here."

"No!" Pascal said, his eyes filling with tears. "I just found you! I won't leave you. I won't!"

At those words, something within him shattered. An intense surge of energy ran through him; a boundless power that grew with each passing second. He didn't know what to say, what to do, how to use it. All he knew was that he wanted to save the people he loved. *I just want another day with him*, he wished—no, begged. *I want him to be safe, for us all to be safe.*

Pascal closed his eyes, forming a circle of light around himself, extending to his father, Pierrot, and the four Carnival folk who'd just reached them. With an angry cry, Mephisto lunged forward. But he couldn't get past the light, for it was like a burning fire, a barrier to keep the darkness at bay. Mephisto's arm rose to cover his eyes.

Paloma's eyes grew wide—like it was her first time seeing Pascal. *Does Paloma even recognize me? Does she even remember who I am? Or has she been spellbound to forget? To hate?*

He shook his head, dejected, and grabbed Pierrot by the arm. With Bati's help, he held his father steady by the shoulder. There was a tear, a flash, and, in the blink of an eye, they were all gone.

Behind them, the orphanage faded into shadow, lit only by the pale moonlight. Pascal could faintly hear Mephisto scream a curse to the sky.

When everyone opened their eyes again, they had landed in a heap in the open area in front of Hugo's tent. Pierrot looked battered and bruised, but he had landed on top of Torto's chest, so he managed to get to his feet first. Immediately, the boy rushed to Harlequin's side and tried to stem the bleeding with his handkerchief.

Pascal, blinking away the white spots that covered his vision, struggled to his feet. Brenson groaned and rolled over, shoving Torto's leg off his head, as Bati lay unconscious with Nomu bent over her, checking her breathing. Nomu laid her head on Bati's chest and closed her eyes with relief, nodding.

"She lives. They all live, but we need a healer," Nomu said, rising to her feet. "I will go get Medic Clara and Cosme. They will be able to help, I think. Branson, if you may, help Harlequin to his bed."

Under Brenson's careful eye, Torto picked up the barely conscious Harlequin and took him inside the tent. After laying him down on the bed, the two left to retrieve bandages and hot water.

Pierrot stood guard at the tent door while Pascal sat by his father and gently peeled back the layers of ragged clothing. Harlequin's suit had been torn by Paloma's dagger. Some of the threads were caught in the wound. As Pascal gently pulled the fabric away, blood oozed out—more slowly now, but the wound had not fully clotted.

"Pascal," his father said faintly, "you did it."

"Not really," Pascal admitted. "It just happened. I knew we wouldn't make it out alive. There was nothing I could do but run away."

"Still, your quick thinking saved my life."

"I don't understand why Paloma attacked you like that." Pascal rubbed his face, trying not to cry at the thought. "Paloma. She—Father, I'm so sorry. I don't know what she was thinking."

"We'll talk more on it later," he replied heavily. "But for now, I can guess that her fear and resentment made her vulnerable to Mephisto's illusions. He will use her just as he used me."

"It's because of her parents," Pascal said, knowing it to be true. "They died during a ravager attack, but how could she have mistaken you for a ravager?"

"Mephisto's illusions. But," Harlequin said slowly, now deep in thought, "Mephisto used to send Darco to recruit outlaws who would do his dirty work. Perhaps there is a faint connection between them that would tie her to him even more deeply. Yes—I would suppose she is under his spell."

"There was red in her eyes," Pascal recalled.

"Yes, the mark of an illusion," Harlequin said, his mouth pulled into a grim, tight line. "She doesn't know what she is doing. Your friend has been tricked, but even so, Pascal, I believe there is still time to save her."

"Is there? And if I find her, what do I do?"

"Talk to her and listen," Harlequin said. "See her the way only you can see her, the way no one else ever has. Remind her of the good that remains inside her heart, and above all, forgive her. After all, she doesn't understand what she has done, Pascal."

"I wonder if I can do all of that."

Harlequin smiled at his son and raised his hand to squeeze his shoulder in silent comfort. Coughing, he leaned back and closed his eyes. His grip loosened, and his hand fell away as he lapsed into unconsciousness. Pascal sat there, tears in his eyes, watching his father sleep—feeling more worried and helpless than he'd ever been in his life.

CHAPTER EIGHTEEN

PALOMA STOOD AT THE TOP OF THE ORPHANAGE'S porch steps and stared down the gravel lane. For a moment, she enjoyed the quiet, standing there alone. There was something comforting about standing there, shrouded in darkness. The faintest hint of cold moonlight filtered through the rags of clouds. For a second, Paloma closed her eyes and enjoyed the bite of the night breeze on her cheeks.

From her position, she could survey the green lawn, now empty of all the guards. Standing here, as though looking over her domain, she felt in control. Only the wendigo remained, but it slowly eased back into the shadowy trees along the east side of the lot.

There was no sign of Pascal and the others. In a blinding flash, Pierrot, Pascal, the Carnival folk, and her parents' murderer had disappeared. Paloma had rushed forward, but her grasping hand had only met thin air. They were gone. The air crackled with residual energy, the aftermath of the mysterious disappearance. She clenched her fists, nails digging into her palms, as she vowed to herself that she would not let this opportunity slip away again.

Upon seeing his enemy escape again, Mephisto let out a frustrated howl. Paloma, on the cusp of realizing her dreams of revenge, understood how he felt. *So close, yet not close enough.*

She promised herself she'd give chase as soon as possible. When Mephisto sent his minions out to search the nearby forests, Paloma volunteered to join them. If her parents' murderer had not been able to transport the group far away, she wanted to be there when he was recaptured.

Mephisto, however, encouraged Paloma to remain at the orphanage and rest. Shadowsoul and the other minions were able to fly, so they would be better scouts than a girl on foot.

Reluctantly, she took a step back, her eyes never leaving the spot where the group had vanished. As Mephisto disappeared into the orphanage to assist Master Darco, who was guiding the children through the portal, Paloma clenched her fists once more. She knew her path was clear, her purpose defined. The chase was on, and she would stop at nothing to avenge her parents and bring justice to their memory.

Moving the children was proving to be difficult. Not only did they have to be dragged from the dorms kicking and screaming, but quite a few of the orphans were ready to fight back. Several boys, led by Danton, broke a window to escape. Even though Paloma had tried to talk sense into them, nobody was willing to listen. Instead, they kept going on about Maldavo. Paloma simply could not understand what everyone was fussing about.

Who cares if Maldavo was killed? Good riddance! She folded her arms and glared out from the shadows of the porch. *He had it coming to him. Maldavo was a traitor and a bully. Besides, all he cared about was power and doing things his way.*

The skepticism in their eyes was palpable, and no amount of conviction could break through the thick wall of doubt. Distrust clung to the air like a suffocating fog. The very mention of Lord Serpentine's name sent shudders through the children. They clung to the familiarity of the orphanage, to the memory of Mistress Alma, who had been their protector and guide. The promise of a better life, of choosing their own destiny, seemed hollow and improbable in the face of their doubts. The situation was made worse by the eerie atmosphere surrounding the portal. It was not a gateway to a bright, hopeful future as they had imagined but a passage leading down into the unknown depths of a dank underground chamber. The stone walls were damp, covered in a sheen of moisture that glistened in the dim light. The air was thick with a musty smell, and the distant echoes of unknown creatures reverberated through the darkness.

Paloma glanced back. One of the front doors was shut, but the other one still stood open. Through it, she could see that Mistress Alma's study door was thrown open, revealing a cloud of smoke and a fire-wreathed portal. It was an unnerving sight, but she didn't mind. To her, the blazing passage led to another life—a place where she would be able to prove herself, where she would come into the full range of her power and skill.

From this day forward, I will work toward a world where there is justice and punishment for wrongdoings.

A familiar silhouette stepped in front of the portal, blocking her view. It was Master Darco, talking in a low voice with Lord Serpentine. Paloma turned back and resumed her survey of the front lawn, but her sharp ears picked up the conversation easily enough.

"In two days," Master Darco said in haste. "Before the full rise of the blood moon, they may attack again."

"Indeed, but we shall be ready. I am growing more powerful by the minute, and Paloma will remain at my side. Together, we will be able to defend Dominion." Lord Serpentine added, "Although, after her blow, it looked as though our old friend may not be moving around so easily, don't you think?"

"The wound looked severe," Master Darco agreed. "I wasn't able to see clearly, though. It may be too late for interference from that quarter. I still worry about the time. If there are any delays…"

"We cannot afford any delays. Fear, anger, and sadness *will*, over time, corrupt a soul. Extra time within the cells may begin to affect the children adversely," Lord Serpentine said. A chilling determination settled over Lord Serpentine as he continued, his eyes glinting with an unsettling fervor. "Every soul we collect must be pristine, untouched by the stains of negative emotions," he emphasized, his words echoing in the chamber. "We cannot afford to let even a hint of impurity taint the gateway. Our master demands innocence, and we shall deliver nothing less."

"Indeed, indeed," Master Darco agreed.

"On the other hand, gathering more would ensure our success. I will leave Killflare and Groundstroke with you to continue with the task of removing the children and placing them in the cells you've prepared. We do not wish the children to be harmed, nor do we wish any to escape, so continue to remove them from the dormitories carefully. Rest assured that upon their arrival at the designated location, they will receive a festive welcome."

"Yes, my lord. And the others?"

"The others, I will send outward to the nearby villages. Perhaps there are children in the countryside that we have missed," Lord Serpentine said. "The more pure souls we claim, the better.

It is my hope that we can locate a few more to ensure that my powers, combined with the blood moon and the transfer of the pure souls, will widen the door for our master."

Summoning? With the transfer of pure souls? Paloma puzzled. *I wonder what that could mean. Is this master of Lord Serpentine so important after all? Why are pure souls needed?* As Paloma pondered, her eyes widened with realization. The blood moon—a harbinger of darkness and arcane power—cast an ominous glow upon the land, and it was clear that its significance was entwined with Lord Serpentine's plans.

There was so much she didn't know—and she didn't like being kept in the dark about the details. Still, she sensed that Lord Serpentine was stronger than he looked, and she knew that when it came to the unknown, cautiousness would yield better results. That was something Maldavo had never learned. Paloma hoped that she would be able to speak with Lord Serpentine soon to better understand what was going on.

"...and that should work," Master Darco went on.

"Indeed," Lord Serpentine agreed.

Paloma wondered what Master Darco had just said, but Lord Serpentine continued.

"Still, Paloma shows great promise. In time, she will come into the full strength of her abilities. Even if her prey has escaped today, I am sure the girl will hunt him down and finish what she started."

At the mention of her fight, Paloma's heart soared with pride. When she gazed at Harlequin's face, she had been transported to her nightmare. The color of his flaming eyes, the sneer, and the shape of his face had been the same. Even more ominous, Paloma had sensed the man's powerful abilities. It brought all her memories back.

Before she had fully realized what she was doing, Paloma had begun to attack him. Her rage and fear had poured out. This wasn't just about justice. This was about making the man pay. In that moment, nothing else mattered to Paloma. Not the presence of onlookers like Pierrot and Pascal, not the gravity of the situation they were in. Her world had narrowed down to the gleaming steel of her blade and the singular focus of her hatred. She moved with a raw, untamed ferocity, her strikes precise and deadly. Each swing of her weapon carried the weight of her anguish, her need for retribution etched into every movement.

When her blade found its mark, slashing across the murderer's chest, Paloma felt a rush of exhilaration, unlike anything she had ever experienced before. It was a twisted kind of joy, a perverse satisfaction born from the agony she had inflicted. For the first time in her life, wielding a weapon filled her with an eerie sense of happiness. The metal in her hands seemed to resonate with her newfound purpose, granting her a grim satisfaction in the act of delivering her own form of justice. The encounter had awoken something within her, a dark and potent force that had lain dormant until that very moment.

She stretched and smiled at the thought of him dying at her hands. She hoped that it would be as painful as what her parents had suffered. Where the man had disappeared and what had happened to him, she didn't know. *If that murderer has survived, I will hunt him down again and finish the job. He will taste my blades of justice.* She couldn't wait.

Still, when she closed her eyes, she could still see the others in her mind's eye—the fear in Pierrot's posture, the confusion among the Carnival folk, and the anguish in Pascal's eyes. He'd protected the man as though the stranger was his best friend. How had someone like Pascal made friends with a ravager and a murderer?

For as long as I've known him, Pascal has always been so happy. He hated fighting. But tonight... Paloma remembered the first look of determination that had crossed Pascal's face and the rising uncertainty he seemed to feel. *Pascal remained. Although he knew he couldn't win, he put himself between me and that murderer!*

He had not only stepped up to fight; he had drawn on something within him to stun them all with a brilliant light. Lord Serpentine believed that the man who had murdered her parents had created the magic that spirited their group away. Paloma, however, wondered if it had been the murderer—or Pascal. After all, Pascal had shown some talent in magic. Paloma, ever sensitive to shifts of power, had seen the light within Pascal's twisted face as he cried out.

It was burned into her memory, the look of Pascal's desperation and, deep within, something else that unsettled her. The more time she spent alone, standing on the top of the steps, the more uncertain she became. If the murderer managed to survive his wounds, she could hunt him down, but first, she'd have to get Pascal back on her side.

Her stomach twisted at the thought of Pascal. There had been an undeniable shift between them. What else had she seen in his gaze? Sadness? Disappointment? She didn't like the way he had looked at her. He was her friend. He should have understood!

It doesn't matter, Paloma tried to tell herself. *But even Pierrot... he looked so scared of me.* He had acted like she was a monster. *But don't they understand? Why was he so frightened? Am I turning into someone else? Is this what—*

Paloma stopped herself before she completed the thought. Of course, her parents would want her to uphold justice. *Wouldn't they?*

She shook her head and glared up at the night sky overhead. The stars glimmered faintly through the thick clouds, and she closed her eyes.

"Loma," Lord Serpentine's voice broke into her thoughts.

Paloma gasped, and her eyes flew open. "Lord Serpentine. I'm sorry, I—"

"Are you alright?" the man asked, looking down at her. "I forgot that you were still standing watch. Would you like a rest?"

"I'm fine, sir." Paloma raised her chin, forcing away the previous doubts. "I was just thinking, remembering."

"I see. Well, if you are feeling unwell, please let me know." He continued on in a solicitous manner. "I do hope your scuffle with that ruffian did not harm you in any way. It would be a shame if you were to be injured before achieving your goals of justice."

"I am well," Paloma assured him quietly. "I can stand guard for a while."

"Good, good." Lord Serpentine smiled and patted her on the shoulder in comfort. "It has been quite a night. Unreasonable people showing up at all hours. It was a shame about your friends, though, Loma. They seemed to be such nice lads... but that is the way of it, isn't it?"

"Kind-hearted people are easily taken in," Paloma said. She shrugged. "If I meet Pascal again, I will try to make him understand. He doesn't know that he's been lied to. Soon though, I'll help him see the truth. When I'm ready, that is."

"That is good to hear," Lord Serpentine said. "I would so hate to see them go the way of that other boy."

"Maldavo?" Paloma straightened. "I'd heard something about it from Nate. Maldavo was killed?"

"The boy was... well, you know how it is," Lord Serpentine said cryptically, his tone veiled with layers of meaning. His eyes, sharp as a hawk's, scrutinized Paloma as if trying to gauge her true feelings on the matter.

"He was a stupid bully," Paloma said. "I'm sure he deserved it."

Lord Serpentine's lips curled into a sly smile; his amusement evident. "Yes," he agreed, his tone silky smooth. "Of course you would understand, Loma. I just hope that your two friends come to realize the truth soon. It would be a shame for such talent to be wasted."

"I'll talk about it with Pascal. I have a feeling that it won't be the last time we will see him and that *murderer*. When we meet again, I will be ready."

"Yes. And what if I told you that I've already thought up a few ideas about how we shall deal with the murderer? If you are going to face that man again, you will want to be prepared. How about we take a look at a few things I've set aside for you."

"But I still—"

"Ah, yes." Lord Serpentine snapped his fingers.

A flicker of annoyance crossed Master Darco's face, his eyes narrowing slightly in disapproval. Lord Serpentine, with a gesture that seemed almost serpentine in its fluidity, assigned another of his henchmen to guard duty. The chosen minion's eyes glowed with an eerie, otherworldly light as he acknowledged the command, an embodiment of loyalty to his enigmatic master.

Serpentine spoke with the headmaster briefly, assigning another of his henchmen to guard duty. As she placed her hand in his, Lord Serpentine's smile widened, revealing the abyssal depths of his intentions. With a graceful bow that seemed to mock the very laws of gravity, he led Paloma toward the portal—a swirling vortex of darkness that seemed to breathe with a life of its own. The air around them grew colder, and the shadows deepened, their tendrils reaching out hungrily as if eager to pull them into the abyss. With a smile and a bow, Lord Serpentine escorted Paloma through the eerie portal to the dark Citadel and beyond.

CHAPTER NINETEEN

"Pascal, you can go in now," Clara said softly. Her gentle hand rubbed the back of his shoulder, bringing his attention to the present.

Glancing up at the medic, Pascal rubbed his eyes and nodded. He didn't remember falling asleep. He looked over at Pierrot, who was curled on his side, still in slumberland. The events finally caught up with them both. Yawning, Pascal sat up. Might as well let Pierrot sleep as long as he can.

The sky was overcast, and the sun slowly peeped over the edge of the eastern horizon, bathing the world in a dull gray-pink hue. He stepped out of the empty wagon that Brenson had found for them and sat by a small fire out front.

The flames flickered and danced, small but fierce. Just like them. They may be a small group fighting a much larger evil, but they were fierce. Determined. In that, they were strong. Though there was one person, he still felt they needed, but was too agonizing to think about.

Paloma.

Pascal couldn't give up on her—he refused. He would get her back. How, he had no idea. But he would. He just needed to sort through this. It wasn't easy. Everything he knew had been flipped upside down in a matter of days, and it was hard to concentrate on anything. There were so many questions spinning through his head. Were Mephisto and his gang still at the orphanage, or had they crossed to Mephisto's Dominion already? What was happening to the other children? Where have Mistress Alma and Michel gone?

Clara's interruption was a welcome one. Wordlessly, he followed her back to Harlequin's tent and discovered that his father had been bathed, bandaged, and propped up against several pillows. At the sight of Pascal, he raised his head and smiled.

Pascal rushed to his father. "You—you're alright!" he breathed, eyes shining.

"I'm on the mend," his father said. "Thanks to your quick thinking, we got back here in enough time to staunch the bleeding and stop the worst effects of the blades. It will be a little while before I can get on my feet, but it looks as though I have escaped death once again."

Pascal eased back onto the stool by the bed. He took his father's broad, roughened hand in his and allowed himself to enjoy the feeling of relief and happiness that swept over him. For a moment, he was content in the quiet of his father's tent and the feel of their hands clasped together.

"From the sounds of it," Pascal finally said, "you won't be able to walk before Mephisto tries to summon Diabolico."

"Walk, perhaps. Fight? Definitely not. There was magic in those blades that have rendered me useless for the time being. Until I can regain enough strength for my body to battle the magic, I'm afraid you're in this fight alone, Pascal." His eyes held an apologetic note of their own, even more so than his words.

"So, I must be the one to go," Pascal said, all his previous questions and doubts crashing into him. His fingers gripped his father's hand hard, betraying his turmoil. "What do I—where do I even start?"

His father's voice was soft and held a comforting reassurance. "To begin with, you need to remember who you are, Pascal."

"Who I am?" Pascal asked in confusion.

"You are my son." Harlequin's golden eyes fastened on Pascal and held his gaze. "My son," he repeated with increasing emphasis. "And as my son, you have the abilities you need already within you, just as I do."

"You really think so? I suppose there's no harm in trying. If I get in trouble, I'll probably just transport myself back here in a panic again."

"There is that," his father said in amusement, "but you needn't panic. If you clear your head and open your heart, Pascal, you will be able to overcome more than you imagine. You won't just destroy Mephisto's schemes, you may also be able to truly understand your friend and bring her back from the dark path she walks."

"I thought I understood her." Pascal shook his head, looking away. "I guess I didn't listen hard enough. If I could just talk to her again."

"When you have walked in the shadows yourself, you will understand better. It is why I can look at Paloma and forgive her. I, too, have succumbed to the darkness inside myself."

"When you were working for Mephisto?"

"Yes." He nodded slowly. "And after, when I gave into despair and left you with Alma. I became rash, incautious even, for a time. I followed impulses of anger and vengeance. Only when I came by the orphanage one morning and saw you playing in the garden did I remember. You looked at me and smiled, and

I saw your mother in you. At that moment, I realized that the most important thing in the world would be to make it a safe place for you. From that day onward, it became easier to return to the light."

"I don't know what my shadow looks like."

"No," his father said. "Mistress Alma took care of you and raised you well. You haven't yet had to confront the darkest part of yourself. But one day, you will face it. Until then, it is important to remember that the greatest magic comes from a pure soul with good intentions. When you maintain your serenity, the magic that resides inside of you will flow out like second nature."

"So, I just keep my soul pure?"

"It's harder than you think," Harlequin warned. "Still, when you fight for your friends—when you fight for true justice—you will find within yourself the strength of a hero."

His memories with Pierrot and Paloma weighed heavy on his mind—the time they'd spent together, the moments they'd shared. Pascal could picture with such vivid detail the way Pierrot's face lit up the first time he juggled his balls or on the night of his first performance.

Thinking of Paloma tore at his chest, given everything that happened. He could almost hear the gentle sound of Paloma's laughter when she wasn't holding onto that edgy exterior she gave everyone else; when she would let go and allow herself to be open and free. A warmth spread through his heart, thinking about her when she was still the girl he'd grown so close to. The girl he wanted to be alone with. And though he may not admit it—at least, not out loud—the girl he wanted to kiss. He knew his feelings for her had started to shift, but seeing her on the cusp of being lost was like a punch in the gut. He needed to reach her in a way only he could. He didn't always have the right words; his actions, though, spoke volumes.

Within Pascal, something stirred. Each memory seemed to echo deep within, awakening a form of energy. It sent a shiver through him, leaving a tingle in his fingers. His chest seemed to expand with a buoyancy and lightness that he couldn't explain. He smiled, realizing what his father meant.

I am my father's son. One day, I will truly be powerful like him. Harlequin. My purpose will be to save others. Maybe I don't feel ready right now, but I have to try. If I don't, then I will regret everything. This is who I am.

Pascal slowly opened one hand, revealing a small, flickering ball of light. It was tiny and unstable, but he recognized it for what it was—a promise of what would one day come.

"There you go," his father said, releasing Pascal's other hand. "I think you understand it now."

Pascal considered his words and slowly closed his fist, ending the illusion. "I still don't know where to go, though."

"You will need to reach Mephisto's Citadel, where his dominion lies," Harlequin said.

"In the mountains? So, I'd have to commandeer an airship," he listed on one finger, counting more, "or Pierrot and I could return to the orphanage to see if the passage they created is still open."

"Yes," his father said, leaning back and closing his eyes. "Either one might work, but if the portal is closed, you will have wasted precious time."

"We still have a day and a half," Pascal pointed out.

"The distance is great, and I wouldn't be surprised if you met some of his henchmen on the way." He launched into a rapid explanation of their abilities and attacks.

Groaning, Harlequin shifted his body. "You have a lot to contend with. But you still have some time to figure out what you want to do."

"And that will be where your talk must end, I am afraid," Clara said, interrupting the conversation as she entered the tent with a tray of damp towels. "It's time to check the bandages, and you'll need to get to whatever it is you need to do, Pascal. Cosme told me to tell you that it is time. Remember her words to you."

"Remember..." Pascal trailed off.

As if from a dream, Cosme's rasping voice filtered through his memory. A boy with a mysterious past faces a dark road ahead, but he bears a light within that he has not yet fathomed. A light that is shared with his friends.

"A light that is shared with my friends," Pascal murmured to himself. "Pierrot." He turned to his father. "I have to go."

"Go with good fortune, Pascal," his father said, giving his hand a light squeeze. "And go with my love."

Pascal nodded once, not trusting himself to speak, and exited the tent. Pierrot stood outside, digging the toe of his shoe into the dirt, hastily twirling the balls in his hand. He folded his arms and looked up in silent determination.

He won't let me go alone. Pascal smiled in relief. While Pierrot was probably shaking inside, he was just as worried about Paloma and the other orphans. The subtle nod Pierrot gave let Pascal know that he wanted just as badly to bring Paloma back to their side, to her right mind.

Pascal let out an anxious sigh, taking away just a sliver of the overwhelming pressure and fear. At least he wasn't alone. He had Pierrot to help him figure things out.

"We have to decide whether we should go back to the orphanage and check to see if the portal is still open or whether we should try to commandeer an airship." He spoke so matter-of-factly, as though driving an airship was something he did every day.

Pierrot raised an eyebrow and squeezed his red ball.

"No to the airship or no to the orphanage?" Pascal asked.

Pierrot squeezed his red ball again and pulled on Pascal's sleeve. He mimed slow walking and jerked his head in the direction of the Carnival's main gates.

"Oh," Pascal said, realizing what Pierrot meant. "Walking and talking is probably a better idea, yes."

The two made their way to the main gates of the Carnival, which opened to the market. The Carnival grounds were bustling, but unlike an ordinary workday, tension filled the atmosphere. The dancers were not doing their regular training exercises, and the food vendors left their stalls closed. There was no sign of the clowns, acrobats, or wrestling dwarves either.

Beyond the gates of the Carnival, the market was in an uproar as well. They came to a stop at the gates and looked down the main street of the market. Usually, at this time in the morning, you would see sleepy shopkeepers creeping out to open their stalls and prepare for the day's work. The earliest food vendors would be open and serving simple meals to long lines of airship dock workers.

Today, everyone huddled in bunches, whispering. Others rushed about bearing pikes, staffs, or any other weapon they might own. Many stared up at the sky apprehensively.

"This isn't going to be easy." Pascal cursed under his breath.

"Pascal! Pierrot!"

He jerked around to locate the voice. Baptiste walked toward them; head tilted in confusion. His clothes were wrinkled and grimy, his hair was unkempt, and there were dark circles under his eyes.

"Baptiste! What's happening?"

"I don't know." Baptiste shook his head, his eyebrows pulled in tight, a horrified expression on his weary face. "I mean, children have been disappearing all night long. Stolen from their beds by monsters who flew in and snatched them. They headed west, but no one has been able to find them. I went to the orphanage, and it's empty."

"Did you check your grandmother's study?"

"She's still not there." Baptiste blew out a defeated breath. "No matter how much I've asked around, nobody knows where she is, and the city guards just dismissed me. I don't know, maybe they'll listen now after everything that's happened. At any rate, I was thinking of helping to search for the children from the sky—wait. Where's Paloma?"

Pascal slumped in his own defeat, and in a somber tone, he said, "It's a long story. Would you be able to help us? Pierrot and I know who's responsible for kidnapping the children: Mephisto. He's taken the children to the Untamed Highlands, to Citadel . That's where we're headed."

"Dominion?" Baptiste's face scrunched in confusion. "I've never heard of it, but I do know my way to the Untamed Highlands, and I could take you there. Come!"

He led them to the main stairs, up to the market's airship docks, and motioned for them to step onto the dock's largest cargo lift. Crates were stacked to the ceiling of the lift. Metal grates rattled shut behind them, and the entire lift rose with a piercing squeal. Pascal and Pierrot watched as the ground slowly fell away.

Below them, four city guards stood at the major points along the two intersecting streets of the market. The market's gates were manned by a guard and a mercenary. Governor de Moura had been spurred into action and was taking the situation seriously. Unfortunately, neither the governor nor her men understood the truth behind the attacks.

Even if they knew, Pascal figured Mephisto would just suck their souls out like he did to Maldavo and gain even more power.

Whether he liked it or not, this was up to them. Pascal looked sideways at Baptiste, who was nervously gazing up at the thick clouds gathering in the sky.

After ten slow minutes, the trundling lift finally docked on the upper level, and the gates slammed open. Baptiste led them over to the dock where The Unbroken was anchored. Together, they rushed up the gangway and began their preparations for the trip. Thanks to his long conversations with Baptiste, Pascal knew that before every flight, the captain had to run through a checklist to make sure everything was in working order.

Baptiste and his now-deceased father had lovingly crafted the airship. Pascal could see the dedication and care they'd put into it, from the well-designed cargo crane that hung off the portside to the plush décor of the captain's cabin.

Beneath the main deck, a large, sloped room where Baptiste usually stowed the cargo stood empty. Along the walls were neatly coiled rope ladders and various hoists and weapons. Not only was *The Unbroken* one of the fastest ships in Pivot, but Baptiste and his usual two-person crew were perfectly capable of fending off any pesky sky pirates.

Baptiste sent Pascal to crank up the airship's gangway and release the anchoring ropes from the dock as Pierrot helped him check off his list. Once everything was ready, Baptiste took the helm and eased *The Unbroken* away from its moorings. Pierrot and Pascal secured themselves to the side of the ship and watched the spires of Pivot pass by.

The airship passed the walls of Pivot, and the deck lurched under Pascal's feet as they picked up speed. Ahead of them lay large patches of grass and swathes of yellow corn and wheat fields. Beneath them, the country roads twisted and twirled about the land like thin ribbons. Horses and carriages raced up and down the roads, and Pierrot pointed out a troop of men marching along. Mephisto had been wreaking havoc in the countryside, too.

The Unbroken passed peacefully over the land. Before long, Baptiste guided the airship toward the first mountain of the Untamed Highlands: Pinewood Summit. Its great slopes, covered in thick pine forest, descended gently down to the hillside, where white dots of sheep grazed.

Beyond Pinewood Summit, Pascal could see the spurs and shoulders of other unfamiliar mountains jutting out of thick mists. Pascal shivered when the cool air pricked his skin.

As if reading his thoughts, Baptiste steered the ship downward and eased it below the clouds, no doubt hoping to cross Pinewood Summit at its widest but lowest saddle of rock. Here, the rock face of the mountain sharply gave way. Only the smallest of shrubs could cling to the stone ledges. Pierrot pointed out a great horned goat perched precariously on a ledge, chewing on a small green bush. Pascal chuckled at the sight, but his smile fell away when he remembered his father lying in bed and Paloma with Mephisto somewhere ahead of them.

They should have been here. They would've liked to see the mountain view, the forests, and the goats. He rested his chin on his arms. *Soon. We'll fix this, and they'll see it soon.*

Lightning struck through the sky in a loud crash, breaking Pascal away from his thoughts. Thick, dark clouds blocked out the sun and cast everything into a shadowy hue. Among the mountains, a heavy fog lingered ominously around their peaks and valleys. Thunder rumbled and crackled as spears of lightning shot down and around the vessel.

Pascal and Pierrot braced themselves against the gunwale as Baptiste expertly veered the airship away from the storm. Despite his maneuvering, the lightning only intensified.

Forks of white light merged like a large net wrapping around the ship.

Hunched over his wooden helm, Baptiste concentrated hard on trying to keep the ship under control as the winds whipped up around them.

"Baptiste!" Pascal called out, "This has to be one of Mephisto's henchmen! It's some kind of dark sorcery!"

"Sorcery?" Baptiste yelled back. "I knew this was no ordinary storm!"

Before Pascal could explain further, a dark blur crossed the decks, swinging Pierrot up and tossing him overboard. Pascal yelled in shock as Pierrot fell over the side of the ship and swung about in his harness, battered by the buffeting winds.

Bracing himself against the side of the airship, Pascal pulled on the rope attached to Pierrot's harness. After a few tiring pulls, Pierrot's hands could reach the edge of the airship's gunwale. Just as he managed to swing one leg over the edge, something slammed into the side of the ship and nearly threw them both off.

Pascal held onto Pierrot with grim determination, pulling him aboard while the ship bucked. A side stabilizer fin tore off and whipped back, cutting through two of the airship's cables. *The Unbroken* shuddered and twisted wildly as another fin tore off.

"I'll have to go to ground, boys!" Baptiste roared. "Hold on!"

A great gust of wind battered the jerking airship, banging Pascal and Pierrot's heads against the gunwale. Baptiste shouted a warning that went unheard through the chaos. Two more cables snapped, and a cloud of bats began to swirl around the ship. *The Unbroken* was now slanted at an almost forty-five-degree angle.

Gripping the side, Pascal woozily raised his head and peered over the edge. They were drawing dangerously close to the face of Pinewood Summit.

The ship briefly scraped against the side of the mountain, sending pieces of rocks bouncing down, sprinkling the ship. Lightning struck overhead, but Baptiste wrenched the ship away before a large boulder plummeted down. Gritting his teeth, Baptiste held the ship on course the best he could as he swerved and aimed downward.

What he was trying to reach, Pascal didn't know, but he watched in awe as Baptiste managed to scrape the floundering airship over the mountain saddle. An ominous whooshing and tearing screamed overhead as the attacks intensified. Deep green pines reared up out of the mist, and smoke drifted behind the airship, but Baptiste focused solely on the spot where he chose to land.

Following Baptiste's gaze, Pascal realized that the forest had opened a little. A strip of green and gray heather was coming up much too fast.

"Hold on!" Baptiste yelled, clinging onto the helm for dear life.

Pascal clung desperately to the rungs that ran along the ship's side, and Pierrot hung onto his side. The ship jolted through the air and hit the ground, bouncing twice before crashing to the ground with a halt. On the second bounce, Pascal lost his grip on the rungs, and Pierrot was thrown forward, slammed against the aftercastle. Pascal's rope harness snapped from the force of the crash, flinging him from the ship.

Everything went black.

CHAPTER TWENTY

Pascal blinked and dragged himself to consciousness, slowly raising his head. With a deep groan, he forced his body to sit up. *I feel like I got trampled by a thousand horses.* His limbs throbbed and ached, though it was nothing compared to the sharp, bruising pains in his side and back. With a swaying motion, he stood, barely managing to get onto his feet.

The mist hung like a thin veil in the small clearing. Through the gray haze, he glimpsed a flicker of red. A fire. He staggered forward to the blaze of the airship's burning balloon that lit the scene with a dull red-orange glow.

Black clouds swirled and crackled with lightning. The thunder echoed among the rocks of the valley. Pascal thought he could hear the distant rumble of an avalanche, but he focused his gaze overhead. Sure enough, two of Mephisto's minions appeared through the mist. One he recognized instantly—Darkwing. The pale-skinned henchman flapped its wings lazily as a cloud of bats circled him, waiting for their command.

Close by Darkwing, something else hovered. Cloaked in shadowy tendrils, the black-skinned henchman was dimly lit by blue flames emanating from its hands. Large horns wreathed in blue flames rose from its head, and its eyes were pure white.

Glancing at the smoking and broken husk of *The Unbroken*, Pascal searched for any sign of his friends. Panic rose within him as he came up empty. Though he tried to focus on his father's words, it was impossible knowing that Pierrot and Baptiste might have died in the crash.

Calm down. He took a deep breath and made his way toward the wreckage. "Pierrot! Baptiste!" he softly cried out, trying not to draw the attention of the henchmen.

It didn't work. Darkwing swooped down, his long, forked tail swinging behind him. The skeletal creature's eyes glowed an unnatural yellow, like a rabid animal.

"Pierrot! Baptiste!" he called again, seeing no movement to indicate their presence. Behind him, the steady beat of Darkwing's skeletal wings drew closer.

At the last second, Pascal dove to one side and rolled forward, dodging Darkwing's punch. He kicked upward as hard as he could, stunning the creature with his kick.

Pascal whipped around to face him. *I need to find the others, but I can't do anything until I subdue Darkwing.* Focusing all his energy on the creature before him, a familiar tingle of light emanated from within him, exploding from his palms. Using the distraction, he jumped and spun through the air, knocking Darkwing to the ground with another kick. The minion scrambled to his feet, but Pascal stunned him with another bolt of light and punched him in the torso.

The creature squealed and cursed as the radiating light seared into his skin. Burns riddled his body which had him twisting and writhing in agony. His cries became wordless screams as he disintegrated, leaving only a cloud of black smoke that wafted into the mist.

An anguished roar sent Pascal reeling as the remaining minion dove, lunging for him.

From somewhere unknown, a barrage of bullets ripped through the air. Pascal's eyes followed them to the source—one of *The Unbroken's* turrets. It swiveled to focus on the minion that barreled down.

Baptiste. He's alive!

"Darkwing may have failed, but you won't be so lucky with me!" screeched the servant. He levitated a boulder and hurled it toward Pascal. "You will learn to fear my power, the power of Haywire!"

Throwing himself into a forward roll, Pascal dodged the heavy stone as it lodged itself into the earth. Parts of the rock broke off as Haywire lifted it again. Pascal darted from one place to another, evading bits of rock and bolts of lightning that Haywire flung at him, hoping Baptiste's turret fire would hit the creature.

Haywire swooped down close to Baptiste but flinched as several stones hit its face. Pascal recognized the aim and smiled. *Pierrot's alive, too. And ready to fight.*

With regained confidence, Pascal captured Haywire's attention, and, like a hawk and hare, they chased one another. Pascal dove from Haywire's attack and swung around, attempting the same in a brutally delicate attempt to give the others an opportunity to strike. Baptiste's aim wasn't the most accurate, but after two hits, Haywire fell to the ground, a puddle of black blood oozing from the wounds.

Pascal raced forward and jumped, executing a perfect flying kick that Paloma had taught him. With a final strike, Haywire collapsed to the ground, unconscious.

For a moment, there was silence as Pascal stood over the minion. *I can't believe we did that!* He looked up as Baptiste and Pierrot cautiously approached with a rope, and they tied him up, just in case.

Leaning against the boulder from earlier, they sat back with their eyes closed, breathing heavily. After a moment, Baptiste stared up at the sky. The worst of the storm had eased, but thick clouds still loomed. Rain trickled down, slowly dousing the fire that had consumed the airship's envelope.

Baptiste's shoulders slumped as he watched his airship, a heavy sigh escaping his lips. Despite the damage, he knew it could be repaired. So much hard work, gone. A family heirloom, in a sense. *The Unbroken* was broken at the end.

"I'm sorry," Pascal said, looking over the extent of the damage that had been done to Baptiste's airship. "I had no idea they'd go after an airship like that."

"It's just a ship," Baptiste said with a shrug, though his voice wavered, deceiving his nonchalance. He sniffled a little but then got to his feet. "I can fix her. It'll take time, though. Time, and tools, and supplies. I've got none of those right now, so from here on out, we're on foot."

"Pierrot and I can walk," Pascal said. "You should go back to town and get started on the repairs to *The Unbroken*. It's a long story, but just trust me that it's better if you let Pierrot and me handle things from here."

"Just you two?".

Pascal glanced at Pierrot, who gazed back silently. Pierrot's face was covered in soot and dirt, but his brown eyes glinted with resolve. Pascal's body ached with bruises, and exhaustion had already settled in, but he wasn't even close to giving up.

"Very well," Baptiste stood and brushed the soot off his trousers. "I'll go back to the city. But before you go, let's see if we can pull some of the ship's weapons out of the hold. I have a dagger or two that might come in handy—Dwarven-forged, you know, made of silver and charmed with spells, or so I have been told." Baptiste seems a bit skeptical about magic. "I'm sure they might help with any other creatures you encounter."

Baptiste limped over to his ship and carefully climbed up the side, disappearing within. After a while, he emerged with a satchel, a compass, a dagger, and a long pike. Baptiste gave Pascal his compass and ran through some headings that would get them to the center of the mountain range safely. Giving the dagger to Pierrot and the pike to Pascal, he nodded solemnly.

"It's all that I can give you, heirlooms of the family, but they should serve you well."

"Thank you, Baptiste," Pascal said with an appreciative nod. "We'll take it from here. Are you ready, Pierrot?"

Pierrot juggled his blue ball and dagger expertly, grinning at Pascal, who chuckled.

"Let's get going, then. We have a long road ahead."

Leaving behind the narrow clearing, the two boys entered the thick pine forest. According to Baptiste, they would have to pass through the forest heading north. As long as they stuck to the correct headings, Pascal and Pierrot would find a wasteland spread in a deep valley on the other side of the forest. Continuing on through the wasteland, they should locate the Citadel, named Dominion.

Time was not on their side, and Pascal knew that the walk would take forever if they got lost. In the forest that Pascal and Pierrot currently trekked through, there were no footpaths at all.

Hours passed, and by the time they stopped to eat a few apples from Baptiste's satchel, the sun was sinking. The long shadows of the mountains began to plunge the forest into darkness. Thick tree boughs obscured their view. Beneath the pine branches, scraggy shrubbery filled in the underbrush. From time to time, they could hear suspicious rustling, the sleepy call of a nighthawk on creaking branches. Still, they continued silently and did their best to avoid scratches from the heavy undergrowth.

The silence was unsettling. Even the creatures in the woods seemed to vanish as twilight passed and the night grew darker. The hair on Pascal's neck rose as he caught a hint of cool air blowing behind him.

We're being watched.

He glanced at Pierrot, who looked just as uneasy. Every now and again, Pierrot stopped to listen to the forest.

"Pascal! Pierrot?" A familiar voice disrupted the silence, and Pascal jumped, startled. He listened again. "Are you two in there?" His eyes widened when he paired the voice with its speaker.

"Paloma?" he called back with a mix of relief and uncertainty. "Where are you?"

"I'm over here!" Paloma replied, not at all helpful.

Is she ... to the left? He hastily pushed back the branches, calling out her name. "Paloma?"

"C'mon, Pascal!" she shouted back. "Where do you think you're going?

"I'm coming!" Pascal stopped and looked around, unable to see more than a few feet in front of him. He realized that Pierrot wasn't behind him anymore. "Pierrot?" he cried out in a panic. "Pierrot!"

Silence.

"Paloma?"

Again, silence.

Why aren't they answering? A sinking feeling came over him, twisting and churning in his gut. His head swiveled in every direction, unable to make out anything more than the dark silhouettes of trees and brush looming over him ominously. Adrenaline coursed through him, lighting up his senses with fear.

Turning back the way he came, he retraced his steps, with only the sound of the branches smacking together and the crunch of them snapping in his footsteps. His heart pounded furiously, drowning out the creaking forest.

Where's Pierrot? Surely, I should've bumped into him by now.

"Pierrot!" he called out with hesitance, almost too frightened to make any noise.

In the distance, Paloma called out, "Pierrot?" Her tone was mocking and cruel. With a laugh, she said, "I wonder where he is! You've left him somewhere, Pascal. Like you always do. Honestly, you should turn back now."

In his ear, he heard a dark whisper. "Turn back, you idiot," and he halted his steps. *What's going on? Is this real? Or is this in my mind?*

"Paloma!" Pascal shouted, his voice holding more courage than he felt, though it was laced with fear. "Is that really you?"

"Why wouldn't it be?" Paloma giggled maliciously. "Best give up, Pascal. You'll never be good enough to save them all."

"She doesn't care for you," the dark voice growled into his ear, wrapping around his mind like a black cloud of despair. "Give up. It's too late. You're going to die!"

"I'm warning you, Pascal," Paloma said. Her voice lilted with amusement. "You should just turn around. You're not going to make it."

"That's not true," Pascal whispered back, brown eyes blazing with determination. "You're a liar, just like your master."

He could hear his father's words playing in his mind. *Don't ever doubt yourself. Always believe in who you are. In the darkest hour, your belief in yourself will spark your power.*

Pascal's eyes glinted with anger. He understood what this was—mimicry. His father had warned him: He'd told him that if you hear the voice of someone you know calling your name, someone you don't expect to hear, it's probably the wendigo, Callisto. Wendigos, like Callisto, use mimicry to lure people to their death. They often prefer attacks from behind because they are sensitive to fire, light, and other physical attacks.

Pascal knew his father was right. That wasn't Paloma. It was Callisto, and it must've gone after Pierrot first. Pascal hoped Pierrot's ability to stay silent and run would save him.

Picking up speed, he moved quietly in the direction of the voice. After several tense minutes, Pascal pushed his way into a round clearing, where a large stone stood wreathed in fog. He let out a breath of relief; Pierrot waited amid the hazy mist with his back to the rock and his dagger in his hand.

Pascal glanced to the left where, from the north side of the clearing, the antlered head of the wendigo emerged through the fog. Slipping back into the shadows, Pascal waited. He caught Pierrot's eye, raised a finger to his lips, and nodded slowly as he hefted his pike. Pierrot shifted his terrified gaze back to Callisto and straightened his shoulders. With each creaking step, the wendigo drew closer to Pierrot. Pierrot gripped his red ball, hurling it right into the center of Callisto's face.

The wendigo charged forward as Pierrot rolled to the side. Pascal lunged with his pike, driving the silver spearhead deep into Callisto's side, the creature howling in pain as the spear sank into its wood-colored flesh. Pascal clung to the pike's shaft and rammed it forward as hard as he could as the wendigo flailed about.

One of Callisto's arms gripped the pike and broke it in half, leaving the spearhead stuck deep within its side. The low voice growled out a wordless wail. Struggling to return to the safety of the shadowy forest, Callisto staggered and fell. Its body began to slowly shrivel up, and after a final shudder, it laid still.

"Sensitive to physical attacks," Pascal said with heavy breath. "Or maybe it was the silver in the spearhead."

Pierrot nodded jerkily, flustered at the sight of the creature. With a shaking hand, he pressed his dagger into Pascal's hand. Pascal looked down at the engraved silver blade and then back up at Pierrot.

"Are you sure?" he asked softly.

Pierrot squeezed his blue ball repeatedly.

Pascal slipped the dagger into his belt and moved closer to the still figure of Callisto. They had been swallowed up by the fog, their long, tangled limbs sinking down among the tall grasses. Darkwing had disintegrated into black smoke, but the wendigo showed no signs of disappearing back to the Netherworld. Pascal hesitated and drew back a step, hand poised over the hilt of the silver dagger.

With a shriek, Callisto twisted suddenly. Long, spiky branches shot out toward them. The wendigo's woody fingertips thrashed in front of their faces, grasping at air.

Pascal and Pierrot flinched. Drawing in a harsh breath, Pascal opened his eyes. The wendigo's branches were retreating, shriveling up. With a deep groan, Callisto shuddered and lay still before crumbling into dust.

With wide eyes, Pascal pulled Pierrot further back. He

glanced up at the darkened sky overhead as the fog dispersed and retreated, returning the forest to normal. It wasn't as late as Pascal thought. The darkness must've been brought by Callisto.

"Let's get going, then," he said. "We're running out of time."

CHAPTER TWENTY-ONE

Pascal's body ached with exhaustion. After another hour of walking, he called a fifteen-minute break.

Pierrot sipped water from Baptiste's canteen as Pascal bit into the flattened sandwich they were sharing. Once they regained their energy, they picked up their pace and eventually pushed their way out of the last bit of forest. As they emerged from the trees, a wasteland spread out before them.

Looking across the vast emptiness, Pascal shivered, and Pierrot hung back a tad. In the far distance, a charcoal-colored rock jutted up from the ground, the distant towers of an ancient citadel resting upon it. Through the mist, it was difficult to see, but knowing their destination was out there lifted Pascal's spirits.

His excitement plummeted when he looked at the barren plain that extended between them and the citadel. Lifeless trunks of blackened, dead trees scattered the land and rose jaggedly into the misty skies. Large boulders and shriveled grass were interspersed with the skeletal remains of shrubs. No birds flew overhead. No small creatures scurried through the grass. And there was no wind.

Pascal lowered his voice as he stepped forward. "Be careful, Pierrot. From here on out, we're in plain sight. We'll have little cover out there, so we'll be easy pickings."

Pierrot nodded and followed Pascal onto the dirt and dead grass of the wasteland. He looked around and hunched his shoulders, keeping close as Pascal crossed a dried-up riverbed, making a straight line through a clump of dead trees. Their feet crunched over dried-up vegetation, occasionally snapping a dead branch. In the distance, a low rumble echoed eerily as a bunch of rocks crashed down the side of a mountain.

After walking for a while, it felt as though the citadel wasn't getting any closer, but they pushed on as quickly as they could. Suddenly, Pascal realized that Pierrot had stopped and was standing at attention; his eyes narrowed as he cocked his head and listened intently.

"What is it?" Pascal whispered, glancing around. "You hear something?"

Pierrot squeezed his blue ball.

"Another one of Mephisto's henchmen, do you think?"

Pierrot shrugged. Then his hand rose, motioning for Pascal to listen.

Pascal strained, trying to hear it. The low rumble from earlier grew louder. Pierrot's eyes widened. He pointed down at the ground with a quavering hand. Something was disturbing the soil in a straight line extending right toward them.

A grinding, guttural voice broke the silence. "You shall go no further, interlopers!" An explosive crash rose through the earth as a large, stone-covered creature emerged from the ground, leaving behind a massive hole.

Pascal's eyes narrowed as he took in the minion. The stone creature towered over them, more than twice as big. Massive, thick arms hung down like one of the monkeys they'd seen at the Carnival, and its legs were short and squat. Beneath a hood of stone, red eyes gleamed from the T-shaped crevice that formed its face. At the end of its arms, shorter stubs of stones stretched outward as it raised its hand into a fist and slammed it into the earth.

The ground beneath their feet rippled. Pierrot instantly crouched down, shifting the center of his gravity lower so that he wouldn't topple over. Pascal staggered back. His arms windmilled for a moment as he struggled to maintain his balance, and he leaped into a backflip, hunkering down like Pierrot.

"Groundstroke," Pascal said quickly in a low voice. "Father told me all about him. Impenetrable skin. Slow-moving unless he is underground. He targets his victims by tracking the sound of their footsteps. Then, he pops out and crushes them."

"Turn back, boy," Groundstroke rumbled. "You may challenge me, but in truth, you are no match."

Pierrot glanced around. Pascal had no time to ask what he was searching for. With a dull, grinding roar like two rocks shifting against each other, Groundstroke lumbered toward them. Just as Harlequin had told him, the stone giant moved slowly, so Pierrot and Pascal easily dodged his swinging arms.

"Scamper about," Groundstroke promised, "but time and experience are on my side."

"We shall see," Pascal replied.

As Groundstroke swung his massive fist again, he half-turned. Pascal leaped forward with a quick series of handsprings and front flips. As he landed each time, he lightly rocketed himself up again. Thanks to his acrobatic maneuvers, he not only avoided Groundstroke's punches, but he also moved behind him to see if his father's memory was correct.

Just as his father had told him, Groundstroke had large gems lodged in the back of both of his shoulders. Each glittering, dark orange gem was the size of Pascal's head and looked like a massive garnet. Suddenly, the gemstones flared with inner light, and Groundstroke dove into the earth, disappearing within seconds.

Pierrot and Pascal froze, knowing that their footsteps would betray them. Pierrot glanced at Pascal and pointed at an outcropping of rock to his left. Pascal nodded in agreement. Two paces away from him, another rock broke through the hard, parched earth. In fact, all around them, various stones stuck out. They would no doubt provide some protection against Groundstroke's attack. Pascal counted down from three on his fingers and sprinted for his rock while Pierrot ran to his own safe spot.

"I got you!" Groundstroke shouted as he rose out of the gravelly soil. His cry of triumph turned into a roar of anger as Pascal jumped away at the last minute.

Pascal grabbed hold of Groundstroke's arm and swarmed up the creature's side like he was scaling a mountain. He drew in a breath and swung his fist at Groundstroke's face. With a sharp cry, he shook his hand. *Damn, that hurt!* Groundstroke's entire body was indeed as hard as rock.

Pulling Pierrot's dagger out of his belt, Pascal tried to stab down at Groundstroke's neck, but the silver dagger didn't even scrape the henchman's skin. A large hand swung toward him. Pascal slid down Groundstroke's back, out of the way of the impact. He stretched desperately and managed to jam the dagger into the crevice near one of the gems.

Groundstroke shuddered and growled, "Your time is coming to an end, boy!"

The stone creature swung about and tried to knock Pascal off his back, but Pascal held tightly onto the dagger and the jagged rock of Groundstroke's shoulder blade. He wrenched on the dagger, starting to splinter the gem on Groundstroke's left shoulder. Pieces of opalescent stone cracked and fell to the ground, a colorful contrast to the bleak wasteland. Groundstroke bucked and burrowed downward again.

Pascal launched himself into a series of handsprings that landed him on a rock nearby. He looked down at where Groundstroke had disappeared. This time, the tunnel seemed to collapse into itself.

Silence reigned.

He scanned the area carefully for any signs of the creature. Several feet away, Pierrot hopped neatly from rock to rock, closer to Pascal, miming a stabbing motion.

"Oh," Pascal whispered, realizing what Pierrot meant.

Reaching into Baptiste's satchel, he drew out Pierrot's other dagger. Pierrot held up his hands, forming a circle, and mimed another series of stabbing motions. Finally, he pointed his thumb at himself and pretended to run.

"You want to be bait again?" Pascal hissed in a whisper. "After last time?"

Pierrot nodded as his hands clung to the blue ball hard, terrified but determined. He took a deep breath and hopped off his rock, running in a large circle. Behind him, the ground rumbled and rippled. A line of overturned earth rose behind Pierrot as Groundstroke drew close to the surface. Pierrot, glancing over his shoulder, gritted his teeth and ran faster. This time, he headed toward Pascal's rock. At the last minute, he swerved, barely avoiding Groundstroke's hand.

Groundstroke shot out of the earth in another explosion of rock, raining dirt and soil all about him. Pascal leaped into the air and swung around Groundstroke's arm, launching himself onto Groundstroke's side as the creature tried to hit him. Groundstroke staggered under his own blow, which gave Pascal the time he needed to find rocky footholds to Groundstroke's shoulder. Once there, he dropped down, grabbed the other shoulder blade, and began to hack at the second, undamaged gem.

Just as Pascal had hoped, attacking the gem finally caused a reaction. Groundstroke howled with pain, falling to his knees.

"Curse you, boy!"

Chunks of gemstone fell to the ground as the minion's fingers rooted in the earth, trying to burrow to safety again. But it was too late. Pascal used the dagger to lever a large chunk of the garnet away, causing Groundstroke to shudder and fall still.

There was a moment of absolute silence, and then Groundstroke's broad frame gave way. Chunks of stones and showers of pebbles rained down as the giant slowly disintegrated into a heap of rubble.

In silent jubilation, Pierrot hopped from foot to foot with his hands raised. Pascal, wiping the dust off his face, grinned back. The two gave each other a high-five and sat down, back-to-back, to catch their breath. There was no sign of any other henchmen at the moment, but that was little comfort. They could appear at any moment.

After catching their breath, Pascal and Pierrot stood and dusted themselves off, took a sip from Baptiste's canteen, and continued on their way.

As the citadel came into view, Pascal could see that getting inside the citadel would be a challenge. The walls look impenetrable. Two sculpted, twisting dragons surrounded the closed-arched portcullis. Behind it, the great gates to the castle had been swung shut.

As they got closer, Pascal hesitated, uncertain of how to continue. Pierrot, however, didn't stop walking. Pascal fell in behind him and followed his friend to the east. Pierrot pointed ahead of them. Where a citadel moat might have once been, the now-empty trench revealed a tunnel. No doubt it would have, at one time, been a sewage tunnel.

Sliding down the steep embankment, Pierrot approached the tunnel and warily peered in. Pascal looked past Pierrot's shoulder, squinting. In the dusky shadows, it was impossible to see more than a couple of feet into the tunnel.

Pierrot held up a hand. Pascal stopped, his foot resting on the tunnel's lip.

Quickly, Pierrot looked around and found a large piece of wood. Laying the thickest end on his handkerchief, he added a few pieces of woody bramble from a dying shrub close by and tied the handkerchief around his makeshift tinder. Pierrot reached into the satchel that Pascal carried and pulled out an old-fashioned metal box, using the flint and steel inside to set his makeshift torch ablaze.

Pascal knocked off the largest bits of fiery wood, allowing for a smoky but slowly burning fire torch.

The two stepped into the tunnel. When they turned the first corner, only the dim glow of their makeshift torch kept them from being swallowed up by the shadows. Feeling their way carefully through the tunnel, they kept an eye out for a hatch or opening into the citadel above.

Something suddenly whizzed past Pascal's ear, nicking him on his earlobe. He looked over and saw a knife! Jerking sideways, he ducked just in time to miss a second knife that whipped over his head.

Pierrot gripped his torch and ran forward, keeping his head low. In the process, his torch flared and lit up the tunnel a little more. Shadows stretched on either side, but Pascal had already seen it—the shadow that didn't move like the others.

Shadowsoul.

Recalling what Harlequin had told him, Shadowsoul was cowardly, always hiding in the shadows. He stalked his victims, striking them when they least expected it. Usually, he preferred to use his claws or daggers. After long years of spending time as a spy and assassin, Shadowsoul had very good hearing and night vision, but that also made him weak and overly sensitive to light.

Pascal gasped in the realization. Immediately, he rose and ran forward. Pierrot followed close behind. Recognizing Shadowsoul's attack pattern, Pascal pushed Pierrot to the left while he began to run along the wall to his right. Bouncing into a backflip, Pascal reached out his arms. His free hand brushed the edge of soft material. *Shadowsoul's hood.*

Bending into a front roll, Pascal continued his pursuit, pushing off the walls to avoid the knives flung his way. Pascal's eyes adjusted to the dark, and he could dimly make out the shifting shadow of his attacker.

Shadowsoul hung back, unwilling to commit to the fight. Pascal gritted his teeth and let his arm with the dagger fall as he eased back. Just as he hoped, the creature lunged forward.

Pascal dropped his dagger, rooted himself into a firm one-handed headstand, and kicked upward. At the same time, he grabbed the dagger off the ground before pushing himself back into a standing position and bringing his silver dagger up in a broad swipe across Shadowsoul's chest. The blade met resistance, thanks to the minion's armor of cloth and hard leather, but it couldn't avoid the beam of light that blasted from Pascal's hand.

Pascal, eyes closed, letting the light illusion linger. Pascal remembered his father's words as he breathed in deeply and allowed the power within him to flow outward. He thought about his dreams, about Pivot, and about his friends waiting in the citadel above him. About Paloma.

Memories swam into focus—the day he taught Danton how to cartwheel, the day Tania had shown him the fairy tale book she loved, the day he built the tree house with Baptiste's help. The day he and Pierrot brought Paloma to the tree house. The three of them practiced for their Carnival performances. From those moments, the light took shape. It was a simple illusion in the form of a small dragon, but its beams flared down the tunnel, lighting up every corner.

With Pascal's light now fully illuminating the tunnel, Pascal and Pierrot could clearly see how frail and thin Shadowsoul had become. With each revealing beam of Pascal's light, he felt a surge of shame coursing through him as he acknowledged the vulnerability of his true form. Before Pascal could grab the assassin, Shadowsoul retreated. With a shriek, he flew down the tunnel like a ragged shadow and disappeared around a corner. The light illusion dimmed, and the tunnel fell back into shadow, but the creature did not return.

"You think he's gone?" Pascal asked in a whisper.

Pierrot nodded beside him; eyes wide.

"Probably gone back to warn Mephisto," Pascal said with a groan. "So much for the element of surprise."

Pierrot tugged on Pascal's elbow and pointed with his torch in the direction that Shadowsoul had disappeared. The two cautiously moved forward, following the direction the minion fled. Each step brought them closer to the heart of the citadel, but there was no sign of a way out.

After some time, however, they reached a dead end. A simple metal grate stood open, marking the entrance to the citadel dungeon proper.

As they walked through, they listened carefully, but there was no sign of Shadowsoul about. Pierrot lifted his smoking torch and motioned down the stone-walled corridor. Their footsteps echoed in the eerie silence, much too loud for Pascal's comfort, though he continued with caution down the empty hall.

On either side, various corridors opened into a labyrinth of halls and chambers. Their own pathway spiraled downward. *I can only guess where that goes...* In the distance, a muffled scream resounded. They froze and shared a look of horror before continuing down the hall with only their torch to guide the way.

Eventually, a shaft of red light shone ahead. It wasn't an encouraging hue, but they moved toward it, nonetheless. As they got closer, Pascal heard a distant murmur. The red hue resolved into swirling tendrils of mist.

When they finally reached the doorway, they automatically took two steps back. With no idea what to expect, neither one was charging through. Taking an apprehensive step forward, a circular courtyard opened up, but they weren't above ground.

They stood at the edge of an inverted tower with a deep drop. Pascal watched in awe as purple and red magic swirled up through the circular center. Above them was a circle of velvety dark sky, giving them a subtle taste of freedom, knowing the exit was within sight.

The Citadel's dungeons.

The dusty cobblestones before them were slowly being devoured by an inky black circle wrapped in smoke and fire. They stepped up to the spiraling staircase and looked up at the first landing, frozen.

A group of Mephisto's henchmen stood around and appeared to be receiving orders. Pascal immediately recognized one of the minions as Anala, the guard from the orphanage.

Anala now had shed her human form and revealed herself as a horned woman clothed in flames.

She must be Killflare. That was what Father called this voracious fire creature.

Beside her, swathed in sleeveless black robes that allowed his six arms to move freely, stood Mechawire, beyond him, a beefy warrior with the head of a boar, broad shoulders, and sharp tusks grunted softly. *Growl*, Pascal guessed to himself. Yet, something in his eyes looked familiar—they looked like Weylin's. *Was this Weylin's true form?*

The slight figure before the three turned around.

At first glance, Pascal realized that the fourth person, the one giving the orders, was a young woman dressed as though she were about to perform for the most nightmarish Carnival act. Around her head was a large, white monster's head that resembled the skull of a bear, with large protruding horns. Between its gaping jaw, a pale face glimmered in the shadows.

Pierrot's wide eyes closed tightly as he took a step back, shaking his head and turning away, his expression filled with terror. Pascal, witnessing his friend's reaction, understood the agony Pierrot felt and the cruel mockery of his past that it represented. The resemblance to the beast that had taken his brother's life was intentional, awakening Pierrot's pain and trauma.

The woman's black and red dress twisted upward in flame-like spirals, with two slits that exposed her black stockings and knee-high boots that had tall but sturdy heels. In her black-gloved hands were two daggers that glowed deep red with power.

Those daggers... No! She can't be—what happened to her? No, no, no! This isn't right!

She raised her head, her face partially hidden beneath the jagged teeth of her mask. But that half-lidded gaze she shot them was all too familiar. Even in the illuminating red glow, where she looked like an entirely different person—he knew it was her.

Paloma.

She smiled widely as though she had been waiting for them.

"Capture them!" Paloma commanded. Pointing her dagger at Pascal and Pierrot imperiously, she added, "I want them alive!"

CHAPTER TWENTY-TWO

"Get behind me," Pascal said in a low voice, stepping in front of Pierrot.

Growl pushed past Paloma and lumbered down the stairs, his beefy hands clenched into tight fists as he snarled and bared his large, crooked teeth. Mechawire unsheathed a longsword while Killflare spread open her right hand and summoned a floating ball of fire.

Pascal's gaze landed on Paloma, his eyes pleading with her to think about what she was doing. Ever since he met Paloma, he knew she was strong. She wasn't like the other orphans. Even the other Rejects who lived on the streets didn't have those same leadership qualities. Maldavo tried but look at what happened to him. No, Paloma was smart, cunning—powerful in her own way. *But she chose to embrace her darkness. Maybe she just needs someone to show her the light.*

"Paloma," Pascal said, an uncertainty to his tone. "Can we talk about this?"

"Talk about what?" Paloma retorted. Still, she raised her

hand in silent command, and the other henchmen drew back a step.

"About what's going on," Pascal said. "What happened to you? Why did you choose this, Paloma? I need to understand."

"What's there to understand?" Her voice was laced with venom, sharp. Hard. Where was that gentle side he'd grown to adore? "The man you protected is a *murderer*, and it's time for him to face justice. I will hunt him down and make him pay. It's all I ever wanted, Pascal."

"I get that. I do." Pascal said, running a hand through his dirty, unkempt hair. He needed to choose his words carefully if he wanted to get her back. No demanding or belittling her view. He needed to make her realize they were on the same side—if she'd just open her eyes. And her heart. "I just... I had hoped that maybe we could do it together. Wasn't that a dream that we shared? To make the world a better place, to seek out evildoers and bring them to justice. Remember?"

With a steady gaze, she watched him in scrutiny. With a shake of her head, she replied evenly, "That's what I'm doing. Bringing justice to an evildoer." She took a step closer, her weapons still in hand, though she wasn't attacking. "My time is now, Pascal. And it could be *our* time, just like we'd planned... if you see reason."

"See reason," Pascal repeated. "Fine. I can do that. But Paloma, *you* need to see reason, too. You don't understand. That man, he's my—he's not what you think he is."

"I suppose you're going to say that I'm mistaken?" Paloma scoffed and rolled her eyes. Her hands tightened around the hilts of her daggers, her grip shaking the blades.

Pascal's mind raced. *I need to think carefully about what I say next.*

"Mistaken, in a sense," Pascal suggested. "It's not your fault, but you've been tricked by Mephisto. He cast an illusion or something—I don't know—but I can assure you that the man you saw wasn't the man you thought he was."

"Highly unlikely." Paloma sniffed. "My intuition is never wrong."

"That's true," Pascal agreed. "But are you listening to intuition or desire? Think about it, Paloma. This is something you feel strongly about. Anyone would want justice! Mephisto is using you for his plan."

"Mephisto understands me," Paloma shot back. "He sees me for what I am and still cares."

"Does he? I see you, and I still care. And so do Pierrot and Harlequin."

"Harlequin?" Paloma frowned.

"The man you attacked was Harlequin." Pascal took a deep breath, hoping his honesty wouldn't come back to bite him. "He's my father, Paloma, and I know that he was not one of the ravagers who killed your parents."

She stared at Pascal. Her lips formed a thin line, and her eyes flickered with disgust and scorn. But beneath her glare, something else lingered. He knew it.

"The puppet show stories were true!" He took another step forward, hands outstretched. "My father has been through a lot. Just like you, in fact. That's why he understands you. He knows what you are going through, and he forgives you—"

"Those fairy tales are true?" Paloma scoffed. "A likely story."

"Fairy tales are akin to lies, that is for certain, Loma," a velvety voice rang out from the dark shadows above. "Brilliant fancies, but this world cannot thrive on fairy tales alone."

Mephisto completed his descent and sauntered in behind

Paloma. He rested his long, pale hands on her shoulders and smiled down at her with a doting expression that sent chills down Pascal's spine. He looked up and met Pascal's gaze with cold eyes.

"Your friend believes in you," Mephisto said to Pascal. "I must admit that I lacked Paloma's vision, but I see that perhaps I judged too hastily. A boy with power—magical power—but of an ancient order." He left Paloma and stalked toward Pascal. Leaning close, he spoke so only Pascal could hear. "So, Harlequin and Columbine had a son. After all these years of hiding, he emerges. How delightful!" Stepping back again, he said, "The power that you hold would be a boon to our cause."

He took a slow step toward Pascal, stopping abruptly in front of him. "I will make you a one-time offer. The Gateway is opening, and the time has come for our lord and master Diabolico to triumph over this world. Join us now, and you could be one of the leaders of his new world order!"

Pascal's jaw ticked, and his lips pressed into a thin line. Pierrot stiffened behind him, grabbing his arm tensely. They stood in silence, Pascal staring hard at Paloma, who seemed perfectly fine with Mephisto's declaration.

"Well, I tried, Loma dear," he said with a sigh. "Though it seems that they will not see reason. How unfortunate." A cruel smile crossed his face. "Then it's time to die, my dear boy. I'll tell Harlequin that you died bravely. Paloma?"

Mephisto spoke her name as both a question and a command.

Pascal tensed in anticipation. Paloma launched forward, but Pascal shot his hand out to knock her wrists aside, redirecting the force of her daggers like his father had done. At the bottom of the inverted tower, the Gateway opened. Quickly, he raced past her up the stairs, kicking at Mephisto—who vanished, then reappeared over the Gateway. He looked on with interest as his henchmen burst into action.

Pierrot dropped the torch at the top of the stairs, momentarily distracting the minions. Growl tried to grab Pierrot, but he rolled forward, grabbed the torch, and darted past Pascal before anyone could react, disappearing into the shadows of the corridor beyond. With a sharp curse, Killflare raced after him, followed by Mechawire and Growl.

"Pierrot!" Pascal shouted, executing three backflips to put more distance between himself and Paloma. "Keep running!"

There was no answer. Not that he was expecting it. Pascal hoped that Pierrot would be able to lose his pursuers in the dungeons. Time was running out. He needed to talk to Paloma—without Mephisto and without fighting. He didn't want to fight her.

But he didn't want to die.

There has to be another way. Maybe I can reach her.

Paloma cautiously stepped sideways, watching Pascal, both waiting for an opening. Above them, Mephisto slow-clapped in solitary applause, amusement written on his face.

Pascal scowled. *The bastard.* He gritted his teeth. Mephisto knew that this was hurting him in more ways than one. *Cruel, manipulative bastard!* If he died here, Mephisto would have one more thing to destroy his father with. And, if his hold on Paloma weakened or if he revealed the truth, she would be crushed as well.

I have to stop this. No matter the cost, I have to stop this now.

"Paloma," Pascal tried again. "Look around you! You're smart. You have to know that summoning Diabolico to this world, creating this 'new world order,' is the complete opposite of what you want. Mephisto isn't working in your best interests. You have to realize that!"

Pascal could tell that her desire for vengeance had cast a shadow over her reasoning. She wasn't thinking straight. He had to help her. It couldn't be too late. It just couldn't.

Paloma lunged forward, twisting and slashing downward with her knives. Pascal vaulted into a backflip and kicked her right hand away, deflecting her blow. He twisted away from her left dagger, jumped up, and brought his leg down. Paloma crossed her wrists and easily defended against his kick.

Pascal used the force of his leg against Paloma's arms to propel himself even further back. He landed on the edge of the stone railing and tried again to talk to her. "Diabolico is going to create a world filled with evil more dangerous than ravagers. More families will be destroyed, and more orphans will be made! That door opens to the Netherworld, and nothing good comes from there."

Paloma jumped and aimed a kick at Pascal, no doubt hoping to knock him off the balustrade down to the bottom floor, where the Gateway was now halfway open. Anticipating her move, Pascal grabbed hold of a nearby stone pillar and swung around to the next arched railing. He leaped upward into a front flip and landed on his feet with his back to the stair wall. The two faced each other on the second level's landing, both breathing heavily.

"Isn't the Gateway and the existence of Diabolico enough proof that the fairy tales are true?" Pascal panted as he struggled to keep his breath even. "Harlequin is real, and he's trying to stop Mephisto from killing innocent people. Don't do something you'd regret. Mephisto is using you! Do you really want to be part of that?"

Something flickered within her eyes. Doubt. Hopeful, Pascal hesitated. Paloma saw his momentary hesitation and took advantage. She darted forward and slashed her daggers, but Pascal whipped out his own and blocked her.

Paloma's arms trembled as she pushed against Pascal, but he grit his teeth and fought back. Both of his hands clasped the hilt of his dagger as the interlocked blades shook between them. Pascal tried to force her blades down and away from him while Paloma tried to sink the blades closer to his chest.

This close, Pascal could see behind the skull-like headpiece that Paloma wore. Even here, in the shadows, the passion that flickered within her hazel eyes reminded him of all the time they had spent together: sitting quietly in the tree house, strolling the market, and performing their routines in perfect synchronization. The way she smiled and laughed. Her confident poise. The tilt of her head. The flood of memories filled Pascal with regret.

I never got to tell her. I never got to tell her how much I cared for her.

Pascal wondered what she saw in his eyes, but as close as they were, he felt as though they were one. Sharing the same space, the same breath, their hearts beating in sync.

If I lean forward, I could finally ... As if reading his mind, Paloma shifted. The pressure on the daggers between them remained the same, but something within Pascal rose with hope.

"Ahhh! This is bliss," Mephisto's voice boomed from behind Paloma. Beneath his feet, darkness swirled within the Gateway, clouds of smoke easing out above the fiery pits beneath. Two red eyes glowered from the shadows of the Netherworld. Mephisto laughed in amusement and triumph. His voice echoed through the inverted tower as if it were within the swirling dark magic that rose to the dark sky overhead.

"This! This is the night that we have long awaited. After all these years, our lord shall finally arrive. What was so rudely interrupted will finally be accomplished. Our long years of struggle will come to an end at my master's arrival, the great Lord Diabolico himself!"

"Listen to him, Paloma," Pascal whispered. "*Listen* to him!"

"And Harlequin?" Mephisto's gloating laugh sent a shiver down Pascal's spine. "Dead? Dying? Unable to be here to witness my triumph, alas. No matter, old friend. I shall find you with my new weapon, and you will finally meet your end."

"Is that what you want to be, Paloma?" Pascal asked. "A useful puppet?"

"You could have been here, dear Harlequin, but no. Instead, you send two boys to fight for you. And for what?" Mephisto's theatrical sigh ended with a sharp cackle of glee. "A shame. A real shame, that. After all those years of work for me, you attempted to reverse your fate, but now we have all we need, despite your best efforts. With the harvest of these souls, our Lord Diabolico shall return, and he shall feast!"

"Harvesting souls," Pascal breathed, feeling sicker than ever. "He means to kill them all. All of them, Paloma! They're going to die just like your parents!"

Paloma's eyes widened as she drew in a sharp gasp. The daggers between them quivered, and the pressure eased a little. He held her gaze. They were so close; he could almost feel the warmth of her skin. His eyes peered down at their hands, reminded of that day at the puppet theater when he had so desperately wanted to hold her hand. And he wanted it now. Of course, he wanted it now.

So many times, I wanted to say something, do something. But it never felt like the right moment. But I'm running out of time. I may not get another chance.

He dropped his daggers and stepped forward, arms outstretched. Paloma froze in shock, inadvertently releasing her weapons. Before she could catch herself, the daggers clattered to the ground as Pascal drew Paloma in. His hands rose to shove the large, monstrous skull from her head.

It fell to the floor and shattered into pieces. His hands rested on her shoulders and slithered down her back as he pulled her in, closing the distance between them.

"I love you, Paloma," his husky voice whispered in her ear; his arms wrapped around her in a tight embrace. "I always have... and I don't want to give up on us or on our dreams."

Drawing back, he leaned his forehead against hers. His heart pounded a rhythmic beat that pulsed through him. Feeling her body pressed against him, he couldn't help but sigh in contentment. His eyes fluttered closed, allowing himself to feel the moment. *After all, it may be my last.*

Soft lips gently brushed against his, and Pascal tilted his head, pulling her in closer. All of his senses ignited at once, the touch of her skin, her subtle, sweet scent. His hand slid up her back and gripped her tighter. There in the shadows, they stood, arms wrapped around each other, captured in a kiss that consumed his body and mind as one.

CHAPTER TWENTY-THREE

I LOVE YOU. I ALWAYS HAVE... AND I DON'T WANT TO GIVE UP on us or on our dreams.

At those words, something woke up within her, a veil lifted. It had always been there, burning like the last embers of a fire. A light within began to flicker again. All her life, she had been searching for hope, for love, for a sense of home.

In her dreams, Paloma always felt as though she were running through a mist, running away from her parents' killers. But if she was honest with herself, she was also looking for something. Recently, she had found herself calling Pascal's name as she ran. And it made sense now, that name. The cause for all her running.

With each passing second, Paloma began to see what had happened in a new light. Every moment she had spent at Lord Serpentine—Mephisto's—side was cast in a darker hue. Looking back at her actions, she was horrified.

What—what did I do?

Paloma gazed up at Pascal, who looked down at her with an expression of love and a tinge of sadness.

"P-Pascal," she gasped, blinking furiously to keep the tears from falling. "I-I'm so sorry, Pascal! I don't know what I was thinking."

"I don't think thinking had much to do with it," Pascal said quietly with his arms wrapped around her, his touch filled with warmth and kindness—the security she needed in that moment. "Mephisto understood the shadows in your heart, and he recognized the emotions you held. He warped your desire for justice and used it against you, but that doesn't mean you were all wrong. I—*we* all forgive you, Paloma."

"Pascal." She buried her head in his shoulder, choking on a sob. A surge of relief washed through her, as tears streamed down her cheeks. "I've been living a nightmare!"

She'd been lied to. Ignored her instincts. Got too swept up in her desire for revenge. But worse was the humiliation of allowing herself to be pushed over that edge, falling for such deceit. Pascal didn't laugh, however. He simply drew her into another warm hug.

When she pulled away, she looked down at herself, at the energized tingle that claimed her body. Pascal's eyes grew wide as Paloma's dress began to change before their very eyes. The black and red became white and cerulean, the twisting, ragged edges softening and curling like the petals of a flower. Paloma had transformed from a hollow-eyed creature of darkness into a stunning young woman.

She glanced up at Pascal, whose eyes flickered with intrigue and delight laced with a hint of desire. Her cheeks flushed, feeling a contrasting mix of confidence and insecurity. With a deep smile, she said, "I no longer belong to him. Like Harlequin, I'm free to walk my own path. My dreams won't be decided for me."

"Yes," Pascal said, leaning his forehead against hers. "And whatever you choose, I want to see it all come true."

Paloma's smile grew. Sheathing her daggers, she looked over the edge of the stone balustrade, and her happiness faded. With fresh eyes, she truly looked at the horrific scene before her. The inverted tower's winding stairs were enveloped in shadows, descending to the black, fiery Gateway at the bottom, opening up to the Netherworld below.

Large, red eyes gazed upward from the gate, but even more horrific was the man who hovered over the opening: Lord Mephisto. The veneer of Lord Serpentine had disappeared as the light from within her shattered the illusion. Without the spell keeping her in his bondage, Paloma looked into those dark flaming eyes and recognized the face of a killer.

Memories flooded back. A cruel, twisted smile, the eyes full of dark flames, the high cheekbones, and the deathly pale skin. In her memories, the mist finally cleared. She saw through the bushes. She was no longer hiding. The fire cast just enough light for her to see a mark on the man's face. It was set like a crown upon his brow. A trident.

She recognized the same symbol lining Mephisto's brow. Fury flowed through her like a crashing wave.

Mephisto's gaze shifted from Paloma to the Gateway, where a massive, claw-like hand emerged from the depths and began to feel around the edges of the gate. A triumphant smile twisted his features, and he glanced back up at Paloma. His hand rose to stroke his short goatee as she glowered at him with disgust and disdain.

"It was you!" Paloma's resentment grew as the realization hit her. "It was you all along! You killed my parents... disguised as a ravager. You lied about the identity of their murderer, and you were using me! Pascal is right, isn't he?"

"About what, dear girl?" Mephisto let out a sigh of disappointment, but the cruel smirk never left his face. "That I used you? That is true enough, but you will admit, Loma dear, that that is the way of things. Everyone knows it, and none understand that better than yourself."

"I am not your *dear*," Paloma spat, her face burning bright with rage, hands edging toward her sheathed daggers. "You lied to me!"

"Well, I take pride in my deceptions." Mephisto shrugged carelessly. "What do you expect? I had, after all, hoped that you would remain at my side for all time. You still can if you will just see reason."

Paloma gritted her teeth and mulled over his words with her blinders off. *I thought I was speaking from my heart, but I was just parroting what he wanted me to say.*

"Look, Loma," Mephisto went on. "You are something else, something different. That is the truth, and I can't deny it. But if you will not see reason, you will end up like your friends…powerful but a liability. And you know what happens to those who lose their value." Mephisto paused, adding with sharp malice. "You will end up like the others, like your parents—*dead*. You don't want that do you?"

At those words, Paloma shrieked. Rage coursed through her veins, pumping through her heart and her limbs, claiming her in every aspect. Her hands flew to her daggers. In a single, fluid motion, she unsheathed them and launched herself at Mephisto.

But before she could strike, he vanished. She passed through him entirely.

The illusion broke into a million shards, and he reappeared on the first-level landing. Paloma landed on the edge of the blazing vortex and raced around back up the stairs. Just as she got close to Mephisto, she threw one of her knives and leaped down at him, but yet again, her blades could not find their mark.

"Just as I expected," Mephisto said with a laugh as he hovered over the Gateway. "Paloma, leader of the Rejects, famous for her intelligence and strategies, also has a dark secret. When she loses her temper, she becomes like any other: easily manipulated. She is no leader. She never has been."

Paloma's eyes glittered with rising anger as Mephisto's words hit their mark.

All her life, she'd been afraid of becoming like Maldavo—letting fear of being vulnerable drive her to do unthinkable acts to keep power and security. She realized that because of those feelings, she nearly ended up becoming a tool for the worst kind of evil. Even now, she struggled to overcome her anger and need for vengeance.

A hand rested gently on her shoulder. "Paloma."

The voice alone instantly drew her to the present. She turned to Pascal, who had moved to her side. Pascal smiled down at her, a shy smile that started in his bright brown eyes. It was a look of trust and reassurance, but it did contain a hint of worry. She couldn't ignore the fear that flowed through them both.

"I get that it's irritating to hear him go on like this," Pascal said quietly. "But he said it, right? He's a charlatan, the master of lies. And any deceiver knows that the best kinds of lies are mixed in with the truth. You have to remember that he's manipulating you. Even now, he has you."

"I know." Paloma released a weary sigh, her head dropping in defeat. With a gentle hand, Pascal raised her chin to meet her gaze. His touch ignited a flame deep within, and her breathing hitched. "Neither one of us can beat him on our own. Together, I think we can stop him."

Paloma nodded, taking his hand in hers and giving it a light squeeze. "Together."

"Let's head back to the second level. Meet him on equal footing, so to speak."

"Our regular combo?" Paloma asked as they hurried up to the second floor.

"No harm in trying," Pascal agreed.

Once they reached the second level, the two hopped up onto either side of a stone pillar. Squatting on the thick railing, they looked at Mephisto. Paloma could visualize the move. She glanced at Pascal and slowly nodded, holding up three fingers.

Two.

One.

They launched themselves through the air. Pascal opened his hand and released a small explosion of light. Mephisto jolted back and froze as if stunned. And as Pascal hurled himself forward into a front flip, he brought his heel down on Mephisto's right shoulder. Paloma kicked at his left side in perfect synchronicity.

Briefly, it seemed as if their kicks had connected with something, but once again, Mephisto's image vanished, leaving only a wisp of dark smoke in his wake. Paloma and Pascal arced through the air in perfect synchronization and landed together at the far end of the cobblestone yard, just barely missing the Gateway.

The hand reaching up out of the Gateway groped wildly, attempting to close in on them. They kicked aside the skeletal fingers and sprinted up to the first landing. Breathing in deeply, they bent over the stone balustrade to look down at the Gateway's opening.

"This is going to get tricky," Pascal panted between breaths.

"But the light illusion you used seemed to stop him," Paloma pointed out. "I wonder why."

"Maybe illusions cancel out other illusions?" Pascal guessed.

"We should try it again." She leaned forward to look further over the edge of the railing. "If we don't, I get the feeling that we'll have a bigger hand to deal with soon."

Pascal joined her and looked down. Behind him, the shadows warped, and unseen to both, a face appeared out of the swirling mass of purple and red.

The corridors that stretched before Pierrot seemed like a maze lit only by the embers of his torch. Maybe it was his imagination, but the walls seemed to get damper and slimier as he progressed further down the stone halls. His ears strained for any hint of a sound, and he could only hear faint echoes of footsteps.

Where are they coming from?

As he stumbled through one set of intersecting hallways after another, he fled down the cobblestones almost blindly. At one point, he tripped and nearly fell, dropping his torch. He gritted his teeth and proceeded to make his way through the dark.

His eyes adjusted to the darkness, and he found a small nook in one wall where large sections of stones had fallen out of place. He slipped into this shadowy niche, keeping his footsteps as silent as possible. A few minutes later, Growl and Mechawire prowled past.

"Where are you, little boy?" Mechawire hissed in a deathly rattle. "Come out now, and you'll be spared the worst of it."

"Yes, yes," Growl grunted. "Come out, boy! Or else!" Then, Growl's voice dropped to a mumble. "Where is Darco? Doesn't he want to be present when our master arrives?"

Mechawire replied, "I guess not," his tone unphased. "Oh well, his loss."

Drawing in his breath, Pierrot kept as silent as possible as the two pursuers came to the next crossroads. Growl thought he had gone right. Mechawire was sure that Pierrot had turned left, so the two parted ways.

Pierrot smiled to himself as relief flooded through him. His decision to draw the three henchmen away from Pascal turned out to be a good idea.

Now to return to Pascal. He'll need all our help. The three of us will be together on one side, united. Just like before.

With renewed resolve, he crept out of his hiding place and ran back down the corridor the way he came. Already, a map of the place was forming in his mind. To others who had ventured through the inverted tower, the place may have seemed impenetrable in its design. Indeed, in several rooms, Pierrot found a few skeletons that spoke of adventurers who'd gotten trapped within the tower—lost adventurers or unfortunate prisoners. The thought sent a shiver down his spine.

Still, Pierrot refused to hide.

Taking his time to move quietly, he followed the simple map that had formed in his head. Sure enough, after taking an indirect path around the tower and down some stairs, Pierrot found himself back at the entrance to the lowest level.

He could see the edge of the Gateway that had opened at the bottom of the inverted tower as he peered out from the shadows. It was a vortex of darkness, edged with smoke and fire.

Within the unfathomable depths of the Gateway, a large hand, curved like a bird's claw, felt its way around the edges of the gate.

The Netherworld. A despicable place where the vilest creatures were spawned. He'd read all about it in a book in the orphanage's library. Back then, it seemed like a spooky fairy tale, but Pierrot knew now it was all too real now in a way he'd never anticipated. At the moment, he was faced with the reality of how large Lord Diabolico must be. The nail of the demon lord's thumb was as tall as Pierrot himself. At the sight, Pierrot shrank back into the shadows.

Uncertain of what to do next, he waited.

Then, just like they'd done at their Carnival performances, Pascal and Paloma came flying through the air. In a whirl of light and kicks, they tried to hit Mephisto, who hovered over the Gateway, but Mephisto was just an illusion. No sooner did they land than the two had to evade the grasping claw of Lord Diabolico. Without a glance at the corridor's entrance, the two raced past and up the stairs.

Pierrot peered around the corner of the corridor's doorway. On the first landing, his two friends came to a halt. Paloma and Pascal were talking to each other. At the sight, Pierrot couldn't help but smile to himself. *They must've made up. Maybe she'll help us fight after all.*

They leaned forward to look down at the hand that rose from the Gateway. Diabolico's skeletal hand extended up to the stone railings, searching for a better hold.

"Mephisto," a loud guttural voice spoke, reverberating around the tower. "Where are the pure souls you promised me? I need those souls to pass! The energy of the gate will not be strong enough without them! Yet again, you seem determined to fail me. Yet again, you do not prove yourself as you say you will."

"M-my lord." Mephisto's demeanor shifted instantly, and his tone of voice took on a tinge of respect mixed with annoyance. It was odd for the children to hear such a tone from someone so absurdly powerful. "They are ready, I assure you! Darco is preparing them now. I simply need to finish off these pesky insects; the better to prepare the way for you. Surely, you understand such needs."

Pierrot shivered. Even Mephisto was but a lowly servant. The thought was chilling. Once again, he battled the feeling of foreboding that settled over him. The creature reaching up was pure evil. He could feel it in his bones. Part of him wanted to run away, but part of him knew he had to stay. He couldn't imagine how, but Paloma and Pascal might need his help.

His emotions gave way to complete terror as he recognized the dark purple and red swirl forming behind his friends' backs. The pale face and the dark eyes that emerged were all too familiar. Mephisto raised his hand, and shadows began to spread outward as he stepped forward.

Images of Maldavo screaming as he was slowly torn apart by Mephisto's powers shot through Pierrot's memory. Without thinking, a voice erupted from Pierrot.

His throat and lungs burned as he screamed.

CHAPTER TWENTY-FOUR

As Pascal and Paloma peered over the balustrade to look at the skeletal hand below, a loud scream pierced the silence. The primal shriek echoed off the stony walls. It became the center of the world.

They whirled around in search of the source of the scream, only to see Mephisto behind them. He'd turned toward the doorway to one of the corridors, where Pierrot stood in the opening.

Pascal and Paloma gaped in shock, eyes wide, as they realized that it was *Pierrot* who had cried out. He'd used his voice for the first time.

"Pierrot," Pascal called out. "Your voice!"

Pascal was thrilled by such an achievement, but there was no time to celebrate.

Mephisto was already in motion. Baring his teeth, he growled in frustration and jetted past them toward Pierrot, who fled into the shadows.

Pierrot can't hide in the tunnel. They'll find him. Killflare,

Mechawire, and Growl stood at the entrance looking victorious, confirming Pascal's fears.

"Paloma, let's go!" Pascal called out.

Bracing himself, he laced his fingers together to create a foothold for her. Paloma smiled and put her foot in his hands. This move was second nature to them. Pascal leaped forward and used the edge of the stone balustrade to push himself toward Mephisto, launching her forward with even greater momentum.

With Mephisto distracted, she kicked him hard and slashed at his back with her daggers. The spelled blades cut through Mephisto's jacket like butter. Black blood oozed from the wounds beneath her blade. Mephisto howled and writhed, unable to break free from his agony.

Pascal tumbled through the air behind her. The skeletal hand swiped frantically at him, enraged at their resistance. Pascal briefly landed on the back of the hand and then leaped upward. After turning a quick somersault in the air, he brought his leg down as hard as he could. And then again. And again. He delivered three successive blows to Mephisto's lower back.

The pain of Paloma's daggers and the force of their combined kicks slammed Mephisto downward. Black blood spurted through the air as he dropped toward the Gateway. Pascal flew to the other side of the inverted tower and grabbed onto a stone pillar, watching Mephisto as he plummeted downward.

"More momentum!" Paloma shouted as Mephisto struggled to stop his fall.

Propelling herself from the stone balustrade, she jumped up and out again, sailing over the Gateway and landing two sharp kicks on his chest.

Mephisto shrieked and threw his arms up in protection. A shining orb appeared above him, illuminating the shadowy courtyard. The explosion of light filled the darkness, blinding everyone. The skeletal hand thrashed about, breaking several pillars, as Mephisto recoiled from the burn of the light. A massive shard of stone pillar crashed downward from the hand, slamming Mephisto into the Gateway below.

"Loma," he cried out, descending to the fiery depths of the Netherworld. "You could have been so ... beautiful."

With a thin screech, he disappeared into the blackness. The dark seemed to grow in gravity when he became a part of it.

The Gateway began to collapse. The glowing red eyes flickered in the darkness of the Netherworld. A deep, guttural voice howled in a violent fury. "Mephisto, you lied to me! You fool! You have failed me again!" An agonizing cry rattled through the disintegrating Gateway. "Harlequin lives and has gained something else!"

Gained something else?

Pascal didn't have time to focus on that as red and purple swirls of magic dissipated like mist evaporating in the sunlight. The hand shriveled, and the voice faded away, a dying ember to the once-ravenous flames. With a deep rumble, the stonework surrounding the Gateway crumbled.

In a last-ditch effort, Pascal leaned over the railing and called out, "What has he gained?"

No answer. Above the cracking of rock, he heard the whisper of a rising wind and the faint call of a voice. It was a woman's voice, high and desperate.

"Commodore!"

Where is that coming from? Pascal hung over the edge of the perch, clinging to the stone as he strained to listen. As he squinted into the collapsing black of the Gateway, he saw nothing.

Then, the staircase fell inward. Pierrot spun around in horror, covering his head from the crushing rocks and boulders. *We have to go.*

Pascal grabbed Paloma's hand, ready to race out of there.

The three minions twisted and thrashed behind them. Mechawire's six arms turned to streaming clouds of black smoke. Killflare's fires raged beyond her control, enveloping her in thick black flames. Growl simply disintegrated, squealing and grunting with anguish.

Pierrot scampered up the stairway, waving wildly at Pascal and Paloma.

"I think he wants us to follow him," Paloma called out.

"Looks like it," Pascal shouted back. "I just want to see ... just to make sure."

"No time!" Paloma cried as an ominous rumble resounded through the tower.

The two swung themselves onto the staircase and ascended swiftly. Ahead of them, Pierrot led the way. Looking around at large cracks that spread beneath each of his footsteps, Pascal wondered if they would be able to survive this. Dust billowed up as the carved stone crashed away. Paloma shot him a terrified glance.

Behind them, the stairway splintered and thudded downward into the Gateway. The staircase, the pillars, the sculpted demons, and the stone railings of the inverted tower all collapsed one by one. As the Gateway slowly drew itself shut, the skeletal hand disintegrated into bony rubble and disappeared under the avalanche of stone. By the tunnel, a pile of black dust was all that remained of Mephisto's minions.

Stone gave way beneath their feet as the three sprinted desperately upward. Pierrot reached the uppermost level first and dove into a tunnel. Pascal could feel the stone falling away beneath him as he leaped upward, and he landed in the mouth of the tunnel just in time.

Yet, when he turned, he realized that Paloma was no longer behind him. The stone stairs had fully given way. Paloma seemed to have fallen with them.

His heart came to a shuddering stop. "Paloma!" He lunged forward, searched desperately for any sign of her.

His heart nearly stopped when he saw her again. Just below the tunnel's entrance, Paloma hung by her fingertips from the broken remnants of a shattered statue.

"Grab my hand!"

Leaning down as far as he could without tipping over the edge himself, Pascal gripped the back of Paloma's hand. Gritting her teeth, Paloma let go of the ledge and grabbed onto him with both of her hands.

"P-Pascal!" Paloma stuttered, eyes wide, as Pascal's arm began to shake.

Pierrot ran over to help, grabbing Pascal and pulling. Pascal huffed and eased himself backward, straining to pull her up.

"I-I have you, Paloma!" he said. His hand held hers with an iron grip. "I won't let you go!"

Paloma nodded, eyes filled with tears.

Emboldened by the support, a support she genuinely trusted in, she swung her legs to find footing and pushed herself up further until her hands were enough above the edge for Pierrot to grab. Together, he and Pascal dragged her to safety.

The three stood on the edge of the gaping hole, gasping and panting. Paloma gave Pascal and Pierrot a smile of desperate gratitude.

"Thank you. Both of you."

The three looked down at the remnants of the inverted tower. Paloma and Pierrot shivered and moved back, but Pascal stood at the entrance of the corridor and watched as the last bits of rubble rained down on the ruins of the Gateway.

Without the connection to Mephisto's magic, the Gateway had closed and kept Diabolico from passing through. He had withdrawn, leaving only a crumbled relic of his presence in the world. Above, the citadel disintegrated. Large chunks of gray and black stone crumbled, burying the Gateway in an ever-growing pile of rubble.

"It's finished," Paloma said, panting.

Pierrot tossed his red ball up and down in silent disagreement.

"Oh," Paloma said, a look of realization dawning. "The others. The children!"

Pierrot beckoned once more.

"You know where they are?" asked Paloma.

Pierrot nodded and tapped his temple with a small smile. The two hesitated and looked back at Pascal, who stood silhouetted against the last flicker of purple and red.

"You coming, Pascal?"

"Yes," Pascal said absentmindedly. "I just…" He shook his head and ran toward them. "Never mind. You know the way, Pierrot?" At Pierrot's confident nod, Pascal smiled. "Lead the way, then. I'll be right behind you."

Pierrot led the others through the maze he seemed to have mapped out in his mind. Working his way upward, he crisscrossed through the labyrinth of tunnels, corridors, and cells. When the three reached the uppermost level, their eyes widened at the sight of evenly spaced, blue-flamed torches set into the wall. Although the torches were growing dim, they could see that the corridors were filled with confused-looking children.

"It's everyone!" Pascal said with relief.

"Probably not everyone," Paloma said. "But we'll see. Let's get them out of here."

Pascal shouted, drawing the children's attention to the end of the corridor. A raucous cheer rose at the sight of the rescuers. Everyone flocked to Pascal, who in turn followed Pierrot to the nearest staircase. They stampeded up the stairs toward freedom, the many footsteps tromping in unison. Once they had reached the surface, Paloma remained with the group while Pierrot and Pascal went down to find more imprisoned children. With each trip, the numbers swelled.

Meanwhile, the last of Mephisto's magic faded. Walls crumbled, and towers disappeared. The ruins of an ancient citadel emerged from the rubble. The children could see the Wasteland and the forest through large gaps in the citadel walls. The entire landscape was surrounded by towering mountains which in turn were shrouded in mist.

Many of the younger children began to cry. Older children wondered aloud how far they'd have to walk to get back to Pivot. When Pascal re-emerged after another search through the dungeons, he noticed that the atmosphere among the children had shifted from one of relief and happiness to one of fear and chaos.

He turned from the group he had just rescued to speak to Tania and Mira. "Paloma will need your help to settle everyone. If we have to walk back to Pivot, we'll need to separate the children into groups. Try to choose older children to be the group leader," he said quietly to the two of them.

The two girls nodded and ran to join Paloma. Pascal glanced down at Pierrot.

"One more area, you said, right?"

Pierrot nodded and led him to the far end, opposite the inverted tower. By now, the blue-flamed enchanted torches had gone out, but Pierrot had relit two of them with natural fire, thanks to Baptiste's tinder box. In the flickering light from the torches, they walked up one corridor and down the next. Like other parts of the citadel, the cell doors had disappeared. There weren't any signs of Mephisto's other henchmen either. They had probably also dissipated into smoke or dust and returned to the Netherworld when Mephisto's hold on Dominion had broken.

"Pascal? Pierrot?" a familiar voice broke into Pascal's thoughts.

"Mistress—Mistress Alma?" gasped Pascal in shock.

The elder woman, looking very thin and grubby, leaned against Michel and a group of older teenagers, Clément, Claudio, and Danton among them.

"You're safe!" Pascal said with relief, rushing to their side. "I was so worried!"

"For now," Mistress Alma said. Her blue eyes glinted with fear and concern. "There is evil afoot in this castle. A demon lord stalks the halls."

"Mephisto?" asked Pascal. "He's, um, gone now. We managed to stop him, so the Gateway collapsed. Nobody's soul is going to be harvested now. The children are waiting above."

Mistress Alma smiled faintly.

"It sounds like you and Pierrot have things well enough in hand," she said. "I'll be glad to shake the dust of this place off my feet."

"Agreed," Michel grunted, his typically broad body hollow and lined with exhaustion.

"Darco may have escaped," Pascal admitted. He didn't want to say it, but the remaining presence of that evil haunted him even now.

"The authorities can take care of that," she answered. "For now, let's get to safety."

When the last group emerged, a cheer rose among the orphans. Other children taken from Pivot and its neighboring villages looked confused, but when they saw the headmistress appear, it was clear they felt relieved. Just being in the presence of an adult had been enough to calm them.

Pascal walked over to Paloma and looked around. Small groups of children had already been formed. "It looks like we got everyone, but it's going to be a bit of a trek back. The Wasteland is spooky but simple to travel across. It's the forest I'm worried about. The trees are thick. It's easy to get lost in there."

"I don't think we have to worry about that," Paloma said. She turned and pointed toward the lowest edge of the mountain's ridge, where the clouds had cleared a little. "Look."

Pascal squinted, and his eyes widened. Three large airships slowly made their way toward the castle. Two carried the black and red colors of the Blackcoat family, but the one leading them, decorated in wine red and deep navy, proclaimed the arrival of the governor's guard.

At the sight of the ships, the children's voices rose in a roar of greeting. Whistles pierced the air as they clapped and jumped up and down. Even Michel smiled and waved his arms. As the governor's guard ship hovered low over the citadel's large central courtyard, a rope ladder unfurled, and a familiar, redheaded young man zipped down with the ease of a professional.

"You did it!" Baptiste said over and over again. "You did it, Pascal! Pierrot! And Paloma!" He reached the bottom. "And

Grandmother!" Baptiste hugged his grandmother hard, then stepped back, hands on his hips. "Now," he said, "who wants to go home?"

For the orphans, returning home was simple. Within two hours, the ships had returned them to the orphanage.

The mansion lay empty when they arrived. There was no sign of Miss Myrrah or Master Darco. Mistress Alma's study was in disarray, books and pencils and paper everywhere. There was no sign of a portal, just as Baptiste had said. It was as if the whole nightmarish ordeal had been just that—a nightmare.

After Michel rustled up a snack for everyone, the children were sent to bed with the exception of Pascal, Paloma, and Pierrot, who remained behind. Once everyone had settled in their dorms, the three met with Mistress Alma, Michel, and Baptiste in her study. Such a meeting held so much less authority than it had in times past.

In one corner, Michel sat beside Baptiste with his hands folded. Baptiste gazed at his grandmother with happiness and relief. Pascal, Paloma, and Pierrot lined up in front of her desk, looking ashamed, frightened, and happy all at the same time.

"I suppose you want an explanation," Paloma said reluctantly. She glared at her boots and scuffed her foot against the floor as her shoulders hunched. No doubt, she was nervous about how Mistress Alma would react to her being on Mephisto's side of the battle.

Pascal squeezed her hand in assurance, hoping to calm her nerves even slightly.

"Some kind of an explanation would be nice," Mistress Alma agreed. "I answered the door, only to find some sort of ruffian calling on me with a proposition. Before I knew it, he had grabbed hold of me and whisked me away."

"Sounds like Master Darco," said Pascal. "He could teleportate himself."

"He whisked away Michel as well," Mistress Alma added, shaking her head.

Michel nodded. "I was nabbed behind the garden. Next thing I knew, I was in the cell with Mistress Alma."

Hearing Michel and Mistress Alma's side of the story was sobering. Pascal wondered for so long what had happened to them, where they'd been. After finding them in the cell, he was relieved they were alive. Yet, the logistics of their respective stories were still quite blurry for all parties.

Slumping his shoulders, he glanced to one side at Pierrot and then to the other at Paloma. Both nodded in silent encouragement, and Pascal outlined their story with occasional interruptions from the others, including Baptiste. He began from the start: when Master Darco had first appeared at the doorstep of the orphanage.

As the story continued, their excitement rose. They explained how the disappearance of the children was linked to Mephisto's growing power and the spreading decay in the north, how they had looked for Mistress Alma to no avail, and how Paloma had been deceived.

"The source of Citadel Dominion's powers was snuffed out, but if Diabolico created a hand," Mistress Alma mused. "I mean, he must've consumed souls. That means that some families will not see their children returned to them. I hope this tale will be a warning to us all. It would do us well to heed the dangers of the world of magic even now, even in this world of such vast progress."

Some children won't be returned to their families. The words repeated in Pascal's mind, breaking his heart to know that despite their best efforts, they still couldn't save everyone.

"What happens now?" Paloma asked with a slight tremble in her voice.

"Well," Mistress Alma said, settling her now-bent glasses crookedly on her nose. "I imagine we will have a time of it preparing for school. It starts next week, but hopefully, we can all work hard and get everything back in order."

"I'll head back to Pivot and give a report to the governor," Michel said, rising to his feet.

"Want a ride?" Baptiste asked. "I've got a horse and cart." After everything, it felt rather anticlimactic to watch Michel and Baptiste shrug on their torn, dirty jackets and disappear outside.

Mistress Alma stared at the three steadily as though reading their minds, but she simply shook her head. Her blue eyes twinkled at them with gratitude and joy.

"Thank you for saving us, you three," she said. "The orphans and I owe you for this. But it would be remiss of me to just let you wander about willy-nilly. No matter how heroic you three are, it's still time for bed. Even heroes need their sleep." With that, she winked at Pascal and motioned them out. "I need some time to clean my study."

After all that, she still sees us as children...

Pascal and Paloma nodded and wished Mistress Alma a good night. Pierrot followed them out silently, his steps soft as usual.

"I suppose I ought to go to bed," Paloma said reluctantly. "I'll see you two tomorrow."

She trudged off in the direction of the girls' dorms.

"She's right," Pascal said and half-turned away.

Pierrot tugged on Pascal's elbow, jerking on the sleeve of his dirty jacket. Pascal stopped and looked down at Pierrot, who shook his head again. He poked Pascal and pointed after Paloma.

"I should... follow her?" Pascal said in alarm. "She's going to bed."

Pierrot mimed walking and tented his hands.

"She's... not going to bed?" Pascal asked slowly, piecing Pierrot's words together.

Pierrot tossed his blue ball. For the first time, he mumbled, "Mm-hm."

Though it was such a small phrase, it was enough to make Pascal stare at him in shock. Pierrot had never spoken to him, and even though it was hardly more than a mumble, it was *something*.

He poked Pascal in the chest and pointed again. Then, he tented his hands once more.

"The...the tree house," Pascal realized breathlessly. "Let's go."

As he turned away, he realized Pierrot wasn't moving to follow him at all. Pascal turned back, his eyes narrowed.

"Aren't you coming?" he asked in confusion.

Pierrot shook his head, his brown eyes filled with a mixture of emotion.

"Oh." Pascal blushed. "But what about you?"

In mute reply, Pierrot unfolded his hands like a book and smiled with a nod.

"Alright," Pascal said. He began to walk away but stopped abruptly. "Pierrot," he called out, taking a few steps toward his friend. "I'm proud of you."

Pierrot's face lit up, and he smiled, pointing at his chest, then to Pascal.

He's proud of me, too. "That's not what I meant. I mean, yes, you did great in battle, but I'm proud that you used your voice. If you hadn't screamed, Paloma and I would've been killed. And just now, I heard you mumble. I know that's a big step for you, but you did it. I hope you'll continue like this...I mean, I hope you'll find your voice more often."

Pierrot's grin widened. After a brief moment of silence, he tented his hands once more and pointed down the hall.

"Alright," Pascal said, patting his friend on the shoulder. "I'll see you later."

Parting ways from Pierrot, he darted toward the boys' dormitory, but instead of going up the stairs, he looped around to the kitchen, slipped out the back door, and squeezed through the hedge. He made his way through the forest to the secret spot where they had spent so much time together. Once there, Pascal scampered up the wood rungs and poked his head above the platform.

At the sight of the hunched shadow sitting on the edge, he suddenly felt uncertain. He couldn't quite figure out why; he was usually quite confident about these types of things. Still, he quietly clambered up into the tree house and sat down by Paloma. She had curled up, drawing her knees to her chest and resting her head on them. Her white and blue dress spread around her like a flowery fan. Gingerly, he edged closer.

"I don't want to talk about it," she said, her voice muffled. She sniffled, swiping at her face.

Pascal's heart sank a bit. Paloma had been crying. That was no good. Crossing his legs, he leaned forward and looked over the tops of the trees before them. Above, the thickest clouds had drawn back, leaving only wisps. Between the clouds, the stars faintly glimmered in a deep blue sky, and the moon, large and full, hung just above the treetops.

"Alright," he said after a beat.

They sat there in silence for a while, but eventually, Paloma drew closer and leaned her head against Pascal's shoulder. She rubbed her face, but the glittering tracks of tears remained. Pascal raised an arm and wrapped it around her shoulders in a comforting embrace.

"I'm afraid," she finally said.

"Afraid? Of what?" Pascal asked, holding her tighter.

"Not what you are probably thinking," Paloma said with a sniffle. "Mistress Alma forgave me. You heard her. She understood, and I won't get in trouble with the city guards. I should be happy, and yet…"

"And yet." Pascal sighed, remembering his father's words. "Over time, this story may fade, like the stories about Harlequin, but our memories will remain within us. They'll always be reminders that darkness will always be within each of us. We mustn't forget such things."

"That sounds… smart," Paloma said with a huff.

"My father," Pascal explained with a light laugh. "He told me about it. He called it the shadow within. Mephisto…Diabolico…they are shadows, but inside of us, we all hold our own darkness. We have to accept that darkness and learn to live with it. I mean, we all know this deep down, don't we?"

"Learn to live with it," Paloma echoed.

"Yeah," Pascal said. "We can try our best. That's all that is expected of us, I think."

"What if our best isn't good enough?" Paloma whispered.

"In those times," Pascal said softly, "I hope that we will be there for each other. To help each other figure it out."

"Oh, Pascal," Paloma choked out with a half-sob, half-laugh. "You silly goose."

Despite her words, Paloma's arms twined about his waist, and she closed her eyes. He leaned his head on top of hers, and they sat there together in silence, watching the moon sink toward the horizon.

CHAPTER TWENTY-FIVE

Some things will never be the same, Pascal thought as he stood outside the tents of the Carnival. *Everything is going back to the way it was, but some things have changed forever.*

This realization hit him particularly hard that week as school started and the old schedule for the orphanage resumed. Between the rumors that swirled about and the Carnival's newest puppet show, Pascal found himself the center of attention on a whole new level—not just from the orphans but from the citizens of Pivot as well.

The new, two-hour-long story starred the silent mime, Pierrot, the athletic acrobat, Pascal, and the powerful dancer, Paloma, as they battled the evil Mephisto and banished Diabolico back to his realm. Now, Pascal and his friends could barely walk through the marketplace without being accosted by a well-wisher. It was an odd change of fate from the way they'd walked through the very same streets before.

Other things seemed to have changed within Pivot, as well. Before, the city had prided itself as a hub for trade and scientific progress, but after the threat of Mephisto and Diabolico, the dragons, dwarves, elves, and fairy folk were given more opportunities to voice their opinions and concerns. Governor de Moura was once again hiring spellcasters to set proper wards around the city. For the first time in decades, the hidden world of magic had emerged from dusty textbooks. On all fronts, Pivot was safer than ever.

Still, as Mistress Alma and the others had guessed, Diabolico's attempted summoning had indeed claimed many lives. Most children who had gone missing before the orphanage was taken over had never returned to play in the streets of Pivot, and their families would never see their sons and daughters again.

No matter how hard they tried, they couldn't save everyone. But for the first time in years, the governor worked to protect Pivot from both magical and non-magical threats. At the same time, however, Pascal couldn't help but notice more as well— the dark corners, the shadows within the shadows, the ruffians that Paloma was always looking out for before. Pascal shoved his hands in his pockets and contemplated the busy scene before him. *It looks the same, and yet...*

The Carnival was in full swing. Clowns meandered past, practicing their juggling. Enzo the Mime felt his way along an invisible wall as he headed toward the main tent. Several acrobats cartwheeled past, shouting at Torto and Brenson, who strolled along, deep in conversation. In the distance, Pascal could hear the clang of wood as stalls threw up their shutters. Awnings creaked in the wind. The eastern breeze was cool, bringing with it the mouth-watering scents of meat pies, fresh pastries, and smoked foodstuffs.

The tent flap behind him shifted aside as his father shuffled out. Leaning on a cane, Harlequin was already on his feet and determined to continue his work at the Carnival, even if he was only announcing the puppet show. The new puppet show was being headed by another performer, for now.

At the sight of his father, Pascal's face lit up. This was one change that he appreciated.

"Are you sure you want to do this?" Pascal asked. "Clara said attending the whole show tonight might be too tiring."

"I can do it," his father replied, leaning on Pascal a little as they slowly walked forward. "I wouldn't want to miss your performance for the world."

"It's not much different from what we did before," Pascal pointed out. "Only the location's changed."

"Are you nervous?"

Pascal hesitated and admitted sheepishly, "A little. Doing our tricks and stuff by the road was … it was fun. Performing as part of the main show, though, is a whole different responsibility. I guess I'm just not used to the idea yet."

The two slowly approached the back of the large, gaily decorated Carnival tent. From this side, Pascal and Harlequin could see a sight few visitors were privy to—the preparation tents that opened into the back entrances of the main tent.

There, Master Barolo stood with Enzo, Crisanto, Cherise, and a few others. Pierrot and Paloma were waiting with them.

Beside Enzo, the mime's organ grinder waited. On a nearby table, bricks had been neatly placed in preparation for Pascal's handstands, along with various juggling props for Pierrot. The daggers that Paloma would perform with had been polished and decorated with brand-new imitation gemstones.

Tonight, Pierrot was wearing a new costume. He had on neatly pressed black pants, a striped black and white shirt, and freshly polished boots. His suspenders and thick scarf were brilliant red, highlighting the blush painted on his whitened cheeks and the red heart drawn at the corner of one eye.

Beside him, Paloma stood tall, wearing a lovely tutu made of feathers and pink tulle. Her hair had been done up in an artful twist that allowed a few loose strands to fall about her face. As always, Paloma had chosen her makeup carefully, using it to turn herself into a beautiful doll with a dark edge that emphasized her large hazel eyes.

At the sight of her, Pascal's face lit up. "Paloma," he said, eyes traveling over her from head to toe. "You look so..." he stopped, then ended lamely, "pretty."

Pierrot tossed a red ball at his head.

"You look great as well," Pascal said to Pierrot. "If our performance is as fabulous as our outfits, I'll be happy."

"Agreed," Paloma said with a slight blush. "And you look fine today as well, Pascal."

"Do I?" he asked, gazing down at his black tights and Harlequin's tunic. His hair was slicked back, save for a few wayward curls that fell over his whitened brow. Like Paloma, his makeup made his face look more doll-like than clownish. Pascal tried to show off his muscles by striking a pose, and Paloma only giggled.

"Let's not waste the show back here." She nudged his shoulder playfully, her smile not leaving her face.

"I'll get the crowd warmed up," Ringmaster Barolo said. "Hugo, Crisanto will help you to your seat. Cherise!"

Cherise bounced forward, launching herself into a series of front handsprings. As she entered the tent, the crowd roared in excitement. With a flourish of trumpets, the ringmaster followed after her, bounding in as though his legs were made of springs. He came to a stop in the middle of the ring and threw his hands up in a grand flourish, throwing off his short purple and gold cape. He unfurled his whip and cracked it. The crowd went wild.

Harlequin clapped Pascal on the shoulder. "Remember to have fun, you three," he said, winking at Pierrot and giving Paloma a broad smile. He leaned on Crisanto and made his way to another side entrance to take his seat.

"You ready, guys?" Paloma asked.

She looked at Pierrot, who expertly juggled his blue and red balls.

Pascal's lips curled into a smile as he stared at her, his heart beating frantically with excitement. She leaned forward to take his gloved hand in hers and squeezed it with encouragement.

"You and me and Pierrot," she said. "We can do this. Just like old times."

"Like old times," he repeated as his grin widened. What a wonderful thought. "Let's give them a show!"

"And after so many rumors, I am sure you are all ready to watch the most unique performance of our marvelous heroes, the great adventurers of Pivot! Let's welcome the heroic, acrobatic Pascal, the brainy, intuitive Pierrot, and the dangerous, multi-skilled Paloma!" the ringmaster cried to thunderous shouts of applause. "Put your hands together for them, folks!"

As each of their names was announced, the three children emerged in turn. Pascal bounded into the ring using his bounciest, highest handsprings. Pierrot was seemingly dragged in by an invisible rope, launching everyone into side-splitting laughter. Then, Paloma waltzed in with graceful arabesques before falling into rolling walkovers and standing front handsprings. The crowd roared with cheers and laughter, as Pascal, Pierrot, and Paloma moved through their familiar routine.

At the end, the three children were called back for multiple encores, one after another after another. Paloma performed a series of daring poses on Pascal's shoulders, and Pierrot mimed a set of cameos taken from the townsfolk of Pivot.

Eventually, the show went on to the next act. Various animals were led out for the nightly parade, and the clowns took the stage. And as much as the crew loved performing, they were happy to rest when their time on the stage was done.

When the night was over, Pascal emerged from the costume tent with his face newly scrubbed clean of paint. He wore his usual black pants, sensible boots, and a navy blue button-down shirt.

Running his hands through his wet hair, he looked around. There was no sign of Paloma or Pierrot.

Looping around in search of them, he stood by the main Carnival tent. Crowds milled around. He recognized more than a few of the children who stood by the stalls. Even Mistress Alma had allowed the children of the orphanage a late night out for this special occasion.

"Beautiful night, isn't it?" A voice broke into the night air. Baptiste, dressed in his finest, stood, arms linked with a lovely blond woman with gray-blue eyes, sporting a gorgeous green and blue dress. Pascal recognized the young woman as Baptiste's beau, Amélie.

"Baptiste!" Pascal smiled. "You came!"

"Of course I did," Baptiste said. "Amélie and I weren't about to miss the best Carnival performance in Vale, were we?"

"Indeed not," she said with a sweet smile. "You three did a fine job, Pascal. Everyone loved it."

"It felt good to perform just for the sake of performing," Pascal admitted. "Less stressful than … well, you know, fighting."

"I can imagine," Baptiste agreed.

"Speaking of which, how are the repairs coming along?"

"Rather well." Baptiste puffed his chest out with pride. "We've done some great work, the boys and me. Before you know it, the airship is going to be as good as new. Even better,

I hope. We added a few more *modifications*. We have the time now in a way we really didn't before."

"So, the journeys of *The Unbroken* are not over," Pascal said with relief.

"Well, it's the *Amélie* now," Baptiste said with a light blush. "Since the airship broke, well, its old name doesn't fit too well now, does it? So, I decided to name it after the best woman I know."

Amélie chuckled and nudged his shoulder, reminding Pascal of Paloma's behavior before the performance.

"The *Amélie*," Pascal mused. "Well, I suppose with a name like that, Amélie will be with you wherever you go."

"And like me, the ship will take care of you and be sure to bring you good luck and safe travels."

"That's the hope," Baptiste said with a wink. "At any rate, I see my grandmother over there. Amélie and I should go say hello to her. And it looks like someone else has come to find you. Goodnight, Pascal... and Master Hugo."

"Oh!" Pascal whirled around to find his father leaning heavily on his cane. "Father, what are you doing out here? Shouldn't you be back at your tent?"

"That sounds rather welcome," his father said with a slight smile. "I suppose I can borrow your shoulder again."

"Anytime," Pascal offered.

For a few paces, the two walked without saying a word. Pascal glanced up at his father, who wore a simple thick sweater with a pair of well-worn pants. He looked a far sight different from Puppetmaster Hugo or even his true form, Harlequin. His hair was ruffled and unruly, and there were lines on his face Pascal hadn't noticed before. His golden eyes shifted down to Pascal, catching his gaze and offering his son a slight smile.

"You did well tonight," he said. "As ever, I find myself so

proud of you. Not just because of how you dealt with Mephisto but because you were able to bring back your friend from the brink of shadow. Just like your mother. She would be proud of you, too."

Pascal smiled back, fighting tears at the mention of his mother. His father's hand tightened around him in a subtle hug. Pascal shook his head, blushed, and rubbed his eyes. He didn't want to lose his cool in front of everyone in the Carnival, but at the same time, Pascal was overwhelmed with happiness.

When they arrived at the tent, his father took a seat and motioned for Pascal to sit down with him. They rested together in silence while Pascal added more wood to the stove. Then, his father leaned back in his chair and started to share his theories about Mephisto. According to Harlequin, neither Diabolico, Mephisto, nor their demon servants could be so easily destroyed.

"I thought they'd be gone after they fell through the Gateway," Pascal admitted.

"Gone?" Harlequin shook his head and offered his son a wry smile. "Gone for now, sure. Evil does not diminish forever. It waits. Neither Mephisto nor his master were finished. And..." He hesitated, rubbing his chin thoughtfully as his golden gaze shifted to the cheerful flames. "And there are other things to investigate. Other mysteries."

"Such as?" Pascal asked.

"The mysteries of the Netherworld, for one. And the worlds that lie hidden within the realms of the unseen. Paths I have not walked for many years. And a voice..."

"A voice?" Pascal immediately thought of the woman's cry he had heard moments before the Gateway closed.

Harlequin rubbed his eyes and shook his head.

"Never mind me. We ought to enjoy the here and now while we can." The older man changed the conversation, setting aside something that weighed heavily on his mind.

Pascal wanted to ask what his father meant, but he held his tongue and contented himself with following his father's advice. Here they were, the two of them seated in plush armchairs before a warm fire. Outside, the noise and bustle of the Carnival provided a comfortable backdrop to the companionable silence.

"What happens next?" Pascal asked. "Besides finding out the mysteries of the Netherworld and getting ready for whatever Diabolico and Mephisto plan, I mean."

"School for you, I imagine, and I shall remain here for the time being." He smiled at the thought. "I think Mistress Alma will agree to allow you and your friends to continue your work at the Carnival as long as you all keep your grades up."

"You think so?" Pascal perked up at the thought and then deflated at the idea of doing homework on time. After everything they'd been through, homework seemed unbelievably tedious.

"It won't be easy, but I think it's important you keep your training up," his father said soberly. "Whatever lies ahead won't be easy, and you will have your powers, which for now, will not make it any easier. You will need even more training, perhaps even some specialized studies in the arts of magic and illusion."

Harlequin rose and shuffled to a great chest. He grunted as he tried to bend over, and he turned to Pascal with an exasperated expression on his face. "If I open my wounds again, Clara will have my hide," he said with a sigh. "Mind opening it for me, Pascal?"

"Oh, of course!" He joined his father, bent down, and lifted the heavy lid off the carved oak chest.

Inside, he saw a jumble of items: clothing, little metal boxes, maps, books, folded papers, and all sorts of miscellany. He pulled out an oddly-folded walking staff and inspected it carefully. The handle was polished, dark-black wood, but the tip of the staff was made of sturdy dwarven steel. It gleamed in the light of the golden fire, revealing deep engravings of ancient symbols in the wood. Unfolding it carefully, Pascal held the now-expanded walking staff in the palms of his hands.

"This is..." Pascal held the staff in his hand.

"It was your mother's," his father said gruffly. "It was one of the walking staffs handcrafted by her clan and passed down. What do you sense?"

"I—I don't know," Pascal stammered. He looked over at his father in confusion. "It just... feels *right* in my hands."

He folded the cane and was about to set it back into the chest when his father stopped him.

"Keep it." His golden eyes glimmered with a mixture of joy and sorrow. "If that is how you feel, it can only be because the staff calls to you, as it did to your mother. In your hands, who knows what power it holds."

"Thank you, Father," Pascal said, eyes shining with happiness. "I'll take care of it. I promise."

"I know." His father nodded. "When Columbine was taken in by Carmen as a little girl, this staff was all that she had. This and a ring. Do you see that silver metal box? Open it."

Pascal leaned forward and gently lifted a silver box. It was a little heirloom piece carved with ancient animals that perhaps Pierrot could identify. Little goat-men blew on pipes beneath gracefully bending, willowy women. Beneath his gaze, the shapes seemed to shift. Carefully, Pascal opened the box and peered inside. A ring sat within, along with a necklace and a pair of earrings made of blue stone.

"One day, when you find someone you truly love, you may offer them that ring," Harlequin said quietly.

"Paloma," Pascal murmured to himself as his fingers traced the edges of the engravings.

It was set with five white diamonds, a ring worthy of any queen. Realizing what he had said aloud, Pascal blushed, shut the box, and put it back in the chest. Harlequin closed the lid with a heavy thud.

"Whoever you truly love," his father said with a slightly amused tone as Pascal refused to meet his gaze. "You will give it to them when the time is right. It is a gift from your mother and me, just as you are our gift to the world. Our legacy. And unlike the material things that remain of our time together, you, Pascal, will change the world in a way no one can imagine."

"Not just me," Pascal said. He turned to the door, where Pierrot and Paloma stood outside waiting. "Pierrot and Paloma will be with me too. After all, if you want to overcome whatever life throws at you, you do it with your family."

AUTHOR'S NOTE

Hello!

Thank you so much for taking the time to read *The Harlequin's Legacy*! Crafting this story has been an incredible journey for me, and I sincerely hope you derive as much enjoyment from reading it as I did from writing it!

I'd really appreciate it if you took a moment to write an honest review. Your reviews help others discover this world and also offer valuable insights to me as an author.

Once again, thank you for giving me the opportunity to share my passion for storytelling through *The Harlequin's Legacy*.

Yours,
Andrés Rosas Hott

Review link